What has love stolen from you?

*I*s there something you always wanted to do but stopped pursuing it when you fell in love? A hobby or dream? What negative effects did falling in love have on your life? What love advice do you have for me?

Perhaps some of you are interested in going on your own Love Quests, taking back what love has stolen. It doesn't matter if you are in love, out of love, searching for love, avoiding love, married, divorced, gay or straight. *True Love* wants to hear from you.

Ca

anything? Then let's turn this on its head. Ask yourself the following questions: 'If you knew you were going to spend the rest of your life alone, you would never fall in love, never settle down, never have children,

what would you want to do? What would make you happy? What would fill up your time, your heart, your soul for the rest of your days?' The answers to these questions are the dreams we need to get back.

boatless with a whole lifetime to fill. I'm going on a quest, a Love-Stolen Dreams quest, to take back what love stole. So, are you with me? Do you want to join my ship?

Pirate Kate xx

I'm going on a quest, a Love-Stolen Dreams quest, to take back what love stole.

WITHDRAWN FROM STOCK

Please send all response letters to:
Pirate Kate: Love-Stolen Dreams,
c/o the *True Love*
London Office
Eton House
18-24 Paradise Road
Richmond TW9 1SR

D0239385

L♥VE IS A THIEF

Claire Garber

H HARLEQUIN®MIRA®

Harlequin MIRA is a registered trademark of Harlequin Enterprises Limited, used under licence.

Published in Great Britain 2013
Harlequin MIRA, an imprint of Harlequin (UK) Limited,
Eton House, 18-24 Paradise Road,
Richmond, Surrey, TW9 1SR

© Claire Garber 2013

ISBN 978 1 848 45213 8

59-0713

Harlequin's policy is to use papers that are natural, renewable and recyclable products and made from wood grown in sustainable forests. The logging and manufacturing processes conform to the legal environmental regulations of the country of origin.

Printed and bound by
CPI Group (UK) Ltd, Croydon, CR0 4YY

Claire Garber was born in Southampton, in 1978, the same year Olivia Newton-John told John Travolta he was *the one that she wanted* and *Space Invaders* were launched.

Claire did nothing remotely of interest until aged twenty-six, when she visited the French Alps and fell in love with every single French man she met. That year she started writing obsessively about her thoughts and feelings, all of which seemed to revolve around love and French boys and heartbreak. Aged twenty-six-and-three-quarters, her friends urged her to do something more 'constructive' with her scribbles, which gave birth to the beginnings of several novels about boys, culminating in *Love is a Thief*—a book she started writing aged thirty-one after her biggest heartbreak of all.

Claire has worked as a freelance winter-sports travel writer, a copywriter and in property, all as a means to fund her writing. More recently she planted some magic beans. She now lives between London and the French Alps.

In loving memory of my mum, Theresa Garber, who died on 11th October 2000—the day my heart was truly broken for the first time

prologue

The bog standard public display of being over your last relationship is when you get yourself into a new one. It's like holding a giant banner in the air that reads:

'Look at me, everyone! I have found someone else. I am OK. Someone else wants me. Someone else needs me. Someone else chooses to be with me. My last relationship was insignificant, barely noticeable in fact, like bellybutton fluff. My ex-girlfriend is just like the fluff from my belly.'

I think it's all crap. I think the public sign you are over your last relationship is when you don't care about the public sign. That said, I do have feelings, and Gabriel starting a new relationship just a few weeks after we broke up, well, that was emotional pain on a level I'd never previously known. Whether or not I believed in the validity of his stupid relationship with an emaciated French girl with fake tits and limited intellectual abilities, he had found someone else, they were on holiday together, and they were taking photos, lots of photos, and putting them on Facebook in an album entitled *True Love* while I was, well, I was bellybutton fluff.

But it wasn't just that I had lost Gabriel, it was that I was so goddamn sad about breaking up with him that even the *thought* of being with someone else made me feel sick. I didn't want to kiss anyone else. I didn't want to have sex with anyone else. I didn't want to share my home with anyone else. I wanted him. So as I couldn't cope with replacing him, and I couldn't speed up the process of healing from him, I just needed to fill up the time.

Because the reality is, I might just be 'that' girl. You know the one. The girl who, for no particular reason, doesn't get the guy, doesn't have children, doesn't get the romantic happy ever after. So I needed to come up with a plan. I needed to get back to basics. I needed to ask myself a few important questions:

What did I like doing?
What *didn't* I get to do because I was with Gabriel?
What *didn't* I get to do because I fell in love?
More importantly, what would I be happy spending the rest of my life doing if love never showed up again?

Now that was a starting point I was interested in.

the beginning

'Hi, this is Gabriel. I can't come to the phone right now but if you leave a message I will call you back.'

In 1990 a man called Tim Berners-Lee created the World Wide Web. He was trying to find a way for particle physicists to access the same information at the same time from wherever they were working in the world.

'Hi, this is Gabriel. I can't come to the phone right now but if you leave a message I will call you back.'

As with so many things in life, the end result turned out to be a little different from the initial objective. The seed he planted grew into something so far-reaching it touched every single one of us in an infinite number of different ways.

'Hi, this is Gabriel. I can't come to the phone right now but if you leave a message I will call you back.'

The Internet now provides us with free accessible education. It can teach you a second language, how to cobble a shoe, how to install a new kitchen or build a satellite that will orbit the moon.

'Hi, this is Gabriel. I can't come to the phone right now but if you leave a message I will call you back.'

You can run your business off it, meet the love of your life on it, find the recipe for a mushroom risotto before fixing your own kettle then learning the origins of the word 'broken'.

'Hi, this is Gabriel. I can't come to the phone right now but if you leave a message I will call you back.'

You can also see images of just about anything you want. I've seen the inside of an atom; the surface of Mars; the expression on Mandela's face the day he was released from prison.

'Hi, this is Gabriel. I can't come to the phone right now but if you leave a message I will call you back.'

But what the Internet has most recently shown me, its greatest gift of all, is a set of photos of my ex-fiancé on holiday with what I can only assume is his new girlfriend. And in these photos, although I'm no Tim Berners-Lee, I'm pretty sure I can see his fully functioning, fully operational,

Internet-connected mobile phone. The very same phone he currently seems unable to answer.

'Hi, this is Gabriel. I can't come to the phone right now but if you leave a message I will call you back.'

'Well, she's obviously not going to get off the floor,' Federico said, to my grandma. They'd stopped speaking to me about 45 minutes earlier. They spoke about me, around me, over me, across me, but never actually to me. My grandma reached down and tried to take the phone from my hand but my fingers were stuck around it like a human claw or a strange device that unconventional men might purchase in Soho.

'Darling Kate, you need to give me the phone,' she said, trying once again to prise it away. I gripped on as if it were my only remaining portal back home. A small circle of people had formed around us. Apparently it's not commonplace for a 30-year-old woman to sit in the middle of Heathrow Terminal Five, surround herself with her own luggage and start weeping.

'Just one more try?' I pleaded with Grandma while Federico wandered from person to person regaling them with stories of the origins of my tears.

'Well, I told her that, yes, I did. I told her when she moved there. I said, "You can't trust the French," and not on account of their political history, of which I am a great great fan, especially that adorable Marie Antoinette—have you seen the film? Fabulous costumes, fabulous, although terribly restrictive of the female form. No, I mean on account of the language barrier. Because how do you ever know if you are truly understanding one another? Who, for example, decided that a *pomme* was an apple? And what if they were pointing to a tree when they said *pomme*, but we were looking at an apple because we were a little bit hungry so we called a tree an apple, and now the French are confused by Tesco's obsession with stocking as many different varieties of edible tree as is genetically modifiably possible to create? Well, it's a complete disaster is what it is!'

'How can he be with someone else?' I pleaded to my audience of 19 women of varying different ages and a security guard called Albert. The other security guard, Jim, had gone to speak with UK Border Control, who were concerned I was a suitcase-laden bomber. 'How?' I asked them again. 'If one person is meant for one person then he must be feeling incomplete and restricted, like a piece in the wrong puzzle. He's in the wrong puzzle!' I said, getting high-pitched and red-faced. And I don't think anyone thought Gabriel was in a puzzle, unless a puzzle was a dirty great metaphor. 'So? What should I do?'

'Perhaps she could try him one more time?' one lady nervously suggested to Grandma. I looked around the human fence surrounding me and they all nodded confirmation. My grandma sighed and rolled her eyes. So I switched my phone to speakerphone and pressed redial for one final try. I held the phone in the air so everyone could hear. I looked at everyone. Everyone looked at me. Then we all looked at the phone.

'Hi, this is Gabriel,' the phone said. *'I can't come to the phone right now but if you leave a message I will call you back.'*

Then everyone went a little bit silent. Actually I don't think you can be a little bit silent. It's an either/or sort of thing. We were silent. And no one would look me in the eyes. So I switched off my French mobile for the last and final time and I handed it to my grandma, who put it straight in the nearest bin.

Then I just sat there, on the highly polished floor of Heathrow Terminal Five, I just sat there, surrounded by every single one of my possessions, and I wept, and I wept, and then I wept some more. If every teardrop were a piece of my soul they would never be able to put me back together.

six months later...

It's the thing I hate most in the world, after eating noises. First place definitely goes to the noises people make when they eat; mostly it's the chewing-swallowing noises I hate, but also the preparation noises: the chinking of knives and forks against plates in a quiet room; the noise as someone opens their saliva-filled mouth; and Lord forbid if someone actually clinks their fork against their teeth when placing food into their noisy gob. But after that, after the food-noise thing, the thing I hate most in the world is heartbreak, and I am surrounded by it every single day at work, because after the 'incident' at Heathrow Terminal Five my friend Federico invited me to work with him at *True Love* magazine.

It was Grandma Josephine's idea originally. She'd said it was important to keep oneself busy when one was feeling broken and empty on the inside. Then she'd said something about paying one's own rent and there were mutterings about inflation and pints of milk. So now I go to work every day, Federico by my side, and once there I am exposed to a multitude of grotesque eating noises and bucketloads of daily heartbreak, although we never let our readers know about the heartbreak. No, *True Love* makes everything look love-covered and golden, and I hate that. I hate the love-covered golden heartbreak.

'Well, it's a twatting mystery is what it is,' Chad said, pacing around the huge heart-shaped table in the middle of the huge heart-shaped boardroom. 'When was the last time we had this much post?' he said on his second circuit of the room. Loosie, his officious 24-year-old American assistant, strode after him flicking through her notebook like an obnoxious linesman.

'Two thousand and one, Chad,' she said, flipping to the correct page. 'Just after 9/11.'

'So what the fuck am I missing?' Chad said, looking to everyone in the room. 'Why are there 27 sackfuls of post? What the fuck did we write about last month?' It was common knowledge that Chad never read his own magazine. He didn't even check the copy before sending it to print. 'Well? What did we advertise?' he asked the room. 'Have Royal Mail fucked up and forgotten to deliver the post for the last 11 years?' He looked from face to face. 'What-the-twat was so exciting about last month's edition?'

Every face in the room turned to me. It was like white-faced choreographed mime at its most terrifying. I say every face turned; Chad's didn't. He'd started on his third circuit of the room, tearing around the enormous table, which was bright pink, glass-topped and viciously sharp-edged. In fact *that* table was more unexpected than the postal situation and had injured 11 members of staff in the last week alone: nine on the jagged edge of its glass top; the tip of the glass heart had drawn blood twice, and Mark from Marketing cracked his knee on it two weeks ago and still walked with a noticeable limp.

'It's not just the post, Chad,' Loosie said, scowling at me, flipping over another page of her notebook as Federico emitted a strange squeaking noise from the other side of the room. If he could have climbed inside his *Nespresso* machine and drowned himself he would have done. I knew the minute the postman arrived we were in 27 sackfuls of trouble and I'd deliberately positioned myself next to the boardroom exit. And excuse me, but I'm not one of those girls who's ashamed of running away. I'm not ashamed of anything after being forcefully removed from Heathrow Airport by mental health professionals.

Loosie opened her mouth to speak and Federico crouched down as if he were expecting an explosion. I leant forward and rested my forehead on the cool surface of the dangerous glass heart. There was absolutely no way we were going to get away with it.

You see, my job at *True Love* was supposed to be the easiest at the magazine, and by that I mean it should in theory be impossible to mess it up. All I have to do is read the letters our readers send us then rewrite them into something more interesting. That's it. Our readers write in (normally in their hundreds) and share stories with us: stories of how they met their one true love; or how much they gave up to save their one true love; or perhaps how they reignited their one true love. I then pick the best ones, call them up, interview them, then rewrite their special intimate moment into a thousand words of tear-jerking genius for an insubstantial salary and absolutely no writing credit. In the writing world I am the lowest of the low. They call me the ghost-writer. I'm a ghost, in the literary sense of course.

Now before we go any further I just want to state, for the record, that I am a hopeless romantic. I am a love lover. I am a princess waiting patiently for her Prince Charming to arrive, on a horse, or a donkey, or even in a London black cab. Or at least I was. Prince Charming was supposed to whisk me off my feet, take me somewhere super and tell me not to worry about the impossibly high house prices or how I will fund my retirement. He was also supposed to be handsome, funny, an emotional mind-reader and have an average to large penis. But the readers of *True Love* kept telling me that getting Prince to turn up at all was pretty difficult, and only the beginning of your prince-related troubles. Because Princey may not possess the above *clearly defined* characteristics; in fact some readers told me their prince didn't possess any at all. But they fall in love regardless only to discover love involves focus; love involves compromise; love involves sacrifice. It's hard to maintain it, difficult to look after, impossible to control. Eventually, almost all our readers lost the bloody thing and became Waiting Princesses again.

Not that we let the public know this. We only showed them the end result, when all the pieces were perfectly back in place. But I saw the void in between. I heard about *'the time I lost him'* or *'why wasn't I enough for him?'* or *'I gave up 15 years of my life for him; he didn't want kids; I gave up my place at university; delayed something; didn't travel somewhere; he doesn't eat spicy food so I haven't eaten Indian for 12 years; he prefers me blonde, skinny, fat, tanned, waxed, hairy.'*

Women seemed to be constantly subjecting themselves to men, not that the men asked them to, I never heard that, just that women seemed to do it anyway.

My grandma always says, 'Don't subject yourself to a man, Kate, subject them to you!' and I think what she means by that is decide what you want in life and get the man to fit to that, not focus on the man's needs and try to accommodate, mould, shape, change, compromise yourself to please him. I always found it a bit confusing because I thought subjects were things we studied at school. But *subjects* or rather *subjecting* yourself is apparently a universal force, like some kind of giant whip, or invisible force field that humans can apply to one another. My grandma knows this stuff because she's a world-renowned feminist, and a prolifically productive one at that. She's written books and papers on just about everything to do to with women, and men, and force fields of oppression. Living with her as a child, I was constantly surrounded by paper towers of manuscripts and books. I ran around them with my best friend, Peter, and we pretended the towers were actually paper trees in paper forests, which was odd because they *were* trees before they were chopped down by a burger company wanting to graze cattle on the newly deforested land, then made into paper for us to build paper trees with...

And that's what I wanted *True Love* to write about— not the cows and the trees and global deforestation; that's more *Time Magazine* than *True Love*. No, I wanted *True Love* to write about the things love took away. I wanted to help women go out and get those things back. I wanted to help them reclaim all the things that love had stolen. And I wanted to ask what they'd do if they were me, a 30-year-old girl who found herself at relationship and life Ground Zero having well and truly missed her own love boat. So I'd suggested this to Chad. I'd said, 'Chad, I want to go out and get back all the things love stole. It's going to be like *Challenge Anneka*[1] but with love and boats and the occasional high five. Please let me do it, Chad, please. Give me something to believe in after my bed for two became a bed for one.'

And I had planned to do that every day. I was going to help people reclaim their love-stolen dreams until the pain in my heart went away and the word Gabriel, or Gabe, or on the odd occasion the 'Ga' sound no longer brought me to tears. Because as Prince Charmings go mine turned out to be gut-wrenchingly rubbish, and I don't think I'm the first girl in the world to think their allocated prince was a little bit shit, but Chad had said, 'No.'

Then I'd starting crying, because since the break-up I've become something of a continuous weeper. Prior to this I thought us Brits were stoic and watertight, but now the tears come fast, in plentiful supply and with the most minimal of provocation.

---

[1] **Challenge Anneka** – British television show. Aired in the late 1980s and early 1990s. Anneka (tall, bottom-length hair, wore jumpsuits and used mobile telephones way before the rest of the world) would be set a challenge. Anneka and her helicopter-flying, mobile-phone-wielding team would then have a limited amount of time to complete the task. Anneka managed such things as repainting a Romanian orphanage, building a seal pool and 'finding' 10 double-decker buses for the National Playbus Association. She was a bit cool, super charitable and also a really really fast runner.

And since then the most controversial thing the magazine had published was 400 words on the physical effects of heartbreak being directly comparable to Class A drug withdrawal (which is totally true, by the way, for any of you feeling violently ill after a recent break-up). No, *True Love* had continued to eulogise the positive benefits of love, teaching readers how to secure as much of it as possible, often through purchasing one of the many products Chad sold advertising space for, and, when they finally did get it, encouraging them to write in and share it with a love-hungry world. Or at least that was our position until last Friday…

And just for the record, before that Loosie starts speaking again, you should probably know that she's had it in for me since I made fun of her funny American accent, and the fact that she speaks with the speed and intonation of a concrete-cracking power drill, and the silly spelling of her name…

'As I said, Chad, it's not just the post.' She glared at me. 'We've received an unusual amount of voicemails; three hundred on the main phone line, a hundred and twenty on the back-up line, and there's something called a *facsimile machine* that keeps ejecting pieces of paper with what looks like handwritten messages. I've called IT and asked them to take it away. We've also received various gift boxes from motivational speakers; have been contacted by the publishers of almost every self-help author in Europe; and the BBC called, three times; and Kate, well, Kate seems to have received an awful lot of messages today too.' You see, I told you. She hates me. 'Yes, lots of people have called saying they want to speak to *Pirate Kate*.' Oh no. 'And most of the post seems to be addressed to *Pirate Kate*—' I looked across the room but Federico was quietly humming to himself and looking the other way '—and everyone seems to want to talk about their love-stolen dreams.'

'Their what?' Chad said, spinning on the spot to face me.

'Their love-stolen dreams, Chad,' Loosie repeated, even though Chad had heard perfectly well the first time. At that moment, thankfully, Mark from Marketing burst in the room. Actually he hobbled on account of his knee injury from the giant heart-shaped table, but that sounds less dramatic, so imagine he burst.

'The servers are down!' he yelled, after bursting.

'The servers are down for what?' Chad said, super irritated, with me.

'For everything, Chad, for everything, the main site, the micro-sites, client side—everything's crashed. Too many people are trying to access them at the same time.' Mark's voice sounds as if he's got an apple pip stuck up his nostril, if you know what I mean.

Chad looked between me, Federico and Mark.

'Everyone, back here, tomorrow, 9 a.m.,' he yelled before marching out of the boardroom followed by Mark, who, for the sake of the dramatic content of this scene, also marched out.

the pianist—beatrice van de broeck—90 years old

What didn't I do because of love? Well, I didn't study piano. It was 1936 and I was offered a place at the Juilliard School in New York. You've probably never heard of it but Juilliard was already one of the greatest music schools in the world. Some of the most successful pianists of our time have graduated from that school.

Well, my father, a very conservative Belgian man, toyed with the idea of allowing me to go but the school couldn't guarantee I'd be able to find work after graduation. To have a daughter move to America was one thing, but for her to become an unemployed musician, well, that was quite another. Ultimately he gave me the choice. To do what was expected of me and marry a wonderful man who I was very fond of, or to go. Of course I agreed to marry. That was the right thing to do, the proper thing. And my husband bought me the most beautiful Steinway piano as a wedding gift. I played it every day until the day he died, God rest his soul.

But after passing up my place at Juilliard I never took another piano lesson. I stayed just as I was; good but not

*great; a pianist but not a musician, not a performer. So if
there had been no husband, if there had been less of an obligation to marry and settle down, if I had been free as a bird
like you are now, you beautiful young girl, that is the first
place I would go. That would be my love-stolen dream. And
if I was there I would cross my fingers and all my toes and
hope that love never showed up so I could stay there forever.*

grandma's villa | pepperpots life sanctuary

'We will do everything possible to make sure you keep your
job. You're the best thing that's ever happened to the ghost-
writing team at *True Love*. Your writing equals a young
Barbara Cartland,' and other such platitudes had spouted
from the mouth of Federico as soon as we realised the trouble I was in. Then we'd jumped in my car and driven straight
to see Grandma Josephine at Pepperpots Life Sanctuary,
the most exclusive old people's home in Western Europe[2].
There'd been no mention of Federico's involvement in
my current predicament. No, we'd skipped over that like
Dorothy sprint-hurdling down the Yellow Brick Road. But
within seconds of actually arriving at Grandma's villa
Team Kate had fractured, with Federico knocking me to
the floor as he pelted down the hallway diving head first into
Grandma's impressive walk-in wardrobe. He re-emerged a
few seconds later screaming, *'Where's the Chanel?'* before

---

[2]You can't really call **Pepperpots** an old people's home. It's more like
a luxury retirement theme park set over 570 acres with its own spa,
floating restaurant, dance studio and rock-climbing centre—the final
stop-off for the brightest, wisest and most physically capable minds
of yesteryear.

dragging most of the contents into the middle of Grandma's enormous open-plan lounge. He spent the rest of the afternoon trying on an assortment of different furs, spinning backwards and forwards on the spot like one of those figurines in a music box.

'Well, I told her to start small,' Federico said, trying on his third fur. 'Didn't I, Kat-kins? I said, "Make Chad think it was his idea," but she went ahead and did it anyway, yes she did, like a boisterous young bullock filled with his first flush of hormones.' He took a sip from a large Margarita and threw on another fur. And just for the record he'd done no such thing. He'd said, 'Go big, Kat-kins!' high-fived me, poured an Appletini down my throat then substituted my diligently ghost-written *True Love* reader story for a two-page advert inviting the readers to get in touch and share their Love-Stolen Dreams. But apparently the truth held no place in Grandma's colossal lakeside villa.

'What we don't understand,' Grandma began, her best friend Beatrice nodding along, 'is why Chad will just *assume* it was Kate.' Beatrice and Grandma were dressed head-to-foot in black Lycra Parkour[3] outfits and looked like Bond girls for the over-80s. 'Federico, you must tell this Chad someone else submitted the advert. He'll listen to you.'

'I see your point, Josephine, yes, I do,' Federico said, collapsing into a pile of dark brown furs, looking like the walnut on top of a giant Walnut Whip. 'But if we are stood

---

[3]**Parkour** – or 'free running' – is a sport in which participants run along a route, attempting to negotiate obstacles using only their bodies. Skills such as jumping, climbing, vaulting, rolling, swinging and wall scaling are employed. Parkour is most commonly practised in urban areas. It is not commonly practised by pensioners.

in *Truth Town*, Josephine, and it feels like we are, Chad doesn't always listen to me in the work environment, no he does not. In fact sometimes that handsome mountain of a man doesn't listen to me at all. But that is a totally different work drama of mine and today isn't about me, it's about Kat-kins, but let's just say if we are touching on the subject, and it feels like we are, that I need to work on establishing better boundaries; emotionally, professionally and *sexually*.' He whispered that last word before sipping on yet another Margarita. I was still dry as a pre-ignited bush fire. 'And Chad thinks it's Kat-kins because she presented the idea to him a few months ago.' He passed Grandma a piece of paper that I recognised as my colourful and mostly felt-tip-based A3 presentation. Grandma unrolled the paper then shielded her eyes.

'I know,' Federico said as he scurried to the other side of the room to try on what looked like a man's dark blue blazer. 'It's like she's taken it to the local preschool and asked a group of mentally challenged under-5s to create her important business proposal for her. Did you do that, Kat-kins, did you?'

'I thought I'd brought you up better than this, Kate.' Grandma tutted, holding the presentation in my face. Personally I think it's hard to quantify whether Grandma brought me up better than a colourful A3 presentation. Certainly she brought me up better than my parents, but they are *really* odd and thankfully almost constantly away. They call themselves *Peaceful Extreme Non-Violent Dangerous Environmental Activists (PENDEAs)* but I know that they are not non-violent and last week I saw images of them on

Channel 4 News. They were wielding machetes on the deck of a recently impounded aid ship entering the Gaza Strip. Dad had face paint on, Rambo-style. I don't know you well enough to tell you what my mother was doing, but let's just say that occasionally she feels exposing her breasts is the best way to evoke peace. So my upbringing was better than hanging about with them, but better than a colourful A3 presentation? I wasn't 100% sure.

'Well, Kate, there is only one way you can save your job,' Grandma said as she threw my presentation in the fireplace and lit a match, the felt-tip-covered page burning with a greeny-orange flame. 'You must find something impressive to write about so that Chad doesn't want you to leave.'

'By tomorrow?' I guffawed. 'I've got more chance of inventing a time machine and catapulting myself back into the past.'

'Well, she could write about that lovely Delaware,' Beatrice suggested. 'People always like to hear news about her.'

'Delaware!' Grandma nodded before punching the air victoriously. 'You must speak to Delaware O'Hunt!'

'Why would Kate be able to interview Delaware O'Hunt?' Federico said, grabbing hold of Beatrice's shoulders. 'Why, I ask you? Why?' He was trying to stay calm but he was shaking her quite violently.

'Because she lives next door,' Grandma said, walking out to her terrace and peering over the fence, 'and normally she pops in for vino before her jazz fusion rock dance class.'

'How did we not know about this, Kat-kins?' Federico shout-whispered. 'The most media-shy actress from the golden age of film living here, next door to Grandma, and you let me come here, drink Margaritas, eat lovely sushi wraps, of which there doesn't appear to be any today,' he said, looking about the place, 'and we never knew about Delaware? This is slapdash, Kat-kins! Totally slapdash!' He placed his forehead against the window overlooking the next-door villa. 'I love her,' he quietly wailed to himself as his breath created misty patches on the glass. 'I completely love her.'

You see, Delaware O'Hunt wasn't just an actress. She's a screen idol of the 1950s. She made more movies than any other actress, starred with all the greats, made plays, musicals, films, won an Oscar, got married, then divorced. She had a tumultuous love life and wore the most incredible clothes. In fact there is nothing in Delaware O'Hunt's current wardrobe that I wouldn't run over hot coals to wear even now she is a proper pensioner. But I can't for a second imagine how love negatively affected the gorgeous Delaware. Love was all around her; love chased her down the street; love made posters of her; documentaries about her; sang about her. She was a world-famous actress, one of the greatest of the greats. It didn't look as if love stole anything at all.

'Darling, she doesn't seem to be in so why don't you pop back at the weekend and I'll arrange for you to have a chat? Federico, if you come early we can go rock climbing together.'

'Thank you, Josephine, thank you.' He was speaking like a 1940s actor. 'I'll be back at the weekend, first thing, first thing I tell you.' He punched the air with Delaware-inspired enthusiasm. 'Oh, and Josephine,' he said, extracting himself from the dark blue blazer that looked in my opinion to be from Hugo Boss Menswear, 'I L.O.V.E. the jacket. It's so on point. Try it, Kat-kins, try it,' he said, passing it to me. 'Girl in Boy is black to last season's pattern on print.'

'Oh, that's not Josephine's jacket,' giggled Beatrice. 'He thinks it's your jacket! No, that's Peter's jacket, isn't it? He left it here when he came for lunch. I remember because I thought it brought out the colour of his eyes. Well, it did, didn't it?' she said to Grandma, who looked uncharacteristically startled.

'Peter who?' I asked Grandma. Beatrice seldom feels the need to contextualise.

'Peter Parker is his full name,' Beatrice continued. 'Isn't that right, Josephine? I'm sure it was Peter Parker because I very much enjoyed the alliteration.'

'Peter Parker as in Spiderman?' Federico asked with re-ignited interest in the jacket I now held.

'No, silly,' Beatrice chortled, 'although he was terribly serious. No, Peter Parker is Kate's childhood friend.'

'Peter Parker!' I turned to Grandma. 'Peter Parker!!!' I was getting a bit shouty. 'You had lunch with *my* Peter Parker? How? When? How?'

'It was a lunch, darling. Can't I have a lunch? Everyone has to eat.'

'Grandma!'

'He got back in touch recently, darling, which has been very nice, if I'm honest. Well, aren't people allowed to contact me any more? And he's been very supportive of me regarding my move to Pepperpots. It was a huge decision to give up the family home, such an upheaval. And I hope I have been equally supportive of Peter regarding his divorce.

It's so hard to maintain a long-term relationship in this current socio-economic climate. I said to him, I said, "Peter, if you are looking for stability in the post-post-modern modernist age you'll struggle."'

'Peter Parker got married? *My* Peter Parker got married? I mean, divorced, I mean, Peter Parker is single?' I really didn't know what I meant.

'I suppose technically I'm all three,' said Peter Parker from behind me.

It was the first time I had heard his voice in over 15 long years.

WHAT DID YOU MISS OUT ON BECAUSE YOU FELL IN LOVE?

Dear *True Love* Readers,

This year, as the clock struck 30 years old, I found myself jobless, homeless and abandoned in France by my French fiancé. I had given up everything in a fight for love, and I'd lost, knocked out in the 7th round, sucker-punched.

With absolutely nothing to my name, no home, no money and no job, I had well and truly missed my own love boat. If I had been younger I would have soothed my broken heart through the tried and tested method of boyfriend replacement and/or alcohol consumption. But this time I couldn't. This time the pain in my heart was too great, the love lost was too huge. For many dark months all I could manage, in between fits of sobbing, was to ponder upon the following:

What on earth do I do next?

Because my One *True Love* had already been and gone; as had all our future plans, our dreams, our as yet unrealised wedding anniversaries, our as yet unborn children. That part of my life was over before it had even begun. So with no guarantee that love would ever show up again I needed to find out what would make me happy in the absence of love. What could I do with my time until love showed up, if love ever shows up at all. **And this is where you come in.**

You see, I have started to make a list of all the things I didn't get to do **because I fell in love;** a list of all the hobbies, ambitions and secret dreams that were put on the back burner the day I fell in love. And I am going to go out and do all those things. I am going to go out, like a pirate on the giant sea of life, and **I am going to take back what love stole.** And here at *True Love* we want to know **what you gave up for love.** Is there something you always wanted to do but stopped pursuing it when you fell in love? A hobby or dream? What negative effects did falling in love have on your life? What love advice do you have for me? Perhaps some of you are interested in going on your own Love Quests, taking back what love has stolen.

It doesn't matter if you are in love, out of love, searching for love, avoiding love, married, divorced, gay or straight. *True Love* wants to hear from you.

Can't think of anything? Then let's turn this on its head. Ask yourself the following questions:

'If you knew you were going to spend the rest of your life alone, you would never fall in love, never settle down, never have children, what would you want to do? What would make you happy? What would fill up your time, your heart, your soul for the rest of your days?' The answers to these questions are the dreams we need to get back.

I have missed my own love boat. I am loveless and boatless with a whole lifetime to fill. I'm going on a quest, **a Love-Stolen Dreams** quest, to take back what love stole. So, are you with me? Do you want to join my ship?

Pirate Kate x x

PIRATE KATE
Please send all response letters to: Pirate Kate; PO Box Love-Stolen Dreams, c/o the *True Love* London Office

NEXT WEEK IN TRUE LOVE:
MR PURRR-FECT
—how a feline companion can take the pain out of living alone
BOTOX OR NOTOX
—should you plump and fill for your special day?
AND HOW TO CREATE YOUR PERFECT
WEDDING DRESS FOR LESS THAN
£69.98

paper towers of paper souls

big red | true love office | london

Jenny Sullivan doesn't work in a wee pod. That's how I knew she was important when I first joined *True Love* magazine; that and the fact that I'd already seen her on a million different billboards, a thousand different TV adverts, a hundred different talk shows. But in terms of my working day, the reason I knew she was important was because she didn't work in a pod. You see, the offices of *True Love* magazine take up the entire top floor of a converted warehouse. They are completely open-plan with one large glass room in the middle, the boardroom, then one corner office for Chad and another for Jenny Sullivan. The rest of the office is dotted with enormous brightly coloured pods each standing eight foot tall with a desk inside and a small arch to get in. They resemble giant dinosaur eggs and make the office look like an incubation chamber in an ethically questionable science laboratory—one growing human clones with above-average writing skills and the ability to sell full-page advertising space. And while there is no scientific evidence that working in giant eggs improves productivity Chad did produce a historical document claiming the Incas had done so. His historical document looked suspiciously like a normal piece of A4 paper stained with tea. And the 'facts' were un-referenceable on *Google*. Nevertheless all the staff at *True Love* were made to work in *Work Evolving Egg Pods*, or *wee pods*; everyone, that is, except Jenny. And I had been hiding inside my *wee pod*, affectionately named *Big Red*, since 09:15 this morning listening to them fight in *True Love*'s boardroom.

'Chad, I'm just saying, Chad, this idea, it doesn't sound very "us", does it?' Jenny said, manically twisting her gigantic wedding ring around her finger, 'because people here are into love, Chad.' Jenny drew a heart in the air with her index finger. 'This magazine is into love, Chad.' She did it again. She could have just pointed at the boardroom table. 'That's why we are called *True Love* magazine, Chad.'

I'm not sure if you've noticed this yet, but Jenny Sullivan likes to overuse people's first names. It's a technique she read about in a book called *'Own it—Take Life by the Bollocks'*. She once said my name so many times I disconnected from it entirely.

'Chad, I'm just thinking of you, Chad.' You see. 'Because we can't *suddenly* start writing about how shit love is, become love pirates, steal love ships and go on bloody love missions. What will our poor stupid readers think?' She looked from Chad to Federico, who was standing like a statue in the corner of the room. Chad, on the other hand, was pacing up and down the boardroom, throwing handfuls of *Haribo* in his gob. 'Because I have other things I can do if this magazine folds, Chad. I'd just carry on with my modelling career,' she said, smoothing out imaginary creases in her clothes. 'Not a day goes by that I'm not asked to endorse some beauty product or fashion brand. It's such a bore,' she said to Federico, as if he'd understand such a burden, even though the only thing Federico's ever been asked to endorse is mouthwash at Paddington Station, and that was more of a general customer satisfaction survey than a traditional *celebrity* endorsement. 'And that's before we take into account my writing career, Chad. My publisher is *constantly* on the phone demanding I write another best-seller. Or I could just take some time out, spend more time being a good wife, fuss over my wonderful husband and—'

'Oh, for twat's sake, Jenny, would you please just shut the fuck up?' Chad said, coming to a sudden stop. 'It would be less twatting offensive if you just put all your awards, and your accolades, and your precious photos of you and your perfect Ken Doll husband, and printed them *directly* onto your twatting clothes, let the fabric speak for you, then my ears wouldn't feel like they were haemorrhaging every time you start twatting talking.'

Federico clamped his hand over his own mouth, his bulbous eyes whizzing between the two of them.

'I get it, Jenny,' Chad continued. 'I get it. You are twatting f-ing great.'

Jenny looked for a second as if she was about to cry. Her bottom lip was a tremble away from a tear. Federico turned away and shielded his eyes. He says that seeing an incredibly beautiful person cry is like seeing a big shit in the middle of freshly laundered sheets. It just shouldn't be allowed.

'Look at the letters, Jenny,' Chad said, pointing to the corner of the room. 'Look at the twatting letters!'

There was a tap on the side of my wee pod. It was Chad's assistant, Loosie. She climbed in, notebook attached to her hand, blocking my view of the boardroom. She harrumphed before speaking just to let me know how tiresome she found me, and everything to do with *everything* to do with me.

'Kate Winters,' she began, 'on the assumption that you are responsible for the advert that ran unauthorised in the last edition of *True Love*, and Lord knows the way you have been pining after your ex-boyfriend we all assume that it's you, that and the fact that no one else would be stupid enough to a) actually pitch the idea to Chad, be rejected, then pursue it anyway and b) publish what is for all intents and purposes an advert actually encouraging our readers to, Lord forbid, get in touch, you have another 29 postal sacks of letters addressed to *Pirate Kate*. They were by your wee pod but Chad, and by Chad I mean me, dragged them into the boardroom. You also have a gift box from a motivational speaker called Bob. He wants to take a meeting with you. And by you I of course mean *"Pirate Kate".*' She made inverted commas with her fingers. 'And you have phone messages: your grandmother called three times wanting to speak to you about someone called Mary, someone called Delaware and someone called Beatrice. She spoke as if I should know who these people are. She also wanted to know why you didn't start work at 9 a.m. Personally I would like to know the same thing. Your friend Leah called, twice, wanting to talk to you about her love-stolen dreams, and a man called Peter Parker called—'

I knocked over my coffee at the sound of his name. Loosie watched me, as if I were poo on a sheet, as I tried to mop it up.

'Peter Parker—' she paused, waiting to see if she could make me spill it again '—spelt his name out for me, twice, very slowly. Please tell…Peter Parker…I am not a retard. And does he know he's got the same name as Spiderman? Don't answer that. Federico asked to see you when you get in, Jenny Sullivan's on the warpath for you, and Chad said to say, and I quote, "Don't even think about starting your twatting day sitting your skinny little arse down or sniffing at a cup of morning twatting coffee before seeing me," and by me I mean Chad—it was a quote. BTW there is a stain on your top that looks like tomato juice, but it could be ketchup. Either way we both know that it's not from any kind of vitamin drink. Kate? Kate, where do you think you are going?'

'I am going to get fresh coffee,' I said, clambering out of Big Red.

'Didn't you hear me, Kate? You need to go to the boardroom. We are having an *Early Morning Focused Focus Meeting*. Go! Now!'

the boardroom | true love

As I nervously slipped into the back of the boardroom Chad was a partial blur, silently spinning himself in fast circles on his special velvet heart-shaped chair. Federico was attached to the *Nespresso* machine and frantically waved as I walked in. Jenny Sullivan was sitting straight-backed and straight-faced at the blood-drawing tip of the glass heart. It looked as if the heart were literally growing out from between her perfect breasts. The rest of the office were skim-reading a *Time Magazine* article that Loosie was silently handing out but with a noisy sense of self-importance.

The 2009 article claimed there was a link between obesity and love. It stated that within a few years of getting married women were twice as likely to become obese compared to women who were merely dating. The research had monitored over 7,000 women and found that unmarried women living with partners for up to five years had a 63% increased risk of obesity. One of the researchers wrote that, 'The longer a woman lives with a romantic partner, the more likely she is to keep putting on weight.' This was by no means the first piece of research to highlight this link, or the more general negative effects relationships can have on women, but it was the only piece of research Chad could get his hands on before our ironically named *Early Morning Focused Focus Meeting*—a meeting that has never once been focused, never once (before today) been held early in the morning and has occasionally involved several members of staff crying. *Afternoon Mothers Meeting* would have been a more appropriate name, or *Let's all listen to one of Chad's never-ending monologues and try to guess how many expletives he will use*.

'I've decided I want to take *True Love* in a new direction,' Chad said, mid spin, the words flying from his mouth as if from a spinning top; the sounds of the beginning and end of his sentence whizzing off in different directions.

'Now, I know I didn't run it past you lot first, but why the fuck would I? So keep up. I'm introducing a new section to the magazine and I'm calling it Love-Stolen Dreams.' He locked eyes with me for a split second of every spin. 'LSD for short.' He grabbed the edge of the glass heart and came to a violent stop. 'I want *True Love* to start having a more balanced view of love and I've decided to start with the twatting fat people.' He got up to start pacing around the boardroom, but his legs buckled under him like a puppet with no master—too many spins—so from the boardroom floor he began his focus meeting speech. 'Now, before any of you get all squeaky and high-pitched I'm not judging the fat, OK, so let's just get that out there for any of you liberalists who are pro the obese and all that. My mum had a lifelong battle with the bulge so I know first-hand how a larger lady can feel. But our readers fessed up, OK. They put it out there. They wrote in, in twatting sackfuls, to say they blamed men for getting fat. Obviously it's not true. I have about as much effect on a woman's weight as a plastic satsuma but we are going to write about it anyway because apparently they give a crap. Marketing guy, put up advertising rates by 15% and call out all the diet-pill companies. In fact call anything weight-loss related: step machines, personal trainers, Paul-twatting-McKenna and his I Can Make You a Skinny Fuck book. We want it all. Yellow WEE Pod, I want a selection of short articles about celebrities whose weight has been affected by love, maybe something about the amount of calories sex burns, but how they got fat afterwards, otherwise we'll lose the fat readers. Blue, black and silver WEES, I want to know about readers who lost material possessions because of love: houses, iPads, cars and so on. Pink WEE, I want you to write about people who cancelled travel plans for love. And I want something about how love killed someone, preferably through starvation, or through having an actual broken heart. We want the readers to go on a roller coaster of twatting emotions. Jenny, read up on queens or princesses, find one who gave up something for love, the right to the throne or something.' Jenny rolled her eyes and huffed so heavily she could have blown herself, on her chair, across the room. 'And, Kate—' I went cold as he said my name '—let's not forget little Kate Winters.' I could feel everyone in the room bristling with delight at the prospect of seeing me publicly fired. 'Kate, you have illegally published something in my magazine. You are therefore responsible for all these twatting letters.' He pointed to the far corner of the room and I turned to look. 'It was the ultimate breach of trust, not only that you found a way to access my copy, ergo millions of our readers, but that you then used that open channel to involve them in your own quest. Give me one magnificent twatting reason why I shouldn't fire you then call the police and have you arrested?'

I didn't know what to say. All I could see were the letters: thousands upon thousands of them on tables in the corner, towers of letters bigger than any paper forest Peter and I had ran around as kids. And each one was a woman, a living breathing woman wanting to share, wanting to speak, wanting to reach out and connect; every letter a different voice, a different soul. Women *did* want to take back their love-stolen dreams. They were like paper towers of hope.

I felt my eyes twinkle at the prospect. This would keep me busy forever.

'Oi! Pirate Kate! Give me one twatting reason why I shouldn't fire you!'

Everyone in the room expected me to crumble, or beg or just pack up my desk and leave. But not now, not with all these love-stolen dreams laid out in front of me. Chad would have to drag me from the building by my ankles if he thought I was going to give up that easily.

'I can give you two,' I said dramatically, turning to face the room, who gasped. 'Actually I can only give you one, but it consists of two words—'

'This isn't twatting charades!'

'How about an interview with the media-shy Delaware O'Hunt?' The room gasped again.

'Actually that's quite a lot more than two words…' Federico muttered. 'Even Delaware O'Hunt is three words, if you think about it, and then there was the rest of the sentence, which takes us closer to ten, although I don't actually know if the O apostrophe gets counted with the Hunt. Does anyone know that?' He looked around the room. 'Anyone?'

'I twatting love Delaware O'Hunt and you know it,' Chad barked, sitting heavily in his heart-shaped chair. 'Kate Winters, I swear to you now, if that interview doesn't materialise, or you piss her off like you've pissed me off, then you will be thrown from the building.' And he meant from the roof. 'You are officially on probation. If you submit anything else to my magazine unauthorised you will be fired. If you come into the office late you will be fired. If you wear a pair of shoes I find offensive you will be fired.' I looked down at my shoes to find they already offended me. 'You are here because of the promise of Delaware and because a certain someone believes you are talented.' Federico pointed at his own head. 'I'm not so sure, so let's see how your Love-Stolen Dreams idea pans out. But you will no longer write anything under your own name.' I didn't anyway. 'You will go nowhere near the copy for next month's edition, and as a special treat you can read *every single one* of the letters you helped generate. I am going to work you so twatting hard you won't know what's hit you. So dive in, go wild, pick your favourites then rewrite them for the magazine, in first person, obviously. And when the Delaware copy is ready email it to Jenny. Obviously it will run under her name. We can't have a nobody writing our main twatting feature, otherwise what do I need Jenny for?' Jenny went a bit pale and locked eyes with Chad, just for a second, before they both smiled sycophantically at each other. 'So!' Chad said, clapping his hands together. 'I will be checking the copy for this edition and I read slow so everyone's deadline is two days early.' There was a communal groan. 'Button it, you lot, and let's take a moment. Close your eyes, take a breath and let's say it together. "Thank twat for the twatting fat people."' He threw his unfinished apple over his shoulder and marched out of the room, Loosie in tow. Then everyone turned to glare at me. I say everyone turned; Federico didn't. He sat in the corner giving me a mini round of applause before getting distracted by something invisible on his sleeve.

'Well, look at you,' he said as everyone left the boardroom. '*True Love* magazine chasing down Love-Stolen

Dreams; a new direction; a new era; an extra-heavy work-load for the rest of the office as a result. Well done you!' He squeaked the word *'Yeah!'* and shook his fist in the air.

Federico was right. It was worth a fist shake and a silent *Yeah*. I had a virtual conveyor belt of love-stolen dreams to busy myself with, taking back what love had stolen; help-ing women reconnect with themselves; spreading happiness and joy and hoping it was contagious like an extra-virulent strain of Pig Flu. And after a few of the postal sacks had been sorted through and skim-read we found Chad had most definitely been right. There did seem to be an awful lot of women who felt their bodies had changed since they'd fallen in love. So Federico and I decided to invite 20 of them to join a *Fat Camp*. We wanted to get back their pre-love bodies. We wanted to make them feel pre-love happy and light. Maybe we could learn why they gained the weight in the first place, because everyone wants to feel beauti-ful and, excuse the pun, worth it, so why did so many of us feel the exact opposite, and why was love bringing about this change?

As I packed up my belongings that morning, on the first official day of Love-Stolen Dreams, I felt a glimmer of excitement, a spark of hope, a hint of happiness, which were all feelings that had been absent in my life for some time. But they were quickly replaced by fear and apprehen-sion as Jenny Sullivan breezed past me in a gust of perfec-tion and skinny hatred, and although I never saw her lips move I swear blind I heard her whisper, 'You'll pay for this, Winters,' as she marched into Chad's office, slamming the glass door behind her.

the story of peter parker—the boy who never smiles

I grew up living next door to a boy named Peter Parker. Not the emotionally burdened alter ego of Spiderman, but the emotionally burdened son of parents unfamiliar with the world of Marvel. Peter is my oldest friend. He was my best friend. And between you and me he was probably my first crush.

our official timeline

Age 2¼ – Peter and I met at our local preschool. Actually I'm not sure you can really *meet* someone at 2¼, more accurate to say we were placed next to each other and shared the use of a black and white Etch-A-Sketch.

Age 3½ – Peter and I discovered the duck pond. There I made him eat 24 tadpoles telling him they were a new kind of Cola Bottle. For the next 11 years he ate almost anything I gave him and I followed him almost everywhere he went.

Age 4 – Grandma tried to make us kiss at my birthday

pool party. Peter refused and burst into a volcano of girl-hating tears. So did I, but for profoundly different reasons.

Age 5 – Peter kissed a different girl at a different pool party, this time voluntarily. Her name was Annabel, she carried a *Care Bear* and she *always* smelt of strawberries. This time I was the only person crying.

Age 6 – The local kids started violently flicking their wrists in Peter's face and making strange saliva-infused whooshing noises. It was one of the toughest years for Peter at school and culminated in a hysterical outburst when our teacher tried to make him wear a Spiderman costume for Halloween.

Age 7¼ – Peter Parker's mum died, quite suddenly, and I was never really told how.

By age 8 I realised Peter Parker no longer smiled. I only saw his front teeth exposed when he played with his pet dog, Jake. Then he would laugh and giggle and occasionally, if he didn't think anyone was watching, he'd do a sort of high-pitched excited scream. We lived next door to each other so I was *always* watching.

Age 8¾ – I made it my official life mission to make Peter Parker smile again because when he did, even for a second, he could light up a room. I etched my promise onto the bark of a tree and pricked my finger with a needle until it bled. As an 8-year-old that was the official way to make a life's promise to oneself. The tree is still standing and I still have a tiny scar.

I was more or less constantly preoccupied by Peter until age 14. He was the man in my life, or at least the unsmiling boy in it. Then, just before my 15th birthday, his father sent him to an international school in Switzerland; the kind of school with no formal curriculum and a lofty focus on developing the individual. Peter didn't say goodbye, he didn't leave a note and I never heard from him again.

peter parker the adult is a handsome, expressionless man. He has thick dark hair, dark blue eyes and sports the complexion of an A-list Hollywood actress. His clothes are always ironed, he smells just the way you'd want your boyfriend to smell and has the ability to retain inordinate amounts of information. Grandma tells me that he completed a Physics degree in Switzerland, a Master's degree in Paris and a PhD in America. He now specialises in the development of renewable sources of energy, and in handsome frowning.

peter parker's favourite thing—dogs and any kind of physical challenge, including sit-ups.

peter parker's favourite activity—running at high speed with a dog and any kind of physical challenge, including sit-ups.

mary the cleaner—68 years old

Mary the cleaner worked for my family for over 30 years. She was plump but not fat, rosy, but not red, jolly, but not funny. When drinking tea, in between sips, Mary always held her mug in both hands against her chest, as if warming her own breastbone.

'Little Kate Winters! Look at you,' she said as she opened the front door of her terraced house. 'My goodness, don't you look lovely? Just lovely,' she said, pulling me inside. 'You know it was just the other day your grandma told me you were back. I am *so* sorry things didn't work out with Gabriel.' She hung my coat over the banisters and turned to face me. 'I remember the two of you at your grandma's birthday. You were quite the smitten kittens. I was sure the next time I'd see you you'd have a trail of beautiful children running along behind you. How are you feeling about it all?' she said, looking deep into my eyes. Now, even though I thought I was fine, and had turned up like a proper journalist with a Dictaphone and giant pack of chewing gum, a child-like lump appeared in my throat and my voice all but disappeared. Because adult women have the ability to reduce me to tears by uttering one simple harmless sentence… 'How are you feeling?' Mary looked startled as tears spurted unexpectedly from my eyes.

'Oh dear, oh dear, you know it was just the same for our Laura,' she said, patting me on the back. 'She used to be with a lovely lass called Carly, who we all adored. Carly was into aromatherapy. Have you heard of it? Well, we were sure there'd be wedding bells and civil ceremonies any day. I bought a hat. But Laura messed it up as only Laura can and ran off with a fitness instructor called Tessa, who, excuse me, is terribly masculine and terribly rude. Well, what's the point of being a bloody lesbian then setting up home with a woman who is the spits of a ruddy great man?' And now Mary needed a hanky and a hug. Eventually we steered the conversation back onto Mary and my idea about Love-Stolen Dreams.

'Well, it made me laugh when your grandma called the other morning, wanting to know about my deepest desires.' Mary took a sip from a mug commemorating the marriage of Prince Charles to Princess Diana. 'I felt like I was on one of those TV phone-ins!' she said, pushing herself further back into her 1980s floral sofa. 'And it's not that I'm unhappy, Kate. I am very content. And I would never want Len to think otherwise, poor old bugger! It's just your grandma's such a pushy what-not. She wouldn't get off the phone until I told her at least one unfulfilled dream or interest.' Mary tutted good-naturedly before offering me a strawberry Quality Street. 'And it's silly that I even think about it. I don't think about it. It's nothing. Well, now I've gone and made it sound like something! Bloody Josephine! For the record I am happy watching a bit of *Top Gear* and sitting with Len while he fiddles with his cars, but, if I was going to spend the rest of my life "alone" as your grandma rather dramatically told me, then I suppose learning about cars would make me quite happy.' She offered me another Quality Street. I took another Strawberry Cream.

'What do you mean you want to learn about cars? Like, you'd want to understand the different makes and models?'

'Oh no dear, I'd want to learn how to take apart and put back together a combustion engine,' she said, straightening out her flannel dress and cardi combo. 'I'd want to train to be a mechanic.' My half-chewed Strawberry Cream nearly fell from my mouth.

'OK,' I said, nodding my head. 'Cool.' Lots more headnodding. 'So, er, have you had any mechanical, combustion-type experiences so far…?'

'Well, I'll tell you, Kate,' she said, tapping my knee, 'I did do a little something about six months ago. There was an old part from one of Len's cars and he was going to throw it out, but I knew it wasn't broken. I was sure of it. So when Len went to work I took the part out the bin, took it apart, cleaned it up and put it back together. I gave it back to him and told him I'd got it from Jim at the scrapyard. Well, I never tell lies, Kate, but I was desperate to know if it worked. And it did! He put it in the car and it worked!' Mary was squeezing her podgy hands together in her lap as if shaking her own hand with praise.

'Wow! Mary, that's amazing! You must be so proud!'

'I felt on top of the world about it, Kate! Still do! It

worked because I had fixed it. Can you imagine that? You see something broken and you put it back together, you fix it, with your own bare hands.'

For some reason the image of my own heart popped into my head, bright red, shattered on a stone floor. I saw hands picking up all the pieces, squeezing them back into shape like a plasticine toy. But all the pieces wouldn't stick; they kept falling off and tumbling back to the floor, like overly floured pastry. I shoved another Quality Street in my mouth to fill the void.

'So, Mary, how did you feel when you were actually working on the part?'

'Well, I'm not sure if it's like this for you, Kate, but normally I have a hundred things going on in my head. While I'm ironing the sheets I'm scanning the room looking for my next job, thinking about what's in the fridge for dinner, wondering what time Len will be back from work. But when I sat at the kitchen table fixing that part I was completely into what I was doing. And that felt…peaceful. When I finished I felt this warmth, right here.' She placed the palm of her hand against her breastbone and left it there for a few seconds. Then she picked up her mug of tea and rested it on the exact same spot. We both fell silent. My red plasticine heart was still in pieces on the imaginary floor in my mind's eye.

'Mary, do you think you might be interested in doing some kind of mechanics course with me? I could organise it all through work. And what goal do you think we should aim for? Would your dream be realised the first time someone pays you to fix a car or—?'

'Well, I never!' Mary flushed bright red. 'Someone paying me to fix an engine!' She shook her head. 'It's not possible, Little Kate. It's a silly idea.'

'Mary, if you find it hard to imagine yourself as a mechanic, why don't you try visualising a version of yourself in a parallel universe, a *Power Mary*, who isn't worried about what Len might think, or the kids, who only has herself to please? What would that Mary be doing with her days? I bet she'd work on cars! Try it,' I urged. 'Close your eyes and imagine a *Power Mary* in an alternate universe.' Mary looked at me suspiciously before good-naturedly closing her eyes. 'What would *Power Mary*'s perfect car-related day be? How would it start?'

'Well, I can't do a thing before I have a cuppa so *Power Mary* would need to start her day the same way. Do they have tea in this universe?'

'I think so.'

'And she'd need her own toolbox, which would be nice, and somewhere to work.'

'Where would that be?'

Mary kept her eyes closed, frowning with concentration.

'Well, there are the arches down near Tessa's gym. *Power Mary* could have an arch down there.'

'And is *Power Mary* by herself or are there other people with her?'

'Well, it would be nice to work with other people, wouldn't it—maybe some other ladies? And *Power Mary* would need to stop for lunch because Len and I do like to eat together. But in the afternoon she could carry on, as long as she finished by four because I like to have dinner ready for when Len gets in. So *Power Mary* could go home, have a quick shower, put her overalls in the wash then make Len a nice stew, although if this is an alternate universe it would be lovely if Len could work a washing machine.'

'Mary, that sounds *so* achievable.'

Mary opened her eyes.

'Me working in a garage!' she scoffed before gathering up the mugs and hurrying into the kitchen. 'Why on earth would I learn to do this at my age?' she said over the sound of frenzied washing up. 'I am who I am, Kate. I have what I have and I am happy. What would poor Len think if I suddenly decided to copy his hobby after all these years? I'd feel like I was taking something from him.' She came back into the lounge with two fresh cups of tea. 'And what if I was better than him, Kate, which, I am not going to lie to you, would probably happen. Lord knows how any of our cars have kept working over the years. No, we are fine as we are. I was brought up to be grateful for what I have and what I have is this.'

'Mary, have you even spoken to Len about this, or asked him if he would mind?'

'Oh no dear. No, not at all.' She opened the box of Quality Street. I found yet another Strawberry Cream in my mouth. It's physically impossible to have too many strawberry Quality Streets. They don't take up *any* space in your stomach, like popcorn and cheese and most kinds of chocolate. 'No, I would never talk to my Len about this. Well, it really is lovely to see you again, Little Kate. Such a treat. And young Peter is back too. You are all back home again.'

'Have you seen him?' I asked, as casually as a World War II interrogation expert.

'Oh, yes, he came straight round to see us when he got back. Such a lovely boy. He's got a PhD from America—did you know that?'

'No, I haven't seen actual proof. So did he say how he was, what he's been doing, why he got married, why he got divorced, why he came back?' Cool as a cucumber.

'Well, he told me about an art exhibition he'd been to recently. Oh, and he told me about his running shoes—did you know they're made from recycled bottles? Such a clever boy,' she mused, chewing on a toffee. 'I remember the tears after he left for Switzerland.' Mine not hers. 'It was worse than when your pet cat Rupert died.'

'Peter's hardly like Rupert the cat, Mary. Rupert was loyal and communicative and didn't leave without writing a note.'

Rupert can't actually write. I was making a point.

'Well, I always liked that Peter Parker. Truth be told, I would have loved it if he'd fallen for one of my girls. Such a lovely young man,' she cooed, placing her mug against her breastbone.

The thought of Peter Parker falling for either Laura or Yvette made my own breastbone warm, but in more of an acidic lung-crushing way than a soul-completing spiritual way, so I sipped on my hot tea to distract myself, but it was slightly too hot so I burnt my own tongue, which had the intended effect.

quest | mary to train as a mechanic

when a rain cloud meets a rainbow

Sport in London is not something I know a great deal about. My normal form of exercise over the last few years has been snowboarding at high speed down a mountain behind Gabriel while he yelled, 'I am in love with Kate. I love Kate!' to whomever he passed before we'd disappear off piste, through a forest, down a secret snow path to a secluded chalet where we'd make love by an open fire before naming all the children we wanted to have while I crossed my fingers, and sometimes my toes, and hoped I'd just been impregnated by my future husband…or something like that…

So 'conventional' sports, involving gyms, training sessions, boot camps and clothes, were as unfamiliar to me as German men; in that they were both a bit foreign and both seemed unnecessarily formal. Someone who did know an awful lot about gyms, training sessions and being painfully over-formal was Peter smile-free Parker, the boy who never dialled. Grandma had called to inform me that Peter was an expert on *everything* to do with fitness; was a triathlete;

an occasional marathon runner and, rather bizarrely, a dab hand on a trampoline. Grandma knew I needed help formulating fitness plans for *True Love*'s proposed *Fat Camp* and said Peter Parker was the only man who'd know how. With less than a week before *Fat Camp* was due to start and with no budget to hire a professional adviser, I had reluctantly called Peter Parker, at Grandma's request, to ask for his sport-related assistance.

I had tried not to bother myself with thoughts about Peter after bumping into him that day at Pepperpots. Actually, we hadn't so much bumped into each other as I had bumped into a chair, tripping backwards at the sound of his voice, landing on my arse and righting myself by completing a slow and wobbly backwards roll. It was an odd and impromptu display of adult amateur gymnastics, finished up with some stuttering nonsense that my mouth wanted to contribute. Something along the lines of,

'Hi, Peter, it's been a long…you just…where did you… why…you didn't ever…' Then I fiddled with my hair before muttering, 'You could have called.'

'What did you say, darling?' my grandma had bellowed as she absolutely can't bear mumbling. Personally I think she's going a bit deaf but she won't hear of it, excuse the pun. She even accused Michael Parkinson of being a mumbler the other day, at his book launch, and they don't come more eloquent and enunciated than Parky.

'I said he could have called, Grandma!' I yelled back. Then, because I'd raised my voice for her benefit, I continued at that level for Peter. 'It's been fifteen years, Peter!

Fifteen years! You didn't call! You didn't write—you didn't even tell me where I could find you.'

Peter had looked at me blankly as if what I'd actually been doing was pointing at his foot and saying, 'That's a shoe, Peter! That's a shoe, that's a shoe, that's a shoe!' rather than having formed a coherent question about the premature and rather dramatic end to our intense childhood friendship. Although in his defence I had just done a backwards roll.

'Well, I've always considered Switzerland to be very insular,' Grandma had continued, nodding her head reassuringly at Peter. 'I can't imagine that I'd keep in touch with anyone if I moved there.' She smiled affectionately, gently squeezing his arm.

'It is very secluded,' Peter confirmed, eyes fixed to the floor.

'Oh, of course!' I'd said, slapping my own forehead. 'Silly me! That's why it's a tax haven! Because there are no phones, or computers, or pens to write letters, or even post offices to buy stamps. Rich people literally disappear there like dropping into a landlocked Bermuda Triangle, and they *never* resurface. I admit I tried the same thing with the Inland Revenue but the bastards just turned up at my office anyway. "I'm Swiss," I told them. "I don't do contact. I'm a landlocked island of secrets," but they made me pay my taxes and they made me do it by handwritten bloody post!' What on earth was I talking about?

'Goodness, Kate, you are getting very shouty. Not all of us can be Anne bloody Frank.'

'I'm not asking him to get under the floorboards and write me a diary, Grandma! Peter, you totally disappeared!'

'He was in Switzerland, darling. You knew he was in Switzerland. Isn't the boy allowed to educate himself? And I don't know why everyone is obsessed with communication these days,' Grandma had said wearily, sitting herself down. 'Social media, they call it. I don't think it's social at all. I think it's nice to be quiet and peaceful and left alone to do one's studies. I imagine that's what Switzerland must be like.'

'I'm not on Facebook,' Peter offered, quite randomly, before reaching over and gently taking his jacket from my hands.

'Well, of course you're not on Facebook, Peter, or I would have found yo…' My voice petered out as I revealed myself to be a bit of a creepy Internet stalker. Peter had stared at me blankly. I'd stared back. He'd practically trebled in attractiveness since the last time I'd seen him. I was fifty shades of grey in comparison to him and I'm not referring to the literary equivalent of soft porn. I'm referring to the drab colourless mist that doesn't even feature on a rainbow. Peter Parker was a bloody great rainbow and I was the grimacing, unwelcome rain cloud in the distance. Switzerland must be the aesthetic equivalent of Lourdes.

'Would anyone like a herbal tea?' Grandma had asked. 'I've got some lovely fresh mint we could use.'

'Grandma!' I yelled, for the second time that evening, before storming off towards the front door with such force I looked as if I were wading through imaginary syrup or performing dramatic high-elbowed mime.

'I'd love a mint tea,' Peter had said as I yanked open the front door. 'I can't remember the last time I had fresh mint,' he said with flat-toned enthusiasm as the door had slammed shut behind me, narrowly missing Federico, who'd pelted after me like an abandoned child.

I'd stood on the doorstep for several minutes, shaking from a mixture of shock and anger, while Peter, my oldest, bestest, long-time, disappeared-off-the-face-of-the-earth friend, and Grandma, my primary carer in the world, sipped on fresh mint tea inside, both of them acting as if it were perfectly normal for him to have reappeared after all these years, which would be fine and excusable if they were script writing for *Dallas*. And why would Grandma allow me to bump into Peter Parker for the first time in 15 years wearing Primark? Why? Why!

Anyway I am completely unbothered by the whole thing. If they don't think I deserve a proper explanation for the disappearance-reappearance I will never again ask for one. I will surreptitiously gather clues, draw wild conclusions, make generalisations then spring them on them at a later stage, probably while pissed. But I will never ask for the facts. Facts are dull. And on the plus side, as I have decided to look for the silver lining of every cloud (or at least my own grimacing, unwelcome rain cloud) I did get to test out my backwards roll, which I've been meaning to do for ages. Traditionally it has always been my weakest basic gym move and Mrs Franklin, my seventh-grade teacher, once said to me,

'Kate Winters! You get back down on that gym mat and you practise that backwards roll. You never know when you are going to have to backwards roll yourself out of a dangerous situation!'

And I think that day in Pepperpots proved to us *all* that Mrs Franklin was bloody well right.

the sport-related meeting with peter parker

I walked into the boardroom to find Federico standing on top of the heart-shaped table in a ninja position doing wrist-flicking impersonations of Spiderman.

'So there's no connection at all?' Federico asked before making a whoosh noise and shooting another invisible web across the room towards Peter Parker. Peter didn't respond. He just stood behind Chad's special heart-shaped chair, cross-armed, stern-faced, handsome. 'Because you really do have the same highly burdened energy, yes you do, a man with a past, a man with a hidden secret, a man who can scale walls and—'

'Please don't do this,' Peter said, without moving a single muscle on his face.

'Well, who needs to be a superhero when you already look like a ruddy great Gucci model is what I say!' Federico said, jumping off the table doing one last mid-air wrist flick that made Peter flinch. 'So, Kat-kins, do you have your notes ready, because our *Fat Camp* auditionees are due any second. Not that they are auditioning to be fat,' he said to

Peter. 'Not at all—they *are* fat, Peter. We are working with genuinely miserable members of the public who are over-weight. Although aren't we all these days? What with all those hidden calories. You need a PhD in label-reading to get through life a size zero. It's like playing hide-and-seek every time so much as a morsel passes my lips. "Is there a calorie?" I say to myself. And then normally I eat it anyway.' His phone started ringing. 'I have to take this. Hello? Hello? Yes, this is Federico.' He shoved me out of the way only to stand three feet away and shout loudly into his teeny-tiny phone. I looked from Federico to Peter, who seemed to be standing at the furthest point away from me on the other side of the room.

'So this is where you work?' he said, looking around the room. 'A writer at *True Love* magazine; saving us from the destructive influences of love…' His jaw flexed. 'How ironic.'

I didn't think it was particularly ironic, but perhaps the lack of irony was in fact the ironic part?

'Well, I'm not sure I'm saving anyone just yet, except myself, from being thrown from a top-floor window.' I chuckled, but Peter didn't laugh. He just watched me, like a statue, or an overly judgemental Greek god. 'Thank you for doing this,' I said, nodding my head like a talk-show host. 'Grandma said you'd be the right person to talk to. "Peter knows sport," she said to me.' I said that last bit in a strange high-pitched imitation of Grandma. 'And she said you were married. "Peter got married," she said.' Same strange voice. 'Although actually she said, "his divorce," then I said, "Peter got married?" and then—'

'I was there, Kate.'

'Yes, you were,' I said with yet more head-nodding. 'You were totally there, for that, for that moment…' I sighed. He watched me. The silence between us was long and heavy and made me want to tear out my own eyes. Peter knew damn well I'd eventually have to fill it. I counted as far as fourteen pink elephants before…

'I didn't get married!' was volunteered into the dead, noiseless space that was eating me from the inside. 'I thought I was going to—there were plans for that,' I said, stretching myself out as if I thought I was at the bloody gym. 'Yep. It was a *serious* relationship,' I said, doing a lunge. 'It was a *serious* marriage plan.' I moved on to a triceps stretch. 'But here I am anyway, not married but writing about love every single day, which I *definitely* prefer.' Three short boxing jabs. 'But you, Peter, you must be an expert in loving—I mean in the emotion, not the sexual act. I don't know how you are with the sex. I've always assumed probably great on the odd occasion that I've thought about it, which is certainly not all the time, maybe once in my teenage years, and then last week when I was watching *Twilight*—' Oh, my God. 'What I meant to say is that you must be an expert in relationships, having been married. I'm sure that you were lovely both as a husband and as a love-maker. Well done you,' I said, shaking my fist in the air, then sighing heavily and looking at my shoes. Why, oh, why was I so excruciatingly odd?

Peter walked across the room until he was in front of me. I was expecting him to perform a quick sidestep and make a dash for the nearest exit but he didn't. He just leant down and gave me a little kiss on my right cheek.

'It's nice to see you again, Kate,' he said, studying my face for a few moments. He was about to speak again when Federico snapped his phone shut and spun on the spot, espresso in hand.

'Well, look at you two! Childhood friends back together again, in London, big grown-up adults in the city. Who'd have thought it?' He took a little sip from his tiny espresso cup.

'Well, certainly not me,' Peter said to Federico. 'The last time I saw Kate she was obsessed with living somewhere in the Amazon and teaching pygmies to Moonwalk.'

Federico clasped his hands together in delight.

'Well, last time I saw Peter he was 15 years old and suffering a bout of embarrassing and uncontrollable erections in Geography lessons.' I chuckled. 'People change.' Federico spat his coffee across the glass heart. Peter looked horrified.

'I told you that in confidence, Kate, as you well know, but you are obviously in one of your argumentative moods and trying to evoke some kind of emotional response, which won't work.'

'So back to *Fat Camp*,' Federico said, studying the potential candidates' headshots that were stuck all over the walls of the heart-shaped room.

'And every adolescent boy suffers from ill-timed erections,' Peter continued. 'It's a normal and healthy part of growing up.'

'Like abandoning your best friend?'

'OK, this really doesn't feel like it's about *Fat Camp*.' Federico giggled nervously.

'I went to school somewhere else, Kate. That's all. Can you honestly say you are still in touch with every single person we knew as kids?' I was still in touch with exactly none of them.

'I wasn't just someone from school, Peter!' Or perhaps I was, because Peter had gone horribly silent and glaring at me, jaw clenched.

'Well, this feels lovely and awkward, doesn't it? Like tattoo removal, and those days when we all pretend we didn't just hear Chad fart in the middle of one of his focus meeting speeches. Although I would just like to say,' Federico continued in a whisper, 'the erection thing, well, I concur. Mine was up and down like a car-park barrier for the best part of three years. I'm sure there are parts of my body that were oxygen starved as a result. I still can't feel my little toe,' he said, looking at his feet.

'Kate, I am here because your grandma asked me to help you. Not to justify educational choices made as a teenager.'

'It happened again when I was living in Miami,' Federico continued. 'Well, honestly, no one wears a stitch of clothing over there and there are some exquisitely attractive Mexicans flaunting themselves on the beach.'

'Kate, I had actually been looking forward to seeing you today. But I had completely forgotten your inability to let things go. And you always have to have the last word.'

Federico clamped his hand over my mouth.

'Kat-kins, we have asked Peter here because we want his

help with *Fat Camp*, which is something you care about, is it not? Peter very kindly agreed to help. Which is a nice starting point for this, and a preferable one to Peter's penile function, which, while I admit I am interested, probably not in this current context. So, Kat-kins, do you want Peter's help or not?'

Peter and I stared at each other.

'Kate, would you like my help or not?'

Out of the corner of my eye I could see the first of the *Fat Camp* auditionees nervously waiting in our reception.

'Yes…please.'

'Then I'll help.'

'Well, isn't that nice? Kat-kins asked Peter *nicely*; Peter said yes. It's like an adult game of *Simon Says* but with obesity problems and two adults with mild to severe anger issues.'

I turned away from both of them and pretended to type something on my phone. If we were playing an adult game of *Simon Says* then a small part of my brain I had absolutely no control over had gone back to thinking about Peter Parker's penis, and I hated that part.

'I have to go,' Peter said, heading for the door, 'but I have a good idea of what you need. Everything will be here by tomorrow.' He marched off through Reception, the entire office watching with inappropriate levels of lust, everyone except Mark from Marketing who shot an imaginary web at him as he passed the photocopier.

The very next day two men from FedEx arrived at the office. They had hundreds of parcels from Peter Parker. He'd sent fitness packs for our *Fat Campers*, motivational books, motivational CDs, handwritten lists of personal trainers, therapists, Women Only gyms, central London park runs, *and* suggested a fitness timetable. He sent over pedometers, booked sessions at running centres for the women to be fitted with proper running shoes *and* booked a session at *Rigby & Peller* for the women to be fitted with proper sports bras. From that moment on until the end of universal time Federico Cagassi was in actual love with Peter Parker—the boy who never smiles.

the story of assumption

A boy met a girl and a girl met a boy, they looked into each other's eyes and they fell in love.

But the girl was from a different land, across a great sea, a land where people loved teapots, umbrellas and rain.

The heart of the boy and the heart of the girl ached when they were apart.

So the girl packed her bags and crossed the great sea, travelling high up into the mountains where the boy lived with many frogs and a selection of friendly snails.

She knocked on his door. He asked her inside. They looked into each other's eyes and they knew they were in love.

Over time the girl became lonely. All her friends and family—the teapots and umbrellas—were all far away. The boy grew sad. He blamed himself for taking the girl away from her beloved afternoon tea paraphernalia. The feelings of blame became feelings of guilt. The boy withdrew from the girl, assuming she regretted her choice.

The girl didn't understand why he no longer held her gaze, assuming he'd stopped loving her.

Their seeds of assumption grew like ivy; every day they assumed a little more based on the assumptions of the previous day.

One day the girl found herself packing to leave, packing to return to the land of rain and crumpets. Her eyes filled with tears, not love, her heart in pieces on the floor of lost dreams. She did not know what was left in the boy's eyes because he no longer came home, too fearful was he of what he would see if he looked at her.

The boy lives in the mountains. The girl lives in the rain. He assumes she's happy now. She assumes the same.

money & the dream crusher—leah—31 years old

OK, *so I am probably not the best person to ask because I hate my ex-husband, he is the devil incarnate, but if you want to know what I gave up for love I would say Every Single Part of My Very Self. For example, my ex's bog-standard response if I wanted to pursue any of my own personal interests, ambitions or dreams was, and I quote,*

'How dare you spend that money on yourself? You are so selfish. We are supposed to be a family.'

He could never see that my happiness and contentment might benefit us as a couple; that an extra qualification might further my career, increasing the amount of money I could earn for us as a family; or that me feeling more complete as a person would have a knock-on positive effect on our marriage. In fact sometimes I think my possible self-development threatened him. At the mere suggestion of me spending money, on anything, he would say,

'Well, if you've got enough money to do that we could spend it on—'

And then there would always be a 'something' for the

house, the car, his hobbies. Once I gave up a place on a Reiki course so he could buy a pet snake and a games console, both apparently for our son, neither of which our son has ever played with; the Reiki course would have qualified me to teach, providing a valuable second income for our family.

Even if we were trying to arrange something nice, like booking a family holiday, most of the things I wanted to do didn't interest him. No matter how passionate I was about a place or country he would say no. And when you are married at some point you get tired of battling, tired of fighting, tired of trying to maintain certain boundaries. So you give in, you agree, you give up. I was married from 22 years old to 30. This is the first time in my adult life I can really identify my own wants and needs and then, with a lot of hard work and planning, start to pursue the things, the longings sitting deep in my soul that are not connected to anyone but me. I've never been so excited about my future.

coffee shop | spitalfields market | london

Good God! I had awakened the beast. It wasn't just that Leah had a lot to say. It was that she wanted to say it all at once, and she wanted to say it all to me. Mostly because I am one of her best friends, but also because I had put a key in a previously unused lock and the door had exploded wide open. If we were in an American action film Nicholas Cage would have been standing by that door of love-lost dreams putting Semtex on the lock, frame and anything else in the surrounding door area. Leah was finally free.

'So I've been working through my list of love-stolen

dreams,' Leah said, extracting an enormous phonebook-sized document out of her handbag. 'And I think that I'm making good progress. I've completed the Reiki course, as you know, and, Henry, Henry, put that down!' Henry, Leah's son, had her iPhone in his mouth. 'And I absolutely loved it, box ticked.' She ticked an imaginary box in the air. So did Henry. 'And I've got some other love-stolen dreams organised. There's a lot to get through,' she said, patting the gigantic document that was in fact her handwritten list of love-stolen dreams. 'But I thought it would be nice to understand why I'd let myself get to a place where I was manically dribbling into my porridge, staring at my ex-husband across the kitchen and wanting to throw Petits Filous Frubes at his head. I mean, I wasn't always a passive-aggressive downtrodden wife.' She was more aggressive than passive but it wasn't the moment. 'So I've decided to do a bit of alternative research, which means that if you do that you won't have a brownie, I told you, Henry, behave or no brownie, so you are going to have to be pretty open-minded when I tell you my idea.'

'I am not here to judge. I am here to take back what love stole.' This has been my mantra since the early shock of Mary's mechanical revelations.

'Well, it was my Reiki teacher's idea really. She thought one way to better understand the obstacles and mistakes of this life would be to understand the obstacles and mistakes of all my previous lives. Apparently there's this thing called *past life regression* and it helps a lot of people make sense of themselves and the things they do.' Henry was presented with a brownie and dropped half of it straight down his front. 'And it's absolutely not something I would have done while I was married, because I couldn't bear his disapproving face, or his voice, or the way he held his cutlery, so that qualifies as a love-stolen dream, doesn't it? In fact it was already on my list.' She flicked to page 17 to show me where *Past Life Regression* had been carefully written in blue biro.

'If I'm honest, Leah, this is not exactly what I was expecting us to be talking about today. I'd found an equestrian centre close to your house. I was going to suggest we go horse riding together. You said you stopped riding when you got married. I think it was LSD 88?'

'It was 87.'

'OK, number 87, but it was on the list. I thought we could go hacking. That's what people do on horses, isn't it? They hack? Computer hackers hack too, obviously, but they do it in a more *let's bring the government to its knees* kind of way, which wasn't really what I had in mind. I was thinking more in terms of a slow trot, through woodland. But if you want to get back love-stolen dreams from the past—I mean from the *past* past, that's very cool. And thorough. Adds a whole new dimension. I like.' I totally didn't get it. 'Well done!' Phew.

'Thank God, Kate! Because I was sure you were going to say no. Federico said you wouldn't do it—'

'What?'

'I said I wanted you to do a past life regression and he said you absolutely wouldn't do it. He said, "Past life regression? Walking, talking fashion regression, more like," then he went on about some cardigan you bought from Deptford

Market last week and how he's had a metaphorical allergic reaction to it. Short version of this story is that he said
you'd say no. He thinks he knows you so well, that Federico
Cagassi.' She typed a message into her constantly beeping
iPhone while Henry fell asleep face first in his brownie.
And just for the record that Federico Cagassi does know me
quite well. He knows me well enough to know I'd rather put
hot coals on my bare-naked tippy-toes than regress myself
into the past, which is why I whispered,

'I don't want to do a past life regression,' into my hair
before bursting into a fit of fake coughing. Which is when
things got a bit awkward…

You see *I'd* never given much thought to what I'd be
asked to do for Love-Stolen Dreams. I hadn't set any guide-
lines or parameters. I just saw myself as a champion of
others, dashing about, problem-solving, drinking protein
shakes and facilitating the journeys of others. But jumping through the windows of time, to right love's past-life
wrongs, well, it was like *Quantum* bloody *Leap* but for real
and I suspect without the help of that middle-aged man who
smoked cigars and had communication devices wired up
to the present.

'Oh…' Leah looked at me with disc-sized brown eyes.
'Oh, sure, of course.' She looked at the floor and started
fiddling with her hands. 'I just thought that you wanted to
help women reconnect with themselves. I thought this was
a selfless quest to take back what love had stolen, not you
picking and choosing a few things that you really fancy
doing, like learning to trot on a bloody great horse.' She was
getting a bit shouty. Henry woke up and crawled under the

table. He knew the signs. 'Remind me again of your new mantra, Kate.'

'I'm not here to judge,' I said through gritted teeth. 'I am here to take back what love stole.'

'That's a great mantra,' she said, draining her coffee mug and starting to pack up her things. I knew what she was going to do. She was going to leave. She was going to leave, without getting properly mad, and I'd feel like a rubbish, disappointing friend and it would be awkward and uncomfortable but she'd *never* mention it again and I'd *never* forget. It would become like a humungous white elephant who sat between us everywhere we went, an elephant called Awkward Stan, and Awkward Stan would always be there, an accessory to our friendship for the rest of my entire elephant-infested life. Good God, she was manipulative!!!

'It was just a little past life regression,' she muttered as she wiped Henry's face with a wet wipe. 'We could have found out what love stole from us in the past to find out why it keeps stealing stuff in the present. The answers are in the past. I just know it.'

'I thought the answers were on this list!' I said, shaking the heavy paper document in her face. She blinked violently as I did it and I knew I'd gone too far. There's never any need to shake paper.

'Kate, all I want is that if you put that iPhone in your mouth one more time I will make you eat the thing, do you hear me, Henry? I will put tomato ketchup on it, put it in a burger bun and I won't feed you another morsel until you have eaten it. Your choice, you are in control of your own destiny. So, Kate,' she said, turning back to me. 'A little regression? Making sense of the future by unlocking the love-stolen secrets of our past—speaking of the past, did I tell you I bumped into Peter Parker the other day? When did he get back?'

'What do you mean you bumped into Peter Parker? Where was he? What was he doing? Did you speak to him? What was he wearing? Did he speak to you? Did he smell nice? How did he seem?'

'He seemed fine. To be honest he spent the entire time explaining to Henry how his juice box would eventually end up as a biodegradable roof tile, which neither of us really understood, well, especially not Henry as he can't count past five. Think about the regression, Kate,' she said as she headed to the door, Henry under one arm, twelve bags under the other and quite a large piece of Henry's chocolate brownie stuck to her bum, which, in retrospect, I probably should have mentioned...

request | regress myself into the past

let's chew the fat of love

'What did I lose as a result of love? My thinness.'
(Susan, 58)

'The effect of love is that there is a whole section of my wardrobe filled with clothes that no longer fit. I am keeping them in case we ever split up.' **(Jane, 33)**

'I've put on weight.' **(Miriam, 23)**

'It's like I didn't value myself any more. I fell in love, we got engaged and leading up to the wedding I had this goal: come hell or high water I was going to be skinny on the day. But after that I sort of gave in to it and the weight started slowly piling on.' **(Clarissa, 38)**

'I got really fat. I am really fat. I stayed fat. Thanks, Love.' **(Rosanne, 47)**

'For me it was hardest after the kids arrived. I just couldn't shift the weight I'd gained. And it seemed selfish to insist that I needed time out a few times a week to go to the gym or for a run; my husband didn't have time to do these things so why should I? And I wasn't really sure what my motivation was. To say it was just about feeling good about myself, feeling sexy and enjoying my body seemed inappropriate. I was a wife and a mother, not a hormone-filled teenager. So maybe love stole my focus? It was certainly that lack of focus that ultimately played a massive part in the destruction of my marriage. I didn't feel sexy. I started to dislike myself and my body. Eventually he felt the same way.' (Hina, 42)

the birth of fat camp

the boardroom | true love

They sat there nervous. They sat there scared. Some of them sat there defensively as if they had already changed their minds in the lift on the way up and now, faced with a hyperactive Federico, who had changed into a white T-shirt that said 'skinny people are happy', were going to do everything possible to stay the size they were. One had her hand in a bowl of red *Haribo*, a second was munching her way through a bag of *Kettle Chips*, a lady in the far corner was nibbling on one of those chocolate diet bars that tells you it's fat free, which of course it is, it's totally fat free and 100% sugar-coated and will make you balloon faster than a hydraulic tyre inflator. In fact the only person in the boardroom who wasn't eating was Chad. He stood silently in the corner watching Federico, who was running from lady to lady telling them they were all *so much more beautiful* in the flesh before grimacing at their headshots pinned on the wall.

Bob, the man we had all been waiting for, finally arrived at 10 a.m. He was a famous motivational speaker from California and was going to be *Fat Camp*'s life coach: the positive voice to help make the positive change that would positively reduce in a negative decreasing way their physical size. He had called *True Love* as soon as my unauthorised advert had gone to press.

'Kate…' he had said, sounding exactly like Woody Allen (and on meeting him I discovered he was the exact same size). 'Kate, this is such a wonderful idea. People become stuck, Kate. They become stuck. To give them a chance to realise their dreams, however small or large, to let life surprise them, in a good way, well, that is truly a wondrous endeavour. I want to be involved.' He then emailed me a hyperlink to a TED talk[4] on achieving change, and a 10% discount for his new book available on Amazon and Kindle.

'Ladies, we all know that certain foods aren't good for us,' Bob began, positively beaming at the room. 'We know that exercise can make you thinner, that if you exceed your calorie intake you'll store the food as fat. We probably also know that a lot of people get bigger when they fall in love. There are literally thousands of studies published on the subject. But I don't want to talk about that. I want to talk about the woman who lives down the street from you, let's call her Catharine. Catharine meets a new guy. She falls

---

[4]**TED Talk** – TED.COM – website with hundreds of inspirational talks from an assortment of incredible people. TED believe in the power of ideas to change attitudes, lives and, ultimately, the world. Their website offers free knowledge and inspiration from the world's most inspired thinkers, including Bob.

in love. She moves in with him. Someone asks you how Catharine's doing and you say "Oh, she looks really well," but what you really mean is that she looks really happy and she looks really *really* fat, because that is what most of us do. Not the Brangelinas[5] of this world—us, the real people, the normal people. We meet someone. We want to stay in with them. We want to kiss them. We want to feed them nice food. We've waited so long to meet this special person we want to *indulge* in it. And we should. And…we…should! Plus our boyfriend says he likes our new curves. We love him so much we find his squishy new tummy so cute and sexy. But when the honeymoon period comes to an end, and it always does, you don't feel sexy and curvaceous any more. You wonder why you can't fit in most of your clothes, why your thighs spread to fill the chair when you sit down, or your boobs barely fit into your bra. And that's before we mention those bat wings under your arms, or your bum that is bigger but also some-how closer to the ground like a blancmange slowly slid-ing off a plate. And his love handles, they're not so lovely any more. And everyone feels a little bit less sexy and a little bit fed up. You have lost your body and somewhere along the way you have lost a little bit of yourself, while gaining a whole load more of yourself if you know what I mean!' He beamed. The room was very very quiet. Bob did nothing to fill the silence. He just looked off into the

---

[5]**Brangelinas** – Brad and Angelina, somehow greater together than the sum of their parts. Ridiculously skinny and beautiful in spite of love, and childbirth and crippling work schedules. In short…not the norm.

middle distance, for ages. Eventually his thoughts came back to the room and he put his hands in a pray position, resting his index fingers on his lips. He looked from face to face before speaking.

'I'm sorry, guys, I can't lie to you. You all seem like really nice ladies, you really do. So I have to admit that I don't know anything at *all* about weight loss.' There was a group gasp and the *Fat Campers* started looking to each other, and to me, to see if he was joking. 'I don't know anything at all about diets. Everyone in this room probably knows more about calories and eating plans. You all,' he said, pointing to the headshots on the wall, 'you *all* already have the information you need to be slim. You could probably open your own healthy-eating university and lecture on it. Fat people always know a lot about food.' He nodded his head, then shrugged his shoulders. 'You have all the facts and yet you are all *so* fat.' He crossed his arms and sat heavily in Chad's red heart-shaped chair. 'And yet you are all so fat!' Bob yelled. This time the group gasp was louder, angry, insulted. Bob bounced excitedly out of the chair and started smiling. 'And that is why I am here!' And now he was speaking fast. 'We don't need to overthink this. Two plus two doesn't need to equal four. We don't need to know the facts. Knowledge doesn't lead to solution. Do you think the smokers of the world don't know cigarettes cause cancer? Of course they do!' he squeaked. 'But they can't stop! Do you think the alcoholic thinks drinking is improving his life, making him smarter, sharper, richer? No! But he drinks anyway. People can't stop. Knowledge doesn't equal power. The fact that you haven't lost weight *in spite* of your

knowledge is not your fault. We are *all* the same. But for
those of you in this room, today marks something new. The
way we will work is in 30-day blocks. Every 30 days, as
in every month, we will try something new. Anyone can
commit to one thing for 30 days. I know a man at *Google*
who lives his whole life by the 30-day rule. Every month he
promises himself he will do something new. In the month of
August he learnt a Spanish word every day. In July he gave
up sugar. In December he took one photograph every single
day and made them into a photo-book. His life is coloured
by new experiences, of growth and development. And he
could pack so much in. One month he made himself write
1,500 words every day. Some days he wrote total nonsense,
but he did it anyway. At the end of it he had 45,000 words.
That's the length of some novels! So he self-published and
now he's got his own book of nonsense!' The room giggled.
'Sounds like fun, hey! It is fun. So we start today, and our
30-day challenge this month is that we will all do one form
of physical exercise, together, every single day. One thing,
even if it's just for 15 minutes. The more fun, the better. No
questions asked. All we have to do is show up every day,
just show up, and we will arrange everything. Everything
you need is here.' He nodded to Federico, who started handing out Peter Parker's gift packs. 'And showing up will be a
common theme throughout our experience together. If you
tell the universe you really want something and every day
you show up for it, you turn up, you drag yourself out of
bed and you yell, "Universe, I am here! I want this! I need
this! But I can't do this alone, help me!" you will be surprised how often the universe delivers. And what you la-

dies don't realise is that you already did just that. The day you wrote to *True Love*, the day you agreed to join this pro-gramme was the day you set an intention, showed up and said, "I want something! I need something! Take notice! Here I am!" And guess what, people? Guess what? We took notice. This is the beginning of your new life. Welcome.' The room burst into rapturous applause while Federico sat weeping in the corner.

'I am a Human Fountain,' he mouthed at me before blow-ing his nose into an enormous silk hanky then running into the middle of all the over-excited ladies and squeezing them all very very hard.

pepperpots life sanctuary

'to be a star you must shine your own light,
follow your own path,
and never worry about the darkness
for that is when the stars shine brightest'

(anon)

The floating restaurant at Pepperpots is one of the most bizarre eating establishments I have ever come across. It's a circular building constructed in the middle of a giant lake accessed by a wooden footbridge that resembles the Millennium Bridge[6]. The restaurant itself stands one storey high, is completely glass-walled and has two enormous decked terraces on either side. And it was here that I had been instructed to wait for Delaware O'Hunt, the movie starlet from the golden era of the silver screen.

It had taken some time to secure a meeting with the elu-

---

[6]**Millennium Bridge** – steel suspension bridge for pedestrians crossing the River Thames, London

sive Delaware. She'd cancelled twice, not shown up once then one day, out of the blue, she'd called and invited me to come and meet. We'd agreed upon the afternoon before Pepperpots' annual fireworks display and I'd arrived early so I could watch Grandma in all her organisational glory. She was coordinating the evening's sparkly event and I could see her on the shoreline assembling a herd of volunteers who just happened to be a gaggle of handsome axe-wielding men. Grandma had them chopping large bits of wood, dragging around heavy pieces of scaffolding and generally doing anything that might result in them getting hot and sweaty and taking off their shirts. As yet another man removed all but his trousers and boots I noticed out of the corner of my eye the legend that is Delaware O'Hunt step gracefully onto the deck. She walked purposefully, no, she *glided* across to meet me. She was rumoured to be close to ninety years of age but looked a glamorous and beautiful seventy. She wore dark glasses and a camel-coloured wool coat and as she crossed the deck in the last of the autumnal rays it felt as if the sun's sole purpose were to illuminate her. Every head turned, in the restaurant, and from lake's edge, and even Grandma, not a gesticulator at the best of times, waved manically in the distance. Delaware waved back before gracefully seating herself on a chair next to me. I on the other hand sat heavily, as if under the influence of a completely different gravitational pull. I shifted my chair to face her. She stayed exactly where she was. Then she began absent-mindedly stirring warm milk into her coffee.

'Kate,' she said to me from behind dark glasses. 'When your grandmamma explained to me your idea I was unsure how I would be able to contribute.' She spoke in a slow and considered way, every syllable carefully pronounced, the words trickling like honey wrapped up in the thickest Texan drawl. 'I am from a different generation from you, darl, so I can speak my truth but I'm not convinced anything I say will resonate with the women of today.'

'I'm sure—' I squeaked before clearing my throat and starting again. 'I'm sure everything you say will be relevant.' I was practically whispering. 'So many women are trying to balance a working life with a relationship, with having kids, with maintaining friendships and hobbies.' I could barely look at her. 'You were among the first generation of women to do this. You are exactly who we need to speak to. You started the revolution,' I said, performing a gentle and uncommitted fist shake while looking slightly past her right shoulder.

'That's sweet,' she said, placing my fist-shaking hand back by my side. 'But it didn't feel like a revolution, that's for sure. Back then, when I was working all the time, I felt mostly overwhelmed, sometimes a little scared and almost always unsupported. It was a man's world and I was a silly little girl who had accidentally ended up with a big career. Certainly to the outside world I had it all. I was acting with some of the greatest actors of the time, with incredible directors, I had to kiss some dashing fellows as part of my day job, most of them gay if the disappointing truth be told, but for the early part of my career I always remember feeling somewhat empty.'

'Do you think that emptiness was because you hadn't fallen in love?' I winced at the sound of my own voice.

'Well, I was certainly aware of love and the lack of its existence in my life. As my girlfriends paired off, which they all did more quickly than me, I suppose I wondered why love had not come into my life. If perhaps I wasn't the type of girl who got to fall in love, that perhaps you couldn't have it all.'

'Were you actively looking for love?'

'You mean going on dates?' She smiled. 'Darl, I went on so many dates I could write you a handbook! And it's funny you should ask because I was reading through some of my old diaries and I came across an entry I had written after one such evening.' She reached into her handbag and brought out an old leather diary. 'If you don't mind I would like to read something to you.' She cleared her throat and began. I felt as if I were watching her in one of her films.

June 5th

I went on another date last night with a man who works in Wall Street. He was handsome in a banking sort of a way and very interested in the play I start next week. But I knew, within 30 seconds, that he wasn't for me. How could I know such a thing so quickly? I should know better than to judge any book by its cover. I am supposed to be a curious individual, an artist absorbing and embracing every single experience. But because I had decided he wasn't The One I couldn't enjoy the rest of the evening. This man never said, "Delaware, come to dinner. I am the man of your dreams." Yet on some level that was my expectation of him, or at least my hope, a hope so hidden that for the most part I don't even know it's there.

How is it possible to miss something you have never had? How can I ever really embrace any moment if I am always subconsciously searching for a thing called love? And what is this overwhelming human desire to define oneself by being in a pair?'

'But you did fall in love!' I squeaked. 'You married Richard!'

'I married Richard.' She nodded before looking off into middle distance. 'I knew the minute he walked in the room that he was the one for me. We met at an after-show party for a play I'd been starring in on Broadway. At the time he was still a young director but with big ideas and absolutely no sense of life's boundaries that constrain the rest of us. He was intoxicating to be around. I had feelings in my body that I was completely at the mercy of, feelings I knew were never going to go away. Thank God he felt the same way. I had a girlfriend who fell so in love with a Swiss man and he resolutely didn't feel the same way about her. What an awful predicament for a woman to find herself in. Your One True Love doesn't want to be your One True Love.'

I loved the way predicament sounded in her Texan drawl, each syllable exquisitely over-pronounced: pre-dic-a-ment.

'So when Richard arrived, when love showed up, how did it affect your life?'

'Well, Richard and I began working together almost immediately.' She nodded. 'To share one's passion with the man you are also passionate about was a dream come true.

He was creatively brilliant and is responsible for some of the greatest performances of my life. He transformed my life on every single level.'

'So falling in love was a positive experience for you?' I knew it. Chad was going to throw me head first from the roof.

'I believe in balance in life, for every high there is an equal low, and so it was with Richard. My career sky-rocketed, thanks in large part to him, but when dream acting jobs came along I didn't want to take anything that would cause us to be apart for long periods of time. I certainly couldn't take roles where he'd been turned down as Director or where I would be working with a director he felt was a competitor of his. So my career, and love life, started to become like a game of chess. For each opportunity I had to predict the next five moves. What would this role lead to? Where would I end up living? How would Richard get to see me? Would me taking the role undermine his confidence as a director? Ultimately the more I moulded and shaped my decisions to stabilise my relationship, the more unstable it became. In hindsight if I had just been consistent, consistently choosing the right roles for the right reasons, Richard would have always known what to expect from me. And I think consistency is underrated in relationships. Your partner being able to predict you, be certain of your choices, of who you are, it has a stabilising effect on a relationship. When you become a smaller version of yourself in order to keep your relationship on track, all that happens is that your partner no longer recognises you. You are not the woman he fell in love with, he starts to lose respect for you, and you lose respect for yourself, the small compromised version of the woman you used to be, and then one comes to resent the other. And so it was with Richard. Love was the greatest joy in my life, and my greatest pain. The breakdown of my marriage nearly killed me. The pain of it ending, the separation from him, the shattered hopes and dreams, it was all too much. I am sure you are aware of the four-year break in my acting career following the end of my marriage. My world collapsed. I don't know why we couldn't be together as a couple. It is one of the greatest mysteries and the greatest sadness in my life. And I know that we will love each other until the day we die. He is me. I am him. But together we are somehow too much and at the same time too little.' She took a sip of coffee. Her words resonated with such depth it was as if she were playing a string instrument in my chest. I struggled to find my voice.

'Delaware, what would you do if you were me and found yourself unexpectedly alone and 30 years old? I mean, if someone had told you on your 30th birthday that you would be alone for the rest of your life, what things would you have chosen to do differently? What advice do you have for me?'

'If I were you and free from love?' She gazed out across the lake. I did the same and noticed a somewhat familiar-looking torso on the shore chopping wood. The half-naked man turned around and stared back. 'Well, I would have made some different creative choices, that is for certain. There are several film roles, films you would have heard of, that I would have taken. And none of my partners ever wanted children, not one of them, which is a strange thing in itself. So I suppose I would have had a child if I had only myself to please and not a man's feelings and needs to take into consideration.' She pulled her coat closer around her. The familiar half-naked torso was now running along the edge of the lake towards the footbridge to the restaurant. 'You know, darl, I don't like to list negatives, to think about what-ifs. I think if I had just gotten into the habit of making good choices for myself I would not have missed out on anything at all, whether there had been love in my life or not. Because when you start making choices with someone else in mind, second-guessing them and their wants and needs, it's like a game of Chinese whispers that over the years slowly unravels into a story you don't even recognise. And you will probably end up losing the one thing you were trying to keep hold of. So be true to yourself. Then everyone else can rely upon that fact.' She paused for a moment before smiling to herself. 'And I wouldn't waste a second of my life worrying about what I look like, that should be forbidden until you are at least in your 70s and even then I think women look goddamn beautiful! I'm sorry, doll, if I've disappointed you. I expect women today want me to tell them to have lots of sex, run along the Great Wall of China and throw themselves out of a plane. But my only true regrets in life are when I let myself down, when I abandoned myself; nothing good ever came from those choices. So get good at being good to yourself. That is what love stole from me. That is what I took back after love had gone and that is what I would want you to do now.'

advice | get good at being good to yourself

Delaware was perfect. The interview was perfect. I clicked off my Dictaphone and took a sip from my now freezing cup of coffee. The half-naked torso appeared at the door to the terrace and marched across to our table, sitting himself down in the chair next to mine. His upper body was horribly lean and muscular in an incredibly clichéd 'I'm so gorgeous and toned' kind of way. And there were bits of woodchip and dirt stuck to his sweaty naked skin.

'So?' He pulled his chair closer to mine. 'Did *Fat Camp* receive the training bags? Have they read all the literature? Did they have their appointment at the running clinic? And the bra-fitting shop? Because they need to be well supported before they start running, emotionally, but also in the breast region. It's important.' Peter Parker was here, naked, and talking about tits in front of Delaware O'Hunt. Brilliant.

'Peter, what are you doing here?'

'Your grandma said she needed help setting up the firework display so I offered. Are you helping?' I looked down at my incredibly smart dress, unsure what part of my outfit screamed *Firework Preparation and Installation Expert*. 'Oh, God, I'm sorry,' Peter said, leaning across me, leaving a trail of woodchips on my dress. 'How rude of me, Delaware—how are you?' he asked, kissing her firmly on each cheek with his big sweaty man face. 'How is the fusion dance coming along? I still can't perfect those moves you showed me.'

'You don't smile but you do fusion dance?' I guffawed. That, as far as I was concerned, was ironic.

'I told you, darl, it's in those hips. You just have to practise. He's a wonderful dance partner, Kate. You should get him to take you.'

'Oh, Kate doesn't dance,' Peter said, brushing the woodchips from my dress as he sat himself back down. 'Sorry about that,' he said as he picked off the last woodchip, which was located very close to my well-supported although disappointingly small right boob. 'No, Kate's practically allergic to dancing. It's an affliction.'

'What do you mean I don't dance? I can dance. I dance! I'm a dancer!!' Peter frowned at me.

'OK… You can dance. I mean, you can't dance but if it makes you feel better I can say that you do.'

'It's not about me feeling better, Peter. It's about operating within the realms of truth.'

'I think you mean the *realms of possibility.* It's *possible* that you could learn to dance with some instruction and dedicated practice. But the *truth* is that you currently can't.'

'You've been away for 15 years! How on earth do you know what I can and can't do? I could have won the bloody Dance Olympics in that time!'

'Well, did you? What year? In what dance category? Who designed your dress? Who did you compete against? What was your most complicated dance move?'

Why was he *obsessed* with the details!?!

'Well, we have had lovely weather today, haven't we, darl?' Delaware cooed. 'And Kate and I have been busy reminiscing—' she patted my knee '—helping me reconnect with my younger self. Although I've been talking nonstop and I know nothing about dear Kate, apart from the fact that you are a dancer,' she said reassuringly.

'She's not a dancer,' Peter muttered. 'Fictitious Olympic appearances or otherwise.'

'So, Kate,' Delaware continued, 'tell me a little bit about you.' For the first time all morning she took off her dark glasses and put them on the table in front of her. 'What exactly are you trying to do here?' she said, looking me directly in the eyes. 'What is this all about?'

I looked from Peter, who was still frowning on account of my truth-bending, to Delaware.

'I want to know what people gave up when they fell in love, so I can help get those things back. It's a quest.'

'I know that, darl. I just don't understand why.'

'Oh, well, I, well…' I shuffled uncomfortably in my seat. 'I, er, I want to—' Peter turned away and pretended to stare at something fascinating on the shore. I turned back to Delaware but spoke more to my knees. 'I would like people to acknowledge the preoccupation you mentioned in your diary.' She nodded along, encouraging me. 'I want people to live more in the moment, to be more present, for people to truly know what they want for themselves. People sometimes forget the things that make them happy when they fall in love. The relationship becomes the source of those feelings. It becomes the source of everything. So I suppose my goal is for people to reconnect with that lost part of themselves and stay connected to it. But I've found that lots of people don't even know what makes them happy. So if I ask them what they'd be happy doing for the rest of their life in the *absence* of love it seems to help them answer from a place of naked truth.' I couldn't help but glance at Peter's body when I said the word *naked*. He was still staring out at the lake. 'And with that knowledge they'll never lose themselves again, whatever happens in their life. They'll be their own energy source, their own sustenance, their own sun, if you will.' By this point I had pretty much faded out to a whisper.

'But, Kate, darling girl, there are a million things you could be doing at this point in your life. Why would you want to spend all your time doing this?'

'Because I plan to live the rest of my life alone, so I have the time. And I think if I could prevent even one person feeling how I felt, going through what I did, am, then it would be worthwhile. So that's why I spend my time doing this, helping others to help themselves, helping others become their own sun.'

'Well, that is very noble, isn't it, Peter?' she said, turning to Peter Parker. 'Peter?'

I looked around to find Peter staring blankly at me. I had an odd and unfamiliar feeling in my chest when our eyes met and Peter looked as if he'd been severely winded.

'I should be helping your grandma,' he said quietly before getting up and slowly walking off.

He spent the rest of the afternoon standing next to the unlit bonfire in deep conversation with Grandma Josephine. He left just before it was lit.

two peas in the proverbial pod of happy coupledom

'Kate Winters! Or should I say bonjour!' Jane Brockley-formerly-Robinson answered the door wearing a Cath Kidston apron and strawberry-shaped oven gloves. 'You lot will have to excuse me,' she said, ushering me, Federico and Leah through her front door. 'I'm just taking something out of the oven. I've been trying out new recipes for gingerbread men and something is always missing. It's driving me crazy. Come through, come through,' she said, marching off. We followed her down the hallway passing a coat stand covered in hundreds of brightly coloured raincoats. It looked like a multicoloured willow tree. Federico and Leah both stifled a giggle.

You see, Jane Brockley-formerly-Robinson, a friend of mine from college, is totally colour obsessed. She always has a waterproof of some description on her person and it is always brightly coloured or highly patterned. I'm actually a fan of colour too. I rarely wear black, or white, and when clashing primary colours were in fashion I was in block-colour heaven. But Jane is the kind of colour wearer that makes you think she wasn't allowed coloured clothes as a child. Every colour of the rainbow and several the rainbow is not even aware of can be found on the raincoats of Jane Brockley-formerly-Robinson. Then there are the plastic coats; hundreds of waterproof coats covered in smiling cats, Christmas trees or flowers. A vomit-inducing collection of colour was Jane's signature style. As was introducing herself as 'Jane Brockley-formerly-Robinson' as if without this extra piece of information a person who knew Jane pre-marriage would forget all about her. Jane's 1998 pink plastic Pac-a-Mac covered in light grey mice building things and driving small mouse cars would be the primary reason no one would forget pre-married Jane; that and the fact that she's ever so slightly boss-eyed.

'James is just through there. Why don't you go through and say hi? I'll be in in a minute,' she said, gesturing for us to walk through an archway from the kitchen into the lounge. There we found Jane's husband, a rotund gentleman called James. His well-fed self was watching rugby on a large leather sofa with a cat they call Nibbles. Nibbles eyeballed me as we walked into the room. James was wearing a non-ironic burgundy cardigan.

'Katie!' he said, getting up to greet me. 'I was saying to Jane just last week that we've barely seen you since your return from France, lovely to see you now, and, Leah, terribly sorry to hear about your divorce. You must be crushed, totally crushed. My second cousin Susan just got divorced and it has totally destroyed her life. And of course he's immediately pushed off with someone else, as is always the way—isn't that right, Katie? Jane said it was the same for you. Gabriel immediately ran off with someone a lot younger. Yes, younger or slimmer I think is the normal way of doing things. You know, I really rather liked that Gabriel. He was terribly attractive. Did you meet him?' he asked Federico. 'Probably almost a challenge for someone like that to actually stay single. Incredible skiing instructor, really incredible—well, these boys start skiing before they can walk. I mean, he could do things on the mountain that I just...' He started welling up. 'Well, let's just say that he skied *up* a mountain once to save me when I found myself in somewhat of a sticky situation. And I remember seeing him skiing down the mountain carrying Katie in his arms a few times. Good God, if I could do on skis what that man could do...' He dabbed the corners of his podgy eyes. 'Britain needs a strong ski team, we really do. Yes, they were probably lining up the day you left, offering him a shoulder to cry on. Don't take it personally, Katie darling. We can't be alone, us men, can't bloody well be alone.'

an emotional interlude

When the existence of a man called Gabriel is mentioned in my new life, by my highly patterned friend's sensitive husband, it feels like a door blasting open into a room I've spent weeks and months tirelessly boarding up, and it scares the crap out of me, because I'd started to forget the room was even there. So I have to start all over again, closing it all back off, nailing it shut, triple-checking the locks are in place so that I can safely turn my back on my past. And that's just in my waking life. Different distorted versions of Gabriel live in my dreams most nights. Gabriel lives in my head, my heart, my subconscious mind and on days like these my defences seem futile, useless, ineffective, because just the sound of his name, seven letters put together to form a noise, can blast open all the doors and windows of the derelict house in my heart. And suddenly he exists again, as powerful as before, and I wonder if anyone ever felt as broken inside as I do.

'Well, do take a seat,' James said, pointing at the sofa. 'Make yourselves at home. Wine, anyone?' He trotted out to the kitchen as we all tried to squish on a sofa meant for two. Nibbles rolled onto his back on the big sofa and stretched out to full length. Then he started a barely audible growl. You see, Nibbles is their pride and joy. He is their baby. If there was an overly expensive local cat primary school they would have enrolled him at birth. But Nibbles is actually a highly duplicitous creature who snuggle-wuggles against his owners as if butter wouldn't melt only to lash out like a sabre-toothed tiger when their backs are turned. That cat is responsible for at least five of the seven permanent scars on my body and once attacked the neighbour's German Shepherd, permanently damaging its right eye. Sometimes when I visit it feels like I'm in the cat version of Orwell's *1984*, Nibbles being *Big Brother* and everyone buying into his bullshit. Everyone that is except me, and that poor one-eyed German Shepherd…

James wandered back into the lounge with a bottle of wine, Jane with a plate of hot gingerbread men. Then they perched on the edge of the coffee table (so as not to disturb Nibbles, who pretended to sleep) and they stared at me, expectantly, as people often do when I visit their houses, as if I am a West End show or human-sized television set with only one channel and more often than not only one volume setting.

'I er, we, I wanted to pop in, to say hi, obviously, and also because I wanted to ask Jane a question. It's a work thing really, a little investigation. I just wanted to know if there was anything you didn't get to do because you met James and, well, fell in love.'

'What do you mean?' Jane looked flustered and brushed her fringe to one side with an oven-glove-covered hand. 'I think we have done everything we've ever wanted to?' she said, looking to James for confirmation.

'There isn't one thing, one small thing that you haven't had a chance to do, alone; a course you wanted to take; or an experience you haven't had? One little thing that was stolen, by love.'

'I've asked Kate to do a past life regression,' Leah said, mouth full of gingerbread. 'But apparently that's not the right kind of request, so now I'm not sure what I'm going to do.' Manipulative.

'And I'm not sure what I'm doing either,' Federico said tentatively biting into the left leg of a gingerbread man, 'but I would consider more ginger, yes, I would, and, I'm just going to throw this one out there, possibly a dash of lemon juice.'

'It's ridiculous to think there's something Jane hasn't done because she fell in love,' James said, puffing out his chest. 'Katie, I had no idea you were so anti-love. There is *noth-ing* I wouldn't support Jane doing. Life began as a couple.

Didn't it, pumpkin?' He patted her on the thigh. 'We've always felt that we became more complete as people when we met each other and in turn had more to offer the world. Jane does an awful lot at the Salvation Army, don't you, darling? So we try to give more love to the world because we have so much love between us.'

Federico had turned green. Leah looked suspicious. Jane still looked as if she'd opened a trapdoor that led directly to the molten hot core of the earth. I watched as she started looking all around her lounge, taking it all in, as if it were the first time she'd seen any of her own stuff.

'Oh, well. I thought it was worth asking.' Jane was still looking at the ceiling. 'I am asking lots of women what they didn't do because they fell in love, then we are stealing those things back, like pirates—' I punched the air and made a sort of oohh-aahh noise that sounded nothing like a pirate, which was embarrassing '—and some women are going out doing things on their own. It's a way to help people reconnect with themselves. My old cleaner is going to train as a mechanic.'

'Because that's an appropriate request,' muttered Leah.

'And what do we have next week?' Federico was off. 'Well, next week is the official start date for *Fat Camp*, yes it is. Twenty of our fat readers; and I mean super fat, fat and miserable, like human Santas, but without the super red outfits, magical flying powers and free mince pies, maybe too many mince pies, but no sledge and definitely no flying ability, are going to start our intensive weight-loss programme, yes they are. Love-Stolen Dreams is going to get back their pre-relationship bodies. LSD to the rescue!' He gave himself a round of applause. 'My idea,' he said, pointing to himself.

He finished by mouthing 'cinnamon' to Jane, then placing his unfinished gingerbread man back on the plate.

'Well, Katie, your job sounds wonderfully frivolous. We do love hearing about your little exploits, don't we, pumpkin? Even if I am not in 100% agreement with this idea. But I'm afraid I am going to have to leave you girls to it as I have a tennis match.' He kissed Jane on the forehead before grabbing his big tennis bag and waddling out of the front door. The moment the door clicked shut it began.

'Gregoire Pechenikov. That's what I didn't do because I met James. Gregoire bloody Pechenikov. He was gorgeous, Kate, totally gorgeous, and desperate to sleep with me. I nearly bit off my own arm the day I first saw him. He walked into the students union on a language exchange from Moscow, had the arms of a rower and he wanted me. He used to hover outside my halls of residence and ask me to explain subjunctives and conjugate verbs. And he used to stand disarmingly close and watch my lips when I spoke.'

'I knew it!' Federico was shrieking and bouncing up and down in his seat. 'Here she is. Welcome back the real Jane Robinson!'

'And Spanish men,' she said, taking her oven gloves off and pouring herself a large glass of white wine. 'I've definitely not had enough sex with hot Spanish men, or twins. I always wanted to have sex with identical twins.' Federico practically dissolved into a puddle of pure happiness on the floor.

several hours later...

'James would support anything I wanted to do—' Hiccup. 'If I stopped doing anything it's 100% my fault. It's my responsibility. And I really like who I have become. What we have created together—'

'Take back the power, Janey Jane,' Federico whispered while performing a slow-motion air grab. 'Take control of the power. Become the energy source, not the plug that drains it. Become a nuclear power station or a renewable source of energy if you are more comfortable with that. I am personally comfortable with the safety of nuclear power.'

'It's just he takes everything so seriously, Kate. Even our love life is serious. James said I can only refer to sex as *making love*. Apparently *sex* is something we did with other people before we met. And he doesn't like me giving him blow jobs, because he thinks it's demeaning, to me. I actually like giving blow jobs. I gave them all the time when I was at college.' She really did; it was like she was sponsored. 'You know, I definitely didn't play around enough before settling down.' Leah choked on a gingerbread man. 'Well, I didn't! Fumbles in your teenage years don't count. When you get older sex gets better. God, if I could have the kind of sex I have now with all the men I fancied when I was younger. Wow! So that's what I'd be doing if I were you, Kate. I'd be having sex with as many hot men as I could get my hands on, hot Spanish men, with tanned baby-soft skin, muscular bodies and thick dark hair. They'd let me give them a bloody blow job.'

'Yes they would, Janey Jane. Yes they would, yes they would.'

'And Gregoire Pechenikov. I'd be having sex with him, a lot. I understand why you are doing this, Kate. I can see how much pain you are in. And you don't know it yet but you will meet someone else—everyone does. It will happen without you even trying and in the blink of an eye you'll be so happy.' She emptied the contents of the wine bottle into her glass. 'James really is the love of my life.' She swayed. 'I know none of you ever understood why—' she looked especially hard at me as she said that '—but he is my man, my James. And I know you'll get a James one day too, you really will, but while you are single if I were you I would kiss and kiss and kiss and kiss.'

'And give blow jobs, Janey Jane. Don't forget the blow jobs.' They all burst out laughing and Federico started doing something childish and inappropriate with a wine bottle.

Why couldn't they operate on a deeper spiritual level? Why didn't they want to become self-actualised, in this present moment, in this present day, with me? Instead they prefer I delve into my past lives, which could be profoundly disturbing on a spiritual and psychological level, and, ex- cuse my English, suck off a lot of different men.

'Jane, isn't there anything,' I begged, 'non-sexual,' I stressed, 'that you like doing but don't since meeting James?'

'Well, James hates dancing. We never dance together.'

'But, Jane, you were great at dancing at college!'

'I know, I love dancing, but we never do it. James has bad knees. But Gregoire Pechenikov could dance,' she said wistfully. 'Oh, my God, that man could dance. One night he took me to this Spanish underground club and we danced salsa until the sun came up. It felt like he was making love to me on the dance floor.'

'Janey Jane, I thought you said you met Gregoire Pechenikov *after* meeting James, did you not?' Federico asked, nibbling at the groin of a gingerbread man. The trap-door to the centre of the earth reopened. Jane's face had invented an entirely new shade of red.

'Jane, maybe dancing could be your thing? You don't dance since falling in love so maybe you could steal the dance back?'

'Isn't that a Michael Flatley show?' Federico asked.

'And I could come with you. I'd be more than happy to take a few dance lessons.'

'Oh, you would, would you?' Leah was off. 'You'll dance for Jane but you won't step through the portals of time with me?'

Federico coughed the word 'hide' followed by the words 'she's crazy' and joined Jane studying the ceiling of the room.

quest | steal back the dance with Jane

advice | kiss lots of different men, with a focus on those of Spanish descent

advice | be generous with the giving of blow jobs

emotional chess

Peter Parker looks good in the morning. I know this because we used to have sleepovers when we were kids, and because I bumped into him at 06:30 one Tuesday morning in a coffee shop near Covent Garden. I was trying to wake myself up with an especially strong espresso and a *KitKat*. As I perched on a stool staring out of the window, metaphorical matchsticks propping open sleep-heavy eyelids, Peter Parker jogged past wearing serious-looking running clothes and bright orange running trainers. He glanced in the window as he sped past, did a double take, then stopped. I stared out. He stared in. Neither of us displayed signs of surprise, shock or astonishment. We displayed no facial expressions whatsoever. It was as if we were exhibits in Madame Tussauds, or mannequins in the 1987 hit romcom *Mannequin*, before they came alive and danced excitedly to complicated set pieces, running all over the department store before making love to each other in a window display covered in fur. Eventually Peter committed to movement, walking back towards the coffee shop, coming in and sitting himself disconcertingly close to me on a stool. Then we both stared out of the window, together, in silence. He took a sip from his bottle of water. I took a sip from my coffee. He wiped his brow with his forearm. His running vest was sleeveless and I was once again exposed to his muscular arms. He looked so stern I nearly reverted to my childhood self, wanting to tickle his armpits or perform a short comedy sketch in order to extract even the tiniest hint of a smile. Who was this fully grown smile-less man? Was he happy? Was he content? Had his smile muscles permanently wasted away as my triceps muscles appear to have done in recent years? I decided I wanted to know more, so I shifted my stool to a more comfortable distance and began.

'Peter Parker…'

'Yes, Kate…'

'I have questions.'

'I thought you would.'

'I have *a lot* of questions.'

'I'd appreciate if you ask them one at a time.' He turned to face me and took another sip from his water bottle.

'When did you move back to London?'

'If I tell you are you going to sit there and try to calculate exactly how annoyed you should be that I haven't been in touch?'

'I can ask Grandma.'

'I've been here for four months.'

'And you've known I was in London for?'

'I've known you live in London for those four months, yes.'

If I'd moved to Switzerland I would have hired Colombo and a pack of bloody hungry tracker dogs to find him.

'And you've been divorced for four months?' A pale band of skin on his ring finger gave away a recent end.

'Marriages don't end on the signing of divorce papers,' he said, absent-mindedly touching his ringless finger. 'They end some way before, or after, some never end, and I suspect some never really even start.' Unhelpfully vague.

'Why did you get divorced?'

'Why didn't you get married?' Deflection, classic Peter.

'Gabriel didn't turn out to be who I thought he was going to be.'

'Well, I don't think I turned out to be who she thought I was going to be—' sharing by copying, clever '—and statistically speaking half of all marriages end in divorce so really we shouldn't be surprised when they fail.' Resorting to the proliferation of facts when asked to comment on something of an emotional nature—smokescreen. 'In fact when marriages fail they are more like a mathematical equation that's been added up correctly, not something that is shocking or wrong—' I was lost and found myself staring at his muscular upper thighs '—and with the advent of television and mass media the spread of false notions of love became pandemic. Did you know that the BBC Television Service was the world's first regular television service? Britain used to be such an industrious country. We invented the steam engine, the sewing machine, penicillin, corkscrews and catseyes, the ones on the road, not the ones in the actual animal. We really don't make anything any more.' See, random facts, factual offerings in exchange for emotional thought. He thinks he can distract me with the demise of the British manufacturing industry. But what *has* happened to our glorious country? And what *were* we talking about?

I looked back out of the window. We both sipped from our drinks.

'Peter…'

'Yes, Kate…'

'Were you sad when your marriage ended?'

'If I think about the reasons why we are not together, then I know we made a good decision. She is very happy and is with a really great man. It was the best decision for both of us.' A well-rounded response; informative, in a way that reveals nothing at all.

We continued to stare out of the window. We both sipped from our drinks.

'But did you feel sad?'

'Kate…'

'Yes, Peter.'

'Why are you in this coffee shop at 06:30 on a Tuesday morning?'

'I have a dance class at 07:15. It's the Love-Stolen Dream of one of my friends, Jane, and—'

'Really? You have a dance class?'

'Yes, Peter, I have a dance class and the dance teacher said that if you start your day with a cha cha cha then the whole day dances for you. She said it in a way that made me think it would be a positive thing, to have a dancing day.' Peter frowned and stared at my feet. For a second I wondered if I'd accidentally put on odd shoes. He turned to look back out of the window. We continued to sip from our drinks.

'Kate, when we were at Pepperpots you said to Delaware that you plan to spend the rest of your life alone. Is that true?'

'Yes.'

'Well, I totally understand that. I am much happier when I'm alone.'

'Peter Parker, you couldn't bear to be alone when you were little. You practically lived with me and Grandma. In fact the only reason we stopped sharing a bed was because the neighbour told Grandma it was inappropriate.'

'It was inappropriate. Teenage boys and girls should not be sleeping in the same bed. A couple more months and you'd probably have woken to find me trying to have sex with you.'

I sprayed my coffee all over the window and started choking.

'God, sorry,' he said, patting me on the back. 'I didn't mean *literally*. I meant, during one's teenage years hormone levels peak to such high levels that it's been argued by some more controversial biologists and anthropologists that one cannot be held responsible for one's actions during those months and years as we operate under the influence of a potent mix of chemicals and hormones. But there were other ways for me to get my point across, sorry.'

'That's no problem,' I said, dabbing coffee spray from my face. 'It was just *such* a silly thought.' That was now permanently burnt onto my brain *forever*.

'Kate, I am not the boy you knew back then. I am an adult male and I am perfectly content alone. In fact my ex-wife said exactly that—she said it felt like I didn't need her, that I never really opened up to her, or to our relationship. She described it as being like my *Insignificant Significant Other*—' that didn't sound very nice '—but the thing is, Kate, I really didn't need her, at all. My life is much less complicated when I am alone. It's more constant. It makes sense.'

'Like a reliable mathematical equation.' I chuckled as I thought about the symbol for pi. I mean, why does π represent a long maths equation? It's so silly. Or is it brilliant?

'Kate, do you remember my dog, Jake?' Peter's eyes sparkled at the mention of his beloved dog. 'Well, having a dog is probably the only thing that would make me happier than being alone. My ex-wife never wanted one. She said they were needy and unstable but they're not. Dogs are loyal and consistent. Providing you walk it once a day, twice dependent on size and breed, and give it the occasional treat biscuit, two simple things and it will love you with all its heart.'

'This is my treat biscuit,' I said, trying to make light of the fact that Peter had just spotted my breakfast, a *giant KitKat* bar that probably wasn't meant for one. 'I find *KitKat*s comforting,' I qualified, hastily wrapping it back up. Peter stopped me, opened up the foil and handed me an extra-large piece.

'Tell me why you like *KitKat*s,' he said, pulling me on my stool so I was once again sitting closer to him. He reached across me for a piece of chocolate; his forearm brushed against mine. He felt warm.

'Well,' I began, trying not to think about his half-naked body or the teenage sex we never had, 'when I was little I used to watch Grandma doing her work. Do you remember how she would spend hours toiling over a new article or piece of research?' Peter nodded before reaching for yet another bit of my *KitKat*. 'Well, I always knew when she'd finally finished her work because she would make herself a cup of tea, take out a *KitKat*—'

'From that big tin where you kept all the sweets?'

'Exactly, and she would sit at the kitchen table, slowly peel back the wrapper of a *KitKat* and savour every single chocolatey mouthful while she gave her work a final, satisfying, read through.'

'So *KitKat*s take you to your safe place?'

'Yes, I think *KitKat*s take me to my *safe place*, although my consumption of them is not dependent on any challenging intellectual endeavour having been completed, just a general sense of neediness. Just yesterday, for example, I was feeling a bit needy because I'd seen a particularly distressed tramp near Trafalgar Square, and I'd thought to myself, "Lucky me, all I have to worry about is unpicking the mystery of love, its absence and effects, across generations and cultures; that tramp doesn't even know where he's going to sleep tonight, poor bastard." So, as an emotional crutch, if you will, I went straight to *WHSmith*'s to buy myself a *KitKat*, and not a regular *KitKat*, the big-bar version. I'd gone heavy duty.'

'Like the one you have in front of you now.'

'It was an emotional time, Peter! Which is why I also bought a notebook because that tramp made me realise I need to be more grateful. So I bought a notebook and every single day I am going to write a list of all the things I am thankful for. It's going to be like a daily emotional *Thanks-*

giving until my neural pathways have re-established themselves as grateful ones.'

It had happened again. The Peter-Parker-induced verbal
diarrhoea where I go on and on and on discovering nothing new about Peter, just unearthing strange pockets of my
own deranged mind, then showing them to him like a mental health 'Show and Tell'. 'So I bought a notebook, and a
KitKat, and today I started to make my list, but if I'm honest one of the things I'm grateful for is the *KitKat*, and the
notebook, and that I know where I'll be sleeping tonight.
Which definitely won't be next to a teenage version of you,
you giant sex pest,' I chortled, then snorted, then went very
quiet before muttering, 'I probably should have just given
the tramp some money, or a sandwich. That probably would
have been more useful to a poor homeless man than me
gorging myself on another bar of confectionery and writing down my thoughts and—' Peter gently placed his hand
over my mouth and held it there until he was sure I had
stopped talking.

'That was a lovely speech, Kate.'

'I thought so. I'd practised it.'

'Especially the sex-pest part.'

'That was more of an ad lib. I was in the moment.' I
gulped down more coffee. Peter went back to looking out
of the window.

'Kate.'

'Yes, Peter.'

'I don't want to bamboozle you with technical terminol-
ogy or self-fulfilling labels, and I'm not judging you, but I
think you should know, your *KitKat* eating, they've found

a name for it. It's called *comfort eating*.' He handed me the last piece of the very food that was filling my void. 'Hit the gym, Winters.' He patted me on the head. 'Enjoy the natural high of exercise. Run yourself to happiness, Kitkat, I mean Kate.'

'You're very annoying.'

'But slightly more succinct than you. Now I'm afraid I have to go. My office prefers I shower and change before turning up.' He gestured to his sweaty sports clothes and I tried not to stare at his partially naked body. I cursed *Nike* for their sparing use of fabric. 'So enjoy your dance class and thanks for the *KitKat*.' He was already halfway out of the door when he stopped and turned back. 'You know, it really is good to see you again, Kate.' He stared at me for a few seconds as if he was about to say something else, changed his mind, then, like a *KitKat* wrapper in the wind, or a tramp discovering a dry and unoccupied shelter, a half-naked Peter Parker ran off to start his smile-free day.

magdalena—43 years old—owner & dance instructor at The Studio dance school

What did I give up for love? Well, I definitely can't be as much of a free spirit. That kind of living-in-the-moment attitude doesn't sit comfortably in a relationship. In fact being changeable at all becomes more difficult when someone else's feelings are involved. And we share our income and assets, which was not something I was previously used to doing. But the biggest thing I gave up for love is my country. I originally left Spain because I wanted to learn English. The opportunities for dancers were all in London so I came here. I planned to work for a couple of years then move home. But after 18 months I met Paul and we fell in love. I wanted to be around him so my move back to Spain got delayed, and delayed, and delayed. And Paul doesn't speak Spanish, he's practically allergic to the sunshine and he would struggle to find a job in Spain.

I truly believe that love is serendipitous. Paul is my happy unplanned opportunity. But if there was no Paul and no love I would certainly have moved home and spent the rest of my life living in Spain.

the studio | covent garden

It was becoming difficult to do anything without an entourage. Federico had insisted on coming because of all the male dancers. Leah had insisted on coming because she said love might also have stolen dancing from her (and because of all the male dancers). Henry was there because he and Leah were a package deal. Jenny Sullivan had come with her husband to prove not only that they could dance, but that they could do it well, and they could do it while being in love. Only Jane was there under the legitimate reason of it being one of her Love-Stolen Dreams.

The dance lessons had been organised by *True Love*, and thirty readers including Jane had been selected to join the *LSD Dance Crew* (Chad's words). There didn't appear to be any obvious pattern to why each of these women had stopped dancing. Neither was there a specific age when they started to disconnect. They weren't even from the same demographic. The only consistent theme was that all the women had forgotten how good dancing made them feel, and this amnesia always accompanied the arrival of love— the love for another overshadowing the love of dance. They didn't need to be mutually exclusive but it seemed that for some reason they were.

'Good morning, people,' Magdalena, the Penelope-Cruz-sized dance instructor said as she strode into the centre of the studio. 'Hola, buenos días and thank you for coming 'ere today.' She curtseyed and clapped us. 'Everyone who works and trains here at *The Studio* is passionate about dance. It is our life. And I've heard that you are also all passionate about dance. So already we have much in common.' She smiled at the room. She wore a full-length Lycra leotard and looked Madonna-hot. 'The purpose of today is for us to get to know each other, to get to know our partners and to get to know ourselves a little bit. So, pupils, please go and stand next to the dancer who holds the corresponding number to you. Say hello. Maybe give each other a little kiss. And I will be back in five minutes to start the class. Bienvenidos.'

We all looked from the numbers in our hands to the numbers attached to the throng of male dancers. It was like a human lottery but with leg kicks. Jane had been given a number 7. I held a lucky number 5. As our allocated professional dancers approached, Federico tried to rip my number from my hand because No.5 (Edmundo) was a ridiculously handsome dark-haired Italian with a body that made me want to collapse on the floor and start weeping. Jane's No.7 was called Julio and was a shy, slender dancer who blushed constantly while nervously looking at the floor. While we waited for Magdalena to return, Federico decided to interview the dancers to discover what love had stolen from them other than their body fat.

'Well, goodness me,' Federico sighed, 'look at you two.' He clapped his hands together doing a mini curtsey. 'Pas de bourrée-ing your way through life, pirouetting past problems, grand jeté-ing across obstacles like modern-day Darcy Bussells but with penises.' Federico beamed at them while Julio looked nervously at Edmundo. 'I bet you love what you do. Do you? Do you love it? Do you? Do you?' He was looking between the two of them like a crazy dog.

'I am never happier than when I dance,' whispered Julio.

'I hear you, just about, but I hear you,' Federico said, high-kicking his leg in the air and immediately pulling a muscle. 'But what I am wanting to know,' Federico squeaked, leaning awkwardly against the wall, rubbing his right hip joint, 'is about your *journey*. Did love ever get in the way of your *Pursuit of Happiness* and I don't mean the Will Smith film, I mean dance, although that film does draw some parallels in terms of life's emotional journey, and Will Smith is of course a very rhythmic mountain of a man, yes he is. So, Edmundo, is there anything you've given up for love?'

'Non!' he snapped, checking his luminous yellow Swatch watch and exhaling moodily.

'What about you, Julio?'

'He gives up everything for love,' Edmundo growled, glaring at poor quivering Julio.

'May I ask,' Jane said quietly from the corner of the room, 'how you managed to stay on track because I've always known I like dancing but it has slowly disappeared from my life, and I can't seem to work out why?'

I knew exactly why and it was bloody well James.

'I fought for it,' barked Edmundo. 'I knew my dream and I fought and I trained hard every single day to get where I am. And I should be training now, not stuck in this lesson to pay the rent.' He spat the words out like pips.

'I was lucky,' whispered Julio, blinking furiously. 'I had a really supportive dance teacher at school. He saw something in me and went out of his way to give me the opportunities he never had. Without that guidance and support I don't think I'd be where I am today.' He pulled hard on his own hair.

'And where is that exactly?' Edmundo yelled at poor Julio. 'Exactly nowhere, I think!' he said, striding off to a different corner of the studio, muttering to himself in incomprehensible Italian. Julio stood head down chewing on his bottom lip. I looked between the two of them and cursed. I couldn't believe I'd ended up with the bipolar, aggressive, shouty one.

'So are we ready?' said Magdalena, returning to the room. 'Then everybody please stand by your partners.'

the dance off

We all took our positions ready to begin. Jenny Sullivan and her husband were just a few feet to my right. He was holding her in his arms and kissing her forehead while she gently nuzzled into his neck and giggled an annoying laugh. They were so perfect and happy it actually made my insides hurt. Edmundo on the other hand couldn't even look me in the eyes. I'd been standing next to him for several minutes but he just kept huffing and puffing and staring continuously at the exit. And Jane's whispering Julio wouldn't look at her either. His eyes were fixed to the floor and I swear I could see tears streaming down his little face. And Jane couldn't seem to look down from studying the ceiling. In fact it was as if the four of us had been given the task of avoiding direct eye contact *at all costs*, as if in the penultimate scene of an action movie and direct human eye contact was the *detonator* for the 700lb bomb buried in the ground below us...

Julio tentatively stepped towards Jane and held out his hand.

'It's ridiculous really,' Jane said, taking his hand, 'but the only hand I've held in years is James'. James is my husband, although he's not much of a hand-holder, more of a thigh-slapper. Well, now I've made him sound like he's in a country and western band. He's not. He's a banker. Your hand feels different.' She fell silent and they both looked at the floor, again. 'You have lovely soft hands,' she said, patting his hand reassuringly with her free hand. Then the music started and Julio spun Jane like a spinning top, whipping her into his arms. They were face-to-face, eyes to the floor.

'Oh, goodness,' Jane sighed.

Then he spun her back the other way. Their bodies were pressed against each other; they moved across the floor in perfect unison, past Jenny Sullivan and Ken Doll, who were snogging the faces off each other, past the other dancers, past everyone, including me, and that's when I realised I wasn't dancing. I turned to Edmundo, who was glaring at me. He grabbed my hand and made my little finger click. Then he spun me violently outwards, expecting me to twirl back in. But I wasn't prepared. My hands were sweaty from the stress. So I sort of lost my grip and spun off towards the mirrored wall, tripping and smacking hard against it. I tried again and managed a twirl, but then accidentally caught him in the chest with my elbow. The third incident was very Chicken and Egg. I think I tripped when I saw Peter walk in. Peter says I was already on the floor when he arrived. Whatever the truth Edmundo spun me outwards, I tripped over my own foot, landed hard on my back at the feet of Jenny Sullivan, cracking my head against the cold wooden floor. I came to to find Peter Parker's warm hands cupping my face, his face inches above mine.

'Honestly, don't worry,' he reassured the room. 'She did this all the time when we were growing up.' This was simply not true. 'Her grandma used to send us to ballroom dancing and she didn't get through a single class without collapsing on the floor.' Maybe a bit true. 'She was like a theatrical Italian footballer constantly vying for an undeserved penalty.' The mostly homosexual room looked confused. 'Obviously that was before her Olympic dancing career.' Bastard.

'Kate, you are going to have to sit the class out,' Magdalena said, trying to help me up. 'Can you make it to the chair?'

'I'll take her,' Peter said, picking me up in his arms, carrying me to the side of the room and plonking me on a plastic chair. 'You were ever so graceful out there, Kate Winters,' he said as he got up to leave.

'What are you doing here? And where are you going?'

'I'm going back to work. I just came to bring you these,' he said, throwing a box of anti-inflammatory painkillers at me. I stared at them in my lap.

'Well, I can't swallow tablets,' I snapped like a petulant child as he walked back out of the doors of the studio not bothering to look back at me even once. He was like an unfinished sentence and we were still on…

I continued to stare at the exit while the rest of the room carried on dancing, all of them ridiculously accomplished, and coordinated, and it felt *a lot* like they were just showing off. But no couple was more accomplished and showy-offy than Julio and Jane. They were doing the most extraordinary tango across the room: Julio executing every move with precision; Jane seeming to respond to him instinctively. She hit every beat perfectly. She connected to Julio. Julio connected to his own thoughts, finding release and freedom within dance. The music reached a crescendo and Jane spun for the final time into the arms of Julio, and there they stopped, both fighting to catch their breath. It took a moment for their alter egos to melt away, then they jumped away from each other like popping corn.

'You are a very good dancer,' Jane said, patting Julio on the back, then stepping back to a safe distance. 'Well done you.'

Julio shrugged and chewed on his fingernails. Magdalena watched them with a smile on her face. She walked over to a notice board and unpinned a couple of flyers, handing one to each of them.

'The national Pro-Am is coming up. A professional dancer pairs up with an amateur. The prize money is substantial and the finals are shown on Dance UK. You two should think about entering. I think you'd have a real shot.' Jane and Julio looked from Magdalena to each other before both very quickly looking to the floor. 'Right, that's it for today. Thank you all for coming, see you at the same time next week, and, Kate…' she said, leading me away from the rest of the group. 'Kate, we probably need to have a little talk…'

That's when she told me I probably shouldn't come back next week but that she knew of a dance specialist called Mustafa who apparently dealt with *people like me*.

'Why haven't I been doing this my whole life?' Jane asked as everyone started packing up and leaving the studio. 'What am I doing baking gingerbread cookies when I could be here dancing a couple of times a week? How did I get so disengaged? It's not like it would even take time away from James—he's at the bloody tennis club!'

'Does anyone know what the Tiramisu was going on between those two dancers?' Federico asked. 'The tension between them was like a tsunami. I saw small villages and islands engulfed by it. I nearly drowned in it. And I am a strong swimmer, yes I am.'

'They used to be a couple,' Leah said, wiping something sticky off Henry's hands, 'but Julio always gets the part when they go up against each other in auditions. So he stopped auditioning so that he wouldn't beat Edmundo, but then Edmundo stopped speaking to Julio because he doesn't respect anyone who puts their relationship before their career. He thinks Julio is weak.' Federico was blinking furiously as Leah spoke.

'How do you know all of this, you mysterious fact-finder of the world of dance? How, I ask you, how?'

'Because Henry wet himself during the class. I got talking to one of the dancers in the baby-changing room.'

'That's why we need a mother-fluffing baby, Kat-kins! I told you this! We need to buy a baby!'

'I am going to enter that competition,' Jane interrupted. 'I am going to enter it and I am going to win it!' She glared at the room.

'So just to confirm,' Federico continued, 'Julio prioritised his feelings over his ambition to twirl? His career is on hold *and* he hasn't got the guy?'

'I think you should enter the competition, Jane,' Leah said. 'I think that's exactly what you should do and I think I might start dancing too. My ex didn't like dancing either. He would bounce around the room to Nirvana after a couple of Stellas but we never had a Frank-Sinatra-Ginger-Rogers moment. We never had that, so that's a love-stolen dream, isn't it?'

'Love-stolen ice cream?' Henry asked.

'No, Mummy didn't say that, did she? She said love-stolen dreams but, nice try, it was an admirable attempt to bring ice cream into the conversation—' Henry burst out laughing '—and great that you are learning to play with the English language. Your father is more of a grunts and snorts kind of man.'

'Daddy snores.'

'Yes, he does, Henry. Another delightful facet of my marriage: sleepless snore-filled nights.'

'Snore-filled rice pudding!' he squealed.

'No, that's not as good. You'd peaked with love-stolen ice creams, and we can probably fit in one love-stolen ice cream before Mummy's reflexology course.'

'Kate…' Jane said, stifling laughter. 'Please don't tell me you still can't swallow tablets.' She pointed to the unopened box of painkillers in my hand and they all turned to look and started giggling. They always do this. They laugh at me as if they are in some tablet-swallowing club, as if it's ridiculous that I might find it difficult, the bastards. Well, it is difficult, and dangerous, and I cursed Peter for drawing attention to an abnormality I've spent *years* waiting for them to finally forget. I looked down at the tablets in my hand, filled with a strange sense of adolescent shame, only to realise *why* Jane had been reminded of my strange *but completely understandable* affliction. Peter had remembered to buy me soluble painkillers. Peter had remembered I couldn't swallow.

Humpty Dumpty sat on a wall,
Humpty Dumpty had a great fall.
All the queen's horses and all the queen's men
Wanted old Humpty together again.

people who live in glass houses shouldn't throw LSD

While we were no closer to understanding *why* the *True Love* readers sometimes missed out on things when they fell in love, Bob (*Fat Camp*'s life coach) thought it would be a good idea if we taught women how to make space in their weekly diaries in order to start achieving some of their goals. So we decided to organise a time-management workshop and host it in central London. When tickets for the event went on sale we didn't think to put an upper limit on the number available. We were even considering holding the event at *True Love*. But over 3,000 tickets were sold in the first two hours so we ended up hiring the O2 Arena and asking Bob to do five different sessions. I had been listening to him speak at the first of these lectures *('Supercharge Your Life and Your Productivity to Achieve Great Change and Ultimate Happiness—Take Back Your Love-Stolen Dreams. Do It—Do It Now!')* when I had a call from Federico.

'Everything has gone tits up in the office, Kat-kins. Jenny Sullivan is *refusing* to write anything for the magazine. She's telling everyone that LSD is bad news. She thinks it's messing with our heads. She thinks it's screwing with our vision of the world. She thinks, and I can't believe I'm about to say this, she thinks we should all stop doing it! Chad's called an afternoon Early Morning Unfocused Focus Meeting. You need to get here, now!'

the boardroom | true love

'This has run its course, Chad. We have written this to death, Chad. I am not putting my name to another feature that says love is shit, Chad.' Jenny was sitting at the point of the glass heart, Chad on his special chair; the rest of the office were squished wherever they could comfortably fit. They'd been stuck in the boardroom for hours, Chad and Jenny at loggerheads…whatever that means.

'Jenny, you are brilliant. I know it. You know it. Everyone in this twatting room knows it. But you don't know shit about the market. OK. It's not finished. This hasn't even twatting begun. We've never had so many readers write in. The post office has had to hire another twatting van to get the post to us. The marketing department is having to hot desk in the stairwell because I need their twatting office to store all the post. We've got the BB-twatting-C calling us every five minutes to find out what our next edition's going to be about.'

'Chad, the BBC calls everyone, Chad. They've had me on speed dial since 1994.'

There was a murmur across the room and Jenny went pale as she realised she may have given away a hint of her true age. Mark from Marketing was desperately trying to do the maths in his head. The murmurs and discontent continued.

Across the other side of the room I noticed Federico furiously blinking as if sending me a message by Morse code. He gestured for me to get up and do something. My chair creaked loudly as I nervously stood up.

'Jenny,' I muttered into my hair, standing as if I were an enormous jacket on a tiny coat hanger. 'Jenny, don't you think it's important that—'

'Kate, I can't hear you, Kate. Chad, I can't hear her, Chad.'

'Speak the twat up.'

I cleared my throat and started again.

'Don't you think it's important that we help women remember all the things they stopped doing when they fell in love; help them go out there and take back what love stole; help them have a bit more faith that they don't have to compromise or put their dreams on hold because love shows up? We should be able to be who we want to be whether we are in love, or we are out of love, or—'

'Kate, please stop talking, Kate,' Jenny said, standing from a creak-free chair. 'I agree with and promote the empowerment of women, Kate. I do. I think *True Love* should be at the forefront of this movement. I want every woman to reach her full potential, Kate. It's my life goal. It is not something you invented the day you turned 30. But what I do object to, Kate, is you. It's obvious that you are doing this because love hasn't shown up for you. You are like a love repellent; a force field; a magnetic destabiliser to relationships and emotions; on some ridiculous crusade to make the rest of us miserable. But what you don't realise, Kate, because you are consumed with your own loneliness, is that some of us are happy, Kate. Some of us have fallen in love. Some of us have not been rejected. Some of us have normal relationships that are positive and empowering and life-changing.' Right on cue Jenny's Ken Doll husband walked through the double doors into Reception. He was carrying a huge bunch of roses, looking as if he had just flown in from the pages of a *Twilight* novel but without the vamp teeth and overly pink lips. He waved at her through the glass wall. 'I can speak for myself and my husband—' she beamed at him and waved back '—when I say that I have resolutely not given up anything for love. My world is complete. I am happy. You are trying to undermine love to make yourself feel better. It is cheap. It is pathetic. It stinks of desperation and sometimes I think you would be more at home working on a reality TV show or one of those day-time talk shows where everyone swears at each other before throwing furniture. I can write you a reference if you like.' She stood statuesque, glaring at me, eyebrows raised, waiting for my response. Chad was nervously looking the other way, gnawing through a red apple and repeatedly glancing at his watch. All the writers in the room were avoiding my gaze. I felt like the skin-peeling leper woman from *Ben-Hur*. Everyone wishing I would go the f*** away, back to my leper cave, to flake and peel out of sight of the rest of the world. Federico mouthed across the room, 'Don't be a Human Fountain.'

'You know what, Jenny,' I said, looking out to Reception, where Jenny's gorgeous husband sat waiting patiently for his wife, 'I think you are probably right.' There was a dramatic gasp across the boardroom. Chad swung round in his chair to face me. He clicked his fingers at his assistant, Loosie. 'I think I am trying to make myself feel better. Maybe I am searching for meaning where there is none. Because I met my One True Love and it didn't work out. I couldn't find a way to make it work. I failed. And at the end of it I was left with nothing. I was bare-naked. Everything had been stripped away from me. So yes, I am a bit of a sad loser. I am a bit desperate. I am trying to make myself feel better. Because I have only ever been in love once. I have only ever looked into a man's eyes once and known I want to create a child with him. I have only ever shared a home with one man. He was it. So my heart is broken, Jenny, broken to shit. And it doesn't seem to want to put itself back together again. And there is no space in it for anyone other than him. There is no space in it at all. So all I have is this, you're right. All I have is this idea, this list of other people's dreams, this list of things that might bring other people happiness, to break up the mind-numbing, endless feeling of pain. Because when I think about not spending my life with him, I can't breathe. This helps me breathe, Jenny. This job, this idea, this is my life raft. It's all that is keeping me afloat. Because I truly believe that if I had been more personally fulfilled, if I had been more connected to myself and my own personal am-bitions, then the loss of him wouldn't have felt so much like I was dying. So yes, Jenny, this is 100% about me and the end of my relationship. You got me, you sussed me out, you exposed me. Well done you.'

The room was totally silent.

Then Federico started a slow clap.

Clap…Clap…Cl—

'Shut the fuck up, Federico. There is no need to twatting clap.' Chad chomped down on his red apple, spraying half of it across the heart-shaped table. 'Loosie, my genius little assistant, did you get all that?'

'Yes, Chad,' Loosie said, furiously scribbling notes.

'I love that girl.' Chad pointed at Loosie. She beamed at him and I saw Federico clutch the *Nespresso* machine for support. 'Fastest shorthand in the city of London. You can't imagine some of the conversations that girl has captured for me with that scrawly mess of hers. She even won some twatting shorthand competition. They gave her vouchers for Harvey-twatting-Nics of all places. As if anyone shops at Harvey Nics. Even the pensioners that live round the corner from Harvey Nics get on the twatting bus and go to Selfridges. Right, people, you all have a job to do. Loosie, type up Kate's little confessional, in first person, obviously. Let's tell our readers why Kate really came up with the idea of Love-Stolen Dreams. Let's reveal who *Pirate Kate* really is. And we need a photo of her looking really desperate—'

'Well, there's that one from the office party—' Federico blurted out before clamping his own hand over his mouth. 'Sorry,' he mouthed across the room.

'Perfect! This is going to be huge! The rest of you writers, you know the routine: I want two articles from each of you and I want them by tomorrow. Jenny, if you don't want to write for this edition then don't. We've got enough material without you. OK, that's it, people. Get the twat out of this office and on with some twatting work!' he said, marching out the room as the rest of the office turned like an intimidating flash mob to glare at me.

'So, Kat-kins.' Federico put his arm around me. 'Pirate Kate. Wow! You have finally got the better of Jenny Sullivan, haven't you, with your very own feature? A named writer for *True Love* magazine. Yeah!' he said, shaking his fist in the air. 'Even if technically someone else is actually writing the article on your behalf. And we will fabricate large portions of your personal history. And Photoshop your picture because you are a little bit too skinny for people to relate to right now, yes, you are. Skinny people are supposed to be happy, and you are very much the exception to that rule. You make misery your full-time occupation. And if we are stood in Honesty Corner, which we are,' he said, pointing to the floor, 'your preoccupation is to the detriment of your work and your dress sense. Ah—' he hugged me '—good talks, Kat-kins, good talks.' He patted me on the head, yelling as he left the boardroom. 'Will someone please find that f-ing awful photo of Kate at the office party, where she looks like she's been in a prisoner-of-war camp? Yes, darling, yes, in *that* dress. In fact *that* dress probably needs a feature writing about it—it could tell us firsthand about the First World War. It's a historical oracle made of cotton and polyester. The history of our very society is woven into that man-made fabric. It's a relic. An actual relic. In fact, can someone call the National History Museum as well? Can we get them in to take a look at it?'

nature vs nurture and the human need to mate

liberty's | london

In order to avoid *True Love*'s tabloid-esque recreation of my own shambolic love life I decided to work in *Liberty*'s, the luxury department store in London and my favourite place to hide out. *Liberty*'s was designed in 1875 and is supposed to make you feel as if you're in your own home. It has large wooden staircases, lots of little rooms, some of them with fireplaces or armchairs; every space filled with something exquisite, luxury, painfully expensive. On the lower ground floor they have a Champagne Bar and a heavenly place called Menswear, and Menswear is filled with beautiful clothes for men, beautiful shoes for men, beautiful accessories for men and lots and lots of beautiful men. I often go to the Champagne Bar, laptop in hand, to work while watching handsome male models as they hold jumpers up against their muscular torsos, or slip on a new jacket, or bend over to try on a new shoe...

Today however I wanted to spend my time researching

the idea of Nature vs Nurture in relation to Love-Stolen Dreams. Because I kept meeting women who lost focus as their lives progressed, this loss of focus more often than not going hand in hand with being in a relationship. I certainly gave up stuff, mostly myself, and all my boundaries; in fact it was as if I held an impromptu garage sale giving away every important part of myself in exchange for a cuddle, or a kiss or a little bit of French love. And Mary gave up learning about something by choice, as did Beatrice, and Delaware missed out, and Leah, and Jane, and thousands of our readers.

So if love, in all its various forms, wasn't necessarily *chicken soup for the soul* perhaps there was a biological need for humans to pair off? Perhaps it was this instinct that was overriding our other instinct, that of self-preservation and self-care? Was it *nature* that was affecting so many of the women who had written in to *True Love*? And if so was there a sure-fire way we could *nurture* everyone back to happiness?

I decided to start my research with *Google* and the *Google* results were overwhelming, in that they overwhelmingly suggested not only that we feel better when we engage in fulfilling relationships but also in fulfilling activities.

Result 1 of 4,235,672—The profound human need for connectedness

   ...Intimate relationships play a central role in the overall human experience... Humans have a universal want to belong and to love, which is satisfied within an intimate relationship...

Result 2 of 4,235,672—Wikipedia-Maslow's hierarchy of needs

...esteem, friendship and love, security, and physical needs. If these needs are not met the body gives no physical indication but the individual feels anxious and tense...

Result 3 of 4,235,672—Human Needs

...all humans have a need to be respected and to have self-esteem and self-respect. They need to engage in activities that give them a sense of contribution. They need to feel a sense of belonging and acceptance. They need to love and be loved. In the absence of these elements, many people suffer from loneliness, social anxiety and clinical depression...

Result 4 of 4,235,672—'What a man can be, he must be.'

What a man can be, he must be, if he wishes to feel truly satisfied. This is a broad definition of the need for self-actualisation and relates to a person's full potential and realising that potential, becoming everything one is capable of being otherwise one will never truly feel satisfied.

'Hi!' A voice from behind drew me back out of my laptop screen like a wormhole.

Peter Parker appeared from nowhere and sat himself down on the stool next to mine. He looked at me with a strange level of amusement.

'OK, so I can't dance. I admit it. I have an allergic reaction to coordinated dance steps. In future I will operate within the realms of truth.'

'Within the *realms of possibility*, Kate, and it's possible you could be a wonderful dancer if you put your mind to it and stopped fibbing about your appearances at the Dance Olympics—which doesn't actually exist.' He leant across me and peered at the screen of my laptop. 'Aren't you supposed to be at work?' he said, reading down the list of my *Google* results.

'I am. I'm researching,' I said, trying to ignore the fact that his face was mere millimetres from my own and he smelt like a man-sized version of a giant chocolate bar. I found myself leaning in to sniff his neck, which he noticed, and flinched away as if I'd stung him. 'I'm, er, I'm reading about *nature versus nurture* and the human need for love,' I said, closing my laptop, praying to God he hadn't seen the other tab I'd had open—the one where I'd been reading about his horoscope and the sexual compatibility of our signs.

'OK, Professor Winters, tell me about the human need for love, which I am deeply suspicious of.'

'You're suspicious of humans or you're suspicious of love?'

'I am suspicious of a human need for anything other than water and basic nutrients.'

'You're suspicious of *all* human needs? Across the board?'

'Need is a social construct, Kate. It's a weakness, and as such I'm suspicious of it.'

'What about the human need to urinate? Does that make you suspicious? And do you think we could have said *suspicious* more times in the last few minutes?'

'You make me suspicious, Kitkat. And yes, we probably could. Suspicious, suspicious, suspicious, suspicious, suspicious. So tell me about your suspicious work.'

'Well, I've been wondering why so many of us get distracted from doing the things we love. Why we opt for the love of others over the love of ourselves. I wanted to know if there was a biological reason for us disconnecting from our dreams.' Peter was frowning. 'I have an analogy.'

'Now I'm suspicious of your analogy.'

'Imagine we are all given a compass at birth—' Peter nodded '—and we plot a route to our chosen destination. But sooner or later we meet someone who wants to come aboard our boat—'

'Is the boat we're referring to the great vessel we call *The Love Boat*?'

'Peter, you can call it what you like—the principles here are always the same. So imagine you meet someone who you quite like—' we both seemed to go a little pink '—and that person, who you like, wants to come aboard your ship, so you make one tiny change, less than 0.005 of a degree, so they can come with you on your journey.'

'Who wouldn't make a 0.005 degree alteration for someone they liked?'

'Exactly,' I said, getting pinker by the second. 'But the thing is, after several weeks, months, years, that 0.005 change has left you miles and miles and *miles* off course, if you can even remember where you wanted to go in the first place. And if you do remember, the about-turn needed to get back to where you were originally going is so enormous it could be detrimental to your relationship with your passenger, who is now well and truly a part of the ship's crew. So I've been thinking, it might be helpful to set up some kind of drop-in centre or Love-Stolen Dreams Academy, some-

where where young women could check in with their compass, if you will, at various different stages in their lives.
I was thinking ages 16, 18 and 25, to make sure they are
really connected to who they are and what they love doing,
make sure that's being translated into their choices at college, university and professionally—a nationwide mentoring
programme, I suppose. Because if the need to have someone on your boat is a biological one, stronger than the need
for self-actualisation, but both are necessary for happiness,
then a mentoring programme might help us stay connected
to ourselves, which would keep us connected to happiness,
which...' I was petering out into more of a mutter. 'Well,
it's a silly analogy, I know that, I just thought, well, there
must be a better way...'

'Kate, that's an amazing idea, really. It's amazing, all of
you, I mean, all of it, it's amazing. And traditionally girls
do outperform boys until their late teens so if you started
guiding them at 16 and continued to do so until their mid-
twenties you'd be on hand during what appears to be the
stage where they get knocked off track.' I knew none of
the above but nodded as if I'd reached the same conclu-
sion. 'You know, I think you should speak to someone at
the Department for Education. They are really open to new
initiatives for kids and young adults.'

'The Department for Education?' I guffawed. 'Peter, I
write for a trashy magazine and hang out in basement champagne bars under the guise of legitimate research. I'm not
governmental material. Who would I even speak to? What
would I say? How do you know they are open to new ideas?

And is it possible for me to ask more questions in one sentence?'

Peter handed me a glass of champagne before taking a deep breath and beginning,

'I went to school with the current Education Secretary. He's a very nice man. He's not above hearing the views of other people. If you think you've identified a weakness in the current education or pastoral care system you should flag it up. It's your duty as a British citizen. I can help you if you like. And, yes, you probably could have asked more questions in one sentence, and have done in the past, although any more and I do find it hard to remember and respond to them sequentially, but I would try, so feel free to bombard me. I'm a Gemini, so there's enough of us to cope.'

Great, he saw the horoscope tab. I gulped down my champagne hoping the bubbles would fill the gapping crater of embarrassment. Peter watched me, slowly sipping on his own.

'Kate…' he said, leaning in towards me. 'If I'm honest, I really *really* didn't know what to expect meeting you again after all this time.' He looked deep into my eyes. 'But you are just like you, just like you were, a grown-up version of Kate but with laughter lines.'

'There are no lines!'

'There are a few lines, Kate,' he said, gently running his fingers along my forehead to the apparent laughter lines around my eyes. 'I like them.'

I realised I was holding my breath and found myself leaning ever so slightly in towards him. 'Kate, I actually have to go,' he said, jumping off his stool, reclaiming the exact distance between us that I'd encroached upon. Which made me wonder if Peter and I were fridge magnets, because every time I moved so much as an inch closer to him he was always repelled back the other way. 'But if you're free later on maybe we could meet for dinner, talk through your idea for a school's programme?' Or my idea for an electronic pulse that negates the opposing forces of magnets. 'Or we could talk about our sun signs?' Embarrassing. 'Your choice, unless you have another important writing commitment in a different champagne bar?'

'Actually I can't tonight. Leah wants me to go and learn about my inner child with her. Apparently it's whiny and incomplete and it's trying to talk to me but I won't listen.'

I started to blush. I mean *who* has to say no to a dinner date with Peter Parker in order to communicate with one's inner child? Me, that's who. I was going to kill Leah. I had been on more of her Love-Stolen Dream than anyone else and she was still banging on about past life regression then guilt-tripping me into going on stupid courses with her.

'So what about tomorrow?'

'Tomorrow I have *True Love*'s annual office cocktail party. Chad is going to be there making sure we all attend. I'd invite you but I can assure you it's not fun. People get drunk, really drunk, and they fornicate. People would try touching you.' I was concerned the drunk handsy lady would be me.

'OK, so no dinner, no fornicating and no drunk-touching, but come and meet me Friday. I'm taking your *Fat Campers* for a run around Hyde Park. Come and join us. It will make you feel as good as a *KitKat*, Kitkat.'

'Peter, please stop calling me that.'

'So I'll see you Friday?' he said, kissing me on the cheek then dashing off before I could say no. I watched him disappear into the art deco wood-panelled elevator as another exquisitely attractive man arrived in Menswear. I immediately recognised him as Jenny Sullivan's Ken Doll husband and he headed straight for my favourite section, Men's Shoes.

I'm not sure if it was the shame of the recent dance class, or because I probably should have been working in the office, but I ducked out of sight and hid. Ken Doll glided into Men's Shoes and was already bending over trying on his first pair when I spotted her. She came up behind him and wrapped her slender arms around his muscular waist. He turned around, bent down and kissed her. It was one of those breathy, slow-motion kisses that make you stop and stare in the street, the man with one arm around the woman's lower back, the other gently in her hair, the couple unaware of anyone else in the surrounding area. It had been a really long time since I had been kissed like that and my heart emitted a little cooing noise as it remembered the kiss of Gabriel. And it seemed as if Jenny Sullivan hadn't been kissed like that either, because the woman Ken Doll was kissing was 100% *not* her.

floating restaurant | pepperpots

'faith is believing something you know ain't true'
(mark twain)

'Oh…my…mother…fluffing…God!' We were at Pepperpots' legendary and liquor-heavy Wednesday evening Happy Hour and I'd just told Federico about Jenny Sullivan's husband trying on 'new shoes'. All I could see were the whites of his bulbous eyes as he processed the information. He looked as if he were doing complicated algebra in his head. 'This is huge, Kat-kins! This is mammoth! This is a walrus at the end of the dinosaur era when the only surviving creatures were small and birdlike. This sticks out, Kat-kins. It's incongruous. That's what incongruous means. It means a ruddy great dinosaur stood with a bunch of small birds. And what are the politics when you see someone cheat? What is the correct response if that person is not an official friend? Do you shut up? Is that what you do? Do you fess up? Do you up and leave?' He got up from his chair walked around it, then sat back down. 'You know, I'd heard rumours about him.' Federico was shaking his head. 'There had been mutterings like butterflies fluttering but I just thought it was jealous gossiping.' He crossed his legs, then his arms, then placed his index finger on his chin.

'Why would Jenny Sullivan's husband even think to cheat?' I asked, hoping Federico might better understand the inner workings of the penis-obsessed male mind. 'What could be better than being with Jenny Sullivan? There is no greener grass; there is concrete, and roadworks and urban scrubland.'

'Perfect isn't sexy, Kat-kins,' Federico said, shaking his head. 'It's annoying. No one wants their imperfections high-lighted by the perfection of their perfect plus one. Would you want to wake up every morning, turn and see some godlike perfect boyfriend lying next to you only to think, "I'm a bit average in comparison"? No, you would not.' I would. 'Perfection makes us behave badly. It reminds us of our imperfections so we act up like the flawed, imperfect beings they've reminded us that we are. She spends her entire life telling us how perfect she is so he has to become imperfect. It's a universal law.'

'Whatever happened to taking responsibility for ourselves? Treating others as we wished to be treated? Turning the other cheek?' Actually I'm not sure that last one's relevant, unless it's a bottom cheek, which seems wholly inappropriate under the circumstances. 'And what about poor Jenny? Does she even know?'

'Kat-kins, if he's been playing around for as long as I've heard rumours about him playing around then she has to know. I even heard a story that he'd shagged a *Dior* model on the *London Eye*, and that's got glass walls, Kat-kins, glass frickin walls! Not to mention there's no bathroom in those little capsules to clean up afterwards. Well, no wonder super-bugs are being passed all over the bloody place with viruses so strong no antibiotics can fight them off—you've got Jenny's husband wandering all over the place shagging in London's landmarks without a washroom or an anti-bacterial hand-wash in sight. He's like a giant germ production centre. His germs are like the *Coca-Cola* of the bacteria world in that they are frickin everywhere transcending language, ethnicity and almost all border controls. MRSA, Kat-kins. It's a killer, a silent deadly killer.' He ordered another Dark & Stormy from the heavily subsidised cocktail menu while muttering to himself about dinosaurs and NHS budget cuts. And I didn't believe for a second that Jenny Sullivan knew about her husband's infidelity. When would burying your head in the sand be preferable to facing the truth? Jenny didn't deserve to be cheated on, not now, not ever and certainly not because she was a little bit too perfect.

'With great power comes great responsibility,' I said to Federico, who rolled his eyes then speed-dialled Chad from his ridiculously small phone. 'We need to help her!' I exclaimed, mostly to myself, and to a nearby bowl of peanuts, just as Grandma and Delaware joined us for what turned out to be a rambling lecture on the most inflammatory of all subject matters…

'…Because I've given this a lot of thought, Kate,' Grandma continued, now on her third large glass of champagne, 'and I think you were under the impression that you had to give up your ambition and personal goals in order for your relationship with Gabriel to work.' Federico was violently nodding his head in agreement. 'So you denied your vagina.'

'Oooh,' mouthed Federico, clutching his groin.

'You became a half version of yourself, a half person, a herson. And what is half a woman, Kate?'

'A half wo-man is merely a man, Grandma.' I groaned.

'Exactly, half a woman is merely a man. You lost the wo of your wo-man in your relationship with Gabriel. I bet his new girlfriend hasn't given up her ambitions and personal goals in order to be with him.' See, inflammatory.

'I bet she hasn't either,' whispered Federico.

'And that's exactly what young Jenny's doing as well,' continued Grandma, rummaging through one of the twenty or so *Liberty*'s bags she'd arrived with. 'She's given up a part of herself to make her marriage work. She's lost her wo.'

'Jenny hasn't lost her wo, Grandma,' I snapped. 'She embodies wo, she is wo, she's the wo that every wo-man wants to be. She loves her job. She's worked incredibly hard to get to where she is. She loves her husband and—'

'And I bet she has worked incredibly hard to get her marriage to where it is,' Grandma said, extracting herself from one of the *Liberty*'s bags. 'Kate, darling, try and imagine the following scenario for me. Can you do that? Imagine you are a brilliant scientist—' Federico immediately put his lensless specs on and gazed at the ceiling with his index finger on his lips '—and you had spent most of your life dedicated to a particular piece of research. Let's say you are trying to find a cure for testicular cancer.'

'Oh, you very much should, Kat-kins,' pleaded Federico.

'So you have been working on a cure for years and you have

made brilliant progress. At times you've felt so close to discovering the cure that you've lived and breathed the work. Then one day someone walks in and says, "Your cure is never going to work. You've got it wrong. It won't work." What would you do?'

'Well, I wouldn't believe them, of course. I'm not going to take the word of one person after years of work. I would investigate.'

'You'd investigate their claims.'

'Absolutely, and then, assuming that I had proved they were wrong, I'd carry on working on a cure.'

'But what if their claims looked to be true? You didn't want them to be true but it looked like they *could* be; a seed of doubt had been planted. Would you just stop work?'

'No! I would re-look at the problem. Re-look at all my research. I wouldn't give up straight away; I couldn't, after all that time, all that work, all *my* time. It would seem like everything I had done had been a total waste. My life's work, a total waste.'

'So apply that to marriage. Apply that response to the most significant and intimate relationship a person may experience in their lifetime. Imagine the work Jenny has put in, the commitment, the energy, the devotion. She believes in the cure. And you wonder why she doesn't walk away just because there are mutterings about her husband. I'm not saying it's the right decision. I'm just saying it seems obvious to me why she wouldn't leave. She is still working towards a cure. She still 100% believes in that cure.'

The air in my lungs reduced in volume by 60%. I could feel that nasty childlike lump in my throat, like a large piece of potato that doesn't want to go down. My tear ducts were on Code Red. And not out of concern for Jenny. It didn't matter how long I had watched the slow deterioration of my relationship with Gabriel, it just wouldn't compute. It didn't make sense to me that it wasn't working, that he wasn't who I thought he was, that we weren't going to go the distance. It was like someone telling me 2+2 equalled 5 or that black was white. I did not want to accept the end. I did not want to move on. I did not want to let go, because I still believed.

Could some of life's most painful and protracted break-ups be a result of us fighting, not for the real relationship, but because we don't want to stop believing in the cure? Maybe the relationships we can't get over are more about the grief of losing the precious dreams we'd created with that person, attached to that person, planned to share with that person than because of the person themselves? Maybe splitting up with Gabriel wasn't painful because of the sadness of losing Gabriel the man. Maybe I felt consuming sadness for all the dreams I had attached to Gabriel. Maybe it was those dreams I had been fighting so hard to save, trying to resuscitate long after the relationship had so obviously died? I was crying my eyes out, thinking, 'This can't be the end. It can't turn out like this. I want this so much,' when really what I wanted was the life and dreams I had attached to him.

'The thing is, darling—' Grandma was now head first in yet another *Liberty*'s shopping bag '—by not admitting that things are as they are, by not seeing the reality of the current situation, Jenny is losing time. That is what love is stealing from her: time, her lifetime. Your grandfather would think it ridiculous the years I spent and continue to spend missing him.'

'And, darl, I did the same thing,' Delaware cooed. 'You know that I didn't work for years after my divorce. But I haven't gained a single thing, either from ignoring the deterioration of the marriage when I was in it, or grieving for it for years and years after. And you can't get that time back.'

'Here it is!' Grandma said, putting all but one of the *Liberty*'s bags to one side. 'For a second I thought I'd forgotten to bring it. Here you go, darling,' she said, passing me the bag. 'Peter asked me to give this to you.'

'Peter did? What is it?'

'As if I know, darling! I don't go rummaging through other people's things.' She smiled at Delaware, who beamed back. Obviously they *did* go rummaging through other people's things.

'Open the card first,' she said, expertly locating it in the bag.

'OK…' I said, looking at her suspiciously then slowly opening the card. They were all watching me on the edge of their seats. Actually Federico was practically on my lap. 'It says, *Happy Birthday*. That doesn't make any sense. It's not my birthday.'

'No, there's more, on the other side,' Grandma said, turning the card over. She could at least pretend she hadn't read it.

Pirate Kate
I've missed fifteen of your birthdays
I can't get them back, but I can buy you presents
See you Friday, 6:30 a.m.
Now you have no excuses.

Peter x

'What's in the mother-fluffing bag?' screamed Federico, waving his hands around his ears like Dustin Hoffman in *Rain Man*. I opened up the enormous *Liberty*'s bag to find a brand-new pair of running trainers inside, my size, obviously, and an assortment of *Stella McCartney* for *Adidas* running clothes.

'Well, he's only gone and bought her bloody *Stella*,' Federico said, fanning his face with the card. Everyone around the table was beaming at me. And I was kind of beaming myself.

an interval

'What did I miss out on because love showed up? My Saturday mornings! Waking up in my own bed; making myself a cup of tea; watching Saturday Kitchen. Since meeting my boyfriend I wake up every Saturday in his flat. So that is what I gave up. Saturday solitude, laundry marathon, Saturday Kitchen and crumpet eating.'
(Gemma, 28)

'I would have accepted a promotion to work on feature films. I'm an art director but only work on adverts and TV shows because films would require me to work away from home. My relationship wouldn't survive long distance so I never pursue jobs in film. I don't regret my decision but certainly that is what my love affair stole.'
(Joanna, 42)

'DIY—a contradiction when in a relationship because you can't do it yourself. They won't let you. They have to meddle. They always know best. Heaven forbid I want to

put a shelf up, or try and fit our new washing machine.
Should be called Do It Themselves. Love stole DIY.'
(Penelope, 56)

'I am getting a nose job. My boyfriend always told me
only superficial people get cosmetic surgery. My nose
makes me bloody unhappy. If it wasn't for him I would
have done something about it years ago. So now I am. My
old nose is walking the plank!' **(Ana, 27)**

grow punctures and slow punctures

What started out as a tiny idea had grown as big as the women who were now getting small. We had passed the midway point of *Fat Camp* and the female participants had been incredible. They had turned up. They had completed every challenge. They were losing weight and they were gaining happy. Some of the women had been so inspired by the change in their own lives that they'd set up mini *Fat Camps* back in their local areas; they were out championing other women to follow suit, taking back what love had stolen, being pirates of their own lives. The BBC had even done two reports on their progress and they'd been given special invites to judge an episode of *Britain's Got Talent*. Things were already looking a lot lighter and brighter for the women of *True Love*'s *Fat Camp*. Today I joined them at Peter Parker's Hyde Park Boot Camp.

hyde park | 06:15

I arrived to find a ten-man camera crew standing around drinking coffee, twenty *Fat Campers* in matching tracksuits, and Federico massaging people's shoulders, handing out protein shakes and jumping on the spot before air punching like a non-Asian Jackie Chan on Red Bull.

'Could everyone please start their warm-ups? Thank you very much, you pretty pieces of lard, you ever-reducing land masses, ever lightening the island that is England, becoming physical and emotional beacons of hope and empowerment for other really really really fat people.'

I stood on the edge of the group and tried to copy the elaborate warm-up. They sat on the floor and started stretching. I did the same. I attempted leg stretches while listening to their laughter-infused chat, trying my hardest not to get mud or grass stains on my new Stella (tracksuit, not beer can).

'Honestly! Look at us all!' one said, bursting out laughing. 'We actually do look like beached whales. That's where the expression came from. It came from us!'

'I was skinny before I met my husband and now look at me!' another one said, struggling to get to her feet.

'You were *never* skinny!' someone else joked.

'I was! I'll bring photos tomorrow. I was a size 10. I played centre forward for the local women's football team until I was 25.'

'Can I ask what happened?' I asked. 'Why you think you started to gain weight?'

'As if I know! I met a great guy then I just kept getting bigger, like that girl in Willy Wonka's chocolate factory.'

'You mean Violet Beauregarde?' I asked, somewhat alarmed. Because Violet Beauregarde didn't just get big. She got big *and* she got purple. It was terrifying to watch as an 8-year-old.

'Yes, just like Violet Beauregarde,' she confirmed, 'but slower.'

'And hopefully not purple,' I muttered, to myself.

'I'll tell you what you were,' interrupted Federico, correcting her stretch. 'You were like a Slow Puncture, but in reverse. You were a Grow Puncture.' They all burst out laughing.

'But something must have happened for your shape to have changed,' I persisted. 'You fell in love and then what?'

'Well, for me,' offered the eldest, 'I always wanted to treat my husband, still do. I love making him nice things to eat, I love spoiling him and I probably have loads of food in the house that I just wouldn't buy otherwise.'

'Me too,' confirmed another. 'I would not make a dessert just for myself. I probably wouldn't even eat meat. But my husband thinks any meal without meat is a side salad. That just wasn't how I ate before.'

'And portion sizes. My portion sizes have got bigger. Before *Fat Camp* they were very similar to his. And women don't need the same calories as men.'

'But,' whispered the youngest of the *Fat Campers*, a pretty brunette with quite extraordinary boobs, 'there are some benefits of our current fat status…'

'Oh, my God, there are benefits!' they all agreed enthusiastically.

'You know, he touched my arm the other day, during the warm-down. I actually got tingles.' They all laughed.

'Well, I can't believe he hasn't got a girlfriend,' whispered a different camper.

'I heard he did have,' said another.

'I heard he was married.' Who were they talking about? They must realise Federico was gay? He was standing behind them applying Touche éclat to a pimple.

'I don't care if he's married, divorced, gay or straight,' said the fattest of the lot of them. 'I'd happily spend the rest of my life lying under that Peter Parker.' They all shrieked with laughter.

'I'd get on him!' screamed another.

'We should all get on him!'

'Yeah! Yeah! Yeah! Yeah!' they all panted.

'NOOOOO!!!!!' I yelled, hands over my ears, rocking backwards and forwards. 'No! No! No! No! No! No!'

Federico grabbed my hand and dragged me away from the startled-looking group.

'What the hell are you doing?' he snapped at me. 'Lying around screaming like that? Rocking backwards and forwards like the lone survivor from a bomb blast, sat in the debris of a shopping mall, all your friends lying around blown to pieces by a disillusioned youth bomber. Have you lost your tiny mind?'

'I don't know. I don't know what happened. It's just, well, did you hear how they talk about Peter Parker?' Little tears pricked in the corners of my eyes.

'Get a grip, Kate Winters! Since when did you become Penelope Prudey Pants? *Fat Camp* is allowed to have sexual feelings, for God's sake! If they want to talk dirty about your precious Peter Parker then they can. They are slimming ladies and they can do as they ruddy well please. How dare you come to my Boot Camp and start yelping in the middle of a warm-up?'

'You're right, I'm sorry. It must be some kind of over-protective, *stop talking about my childhood friend* knee-jerk reaction, like an allergy, an allergic reaction to sexual talk about Peter Parker, like a Peter nut allergy, a pallery.'

'Stop talking, Kat-kins. Stop talking. And please remember that warm-up is a time for contemplative thought and muscle preparation. Everybody knows that. It's not a time for yelping and wailing. Shame on you!' He stomped back to *Fat Camp* while I stood alone at the edge of the group. I could feel the eyes of *Fat Camp* burning into my back, probably trying to turn me into a Grow Puncture, bastards.

hyde park | 06:30

Peter Parker finally arrived. I say he arrived—he sprinted, at high speed, across the entire length of Hyde Park. I watched him approach. He ran like a racehorse; graceful, powerful and straight over to the perverted *Fat Campers*. He didn't even come over to say hello. I went to wave but changed my mind halfway up.

'Are we ready, ladies?' he said, jogging on the spot. 'Right, everyone down on the floor. We are going to do the same routine as yesterday: stretches, press-ups, squats, burpees then the 10K run.' I had no idea what he was talking about but Federico signalled for me to get on the floor. I looked around to see *Fat Camp* had their legs in the air doing sit ups.

'It's muddy,' I mouthed at Federico as he rolled his eyes and pretended he didn't know me. The next thing I know I had been picked up and was once again being carried in the muscular arms of Peter Parker.

'You are supposed to be working out, Kate,' he said, walking me into the centre of the group, then kneeling down and slowly laying me out on the ground.

'Peter, you always seem to be picking me up and carrying me somewhere.'

'Carrying you metaphorically or literally? And you're very light. It makes me look masculine and strong in front of all these ladies. It was you or Federico and he doesn't smell as nice.' He sat back on his heels, taking in my running outfit. 'Do you like your presents? Does everything fit? Because it's important to have the correct kit; good support for your feet and your—' He looked at my boobs then stared at the sky.

'Everything is the right size. Thank you.'

'Do you understand the exercise routine?'

'Not one bit.'

'Then follow me,' he said, about to jump to his feet, then stopping himself. 'Oh, your strap is twisted,' he said, leaning back down to straighten the strap of my perfectly fitting sports bra. He hovered above me as he fiddled with it, his face directly above mine, his lips mere inches from my face. When he'd finished he realised how close we were, but he didn't pull away like a fridge magnet. He just looked down at me, exactly where he was. I found myself staring back, into his blue eyes, into Peter Parker. Then he leant down, very slowly, and very deliberately, and he kissed my cheek, lingering there, his face against mine, cheek to cheek. I could smell the washing powder on his clothes, his skin, his shampoo; it was like a Peter Parker scent explosion in my nose. My heart felt as if it were doing something calamitous in my chest and I hoped to God Peter Parker couldn't hear it. Then 'TWENTY MORE, PEOPLE!' was *screamed* in my ear and Peter jumped back up to his feet. 'Then I want you all to sprint to the Serpentine and back. Last one back will have to do it all over again and you know I mean it.' The *Fat Campers* started scrabbling to their feet. 'Go! Go! Go! Go!!' he yelled as they all sprinted off. But I lay completely still on the ground, staring up at the morning London sky. I touched my hand to my face where I could still feel his kiss; the kiss of Peter Parker, the boy who never smiles.

a friend in need

As the *Fat Campers* left with Federico to film their post-workout video diaries for *True Love*'s *YouTube* channel, Peter and I went to have coffee. We found an empty park bench. We sat down. He slung his arm along the back of the bench, absent-mindedly playing with the hood of my tracksuit. It made my neck tingle, wondering if at any moment his skin would touch mine. I'd only completed half the Boot Camp but had managed to end up sweaty and crazy-haired. I would have paid good money for a hand mirror, a hairbrush and a couple of minutes of privacy to smarten up. I wondered if I would ever look as glamorous as the sprinting, problem-solving goddess that is Anneka Rice. Peter didn't look puffed out at all. He looked shower fresh, handsome and tall; a tingle-creating triathlete dressed in tiny swatches of *Nike*.

The reason I'd asked Peter Parker for coffee was work-related. I needed his advice and I hoped that today he would be as prolific and prophetic as Peter normally was.

But as he affectionately tucked some of my crazy hair-frizz behind my ears I struggled to focus on the work at hand and not on my overwhelming desire to throw myself on the ground on the off chance he'd give me another kiss. You see, I wanted to help someone who probably didn't want my help. The someone in question was Jenny Sullivan. The chances of her listening to me were zero. So I needed another way, or more specifically I needed another brain. Because I couldn't stand by and do nothing. I couldn't pretend I hadn't seen that kiss. There was a code of conduct in *Liberty*'s Menswear Department and Jenny's husband had crossed the line. I wish someone had helped me when Gabriel had crossed that line. I wish someone had stuck their oar in, given me their ten pennies' worth, confirmed that the situation definitely wasn't OK. So it was my duty to help Jenny Sullivan. It was my duty to help her help herself.

'So just to clarify, Kate,' Peter said calmly, taking a sip from his coffee. He was focused and handsome in a way I never seem to achieve—not that I want to be considered a *handsome lady*, just purposeful. 'There is this nameless person—' I decided anonymity would be professional; it's what Anneka would have done '—and you have decided that you want to find a way to help change their life but make them think they decided upon this change themselves?' Concise and brilliant.

'Exactly, Peter,' I said, nodding along with a smug smile. 'That is exactly what I want to do.'

'You want to change someone's life because in your opinion they would be happier living it a different way, in your opinion?' That sounded a teeny bit more manipulative than I would have liked. 'Even though they might actually be happy with the life that they have chosen for themselves.' Is this how Hitler started?

'The thing is, Peter, sometimes people are scared to admit what is staring them in the face. They're scared of change; scared of the unknown. So they just need a bit of help taking the first step. I want to be the step.' Hitler didn't want to be a step. He wanted to be an all-powerful master of the human race.

'So how are you going to show this nameless person the error of their ways? And what is it that you want them to change? What if they're not capable of making a change? Or don't want to?'

'Well, what's currently going on in their life is not to be envied; pretending everything is perfect and complete when clearly it's messed up and empty. Just because you tell everyone a thousand times a day how great your life is doesn't make it so. Sometimes it's better to just throw your hands in the air and say, "I'm scared, I'm in pain, things really haven't turned out the way I wanted them to and I don't know what to do." My mum always says, "Do unto others as you wish to have done to yourself," so that's what I'm trying to do.'

'Your mum says that?' He frowned and removed his arm from behind me. He looked out across the park. I also looked out across the park. We were like Greek philosophers, pondering, pausing, taking a moment and gazing. Move over, Socrates.

Peter turned to face me. 'Is this about me, Kate?'

'What?'

'Because you think I should be living my life a different way?' He was glaring at me. 'Because I promise you, Kate, you know *nothing* about my life and you know *nothing* about the choices and circumstances that got me here.'

'Peter, I never said that. I don't think that, I just—'

'And they were good choices,' he said, nodding his head. 'They were *really* good choices. Just because I am self-sufficient and self-contained doesn't mean there is anything wrong with me. And under the circumstances there was no other way I could have been. And I like it, actually, I like who I am. I'm not frightened of change,' he said, poking his own chest. 'I make change. I am change!' What the hell was he talking about? Where was this coming from? Where was it going? This didn't feel like ancient prophetic Greece. It felt like the bloody crucifixion when Jesus got all strung up and it totally wasn't his bloody fault. 'And I have never once judged you, Kate, and your choices and mistakes. Yet you see fit to judge me and my life, like your vision of the world is the only correct one. I don't even know why I am surprised really—' He started packing up his sports kit ready to leave. 'You, Winters, always think you know what's best for other people, always do what the hell you want.'

'What are you talking about?'

'Kate, you can't keep focusing on me like this. You can't. You've been doing this since we were kids. Trying to save me or help me or change me. You need to take a step back. We both need to take a *big* step back. You need to focus on your own issues, not constantly trying to piece me back together after Mum's death. She died, OK. She died. I am over it. You need to get over it.' He finished packing his bag, then sat staring out at the park. 'I think it was mistake,' he finally said, 'to get back in touch with you. It was mistake.'

'What on earth do you mean?'

'It's not good for me.'

'*I'm* not good for you? Peter?'

He wouldn't look at me. His jaw was clenched.

'I hope everything continues to go well with your Love-Stolen Dreams column.' He kissed me lightly on the cheek before getting up and walking off across the park. He didn't even take his coffee with him, leaving it on the bench next to me.

'Well, you really took the wind out of his sails!' Chad said, appearing from literally nowhere and sitting himself down on the bench. 'Although I can see his confusion. You didn't exactly spell out that you were trying to help Jenny.' I looked at him with surprise. 'Federico likes to share,' he qualified. 'Although I'd rather he twatting didn't. And she won't appreciate your help, Kate. I can tell you that for free. She made her choice. She gave up one thing so she could have something else. Her husband, her marriage, it's part of her twatting brand, *brand Jenny*. And she would stab her grandmother if it meant keeping her career on track. I wouldn't want to be the person to take that down.'

'I don't want to take her down. I want to help her.'

'The first thing you need to realise is that you can't have it all, Kate. LSD should have shown you that. The magazine's never been so successful because it's impossible to have it all. We don't live in a twatting fairy tale, Kate, Jenny made her choice; she lives with his infidelity and she has the lifestyle and success she wants.'

'I don't believe you. I don't believe this is what she wants and I don't believe you can't have it all.'

'Well, she won't appreciate your efforts, Kate, like a certain someone who's been sat in our office since 7 a.m. this morning.' He picked up Peter's coffee and started gulping it down. 'Those fatties are doing well, aren't they?' he said, leaning across me to grab a handful of my breakfast muffin.

'You were watching Boot Camp?'

'I watch all their training sessions, Kate. And don't look so twatting surprised. I do give a twat what happens at my magazine. I tell you, my old mum would have loved this,' he said, pointing at *Fat Camp*, who were laughing in the distance with the camera crews. 'She was terrified of sport, didn't want to look ridiculous in front of my old man. But if she'd had this, all these other ladies to be with, I think it would have made a difference. When you have money, Kate, you can always buy what you need: personal trainers, gym subscriptions, twatting therapists and dieticians. You can even buy love, or at least sex but it's the same twatting thing. Money is the key to any lock. But without it, well, people need things like this. And I think *Fat Camp* have worked well hard. We should give them a treat, nothing sugary of course, something to make them feel glam.'

'Did you just use the word *glam*?'

'Shut the fuck up, Kate.'

'And what did you mean when you said someone's been in the office since 7 a.m.?'

'The husband of your dancing mate is in the office; waddles when he walks; always carries a tennis bag. Well, he's in the office and he is well twatting annoyed with you.'

why can't *I* give you all that you need!

boardroom | true love

As I walked into the office I could see Jane's husband James in the boardroom. He was pacing up and down, occasionally picking up a handful of red *Haribo*, gobbling up a sweet per step, and Chad was right: he did look pretty angry.

'I've got a bad knee, Katie! OK! A bad bloody knee! It's my cruciate ligament. It could tear off my kneecap at any moment, just like that.' He did a wild arm movement. 'Just like that!! I can't bloody dance, Katie, and now you've got my wife sneaking off twice a week to get all sweaty with some lech. They are competing in a bloody dance competition together! And every time I see the man he goes bright red and looks at the floor. Every time! He couldn't look more guilty! Bloody pervert! Honestly, Katie, honestly, I thought you were a friend to us both. I can't believe you arranged all this.'

'James, she's not sneaking off. She told you she was going. We both did. And she's invited you to *all* the practices. And I find it hard, no, impossible to believe that Julio is after Jane.' What a drama queen.

'Any man would be lucky to be with Jane Brockley-formerly-Robinson.' He shoved another hundred *Haribo* in his mouth, powering up and down the boardroom on his severely injured knee.

'James, firstly, Julio is gay, so that should put your mind at ease regarding his apparent sexual pursuit of your wife. Secondly I *am* your friend, and Jane's friend. We've all been on holiday together; you stayed with me and Gabriel in France; we've been skiing together, been for hikes, we've even got drunk together quite a few times.' He was nodding his head in agreement. 'All in all we've spent quite a bit of time together, over the years, which is why I know your knee is just fine.' At the suggestion of a lie James huff-puffed himself out like a red-breasted robin. 'And I've even seen you dance a couple of times, James; at your wedding, and on a few nights out. You even danced in a cage that night in Brixton. Do you remember? You took off your top and the bouncer threw you out.' He chuckled to himself. 'So why do you tell Jane that your fully functioning, tennis-playing, skiing, drunk-dancing knee is not working?'

'Solo dancing, Katie, I can do solo dancing, and the Macarena, but that's more of a modern disco take on a line dance than a traditional two-person dance. But couple dancing, well, it's like my brain has an implosion. I just can't do it!' He sat down heavily in Chad's heart-shaped chair. 'I had dance lessons for six and a half months to prepare for my first dance with Jane at our wedding. Six and a half months, to learn a three-minute routine!'

I actually thought Jane and James did a regular 'old school' slow dance at their wedding, when you loop your arms around each other's waist then rock from side to side like a giant human metronome...

'It's just the thought of her doing something with another man that I'm not able to. It makes me feel so inadequate. I can't be a bloody dancer. I can't go by the name of Julio and do the ruddy splits, OK? And if that's what Jane needs I'm going to end up divorced. What have you done to me? What have you done? I am happy for men to flirt with her. I want her to feel good about herself. But this, this bloody idea of yours, it makes me feel so, so, lacking, like I am not enough for her, like I am fundamentally, biologically, genetically lacking something that would make Jane happy.' Bollocks. That was never the plan. Chad was right. I was pissing everyone off.

'James, I know,' I said, grabbing him by his shoulders, 'I *know* that she would much rather be dancing with you. So, I have an idea, why don't we go to dance classes? We could practise in secret and then one day, when you feel ready, we could surprise her. I've been recommended a dance guru— his name is Mustafa. Apparently if we can't learn to dance with him, then—' I gulped '—no one will be able to help us.' James looked up at me, astonished.

'Kate...are you also...?'

'Yes.' I nodded. 'I have also been afflicted, but together we will succeed.' We high-fived, then immediately felt a bit embarrassed. Brits just can't seem to pull that off. James' face fell.

'Jane would hate it if she thought I was suddenly trying

to be a dancer like her. She'd think I was bloody stalking her, or copying her, or that I didn't trust her and was trying to get better so that I could step in and stop her seeing Julio, which isn't what I want! I just don't want to feel so bloody inadequate.'

'James, how would you feel if one day Jane turned up at your tennis club, put on a pair of Green Flash and started knocking the ball around?'

'I would bloody love it!' he exclaimed. 'I have no idea why she's so anti-tennis. I've always wanted us to play together.'

'What if she was rubbish, which, by the way, she *really* is?'

'Why would I care about that? I'd just love to share it with her.'

'She doesn't come because she thinks if you see her play tennis it will be a massive turn-off for you. You'd be embarrassed by her, especially as you are always playing with that Cat Henderson. She's a tennis pro! How can Jane compete with that?'

'Cat Henderson is chronically dull, Kate, and, between you and me, is a ruddy great lesbian. No one says it out loud, mind you—the club's very traditional.'

'James, you know I think it's important couples do things separately, but in this instance I think you should come to at least one dance class. Get over yourself, James. Be brave. Be a man!'

Well, at the mere suggestion that James might not be a man he agreed, and I made a mental note to always challenge a man's gender when wanting him to do something.

'Katie…' James said, spinning himself on the chair like a little boy, 'I don't know what love means to you, or feels like for you, but…I just wondered—' He came to a stop. 'Have you ever loved someone so much that you just want them to have everything, everything in the world?'

'Yes, I remember what that feels like.'

'And wouldn't you want to be the person who could give them everything?'

'Yes, I probably would.'

'I'm sure it's my ego at work. I've read Freud, and Jung, and I did a semester in existentialism at Cambridge. I know that if you love someone you have to be brave enough to let them go. It's such a total cliché and it sounds so simple and easy until you've been in love, until you've woken up every morning next to this *being* who you treasure above all other things, above your own life. Then the thought of not being able to complete them, well, it's terrifying, Katie, totally bloody terrifying. And I know I sound like a ridiculous old fart, but I am in love! I have been in love with Jane from the first moment I saw her. My life is in colour with her, without her it would be in black and white, so I want to be able to provide everything for her. I want to be her Julio. And the fact that I can't is…well, it's bloody painful.' He started spinning again, spinning in the giant heart-shaped chair. 'I just wanted to make my pumpkin happy, that's all. I wanted to be the one who brings her the most joy.'

I watched him spin for a few minutes, playing around with the idea before I committed to saying it out loud.

'James…there is probably something you could do for

Jane that Julio definitely can't. And I suspect it would make her a whole lot happier than Spanish dancing ever could…'

James came to a violent stop and stared up at me from the chair. He was all ears, and eyes, and podgy tennis legs.

mechanics r u!

Mary the cleaner, after much persuasion and a certain amount of emotional blackmail, had finally agreed to go on a basic mechanics course. I had attended the first few classes with her and they had been a pink-jumpsuit-wearing revelation. The mechanic school was on an industrial estate in South East London in a warehouse that had been painted bright pink. On arriving for the first class we'd been ushered into a locker room and instructed to change into their uniform. Before you could say 'brake fluid' we were all wearing bright pink overalls with *Mechanics is Me* written on the back in gold italic writing. It felt very Pink Ladies from *Grease*.

We were then asked to stand in a semi-circle in the middle of the large garage. There were five other ladies there (1 x widow, 3 x divorcees, 1 x stage 4 singleton[7]); three

---

[7] **Stage 4 Singleton** – Diagnosis: Terminal. Treatment is possible with mild interim improvement but long–term prognosis will remain unchanged. The pack animal has gone lone wolf and it's unlikely that any attempts at re–entry into pack life will be successful.

old cars (not a metaphor); a huge tool area (ditto); a small kitchen area and even a laundry where you could wash and dry your dirty overalls. Our teacher that night was a man called Jefferson who ran like a fairy around the periphery of the room before coming to a stop in front of us.

'I'm an actor slash voice-over artiste slash mechanic,' he said as he pirouetted on the spot. 'Welcome to the school. Welcome to *Mechanics R U*—' he took a bow '—and I know, we've stolen our name a bit from *Toys R Us*, in that it's a play on words, or rather a play on their words, but the emphasis is on you, as opposed to us, because we are already mechanics and we are empowering you, so *Mechanics R U* is like a subliminal non-subliminal message reinforcing who you are *becoming*, not who you were. Consider me your conduit to the mechanical world.'

Yes, I had managed to take Mary to a class run by a spiritual, pink-overall-wearing out-of-work actor. I turned to Mary to apologise only to find her nodding along, ferociously agreeing with every single word Jefferson spoke. It was like bearing witness to Moses speaking to the people before parting the Red Sea, or Antony Robbins[8] during one of his *'Unleash the POWER'* lectures. Everyone in that room was in rapture.

'You,' Jefferson said, pointing at Mary. 'You are a mechanic.'

Mary then burst into actual tears and everyone started clapping.

---

[8]**Tony Robbins** (Antony to his friends) – millionaire inspirational life coach guru person. He can release the power within you, for a small sum of money, and an annual subscription.

'You,' Jefferson said, pointing at a different woman. 'You are a mechanic.'

This woman also burst into tears. It was like being in an episode of *X Factor* with everyone wanting everything a great deal and it all being terribly important.

'So,' Jefferson said, clapping his hands and bouncing into the centre of the workshop. 'Let's accelerate to success.' Then he ran past everyone making us all high-five him.

By this point Mary was flushed bright red. She beamed at the other women in the group. They all beamed back, all of them red in the face. Everyone in that room was blushing, including Jefferson, excluding me. But then I was embarrassed because I wasn't blushing, so I blushed. It was confusing. Then Jefferson showed us how to open the bonnet of a car and encouraged us to touch and feel the engine as much as possible.

'The engine is the heart of the car. Bond with your machine,' he'd said as he furiously jabbed the oil stick in and out of the engine. Mary had looked like she was going to pass out.

And since that day Mary had been attending religiously, secretly practising in the garage at the bottom of her garden, honing her skills, becoming the mechanic she's always wanted to be. I only got as far as week three and was asked to leave after an incident involving a Skoda and a blow torch. Then one morning, quite out of the blue, Mary had called sounding guilty and vague. In a hushed whisper she'd insisted I come straight to her house. She told me to wear old clothes and to bring the emotionally unpredictable Peter Parker, which is what I then tried to do.

goldman apartments | london

When I arrived at Peter's apartment, in a private development that overlooked the River Thames, a stone-faced concierge let me into the building. I took the lift up to the top floor and found apartment 41. I knocked on the door and I waited. Eventually, after several long minutes, Peter Parker opened the front door. But he did not resemble the Peter Parker that I knew…

To say that he looked ruffled would be a Shard-sized[9] understatement. He looked as though he'd been tickled nonstop by a gang of parentally unsupervised children. He was bright pink in the face, sweating, and his hair was shooting off in every direction the poor hair follicles would allow. He was also still in his pyjamas.

'Kate?' he said, stepping out into the hallway, pulling the door part-closed behind him. 'What are you doing here?' he said, trying to pat down his hair.

'I need you to come to Mary's with me. I think it's some kind of emergency. She's been fixing cars and I—' I tried to walk past him into his apartment but he sidestepped and blocked me. So I tried to peer past him. But he towered above me ensuring I couldn't see in.

'Peter, what's going on?'

'Nothing's going on, Kate. Why would you think something's going on?' He glanced back at his front door to make

---

[9] **Shard** – tallest building in London.

sure it was pulled to. Then he put his hands on his hips and tried to look super casual. 'I've been working out, doing exercise.' He shrugged before jogging on the spot, then stretching. He was so red and so sweaty and so out of breath. He hadn't once looked like that at Boot Camp.

'Peter, is this about the park? Because I wanted to speak to you about that. I wanted to apologise for the misunderstanding, because it was a misunderstanding. I was actually trying to talk to you about Jenny Sullivan—she works in my office. It wasn't about you, or a critique of your life choices, of which I know nothing because you haven't been in my life for over—'

'Jenny Sullivan? The celebrity?'

Unbelievable. The woman could scene steal from a mile away.

'Peter, I've missed you over these last few weeks, which has come as a bit of a surprise if I'm honest, and I think it's unacceptable for you to just disappear all over again, and I really do think Mary needs our help so it would be great if we could go together and...'

I petered out. Peter wasn't listening to a word I was saying. He was compulsively checking his watch, then wiping his sweaty brow. I tried again to look into the hallway of his apartment but again he blocked my view, fully closing the door.

'Peter, why are you so sweaty? You look like you've been doing Hot Bikram in your flat. And why can't I come in?'

'It's been proven, Kate, that even 30 minutes of moderate exercise every day can create a level of endorphins in the brain equal to that of—'

'Is there someone in your flat with you?'

'There's no one in my flat. Why would you think some-one's in the flat?'

'Well, look at you. You look like… Well, you've obvi-ously been *physically exerting* yourself.' Physically exert-ing in this context meant something naked and breathy that culminated in a whole lot more than a release of endorphins. 'It's OK if you have someone in there and you don't want me to meet her.' I had *no* idea Peter Parker had a girlfriend. In fact I had no idea what Peter did outside the time he spent with me. Maybe he was seeing that young heavy-chested woman from *Fat Camp*? God, I wish I had boobs…

'I'm not with a girl. Why would you think there's a girl? There's no girl.'

'Peter, no one else in the world is still in their pyjamas at this time of day, flustered, sweating and red-faced unless they are…*entertaining.*'

A drop of sweat dripped off the nose of Peter Parker. He ignored it. I looked at the small patch of moisture it had made on the hallway carpet. The woman in his flat must be some kind of insatiable sex princess to have created this flustered, hair-ruffled, fib-telling version of Peter. This must be what Peter looked like during sex. This was *Sex Pete*, a person I have no experience being in the presence of. In fact the only time I've been in close proximity to Peter and another girl was when we were five years old and he kissed strawberry-smelling Annabel at that pool party. She had buck teeth. The old memories came flooding back. Why, oh, why did he kiss strawberry-smelling Annabel????

'Kate, can we do this another time? It's really not a good

moment for me.' He leant down and gave me a quick kiss on the cheek, then slammed the door shut in my face.

I stood there for several minutes just staring at that door; wondering if he would come back; wondering if I should put my ear to the door to try and identify any noises or voices inside; hoping that he wasn't watching me through the peephole. Eventually I walked back to the lift, occasionally looking back down the hall, expecting him to run out and invite me in. But he never reappeared. I took the lift back down to the luxurious marble-floored reception, walked back past the stone-faced concierge, back down the busy street, back to the dirty smoggy tube and finally I arrived at scary Mary's, alone.

OK, I admit it!!! I may have asked the stone-faced concierge, 'Is there a girl in Peter Parker's apartment?' to which the stone-faced man raised his right eyebrow very high. He had obviously been sworn to secrecy, part of his job description I suspect, or some misplaced male allegiance with the highly sexed Peter Parker, so I left none the wiser, certainly none the happier and still unclear about the events in Hyde Park.

scary mary's and the mess of the mechanics

When I arrived at Mary's the house appeared deserted.
There were no lights on. The curtains were all drawn, and
Len's car wasn't there. The front door was on the latch so I
let myself in and called out for Mary.

No response.

I wandered down the garden to the garage where Len
kept his old cars and found Mary head first in the engine
of an old white Ford Capri.

'I couldn't help myself, Kate,' she said, peering out over
the bonnet. 'It's been sat in here for weeks, sat in this garage,
him tinkering away every night, never fixing the bloody
thing. And I thought, *I can do that. I know what's wrong
with it.* So when he went to do his post round yesterday I
came down and I had a go. Thirty minutes later the car
started, for the first time in seven months. But I couldn't
stop there, I started tuning and fine-tuning and then I started
changing the oil, the air filter, looking at how the carburet-
tor turned over. Before I knew it, it was as good as new.'

There had been a transformation in Mary. While she still

snacked on Quality Street and occasionally warmed her breastbone with mugs of tea she also moved expertly from one side of a car engine to the other. She was focused. She was capable. She was a mechanic.

'Mary, that's really great. Congratulations. I bet Jefferson would be impressed. You should call him and tell him.' Mary looked up from the engine.

'You are a genius, Kate. Jefferson could put the car back to how it was. I'm going to call him right away.'

'Mary, wait! What's going on? Why would you want Jefferson to break the fixed car?'

'Kate, if my Len came back and the car suddenly started working it would be a bit of a mystery, but knowing Len he'd accept the car fixed itself. But if he comes back to find new spark plugs, clean oil, all the pistons replaced, how could I explain it? So I wanted you to put it back to how it was. If you could do whatever it was you did to that Skoda it would keep my Len busy for the next six months.'

'I did exactly what the instructions told me!' I said defensively. 'It's not my fault the car was misdiagnosed before the lesson.' Mechanics can be a cliquey judgemental bunch.

'Kate, my love, just get some overalls on and get under the car, please. And why isn't Peter Parker here?'

But before I could put my engine-destroying hands on the poor car and open up about the strange events at Hyde Park and at Peter's apartment I spotted a smiling Len tottering down the garden towards the garage.

'Er…Mary…we might have a small problem…'

'Oh, goodness me, Len's home—' Mary shoved a toffee Quality Street in her mouth and started manically chewing. She crossed her chest then looked skyward. 'Dear Lord, this really is your moment to shine, your moment to prove to me without a doubt that you exist because we are still on very shaky ground after the lack of a lottery jackpot win and my second cousin Janet's breast cancer.'

Len opened the garage door and stepped inside.

'Well, hello, love! Hello, little Kate! What are you two doing out here? You been showing Kate my handiwork? Kate, you can't imagine how hard this one's been. I've been working on it for months and the old girl still won't come back to life. I keep saying to Mary it's like the Tin Man in *The Wizard of Oz*. I just need to find out where its heart is.' He beamed at me and wandered over to his wooden work-bench, hung up his jacket and started picking up some tools. 'Now where are my overalls?' he muttered to himself, patting his pockets absent-mindedly as he scanned the garage, his eyes stopping on Mary. 'Mary, love, why have you got those on? You're not going to get your good clothes dirty just by being in here.' He chuckled and rolled his eyes at me. Then he saw Mary's hands; dirty, oil-covered. 'Mary? What have you been doing, love? Did you accidentally drop some-thing in the car?' He walked towards the car and peered into the engine. 'Whatever it is I am sure we can find—' The new parts she'd fitted sparkled like Christmas lights against the ancient dirt on the old engine.

'Mary, what is this? What's going on?'

'Kate,' Mary said very quietly, 'I think you should leave.'

Len looked from me in my clean and normal clothes to oil-covered Mary, confusion engulfing his smiling face like fast-moving storm clouds covering the sun. I back-stepped

my way out of the garage and pulled the door closed behind me. Then I ran back up the garden to the house as fast
as my little legs would carry me. Just as I reached the back
door I heard the engine of the car roar into life.

'Mary!!!' was the last thing I heard as I sprinted away.
I prayed to God (the lottery-withholding one) that Mary's
imagination was as capable and fast-thinking as her mechanical mind.

the objectionables

I arrived back in the office to find Federico in the board-room interviewing yet more Love-Stolen Dreams candidates. Jenny had rather obstructively arranged this particular meeting with a group of women we liked to call 'The Objectionables'. Because while these women would go as far as admitting they had unfulfilled dreams and ambitions, they resolutely refused to connect them to love. One such woman was Annie.

'Look, I work hard,' Annie asserted from the tip of the vicious heart. 'I am in an office all day with people, but I am away from the people I love. So after work I'm not going to choose to do something alone. I want to spend time with my friends and my boyfriend. Any dreams I'm not currently pursuing are just down to a lack of time.'

'You see…?' Jenny Sullivan said smugly. 'There is no story. Love isn't taking anything from anyone and I don't know what the bloody hell Chad is going to say when you two try and make this into an engaging and entertaining feature. Fire you both, I think, and about time.'

I couldn't believe that trying to help Jenny Sullivan was the tiny gust of wind that had sent the house of cards that is my friendship with Peter Parker tumbling to the ground.

'Because the fact is,' Annie continued, 'I don't know anyone interested in clothes design. None of my friends want to learn to knit, or pattern cut, and my boyfriend would actually weep if I made him come to the cobbler course I saw advertised last week. These are things I'd have to do alone, so I *choose* to put them on the back burner.' She crossed her arms and beamed at Jenny, who beamed back.

'You are very smart, Annie.' Federico nodded. 'Very smart. I hope that boyfriend of yours can see the catch he has in you, the big fish on his hook, the 200lb salmon gasping for air as it's taken out of the pool of life and left to die. So when will you put them on the front burner?' He put his spectacles on (heavy dark frame, obviously no lenses in them) and blinked his eyes several times as if refocusing. Refocusing on what I didn't know. There was only pure air between him and Annie, the 200lb dying salmon fish.

'Well—' Annie looked anxiously over to Jenny '—I don't have an official plan. But maybe when I have kids? I'll be at home for at least the first 6–12 months so I'll probably take some courses then. Or maybe when I retire? When I retire I will do more.' Annie had just turned thirty.

'When you have kids or when you retire…' Federico was frowning and scribbling furiously in a notebook. 'And what if your husband doesn't want to do these things, Annie-pants—may I call you Annie-pants? What if you don't have time when you have kids, which, sorry to burst air bubbles, Annie-pants, you won't. What if you reach retirement age and your husband says, "No, Annie. No! I don't want to learn how to hand-knit jumpers and double-stitch curtain hems. I want to sit around and fart and touch myself and play golf." What if you don't reach retirement age? What about that? You never know, Annie-pants. You just never know. And then of course you might get divorced. What is the statistic? Is it one in three marriages that end in divorce?'

'It's one in two,' I corrected him.

'One in two, Annie-pants! One in two! That's a coin flip, Annie-pants. That's a freakin coin flip! Although this is all a moot point because your form here says that you are not yet married, which means we are talking theoretically about the man you live with out of wedlock. Which brings us back to you being alone, doesn't it, yes it does, and you having to get over the fact that you need to start doing some of these things now even if it means occasionally being alone. Otherwise you may never do any of these things at all.'

'I guess…I just…' Her bottom lip was trembling. Federico continued regardless.

'And you say that you don't want to be alone after working all day, isn't that right, Annie-pants? But what exactly are you doing post 6 p.m.? Are you and your boyfriend at home doing hobbies together? Are you constructing great structures from clay or perfecting the art of Kama Sutra? Are you engaging in stimulating conversation? What happens at your house of joy from 6 p.m. onwards? Because whatever it is, Annie-pants, I want a part of that action, yes, I frickin do!'

'I, er…well, I am at home. We are at home. Mostly watching TV… It relaxes me.'

'You are watching *TV*?' He squeaked the word *TV* in such a way it set my teeth on edge.

'Yes.' Her response was more of a whisper.

'Five nights a week?'

'Yes. Although Tuesdays I sometimes do Pilates.'

'So, to sum up, you do less because you have a boyfriend and you want to devote time to him. But you will do more apart from him, as and when you become more committed to him?'

'Yes, it's a choice, to delay things—my choice.'

'So would you do more if you were single?'

'I'd have more time,' she said, looking at me, as if I were the Goddess of Time, as if I had a ruddy great clock around my neck and a sign on my head that said *Single and Time Rich*.

'Annie-pants, I want to play a game with you, can I? I want you to imagine that you are going to spend the rest of your life totally alone. Are you imagining this lonely existence?'

'Yes,' she breathed, dabbing her eyes.

'Is there anything at all that might take your mind off the horrific endlessly black loneliness? What could you do with your day? What consumes you and engages you so much that you could forget for a few seconds about your lonely life of solitude? Is there anything, anything at all?'

'Well…I really like clothes, and shopping. So spending every day designing and making clothes, or shopping for them, that would probably stop me thinking about my boy-friend. Stop me thinking about anything actually.'

'Oh, for goodness' sake,' Jenny snapped before storming out of the boardroom.

'Maybe I could open a shop selling clothes?' Annie-pants said excitedly. 'Then I'd have to buy the clothes for the shop and make clothes for the shop and people would come to the shop and we'd talk about clothes. So that would be great, re-ally great, if I was going to be alone for the rest of my life.'

'Annie-pants, I am so happy I am literally about to pee my pants. That is your Love-Stolen Dream. You are going to be the next Alexander McQueen. No sudden depression-induced suicide though, Annie-pants. Long live you and your suicideless life. Sooooo, would you consider spending one evening a week taking a short course in clothes design, or pattern cutting, or fashion buying? You'd still be home before 10 p.m. to watch TV with your dreary boyfriend who, FYI, you should not have moved in with before he proposed. You can Skyplus any TV shows you don't want to miss and I promise absence makes the heart grow fonder. Your boyfriend will find you more interesting if you have eyes for something other than him, even if it is buttons and haberdashery.'

'Well, that would be really nice because sometimes I don't feel like my boyfriend really *sees* me, you know, he doesn't always notice I am there, even though I'm there, the whole time...'

'Annie-pants, don't even start with semi-invisibility. There is a certain someone who may or may not work in this office who has the ability to see right through me. And not in a spiritually connected way, no, in an "I'm totally oblivious to your existence" kind of way. So Thursday nights works for you? Loosie!!' he screamed out of the boardroom door. 'Loosie, find a Thursday night course close to where Annie lives or works. Annie, please send us an update in five weeks' time, less than 2,000 words, more than 500 and understand that it will be rewritten by one of the writers here but will of course remain in first person so that all our readers think you've written it. Next!!!!!!' he yelled as a confused-looking Annie was escorted out by Loosie.

'That's quite a system you've got going on,' I said, sitting myself next to him.

'Kat-kins, Chad told me to find LSDs to write about and that is what I am doing. I am uncovering their ambitions and putting them on the road to happiness, which is what you wanted, is it not?'

'But don't you ever wonder why they are not on the road to happiness in the first place? Aren't you getting tired of discovering woman after woman after woman making the same mistakes? And some of them aren't even grateful.' I was thinking specifically about Jenny. 'Some of them don't even want to change their lives for the better. And if someone already knows what makes them happy why are they sitting at home watching TV?'

'Kat-kins, I'm not sure what's going on with you and your angsty, angry energy right now. I'm not sure I care. And I don't know what's going on with women in general. I'm not sure I care about that either. In answer to the last of your gazillion questions I suspect the women think they have a lack of time, like Annie, or a lack of money, like Leah, or maybe there is lack of inspiration, like me? Or maybe, just maybe, the road to ultimate happiness is actually the TV? Seriously, Kate, what's with the unending list of questions? You spurt questions like a first-year medical student who has just been asked to perform her first appendectomy. Do I look like an *Attending* on *Grey's Anatomy*? Do I look like a handsome, highly trained medical professional with a complicated and intriguing personal life?' He wanted me to say yes and deliberately put his glasses back on. 'I am on a quest, Kate, your bloody love quest, to take back what love stole, not to find out why love nicked it all in the first place, or, more to the point, why we all ruddy well gave it up.'

Loosie marched into the boardroom with my mobile in her hand.

'Sorry to interrupt what I can only assume is another one of your dreary love-related conversations but your phone has been ringing off the hook. There's someone called Mary on the line. And FYI, she sounds ODD.' Lucy thrust the phone in my hand and marched out. I could hear deep breathing on the line.

'Mary? Is that you?'

'Oh, good Lord, oh, good Lord and little baby Jesus.' More heavy breathing.

'Mary, what's wrong? Where are you? Is Len with you?'

'Kate, you need to come to the house. And you need to come now. Meet me in the garage.' She hung up.

Well, this time I definitely wasn't going alone.

mary's house

'It was in the *Daily Mail*, Kat-kins, last weekend, last frickin weekend. "Wife Murders" it was called. I swear to God,

Kat-kins, if you are taking me to the scene of a crime I will kill you, actually kill you. I learnt a very dangerous life-preserving move from my colonic therapist and I didn't plan to use it but by God I will, you be sure of that.' The front door slammed shut behind us. 'Oh, my God!' Federico squealed before grabbing hold of me in a bear hug. His head was darting from left to right.

'It was just the wind, Federico. Please, calm down and let me go.'

'Over seventy per cent of murders are committed by an acquaintance, Kat-kins,' he whispered in my ear as we walked down the hallway. 'Over seventy per cent! And almost *all* of those are by angry spouses. It was in the *Daily Mail*, Kat-kins. Last weekend!'

'I heard you, Federico,' I said, slowly pushing the lounge door open. I could see cushions all over the floor but still no sign of Mary. 'Federico, it looks like there has been some sort of kerfuffle in here.' Kerfuffle is a word I rarely use, but it had been applicable twice today. Everyone seemed to have strange kerfuffle-esque activities going on in their houses. Well, everyone being Mary and sex-crazed Peter Parker.

'We could very easily fall into that seventy per cent,' he said, following me into the lounge, then becoming immediately distracted by a selection of family photos on the walls. 'Just by being here we are at risk,' he said, rummaging through Mary's ornaments. 'Ooh, look! She's got a Charles and Diana dinner set! I'd cut off both of my big toes for a Charles and Diana dinner set. And the big toes are the important ones, yes, they are. The other ones are practically redundant, like our appendix, and pubic hair. In a few years we won't have the other four toes, or the appendix, or pubes. It's an evolutionary fact. Ooooh, Quality Street. Do you think Mary would mind if I pinched a Strawberry Cream?'

I left him talking to himself in the lounge and walked through the kitchen and down the garden to the garage. There I found Mary. She was sitting on an old wooden chair sipping from a mug. She had an old oily dust sheet wrapped around her and very little else on. There was no sign of Len.

'Mary?' I said tentatively, stepping inside. 'Mary, what's going on?'

All the doors of the Ford Capri were open and the engine was running. I walked over to the car and switched it off.

'For the rest of my life I will never forget the sound of that car engine,' Mary said, looking at me for the first time since I walked in.

'Mary. Where is Len? What's going on?'

'Well, he knows. Len knows. He knows I have been lying to him, he knows I have been secretly training as a mechanic and he knows that I fixed the car.' She walked over to me and gave me the mug, which was actually filled with some kind of alcohol. She then sat herself in the driver's seat of the now silent car. I sat beside her. She seemed to be in some sort of dream state.

'Kate, I never knew it could be like that, you know.' I didn't but the passenger seat felt damp and sticky. 'I never knew that…I didn't realise that…Kate, people can be so different to how you thought!'

'That's very true,' I said, thinking about Gabriel, and Peter Parker.

'Oh, my goodness, that is true,' Federico said, mouth full

of Quality Street. Somehow he had managed to get into the back seat of the car.

'And then you wonder,' she said, turning to face us, 'how it was that you went so long without seeing it.'

'I agree, Mary, I do, I do, they just reveal themselves from nowhere,' Federico said, gently squeezing Mary's shoulder. 'Chad does it all the time, yes, he does, and mostly it makes me weep. Did Len reveal something to you, Mary?'

'He revealed his whole self!' she squeaked, turning round even further so that she could speak directly to Federico. I was pretty sure I could see what looked like a giant love bite on her neck. 'He couldn't stop himself!' she said, wide-eyed, to a wide-eyed Federico. 'He just went, sort of wild.' She was gently touching the love bite on her neck. 'At first he was angry. He said he couldn't believe I would keep se-crets from him. He said I had betrayed him by going be-hind his back—'

'Which is sort of true, isn't it?' muttered Federico before I could smack him over the head.

'Len said that he didn't know me. I wasn't the woman he'd married. But then, then his curiosity got the better of him, and he wanted to know how I'd fixed it. So I started to explain. And the more I talked, about oil and nuts and bolts and screwdrivers, the more, well, *excited* he became.'

Oh, God. Mary was about to share a sex story with us. I started humming and stared at a fixed point ahead.

'The next thing I know I am bent over the bonnet and Len, oh, my Len, he was magnificent.' Federico was clap-ping his hands and jumping up and down in his seat. 'We have never ever had sex like it!'

I hummed louder but the nausea was taking hold. I couldn't listen to stories of Len bending Mary over a Ford Capri in their twilight years.

'We've done it everywhere,' she continued. 'Everywhere,' she confirmed. 'I feel like Kim Basinger in *9½ Weeks*.' And now I had visual images of Mary and Len watching *9½ Weeks*.

'He was just so masterful.'

'He looks like he could be masterful,' encouraged Federico.

'And every time I mentioned part of a petrol engine—'

'I can imagine, Mary, yes I can, yes I can, you magical queen of the mechanical world.'

'Oh, goodness, Kate,' Mary said, putting her hand on my forehead. 'You don't look at all well. You are very pale, my dear, and very clammy. Are you going to be sick, my love?'

'Don't do it near me! Don't do it near ME!' Federico screamed, covering his eyes and holding his nose.

'I just need a bit of fresh air,' I said, running from the garage and promptly throwing up in the neighbour's hedgerow. It was over before it had started, like my dance career, but I stayed sitting in the cool night air, breathing it in, trying to calm myself down, because something had just malfunctioned in my brain. Mary's sex story had made me think about something else, something that caused a shortness of breath followed by a panic-filled urge to get outside, launch myself into a hedgerow and vomit. It was the thought that Peter Parker had, that very same day, had a similar wanton sexual experience with some woman in his flat: passionate, sweat-producing, hair-ruffling sex. There was a woman somewhere in London who got to be that intimately close with my Peter Parker. And that thought, that made my stomach hurt in a painful, vomit-producing way. But what I didn't understand is why I even cared.

Had I accidentally got emotionally attached to Peter Parker since his reappearance in my life? Was he filling a void that I should be filling myself? Had he become some kind of great-smelling, man-sized-handsome-well-groomed comfort blanket? And if so I needed to work out how to break these invisible bonds. I needed to once again stand on my own two feet. I needed to search *Google* for 'invisible bonds' and find out exactly how it was I could break them, so I could get back to my pirate quest and stop chucking up in people's begonias. Actually it wasn't a begonia. It was just a hedge. I've just never used that word in a sentence before. Begonia.

an interval

a short message from my beloved bikini waxer

I am Hindu OK. I am from India. Yes, London is my home. Yes, I love it here. Yes, I will never leave. But India is my home. My husband is Indian. I am Indian. My children are Indian. And when we marry. We marry! I will be with my husband until my dying day. He is going to be there whether I like it or not. And he is my best friend. But, Kate, do you think for a second that I am wanting sex with him after 18 years of marriage? I am not. He is. I am not.

And I tell you this, Kate. I speak to a lot of women. My clients here, they are my friends. Like you are now my friend, they have also become my friends. We have a special bond. It's true eh? How can we not have a special bond? And I ask my clients, I say to them, 'Am I normal? Do you feel like this too?' and they say the same. They want to have sex with their tennis coach, or their yoga teacher or the man who delivers their groceries, but they are not lying at home thinking about having sex with their husbands. Kate, we've been with them for more than a decade. I am telling you, as a woman, as your friend, for other women, go out there and enjoy your life now.

Love is so wonderful. My husband is so wonderful. But if I could go in a dark alley and have a fondle of the man who teaches my Pilates class, Kate, I really would. Go enjoy yourself, Kate. Touch everyone! No man is worth how sad you are currently feeling. Get back out there!

frog princes and frog princesses

It had been over a week since Mary and Len's; a week since Peter's apartment; a week since the discovery of certain invisible bonds; but nothing had been severed and *Google* had provided zero results. So I decided to head to Grandma's to ask her advice. She'd been pestering me all week to visit. She had a new idea for LSD and had called my office every day telling me how, done right, it would dramatically improve my quality of life. Whatever it was I was going to embrace it and participate in her new obsession in the hope she could release me from my own.

grandma's villa | pepperpots

I arrived at Grandma's villa to find Grandma, Delaware and Beatrice all rather pissed.

'Darling, we are bored,' Grandma began from the head of the large wooden dining table. They had been on the Margaritas all day and looked unusually dishevelled.

'That's what you've been calling me about every day this week? You want to tell me you are bored?'

'In a way, yes.' She poured me a drink and dragged me onto the seat next to her; a glassy-eyed Delaware sat on my other side. 'Kate, darling, when you get...*older*—' Grandma hated the word '—some things in life become less frequent. You are less noticed by the opposite sex. The hours spent with girlfriends giggling about your latest love interest, a first kiss, what he meant when he said he thought you were different, those hours no longer exist. Those experiences no longer exist.' I couldn't imagine Grandma ever giggling over a man and the meaning of a sentence he uttered other than to critique its grammatical content. 'The excitement of first love or first lust is gone for us.' They all over-zealously nodded along. 'Obviously on a practical level there are ways of ensuring one is still sexually satisfied—' There was a smash of glasses from the kitchen and Pepperpots' Vietnamese pool boy—who my grandma had an unusually close relationship with—popped his head around the corner.

'Sorry, ladies,' he said, pronouncing the *s*'s as if they were *th*'s. 'So sorry.'

'I think, darl, what your grandmamma is trying to say,' Delaware said, taking my hand, 'is that *you* are not too old.' They all looked at me, wide-eyed, Beatrice swaying heavily from side to side. 'Now I know, sweetie, that your heart is so broken right now, darl. I've been there.' She was breathy, like Sue Ellen in *Dallas*. 'I've really been there. But sometimes you have to move on even before you are ready to move on. You have to get back in that ring and you have to throw that first punch even if you don't think you've got the strength or the desire.'

'I read a book recently—' we were back on Grandma '—about devaluation. Actually the book was on global economics, not one you need to read cover to cover but one that is applicable in this instance. You need to *de-value* your experience with Gabriel. You need to *devalue* what he is and was to you. He needs to become one of a number of men and experiences in your lifetime. And there are two ways we are going to achieve this. One is by making a list of all the things you loved about Gabriel *and* all the things you like about other people. You might love Federico's fashion and creativity, or the way George Clooney swoons, or Peter Parker, there must be something you love about Peter Parker?' I had a flashback to the last door-slamming time that I'd seen him. 'You might even love Chad's unwavering self-belief. Put all these qualities on that list and make a description of your perfect man with all his perfect qualities. And you will immediately see that Gabriel only forms a small part of that list, a very low percentage. And that is how we start to devalue him and what he brings to the table. He doesn't bring every-thing to the table. He never did.'

'If I was you, darl, I would also cut out some photographs of different men, maybe there are some actors or singers you think are beautiful, we could get some pictures from a magazine and stick them on this list too.'

'Great idea!' Grandma shook her fist in the air with ex-citement. 'Great idea! A list with pictures, a list showing you that Gabriel is one of a number of beautiful men, with limited qualities and abilities.'

'Next, darl, you need to *physically* move on.'

'Like move countries?' I was confused. 'Because I have already moved, twice if you think about it, once to France and then once back from France. I don't really want to move again, not just yet.'

'No, we mean that you need to start seeing other people.'

'Oh. Well, I don't want to. I don't have the time. I don't have the enthusiasm. I can't. I don't want to. I won't. No.' The response felt more reflex than conscious.

'We thought you might say that, didn't we?' Grandma said to Delaware. 'So we are going to take baby steps. What we would like, and, yes, this is a formal Love-Stolen Dreams request before you try and wriggle out of it, is that from now on, every time you go out and do something related to your Love-Stolen Dreams column you can't come back until you have kissed someone there.'

'What?'

'Not in the French way, darl, unless you want to. Just kiss someone, on the lips, or the cheek if you prefer, a quick peck, that's all. I bet the last kiss that had meaning for you was a kiss with Gabriel, wasn't it, darl?'

'I guess so,' I said, blushing bright red, touching my cheek where Peter Parker had kissed me in Hyde Park. Delaware looked at me suspiciously. Grandma took over.

'Well, if you kiss someone on the lips every day or week or two weeks it will devalue kissing in general, normalise it, and you are increasing your odds because the more frogs you kiss, the more likely you are to meet a prince and in the interim you are entertaining us with the kinds of experiences and conversations we are no longer privy to.'

'I don't want to find a prince and I don't think me looking for one is in any way complementary to my current objectives. In fact it feels contrary to what I am telling everyone else to do.'

'Darling, your objectives were to help people realise their potential *within or without a relationship.* You were never anti-relationships. And you might meet someone one day and when you do all these experiences will help you stay connected to yourself. So we think it's valid if you kiss as many people as possible. Now we would also like where possible if you took photos of everyone you kiss and we will stick the photos on here.' She pressed a button and a screen dropped down from the ceiling with a world map on it. There was an A4-sized headshot of me in the middle (11 years old, train-track braces).

'Seriously, Grandma? That was the only photo you could find?'

'This is going to be our record of your Love-Stolen Dreams kissing journey,' she said enthusiastically.

'That is just classic, yes, it is, yes, it is.' Federico wandered into the kitchen followed by Leah, who was bellowing into her iPhone. 'Well, hello, campers!' he said with jazz hands. 'And that photo really is Cadbury's Dairy Milk in that it is never going to get old and it is never going to stop making me feel good, no, it is not.' He grabbed a jug of Margaritas and started topping up all their glasses. 'So, Lady Bears, Leah asked me to bring her here because she is going to teach us how to crystal heal and I am cherry bakewell ex-cited about it.' Leah was still talking on her phone.

'No, no, he can't stay up later than 8 p.m. No, he can't. Since when did an under-5 become the more knowledge-able in the parent-child relationship?' She rolled her eyes at us. 'Well, of course he'd say I feed him ice cream before bed. He says a lot of things. Last week he told me he cre-ated a spaceship and flew it into the ear of Grandpa Jim, but I didn't call *Science Weekly* and schedule an interview for them with our spaceship-building son. I told Henry he was a clever boy, then I made him finish his mashed pota-toes.' She held her hand over the mouthpiece and whispered, 'It's my ex's turn to have Henry,' before wandering off into the lounge. 'No, no, he can't watch that film, no, no, I have never let him do that before—'

'Who wants more Margaritas, Lady Bears?' Federico said, pouring the last of the jug into Beatrice's glass before we all realised that she was in fact asleep head first in a plate of cold pasta.

'More Margarita!' yelled Grandma, before zigzagging her way to the kitchen. Federico copied her. Delaware stayed in her seat next to me.

'Sweetie, humour us. Do you think you could do that? Make us smile. Let us have a little glimpse back to the past. You never know, you might just enjoy it. And I really think this will help you move on in ways you can't even imagine or appreciate just yet. I truly believe this is the best way to sever the invisible bonds that can keep us connected to an-other person. So please trust me because we are trying to set you free.'

request | kiss a frog every time I come to a pond

Grandma's newest request had made me feel dizzy, dizzier than the earlier Margaritas. I didn't like the idea of kissing a bunch of low-life punks every time I went out to take back some Love-Stolen Dreams. Captain Hook didn't have to snog every dirty crim he ever met. He was the captain of his own ship; the master of his own destiny; he would have made Love walk the plank then held his pistol in the air yelling, 'ooohh ahhhh,' before feasting on red wine and giant chicken legs. No, this whole kissing idea was a real headache for me, an *actual* headache, so with a migraine beginning to caress my left temple (as opposed to me caressing everyone I ever did meet) I disappeared to find some painkillers before my enforced session of crystal healing.

grandma's walk-in wardrobe

Grandma has *never* compromised on closet space. Her walk-in wardrobe offers me comfort on a level not even a *KitKat* can compete with. It is cavernous and never-ending like the wardrobe that takes you to Narnia. Familiar items of clothing hang from the rails that line the walls: vintage fur coats; hundreds of boxes of shoes; delicious *Chanel* suits; beautiful pieces of jewellery displayed in silk-lined cabinets. There are also items from my past. Grandma has carefully packed away my christening outfit; pictures I painted her; misshapen clay pots I made at playschool. Grandma still used them. One for buttons, one for foreign currency, one was filled with odd pieces of ribbon. There was a tatty friendship bracelet I'd given her aged seven; the hospital wristband from my birth. There is even a small piece of fabric that I'd sewn her initials onto. And somewhere, somewhere in this delightful walk-in wardrobe was an impressive medicine box that very much blurred the boundaries of current British medical legislation.

I was on my sixth unsuccessful box when I discovered them. Not the Asian pain medication I sought, but a box filled with letters; hundreds of neatly packed letters, batches of them tied in ribbon. Some were incredibly old, some more recent, with stamps and watermarks from all around the world, all with the same handwriting, all of them addressed to Grandma but not to our house, to a PO Box address I didn't recognise. I'd never seen any of these letters before. I pulled out a handful and noticed the handwriting; slanting slightly to the right; angular and precise. I chose a letter with a postmark from 10 years ago and carefully opened it.

Dear Josephine,

I am settling in well in Paris, thank you. There is an amazing research facility attached to the university, and the apartment is wonderful. In fact everything has been impressive so far, with the exception of my French. No amount of lessons could have prepared me for the speed everyone speaks. Most of the Parisians are rude and switch immediately into perfect English. Occasionally they are patient. In the café where I have breakfast every morning the waiters allow me the time and good grace to try to order in French. I've seen them laugh a few times but in general they try to help. And there is an amazing teacher at college who speaks French with me for a few hours

*every Wednesday, it's part of a language exchange
programme. It's strange because, although they are
not the same age at all, there is something about the
teacher that reminds me a little bit of Kate, which has
made me feel slightly homesick. How is she?*

Who was this person? Why were they asking about me?
I flipped to the last page of the letter.

*I'll send you the dates when I am next free to meet. I
hope all is well there.*
Love, Peter Parker

'Ah! It's like your childhood all over again!' Grandma
beamed as everyone trudged into Grandma's room to find
me. 'She used to spend hours playing in my wardrobe as a
child, didn't you, darling?'

'What's that?' Leah said, grabbing the letter out of my
hand. 'And why are you so pale? Are you going to throw
up again? Federico said you did the same thing at Mary's.
Are you pregnant?'

'As if,' Federico said, trying on one of the fur coats. 'It
would be God's child if she was.'

'I was looking for painkillers,' I said, looking up at
Grandma. She looked from me to the box of letters on the
floor.

'Well, that doesn't look like the medicine box, does it?'
Grandma said, grabbing up the box and then the letter from
Leah's hand. 'And, darling, you know better than to read

other people's letters. I thought I had brought you up better than that.'

'Grandma?'

'Now where are these painkillers?' She started rummaging through the cupboards, pulling out a big box, opening
it up on the ground next to me. 'Painkillers, painkillers,'
she muttered as she picked through the contents of the box.

'Grandma…?' I felt nervous to even ask the question.
'Have you been in contact with Peter Parker the entire time
he's been away?'

Federico gasped. Leah looked as if she was holding her
breath. Delaware swayed and tripped backwards into the
Chanel suits. Grandma stopped very still, staring into the
box of drugs.

'Grandma, how could you not say something? *Why*
wouldn't you say something? You saw me! You saw how
upset I was when he left! He just vanished, without a word,
my best friend, he totally disappeared, and you were in
touch with him the whole time?'

The oncoming migraine was beginning to thump against
my skull like an attention-seeking child. Grandma took
two tablets out of a box and placed them in the palm of my
hand, gently closing her hands around my own. The tablets
weren't soluble.

'Kate,' she said quietly, 'I don't think this is the moment
for us to talk about this. In fact, I don't think I can have this
conversation with you. It's not my place to. So, get yourself
a glass of water to take those tablets, no one ever thought
clearly with a headache, and then I think it's time everyone left. I'm sorry, Leah. I know you were looking forward

to healing us but I am suddenly very tired. We'll have to do it another time.' She left us in her wardrobe; Delaware amongst the suits; Federico, Leah and I just staring at each other.

'Kat-kins,' whispered Federico. 'Literally…what the mother fluff just happened? That was intense, wasn't it? Did anyone else feel that? That was episode-ending, in a dramatic way, and I'm thinking to myself, I'm thinking, why does no one give a peanut butter sandwich that Beatrice is still asleep in a pasta ready meal for one?'

the golden swan—federico cagassi—41 years old

*I guess I couldn't avoid doing this forever. So, my name is
Federico Cagassi and love has taken away my career pro-
gression. You know, I know, we all know that I should be
at a more senior level at* True Love. *I should be Editor. I
should be Chad. But as I want to work with Chad, not without him, I have chosen to work under him. So that is what
I have given up for love, yes it is, yes it is, yes it is.*

*Firstly I want to state for the record that it's not all bad.
I think of* True Love *as my baby. I spend almost all my
waking hours working on it. I still get shivers every time
I walk past a shop window and see our newest edition on
the shelf, or someone reading it on the tube, or the day
our server went down because we had so many hits on the
Love-Stolen Dreams website. So in many ways I haven't
given up anything at all, except perhaps a job title and a
bit of extra money, a lot of extra money actually, and invites to parties—Chad gets all the invites to parties. And he
gets the freebies. I get some: the ones he doesn't want. Just
last month I walked into my apartment and for a second I*

thought I'd taken a wrong turn and accidentally ended up in the gift section of Harrods, there were so many presents in there. But Chad always gets first pick, first dibs, at the invites and at the freebies. I didn't get a look in when the new iPad arrived, no, I did not.

The thing is, Kat-kins, if I did something about this, if I applied to work somewhere else, I'm not sure I'd see that much of Chad. I don't know if we'd continue to spend time together. And I am not ready to find that out. I want to avoid that reality because my heart is fragile like a butterfly made of gold leaf. I am a golden butterfly of fragility. And so I remain sub-editor and beat my golden wings every day unnoticed, an ugly duckling who is in fact a swan but is standing behind an aggressive and large goose who gobbles up all the Haribo *from the children who come to visit us at the park where we float in the pond of life. I am a golden swan. A golden swan who is still a sub-editor. Love has halted the self-actualisation of Federico Cagassi. And Love is mother-fluffing powerful.*

pink wee pod | true love

'It's always about you. It's like it's your birthday every single day of the year and everyone is like, "OK, I will put my super-important personal stuff on hold because it's Kate's birthday. We can't focus on our quest, on our questions, because she has so many of her own and she is so fragile and broken and sad and it's her birthday so we are just going to have to bloody well wait." And we do wait. We do. But the birthday goes on and on and on like some kind of endless Jewish shiva where everyone is just dying inside, desperate for a change in fabric colour, and a change of scene, and to hang out anywhere that doesn't have a body-filled coffin in the front room. Well, I can't wait, Kat-kins! I can't mother-fluffing wait. I need your time and I need your focus. It's just a few days of interviews and then you can go and chase down your call-rejecting Peter Parker and find out why he can in fact be Anne-bloody-Frank, just not for you, for your glamorous gran. So are you ready? Then let's go, because we are already 40 minutes late.'

I should have seen it coming. Federico had started to lose the plot when we began researching the male perspective on love-stolen dreams. We'd received a lot of letters from distressed boyfriends asking for help. I caught Federico smuggling them out of the office to read at home. This was further compounded by research I'd been doing into divorce rates, because it seemed that the petitioner in over 93% of divorce cases was the wife—93%—that's almost all of them. And of this 93% almost none were contested by the husbands. If men were so unhappy they didn't want to fight to save their relationships it seemed important for us to understand why. So that's exactly what we decided to do.

the boardroom | true love

The men in the boardroom were younger than I'd been ex-pecting. Many of them in their twenties, some in their thir-ties, one forty-year-old, and Mark from Marketing, who was hovering by the snack corner eating a blood orange. Two in particular were the most vocal. They were dressed in expensive-looking sports brands, with heavy-duty accessories, and looked as if they probably owned a record label with a *Crib* on *MTV*. JC spoke on behalf of his forlorn-looking friend Bo, who sat nodding his head to music that I just couldn't hear.

'His girlfriend is hot, man,' JC told me. 'She is hot!'

'Yeah, she is hot,' confirmed Bo.

'Do you remember how she used to cuss you down when you were chasing after her?' he said, jabbing Bo's arm.

'She used to cuss me down.'

'You were all like, "Hey, honey, you is so fly, I gotta be wiv you" and she used to cuss you down. She was so funny, man! She had it, you know. She had it. And she was funny.'

'Yeah, she was funny,' agreed Bo.

'But she is not funny now, man.'

'She is *so* not funny now.'

'Now she hangs around you like a prop, like an accessory. She's all bovvered about what you want and what you like. I'm not bovvered about you and you is my best mate.'

'I'm not bovvered about you either.' They high-fived in a complicated male way.

'I bet if you said to her you like women to wear gold, she'd wear gold. Or if you said you want a cake, she'd go bake you a cake.'

'She did bake me a cake! For my birthday!'

'Did she?' JC was surprised. 'Was it good?'

'Yeah, it was all right. It was a cake. But she said I didn't look like I was really enjoying it. So she got in a mood and we had a fight.'

'You see, man! You see!' JC was talking to me now. 'She wasn't like that before. She was funny before. And hot. Well hot.'

'All right, man, I get it, you can stop going on about how hot my girlfriend is.'

'*Was* hot. I said was hot. Now it don't matter what she looks like cos all I can see is that moody face every time I turn up to take you out. And those doe eyes every time she looks at you.'

'She didn't look at me wiv doe eyes after the cake.'

'I can't believe you didn't save me a piece, man.' JC turned away from his friend. 'I love cake.'

'I promise you, if you'd eaten this moody cake and seen those moody eyes you would not be lovin' cake.'

'So we need your help,' JC said to me, 'because it's not just his girl who is like this. They are all like this. I had one too. *Had* being the operative word. So you need to like distract them or give them something else to focus on or give them a handbook on how not to be miserable. Because *I* am not the answer. And *he*,' he said, pointing to Bo, 'he is not the answer. We are just blokes, not characters in a film or in one of dem books she reads.'

'I tell you, man, if she heard us saying this stuff to this lady she would cuss me down.' Bo looked worried. I was worried too. Since when had I become a *lady* not a *girl*?

'No, she wouldn't, my man, no, she wouldn't. *That* is the point. She wouldn't cuss you down—she'd just cry. So you have to speak to his girlfriend,' he said, turning back to me.

'And if you could also help my wife I would very much appreciate it,' said Mark from Marketing, whose presence I'd assumed was work-related. 'Because she is angry with me almost all the time.' The boys were manically pointing at Mark but looking at me. 'Mostly she is annoyed because

I am not responding in the correct way to the things she is doing. Apparently she is doing all these things for me and I am not giving the appropriate level of enthusiasm or the correct facial expressions. So she spends a large percentage of her time annoyed and frustrated, and occasionally crying.'

'They is always crying!' said Bo.

'And it seems I am responsible for all these emotions, all this unhappiness. When we met I was responsible for making her feel happy and content. Now I do the opposite. Apparently I am very disappointing and annoying. And I'm not entirely sure what has happened but apparently it's my fault so I would like to try and fix it. Although it seems to me that she was much happier before she met me so maybe it would be better if we were apart.'

'Well, his girlfriend was definitely happier before him,' said JC.

'Yeah, she was.'

'She was happy *and* she was funny.'

'And she used to see her mates more,' said Bo. 'I'd ask her out and she'd say, "No, thanks, I'm with my mates." But now, now she waits to know what I'm doing before she makes her plans. And then, if I don't know what I am doing, and to be honest wiv you I am not a big planner, she gets annoyed because it means she can't make a decision about what she is doing. And she's a planner.'

'It's warped, man. It's totally warped,' said JC.

'My wife does the same,' confirmed Mark. 'She almost always has a diary or day planner in her hand and is constantly asking me to commit to something or other. Sometimes I think she's trying to trip me up so she can get more annoyed thus proving what a total and utter waste of space I am. Just yesterday I had to confirm a dinner eighteen months in advance. Eighteen months in advance! I think we all know how that is going to end.'

'She needs to Jack and Gill,' said JC.

'She really does,' confirmed Mark.

'So you gotta help us, lady,' said Bo, 'because my girl, she is so fly. She is *so* the woman. She is *the* woman. I want her to be *my* woman. But right now she is this other woman. And I don't really like this other woman. I want my girlfriend back,' he pleaded.

'I'd really like my wife back too—' Mark nodded '—because right now the lady that works in Tesco's is more excited to see me every week than my wife is. And it feels somewhat pathetic going to the supermarket to receive a warm smile and some nice conversation.'

'You see!' Federico said, turning to me. 'It's a bloody big mess is what it is. So what the custard creams are we going to do about it?' He drummed his fingers on the heart-shaped table and waited, along with the rest of the room, for my response. So I pretended to hear someone call my name, then ran into the yellow wee pod and hid.

Because we'd never once considered how women were actually conducting themselves in relationships. Could Mark's wife really be that angry with him? Or was she really angry with herself? And if the girl in Tesco was consistently more pleased to see him than his wife, who's to say that at some point that shop assistant wouldn't become more than just a friend? There were hundreds of American studies claiming that infidelity occurred in nearly half of all failed marriages. And almost all of these studies agreed on one thing: that infidelity was ***not*** the primary reason for the divorce. It came about as a *reaction* to problems within the marriage. These could be anything from resentment, to boredom, to the above-mentioned anger. Maybe these feelings were because the women felt they had given too much, put in too much, unbalanced their own lives for their relationship. Was love the problem or was it that we were unable to multitask?

It seemed now more than ever that an LSD drop-in centre or a mentoring programme for young women was absolutely necessary, otherwise I had to rely on women contacting *True Love*, by which time it could already be too late. So I needed to pitch to the Department for Education. I wanted women to have it all. I wanted women to make a change. So I needed to get in touch with solution-providing, letter-writing, secret-keeping Peter Parker.

goldman apartments

The beginning of our doorstep ritual started the same as always: with a knock on the door of apartment 41, a long wait, and Peter looking as if he'd been doing interval training in his flat. No sooner had he opened the front door than he was trying to close it again, with me on the other side. I felt like the brace-wearing kid at college, the one no one wants to let into the party. So I decided to act accordingly, and brim with nerd-like enthusiasm, deflecting any sign of rejection with a skin so thick there was every possibility the *X-Men* would seek me out and try and recruit me.

'Hi, Peter!' I beamed. 'I was just passing and I thought I'd drop in.' Three tube changes, one bus, 17-minute walk.

'Actually I'm in the middle of something, Kate,' he said in a flat, irritated tone, 'so you probably should have called first.' We both knew about the eleven thousand messages I'd already left on his voicemail.

'It wouldn't take up a lot of your time, just a little chat.'

'As I said, Kate, I'm in the middle of something so…' He didn't bother to finish the sentence, so we stood there in silence. 'Why don't I walk you to the lift?' He grabbed me by the arm and marched me down the hallway. He pressed the lift-call button and stood cross-armed as we waited for it to arrive. The doors pinged open.

'Good to see you, Kate,' he said as he pushed me inside. The doors started closing. I hit the button to reopen them. So Peter Parker stepped inside, took my finger off the hold button and pressed G. The doors closed, with both of us inside, and we started to descend. Peter crossed his arms, huffed and remained silent. It had been a brilliant and seamless start.

'I didn't mean to bother you, Peter, really. I was just a bit worried because I haven't heard from you in a while—' he was watching the floor numbers decrease, my time evaporating '—and I had a few questions, about creating a proposal for the Department for Education, oh, and a box of letters I found at Grandma's…'

'Aren't you off to New York soon?' he said without looking at me.

'Er, yeah, yes, I am actually, with Beatrice, we're going to the Juilliard School, which is actually one of the things

I wanted to tell you about, along with the letters, and the drop-in centres and a stupid idea I'd had about fertility preservation and—'

'Whose fertility preservation?' He glared at me. 'What's wrong with your fertility?'

'Well, nothing, yet, I don't think. It's a ticking time bomb, obviously. It's just I've interviewed some women recently at *True Love* who were going into an egg-freezing programme and—' Why was I talking about this? How had he managed to change the subject?

Ping. The lift told us we'd reached the ground floor. The doors slid open to reveal the stone-faced concierge. Peter Parker held the door open waiting for me to leave. I didn't move. So he huffed angrily and the doors re-closed. The lift started going back up to the top floor.

'Kate,' he said, super irritated, 'I am busy at the moment. OK. I have a lot of things I am trying to sort out. I need time to do that. And I need space. And that means I am and will continue to be less available to you. OK? Did we have some pre-arranged number of hours that we were supposed to see each other every week?'

'No, I just, I had a few things that I thought you might be able to—'

'I won't be able to help.'

'Well, that must be difficult for a man who prides himself on assisting others.'

'Excuse me?'

'Well, normally you spend all this time helping other people, building bonfires for Grandma, *Fat Camp* runs at Hyde Park—you're always involving yourself in the lives of others and none of us knows a thing about you, or where you've been, or what you've been doing, or why you've been writing thousands of letters to my grandma. I mean, who the bloody hell are you?'

'This from the girl who is going to spend the rest of her life taking back what love has stolen, from *other* people. Talk about being disconnected from your own needs.'

Ping. The lift told us we were back on the top floor. Peter stepped out into the hallway. This time I held the door open.

'Peter, I didn't come here to fight with you. So can we please just go in your apartment and sit down and talk about this like adults? I have questions that I think deserve answers.'

'I told you, Kate, it's not a convenient time for me right now.' He stared me dead in the eyes and I noticed how completely exhausted he looked.

'Peter, is any of this, any of what's going on, to do with what's going on in your apartment, I mean, the woman in your apartment? Because you don't need to keep things from me. I'm a big girl. I can take it. And I need you to explain about these letters.'

'There's not a woman in my apartment, Kate! Why do you always think I am talking about women?' He was getting snappish. 'As if that was the only option!' He was glaring at me. 'Go home, Kate. Let this go. Let *me* go.' He marched off down the corridor. 'It's better this way, Kate. Trust me. Just go home.'

The doors of the lift closed. My brain was still trying to piece it all together. Why was it better if I left? What did he mean when he said having a woman in his apartment *wasn't the only option*? What was the other option? That he had a ruddy great man in there and was training for a world championship wrestling match?

Oh.

Ohhhh.

OHHH!

Shit the bed. Was Peter Parker gay? Let's look at the evidence. Smart, self-sufficient, intellectually brilliant man; immaculately dressed, great skin, dry sense of humour, failed marriage; I hate to admit it but he's a superb dancer; has an apartment that I would literally kill another human being to live in (goodness, this list is getting long); fantastic in the kitchen; endlessly patient with me and all my girl stories, troubles, problems and issues—well, at least until very recently; always, always smells great. Peter Parker was gay. My Peter Parker was most definitely gay. And he was in his apartment quite literally testing it all out; working out which bits go where; getting hot under the collar; making himself bright pink in the face.

And then they were off; my wholly independent tear ducts were sending large and frequent tears down my flushed cheeks. I wanted to be happy for him. I wanted to be happy that he was finding himself; that he was on the road to ultimate happiness, civil ceremonies and adopting an Ethiopian baby, but I felt desperately, inexplicably sad. And I still knew nothing about the sodding letters, or why I should *leave things alone*, or why being gay meant we could no longer hang out, or what on earth boys did together that made them go so red...

My phone rang. It was Leah.

'Hey, Kate, I have booked us onto a karmic self-awareness course. It was number 17 on my list, remember? And I still haven't forgotten about the past life regression. Oh, and I've decided to set up my own alternative therapy practice. Obviously I've got years of training ahead of me but I am going to become Dr Leah one day. Maybe they will give me my own TV show? Anyway I just wanted to say thank you for setting me off on this path. I don't know what I am doing, how it's all going to work, but I really *want* to do this, you know, and *that* is the point. So thank you! Thank you for starting me on this journey, opening me up to this new side of myself. God, I feel free! And scared, really really scared. And I can see you. Henry. I can see you. Put that down right now or Mummy will go to her angry place. Kate? Kate, are you there? Are you crying? Kate? Hello? Hello?'

The line went dead. I'd lost my signal. I was going down, way down, to Ground Zero.

i've got sno balls—sue—60 years old

My boyfriend is good at everything. And I mean everything! And so sometimes when he tells me about things he likes doing I agree, which I think constitutes lying, but the lie is always based on a modicum of truth so it doesn't really feel like a lie. Take a few months ago. He was going on and on about how much he loves skiing, really loves it, like if he had to make a list of the three things that made him happiest in the world skiing would make the top two. Now I took my kids skiing once when they were young so I said, 'Me too, I LOVE skiing! It's so much fun,' which again is sort of true. It was fun, for the kids, and my ex-husband. And I loved watching them all speed down the mountain. But my personal experience on the piste was terrifying and ended 37 minutes after it began involving several falls and a life-and-death situation on a chairlift and I have not set foot on the snow since. In fact I have done everything possible to avoid setting food on snow, until now...

So my boyfriend exclaims, 'You know what would be fun?

If we go skiing together. I'd love to go skiing with you. It would make me so happy,' to which I squeaked, 'Me too!'

Houston, we have a problem.

Obviously problem number 1 is the impending skiing holiday itself where my wonderful boyfriend realises I have fibbed, not only about my skiing ability, but also about my enthusiasm for his beloved sport. He will realise I was trying to either impress him or please him, the result being he will feel neither impressed nor pleased and he will think I am needy and insecure.

Problem number 2 is me because what I didn't realise until reading Love-Stolen Dreams is that during my first marriage, I played a certain role. My ex-husband was good at all sport. In fact he was also good at everything, and I loved that about him. Show him a new sport or a physical challenge or ask him to master anything and within 30 minutes he could do it. So when we went on holidays involving sports, skiing, for example, I would always hold everyone up. I was never as good as my ex-husband and the kids and I didn't want everyone waiting for me while I snowploughed my way down the baby slope screaming. So I ended up sitting everything out. I became really good at watching from the sidelines. I got good at saying, 'I'd rather read my book'; 'I'm happy just watching'; 'It's not really my thing.' I got so good that I started to believe my own bullshit. I forgot I used to be a different way.

So I confessed to my current boyfriend about my moderate fib, which he thought was hysterical. But I didn't book a ski holiday for the two of us. I booked a ski holiday just for me. I want to spend some time overcoming my fears

and getting back the part of me I lost during the marriage.
I don't want to read a book. I am not happy sitting on the
sidelines. I might not be good at skiing, or even learn fast,
but I am going to go and learn how to do it properly, at my
own speed, just for me. And I'd like Pirate Kate to join me.
So, fancy some skiing in the French Alps?

1813 meters above sea level | french alps

The ridiculously fit ski instructor waved at me then saun-
tered across the mountain-top bar. He was dressed head-to-
foot in red, still covered in snow, and walked with a swagger
that ski boots cause and ski instructors perfect. He was
yet to remove his goggles and hat but looked so much like
Gabriel I found myself tearing away at the collar of my ski
jacket, trying to make my throat feel less constricted and
starved of air.

'Here he is!' Sue said excitedly, four days into her Love-
Stolen Dreams skiing holiday. 'My star! My teacher! The
man who has taken away *all* of my fears! Kate, I would like
to introduce you to Julien.' The ski instructor arrived at our
table just as I had a few minutes earlier.

'Hello, Sooo,' he said, kissing her politely on both cheeks.
'And you must be Kate?' He took a ski glove off to shake my
hand; his melodic French accent making me feel warm in
my body, like muscles relaxing at the hands of a masseuse.

'May I sit next to you, Kate?' he said, pulling out a
chair. 'And please excuse me because I am still in my work
clothes.' He took off his other glove, then his goggles and
finally his hat; thick dark hair tumbling out. He ran his
fingers through it and tried to pat it down. 'Hat hair!' he

said, looking at me with dark chocolate eyes hidden under a canopy of a thousand thick lashes. I patted my own messy hair as if to empathise but Julien was already busying himself removing his outer layers of clothing, loosening his ski boots, laying things out to dry. I watched enviously. There was something about a ski-instructor outfit that appealed to my sensibilities. And I don't just mean in a sexual way. Eventually Julien sat himself on the chair next to mine, shifting to face me, our knees ever so slightly touching.

'It's so nice to meet you, Kate,' he said, staring me straight in the eyes. He didn't look anywhere else for an impossibly long time. I on the other hand was trying to look *everywhere* else. 'I am *very* excited that you are here,' he said, gently touching my right knee. I nearly leapt five feet up in the air and grabbed the table to keep me steady. Because ski instructors *are* my kryptonite, I have zero immunity, attract them like flies but don't have a gang of disaster-preventing busybody friends to bail me out when under attack.

'Julien, I was just explaining to Kate, as I said to you, that my ex-husband was good at everything, and I mean *everything*. And I loved that about him—that's why I married him. He was brilliant at playing sports, especially extreme sports, and he completely fell in love with the mountains…' While Sue was speaking Julien had started fiddling with something on the collar of my ski jacket. He was so close to me I could smell the washing powder of his clothes mixed with aftershave and man. Let's just say I was struggling to pay attention to my Love-Stolen Dreamer. 'So as soon as our kids were old enough,' she continued, 'they would go off with him, throwing themselves down ski slopes having all sorts of fun. But I am a lot slower than them and I got fed up with everyone having to wait. And I promise you, Kate, there is nothing worse than a group of energy-drink-filled teenagers groaning as you snowplough towards them at three miles an hour. And my then-husband, who I still wanted to think of me as a sexy goddess, giggling in the background calling me "slow old mum"! It was soul-destroying…' Julien stopped fiddling with the collar of my ski jacket, content he had fixed the mysterious non-existent problem, then started looking about my person for other things to do. 'So to avoid feeling like that one day I just opted out.' Julien was now on his knees adjusting my ski boots, which was the closest thing to a proposal since, well, since Gabriel, which actually made me feel a bit nauseous. 'But what I didn't realise, Kate, was that day, that was the beginning of a pattern of opting out that spanned two decades. Two decades! That's well beyond our separation and divorce. My ex-husband was the adventurous parent; I was the watchful mother. Our roles were defined and became set in stone.'

'But we 'ave changed all that this week, 'ave we not?' Julien said, finally switching his attention onto Sue.

'Oh, it's been amazing!' she squealed, looking from Julien to me. 'Oh, Kate, I love it!' She couldn't stop smiling. 'I actually love it.' She literally couldn't close her lips over her teeth. 'I LOVE IT!' she yelled, air punching. 'I feel like I've got back a part of myself I'd totally lost. It feels like being with an old friend again, who makes you laugh and smile and reminds you who you used to be. It's so long since I have been this person. So long since I felt like *this*

person. I like *this* person! I like me!' She laughed, sat back
in her seat, then slapped her own thighs.

'And you, Kate?' Julien was back on me. 'Do you like
who you are?' He stared only at my lips when he spoke.
'Are you happy like Sue?'

'Well, I, er, I think, I er...' Why couldn't I just say *yes*
like any normal miserable person would have done?

'Well, perhaps the surprise I 'ave arranged for you will
help. Come, come, it's going to start any minute.' Julien
wandered out of the bar carrying his skis and my skis while
Sue beamed excitedly and nodded for me to follow. I was not
entirely sure what they had planned, and when I say that I
mean I literally had no idea. As far as I was concerned I was
going to informally interview them tonight, then shadow
her ski lesson tomorrow. But I am all for surprises and unplanned presents, unless it's the kind of surprise my pet cat
Rupert used to leave for me, because I am not and never
will be good with partially dead, headless mice.

Outside the snow was tumbling down in heavy flakes,
the last of the daylight quickly ebbing away. Julien laid our
skis on the ground and beckoned me over.

'So,' he said, clipping me into my skis and handing me
my ski poles. 'Tonight there is a night-time torch-lit descent.
All the ski instructors do it every week—it's for the tourists. We go to the top of that piste there—' he pointed into
the darkness '—then we ski back down 'olding flares. As
we come down ze mountain in the dark it will look like a
giant snake of fire. The tourists love it.'

'I'm not good enough to do it yet,' Sue said, handing me
a giant unlit flare, 'but I'd love you to do it for me, if that's

OK, then you can tell me what it's like. I promise as soon as I am good enough I will do it myself.'

'Yes, you will, Sue,' Julien confirmed, gently squeezing Sue's arm. 'You will do it with me, next holiday, I am sure.' Julien looked back to me, his eyes anything but innocent. 'So, Kate, will you come with me? I'd love you to, really— let's come together.' I looked from his wanton eyes to Sue, who was positively beaming at me.

You see, my reluctance at that moment was down to past experience, because I was already *very* familiar with this kind of night-time fire-lit mountain descent. I'd done it before, with Gabriel, and we *always* ended up having sex in a forest on the way down. What if this was some kind of ski instructor sex trap? Or sexual initiation into a new ski resort? Or my grandma's idea to get me back into a saddle I totally didn't need to be in?

Julien suddenly clapped his hands together and said, 'Then it's agreed!' before grabbing my hand and pulling me along next to him; down the deserted piste; down to a lone chairlift; down towards the very limits of my powers of personal restraint.

We arrived at the chairlift to find about 50 other ski instructors already there, waiting to be whisked up the dark mountain. Julien and I took a chairlift together, alone. He immediately slid across the seat until he was next to me. He put his arm tight around me.

'I don't want you to be cold, Kate,' he said as he pretended to check the zip of my coat was pulled up, that my hat was on properly, that I was as close as possible to his kissable bloody lips. 'So you write,' he said as he tucked some of my hair up into my hat. His face was so close to mine that we were talking nose to nose.

'Yes, about love.'

'That's my favourite subject.' He smiled, exhaling as he looked longingly at me. He was the exact opposite of Peter Parker the gay fridge magnet.

'So, Julien,' I said, eyes fixed straight ahead, 'have you ever lost anything because you fell in love?'

'If I lose something because of love it's normally the love itself.' He smiled at me. 'I don't have a lot to lose, Kate.' Good looks, athletic body, ability to ski to an Olympic standard—could he be more glass half empty?

'So what did you lose, Kate?' he said, pulling me closer again.

'Well, I think that I lost this,' I said, gesturing to the view of the mountains, but Julien carried on staring at me, so I sat in silent meditation for the rest of the journey up. As we reached the top of the lift he grabbed me by my hand.

'Let's go over here,' he said as we slid off the chairlift, pulling me past the group of assembling ski instructors, stopping some 40 metres away on a darkened cliff edge.

'Kate, you are very honoured,' he said, unclipping our skis. 'This is a very special place. Come, I invite you to join me on my rock. Please take a seat.' He pointed at an *actual* rock.

'Shouldn't we wait over there?' I urged, backing away.

'No, no, we have time. I have a present for you. Come.'

I sighed and followed him over; there was only so long I was going to be able to fight it. I was a flame. French ski instructors were moths. Or perhaps it was the other way around. However it worked I always ended up in bed with one. It was an unwritten universal rule, like gravity and post-35 cellulite. So I sat down on his rock (*not* a metaphor) and he sat down beside me as close as he could physically manage and put one arm around me, pulling me in to him. We were huddled so close together I felt myself quite naturally curling into his embrace, beginning to rest my head into his shoulder, turning my head into his neck. How could I be so physically overly familiar with someone I had literally just met? It's just, he was so like…

'Kate, look,' he whispered in my ear. He turned my face to look out at the view, pointing down the mountain. I followed his gaze. The ski resort was about 1000 metres below, lit up against the darkness of the night like a tiny Ewok village. And the mountains in front of us stretched for miles; hundreds upon hundreds of peaks, the last of the setting sun far away in the distance. I touched my hand to my breastbone and thought of Mary. For the first time in as long as I could remember, looking at this view, I felt peaceful.

'Here,' Julien said, handing me a small plastic cup. 'It might be a little warm,' he apologised as he unzipped his jacket and took out a bottle of champagne (it's a mystery, all the things they can keep in there). He poured me a glass then gently rubbed my back to take the edge off the cold.

'So, Kate, do you like who you are when you are 'ere?' He gestured to the view in front of us. I looked from his beautiful face to the view.

'I love who I am when I am here.'

'Then my job is done,' he said before stroking the side of

my face, his lips hovering less than an inch from my face. I felt as if I were dissolving into him, into the moment, into the rock where we sat, and I am sure beautiful Julien knew this. I must have been the gazillionth girl he'd captured, put on his rock and fed slightly warm booze to. Not that I was complaining; chilled champagne is overrated.[10]

Julien and I stayed on that rock for a long time, him wrapped all around me, me making no attempt to fight him off. We stayed long after the other ski instructors had lit their flares; long after they had skied off, one after the other, a slow-moving snake of fire curving down the dark mountain; long after the fireworks exploded thousands of feet below. I had to keep reminding myself that I was in fact on a work assignment paid for by my financially obsessed boss. Chad would be expecting a world-class article from me, or at least a largely fictitious interpretation of what may or may not be a run-of-the-mill middle-aged lady's ski holiday, but I definitely couldn't leave empty-handed, empty-headed, with another ski instructor notch on what was an already well-carved post. Although…over 11,000 *True Love* readers had written in advising Pirate Kate to enjoy as many other pirates as feasibly possible before settling on just one ship, so in a way I was working by not working…

'Maybe we should ski down the mountain now, Julien?' Good girl. 'I think I should do some work before tomorrow.' Chad would be proud.

'Kate, you can work another time—you can work all the time. This is for now, this moment, this view, us 'ere alone. Be here, with me. Just be. It's important to live a bit in the

---

[10]It's not; it's not overrated. It's bloody lovely. Especially when cold.

moment, is it not?' Damn him, yes, it was. And it was one of my newest mantras. 'Kate, we are safe to ski down a bit later. I know the mountain,' he reassured me, leaning in for a kiss. 'I promise you, Kate, I promise, I *really* know the mountain at night.' I *really* knew the mountain at night too and it involved kissing, and over-the-thermal touching and very occasionally a bit of frost bite on the bum.

mirror mirror on the wall

the following day | french alps

French boys *do* breakfast. I woke to fresh espresso, to crois-
sants, to a little flower left on my pillow and a note telling me I was wonderful and to meet him on the mountain.

French boys *do* the morning after. As soon as Julien saw
me on the piste he skied straight over. He beamed at me as
if I were a marvellous creation he'd been toiling over all
night, which was sort of true.

French boys *do* compliments. I spent the entire morning
being told I was the best thing *ever* and that everything I
did was *brilliant*.

French boys *do* epiphanies. Or at least they can stimulate
epiphanies, and when I say that I am not trying to be crude.

I had spent all morning skiing with Julien and Sue,
watching him teach her, watching her grow in confidence
and self-belief. Sue literally whooping with joy every time
she made a turn.

'I can do it!' she kept yelling to me. 'I can bloody well

do it! Woohoo!' she'd shout before losing control, skiing off towards a tree and bursting out laughing as she fell to the floor.

After her lesson Julien asked if I wanted to help him teach a beginner ski group. As I held the hands of the different students, helping them make their first turns, picking them up when they fell off the button lift, reassuring them that everyone has to be crap before they can be great, I finally started to feel *The Thing*.

The Thing is what Mary feels when she's fixing cars; *The Thing* is what Annie-pants feels when she sees clothes; The Thing is what Leah feels when she does her therapies or Beatrice feels when she plays the piano. In the ski lessons I felt content in a way that wasn't connected to anyone else, couldn't be taken away by anyone else, wasn't dependent on anyone else. The mountains, the ski lessons, the ski-instructor boyfriends... I was starting to develop a theory and it involved a mirror mirror on the wall.

Because what if we are attracted to people whose qualities or lifestyle we actually desire for ourselves; qualities or skills that perhaps we have not embraced in ourselves? So we choose to date or marry someone who does have these qualities, skills and achievements, as if proximity will be enough. Sue had serially dated ridiculously capable physically accomplished men; Mary married and then watched Len work on cars; I dated a bilingual ski instructor but I never went off and became fluent in French myself or qualified to teach skiing. I happily lived with Gabriel, enjoying his life choices rather than making them my own. A bit like being a Gatsby-esque nosey neighbour living adjacent to my dream house and dream life, or an overbearing parent living vicariously through the successes of her kids, or a sycophantic fan who sleeps every night with a discarded cigarette butt that may or may not have been smoked by her star. Julien was a *Sign Post*, just as Gabriel had been before him. They were the mirror showing me the reflection of what I think I had wanted for myself all along.

important disclaimer: Just because you realise something is a mirror doesn't mean you have to give it up straight away. Mirrors and sign posts can be fun. I for example may have re-looked at the mirror (Julien) one or two times (more) before flying back to London. Well, it was a watershed moment, wasn't it? The first kiss after Gabriel, the first intimate naked moment after Gabriel, the first other things that are not appropriate for the page...

On my last night staying in France, after looking in the mirror a few more times, self-indulgent I know, then taking a few photos of the mirror while he slept (for Grandma, obviously) I fell into the deepest sleep I think I'd had since leaving Gabriel. In the arms of Julien, a man who, if I am honest, wasn't the greatest conversationalist on planet earth, I felt as if I had finally turned a corner. Or at least I did, for about 4½ hours...

voices in the night

The call came in the middle of the night. My mobile ringing off the hook. Julien stirred next to me, my hotel room in total darkness. I fumbled for the phone, sending a glass of water to the floor.

'Hello?' My voice was barely there.

'Kate?'

'Who is this?'

His voice a whisper.

'You sound just the same, Kate. It's so good to hear your voice, so good.'

My heart was thumping in my chest.

'I miss your voice, Kate. I miss you.' A breath. 'Are you there, Kate? It's me, it's Gabriel.'

The voice of the man I loved. He was crying. French words more like weeping French breath.

'I don't know what happen, Kate. I don't know what happen.' A breath. 'Why aren't you here? Why did you leave me? I miss you.' A whisper. 'I miss you.'

Silence. I'm holding my breath. Eyes wide open. The darkness of the room.

'She's pregnant, Kate.'

I felt the words puncture.

'She's pregnant.' A breath. 'She wants to keep it.'

More silence.

'I don't know what to do, Kate. I miss you. I miss you, Kate. I don't know why you are not here.' Silence. 'She is here. I have to go.'

The phone line goes dead. As does a piece of my heart. And I tumble helplessly back to the place I'd existed before the kiss of Julien.

Back to the reality of my life without Gabriel.

some things are better on ice

'My relationship just ended. I can't imagine ever meeting anyone else, or even wanting to. But I have always wanted to have kids. This is already such a painful time. My ex-boyfriend was my best friend in the whole world. I have lost him and possibly I have lost the chance of having a family. It is a second heartbreak on a gigantic scale.' **(Milene, 33)**

'I didn't plan it this way. My relationship ended after 11 years when we were both 35. He has since gone on to meet someone else and have kids but my time had passed. I am now unable to have children. Nature doesn't wait until we find that we are ready.' **(Anon, 48)**

'Having children was always something I just assumed I'd do. I've enjoyed every part of my life to date; the travelling, my work, my friends. But I can't say I ever found The One. So I feel like I've been left with a number of really unappealing options, like deciding to get pregnant

now, alone, or letting myself get pregnant in the wrong
relationship, of which there have been many, or never
getting pregnant at all.' (Aggie, 37)

harley street | london

Dong.

As with so many things in life, the moment you think you can't have something it's all you can bloody well think about.

Dong.

The morning after the midnight call from Gabriel I flew straight back to London on a mission. I had one thing and one thing only on my mind.

Dong.

I knew I couldn't let the end of my last relationship, or rather the timing of that end, remove any chance I had of having children. I might not be ready now, maybe not for years, but love (or the misplaced love I felt for another) wasn't going to steal away something I might want for my future.

Dong.

So as my biological clock made a colossal DONG I decided to create space in the future for the *possibility* of starting a family. Actually I wasn't going to create space in the future, I was going to create space in a deep freeze so that the family I hoped to have one day could live in frozen safety until the time was right for release. It seemed to draw parallels with the plight of *Han Solo* in *Return of the Jedi* when he was put indefinitely on ice by the giant glow worm that was Jabba the Hutt. I hoped for the sake of my future children that their defrost didn't coincide with an inter-galactic war or result in estranged siblings with an unnatural level of attraction for one another...

the office of dr patel | harley street

I'd made an appointment with a world-renowned fertility and embryology specialist called Dr Patel. On meeting him I realised Dr Patel had exchanged his sense of humour and dress sense for intelligence. Brilliantly bright, to the point of communicating like an android, he dressed in a variety of different shades of brown, as if colour or pattern may somehow distract his patients from his mind.

'The process is long, Miss Winters,' he said after welcoming me into his office. 'The process is expensive.' He signalled for me to sit in a brown plastic chair. 'There is preparation. There is harvesting. There is storage. There is thawing.' He listed them on his fingers. I did the same. 'And there are no guarantees of success.' I looked around the room at all his certificates. It looked to me as if he'd been very successful indeed. 'First we would need to take some blood to assess your current fertility levels. The higher the result, the more eggs you have left.' I winced at the thought that my egg supply was running dry and there was no supermarket on earth that could supply me with more. I was like a drought-affected river in Africa, the animals wanting to drink from me and there being nothing bloody left. I clutched the edge of Mr Patel's desk for support. I felt the imprint of a thousand different women's hands placed there before me. Dr Patel poured me a glass of water and told me

to relax. Dr Patel had lots of water. He was like a fountain
of hope but in brown.

'Subject to you being a suitable candidate,' he continued,
'there would then be various different stages culminating in
collection of your eggs, which is called harvesting.'

'Mr Patel,' I whispered, 'I've never had any kind of surgery in my life. And I've certainly never been harvested,
to my knowledge.'

'Oh, you do not need a surgery for the harvesting. You
will be lightly sedated while a fine needle is inserted into
your vagina and up into your ovaries.'

'Oh, God.' I felt as if I was slipping closer to the floor. A
needle up my vagina! I'd need more than sedation. They'd
need to chain me down and lobotomise me, if that's even
a word.

'The successfully harvested eggs would then be stored
for up to ten years in liquid nitrogen.'

'Like *Han Solo* in *Star Wars*?'

'Is she a patient at this clinic?' he asked, typing her name
into his computer until he saw me gently shaking my head.
'The eggs would then be thawed when you decide you want
a baby. We inject them with sperm, insert them into your
uterus and then, if successful, you'd be pregnant.'

'Wow. I'd be pregnant.'

'If successful.'

'Well, how successful is it? How many women have had
babies this way?'

'200. Worldwide.'

'200? Worldwide? Only 200 babies worldwide! It doesn't
seem like an awful lot, Mr Patel.'

'It's Dr Patel, Miss Winters, Dr Patel, and 200 is more than zero, is it not?'

'And presumably the younger I am when I freeze my eggs—'

'Time is not your friend, Miss Winters. Time is not your friend.' Bastard.

'Well, is there another way?'

'No.' Great. 'But a more successful process is freezing an embryo. Embryos can better withstand the thawing process and there have been huge successes with babies going full term.'

'You mean extract my eggs and fertilize them with someone's sperm. Make an actual embryo and freeze that? And who would I make an embryo with? Because I don't mean to insult your intelligence, Mr Patel, but if I already had someone to make a baby with I don't think we'd be having this chat.'

'Is there someone platonic in your life that you would be happy to create a child with? Healthy family tree, good level of intelligence, good skin, teeth and so on; someone unlikely to marry and have children of their own. If not we can recommend a donor but the laws are changing regarding anonymity and children are seeking out their donor parents. It can be distressing for them later on. Have a think, Miss Winters. You don't have to be romantically involved with this person. Just someone who you have a good stable relationship with, perhaps someone who doesn't want a child per se but would support you wanting one.' He looked at the brown wooden clock on the brown wooden wall in the brown-coloured room. His office was in the autumn of its life, like my ovaries. 'I think we have gone as far as we can today. So please, read all the literature, take your time and if you have any questions call the clinic.' He handed me a pink leaflet with the words 'IVF is for us!' blazoned across the front and a really happy couple high-fiving. 'Let me show you to the door, Miss Winters,' he said, standing up from his brown chair and walking out through brown corridors to the brown front door. He opened it onto a noisy, rainy Harley Street, a stark contrast to my thoughts of eggs, sperm, fertilization and lone parenting.

'Thank you, Mr Patel,' I said, shaking his hand and stepping out into the rain. I was about to walk off when I remembered something. I turned and stopped him from closing the door.

'Is there something else I can help you with, Miss Winters?'

'It's a bit awkward, Mr Patel, but would you mind if I just gave you a quick kiss, on the lips? I can't leave until I do. It's for my grandma.'

'Very well, Miss Winters, but please remember, it's Dr Patel, not Mr.'

I leant in and gave him the briefest, quickest, barely lip-touching kiss on the lips.

'Are we done now, Miss Winters?'

'Yes, I believe we are. Thank you.'

Mr Patel closed the door and I stood on the steps rummaging in my handbag for my umbrella. On opening it I remembered why the last time I'd used it I'd made a diary note to buy a new one. Only two of the prongs still extended out fully with less than 50% of the umbrella's rain-resistant material still attached. It left one strip of possible rain protection that would have been insufficient for a single piece of pre-cooked spaghetti. Resigned to the fact that I would be soaking by the time I got home, I turned to walk to the tube only to find Peter Parker standing on the other side of the road. Force of habit led me to wave enthusiastically until I noticed he was glaring at me and looked for a moment as if he was going to walk off. Instead he sighed heavily, checked for traffic, then strode across the street towards me, towering above me with an enormous and structurally sound umbrella. He exchanged his umbrella for my umbrella equivalent of a shanty town. A large drop of rain immediately plonked on his nose. He didn't flinch.

'So,' he said in what was his most flat and irritated voice yet. 'Your grandma tells me that not only do you battle the evil and conspiratorial forces of love, but now you kiss everyone who stands in your way. I assume I just witnessed another example of your kissing crusade, or have I just interrupted you on a date?'

'No, it wasn't a date, Peter, it was a… You know what, it doesn't matter what it was. And Grandma wanted me to kiss people because she thought it might help me move on from Gabriel, something to do with frogs and beating the odds and making him one of a number. And it makes her and the girls at Pepperpots happy so it's the least I can do really, bring a little joy.'

'Ah, yes, I've seen photos of the joy you brought in France.'

How was it possible he already knew about Julien the heterosexual love God?

'What is your problem, Peter? I didn't particularly want to kiss most of these people.'

'Most of them?' He raised his eyebrows. 'And yet you do it anyway. You do as you please without concern for the consequences.'

'I am constantly concerned about the consequences of my life choices actually, and the kissing seemed to be in the spirit of things, me doing things I wouldn't normally do, pushing myself out of my comfort zone, seeing as I'm asking everyone else to do the same.'

'Maybe things worked better when they were left alone. Did you ever think of that? Maybe things were just fine and functional and made sense before this stupid idea and all the ridiculous and irrational decisions people made as a result of it!'

'What?'

'I read your article, in *True Love*, about you and Gabriel.'

'Oh…' I'd totally forgotten about that.

'About how you compromised yourself and—'

'Peter, that was a *massively* exaggerated version of the truth—' by about 1% '—and actually I didn't even write it, Chad's assistant did, Loosie. I know it's a bit confusing how we all seem to write under each other's names but Chad always seems to come up with some compelling reason why it makes sense. In fact the only person who writes under her own name is Jenny Sullivan, although she seems to put her name on an awful lot of my work these days, like the Delaware interview, for starters, and—'

'Kate, I can't believe you had all these people in your

life, all working hard to make sure you remained happy and safe, and you just threw it all away with Gabriel, losing yourself in some relationship. And you go from one extreme to the other. First you throw everything away, now you're reclaiming everything; flipping between two extremes isn't progressive, Kate; kissing bloody ski instructors isn't progressive.'

'So what if I kissed Julien?'

'I don't like it, Kate!' he shouted, before looking a little startled. Then he turned on his heel and marched off down the street, chucking my shanty umbrella in the first bin he passed.

'What is your problem, Peter?' I screamed down the street after him. I'll be honest with you, it was a bit like a scene from a trashy soap opera, and strangely liberating, until I noticed Mr Patel staring angrily out of his office window. He was jabbering into his phone, probably calling the cops, reporting me for disturbing the peace.

'What are you looking at?' I yelled up at him, like a thug, totally forgetting myself and my social graces. 'Sorry, Mr Patel,' I wailed up. 'I'm so sorry!' My voice was wobbly, my personality shifts like watching the therapy tapes of a schizophrenic. Peter was right: I catapulted between extremes. 'I don't know what's come over me, Mr Patel.'

'It's Dr Patel!' he yelled back down. '*Dr* Patel!'

'It's my hormones, Mr Patel. I think it's my hormones.' People on the street started stopping to watch. Mr Patel snapped his office blinds shut.

'Damn!' I yelled, dramatically lightly kicking the iron

railings, punching the air, knowing that's what Tom Cruise[11] would have done. 'DAMN!!' I yelled again, picking up my bags and my structurally sound umbrella and making my way back to the tube. 'Show's over, people,' I said to by-standers as I passed them. 'There's nothing to see, folks. There's nothing to see.'

And there really wasn't anything to see, except a slightly deranged woman arguing with a so-called friend while deal-ing with imminent infertility. I swore that day that if Peter Parker had just ruined my only chance of getting Mr Patel to harvest me he would bloody well have to impregnate me himself.

---

[11]I have an obsession with **Tom Cruise** and his attitude to life. He is passionate about everything he does, enthusiastic, dedicated, com-mitted. If you asked Tom Cruise to wash up dirty dishes, he'd wash them up so hard those plates would gleam. If he gets angry, he's like a raging bull. Tom Cruise commits to everything 110% and I aspire to be more like that. So when questioning my own attitude to life or when facing its hurdles, obstacles, the odd broken heart, I ask my-self the following: 'What would Tom Cruise do?' then I try to embody the spirit of Tom. More often than not life starts to feel pretty damn good. Try it. Say it. 'What would Tom do?' Feels good, doesn't it? I love you, Tom! I actually love you!

'we forge the chains we wear in life'
(charles dickens)

Finally it was time for Beatrice's Love-Stolen Dream. A trip to New York had been arranged by *True Love* and Loosie had been responsible for organising every detail. She had liaised with the Head of Student Care (Huck Snuffleupagus) and the Principal of Juilliard (Herbert Birdsfoot) both of whom were delighted to welcome Beatrice to the school, neither of whom were offspring of *Sesame Street* characters.

Beatrice had been invited to stay for three days and had been given carte blanche to attend any lectures and classes she wanted. So we flew out on the last New-York-bound flight from Heathrow late one Sunday night, Beatrice quickly falling asleep after take-off. As I watched her sleep, in a way that does not resemble a stalker, I wondered what her life would have been like if she had made this flight all those years ago. Then I wondered if she would have flown or taken a boat. Which made me wonder about the history of the commercial jet plane, which consumed my thoughts for the next five and a half hours. Before I'd even managed to watch the new *James Bond* or *Twilight: Breaking Dawn—Part 2* we had landed at JKF and a car had whisked us across town to the Juilliard School of Music.

'Super great to meet you both,' said Head of Student Care Huck. 'We are honoured to welcome international guests to our school, especially fellow musicians. Beatrice, we have a great programme lined up for you this week. We even managed to get our hands on your original application to the school. Super great choices of music. And some tough ones! I hope we get to hear those magic fingers play this week! Kate, do you play?' He pursed his lips so tight they went white.

'An instrument? No, no, not really. I used to play the recorder at junior school although I never passed any proper exams, and Peter Parker to this day says that I gave him tinnitus, which I don't think you can actually catch or be given by an untalented recorder-playing friend. He has a dry sense of humour.' I chuckled, to myself. 'Well, he did have—he seems to be harbouring a lot of repressed anger of recent weeks, and hidden homosexuality, but I'm pretty nifty on a set of bongos. I've been told that *a lot*; bongos or a tambourine, any kind of percussion instrument actually, but that is normally when I've had Red Bull and, er, well, something else that goes with Red Bull that is associated with fun and parties. Alcohol. When I am a bit pissed I have rhythm…apparently…' At this point I knew I should *never* have started talking and Huck's right eyebrow was raised so far up his forehead I was concerned it would ping off and attach itself to Beatrice's face, forming a small Hitler moustache. 'That's probably not what you meant when you asked if I play an instrument. No, I do not play any instruments, at all. I am not musical. I am *not* a musician.' Phew.

'Well, don't let us keep you,' he sneered at me. 'Us musicians have a lot to achieve in the next few days. You can see Beatrice in the evenings after class, except for Monday and Tuesday evenings when the college prefers that students eat together. And tonight we have arranged a welcome dinner. So we don't really need to see you until Wednesday night, after 9 p.m. if possible, although our Wednesday-night concert recital ends at 10 p.m. so you could just pick her up on your way to the airport.' Huck then marched Beatrice off to music camp leaving me with three clear days to please myself in my second-favourite city in the whole wide world.

madame butterfly does happiness

One of the non-redtop newspapers that feels very much like a redtop, or a women's magazine, but is blacktop and serious-looking, recently published an article entitled *'Giving In to Temptation'*. It claimed that resisting treats is bad for us and self-regulation makes us feel dissatisfied. In fact resisting temptation all the time can actually make us feel angry. If on the other hand people give themselves a little bit of what they fancy from time to time it can help people connect with themselves and build self-esteem. On researching the article further I found that the professor in happiness quoted in the article, Madame Butterfly, actually lived in New York so I arranged to meet her.

It's not that I'd been feeling blue of late, I hadn't, but I hadn't been feeling pink either, or yellow, or whatever the colour is that happy people feel. In general I'd been feeling grey, grey to black, or whatever colour represents a general feeling of numbness and apathy. Work was keeping me occupied, blocking out thoughts of Gabriel and his imminent fatherhood, and distracting me from the oddities of Peter

Parker, but outside work, when I let myself stop for a few minutes each day, that time didn't feel so great, and like Pavlov's dog I'd come to recognise that non-work time felt rubbish, so now I rarely stopped.

greenwich village | new york

Madame Butterfly's office was in a vacant school in Greenwich Village. Children's paintings still covered the walls as I walked down a long corridor to meet her. There were colourful butterflies made of glitter, crayon suns popping out from painted mountains, stickmen families, stick pets, stick Christmases with colourful stick presents made of gold. The stick people were happy with smiles bigger than their stick heads and they all seemed to be living in the stick mountains. Madame Butterfly's waiting room was at the end of this painted corridor of happiness, a square room with a small table in the middle, chairs around the periphery and a high shelf that ran all around the room. The shelf was covered in small stuffed animals, mostly birds, a few mice, a squirrel and one toad. This was where taxidermy animals came to retire. All the glass eyes were on me, me and my greyness.

Madame Butterfly opened her door and the wind chimes that were attached made noise as she wafted into the room, all floating scarves, a floor-length shapeless dress. She smiled in a vague way that made her look as if she was smiling at the whole waiting room, including all the animals, who, on closer inspection, had the same wide-eyed look.

'It's so great you are here,' she said, to all of us.

After a cursory introduction about who we both were,

and a toilet break for me because I felt strangely nervous, she asked the most simple and yet most difficult question I'd been asked in a long time.

'So, are you happy, Kate?'

'I, er, well, things are moving in the right direction. I am definitely ticking boxes. I have a good job and I work very hard and—'

'Do you feel happy, Kate?'

'As I said, I think I have made some good decisions for myself recently, tough decisions, but adult ones, that I will reap the benefits of at a later stage.'

'OK, but can you tell me how you feel?'

Like I am freefalling out of control into an abyss of nothingness.

'I don't know how I feel.'

'When was the last time you felt 100% joyfully happy?' An image of Gabriel's smiling face flashed into my head, followed by an image of him holding a baby. I tried to squeeze them back out.

'I don't remember.'

'Well, let's tackle this a different way. When did you last cry?'

'I haven't cried for weeks actually, which is strange, come to think of it, as I was a bit of a crier before that. Crying is not the issue. My eyes cry whenever they feel like it, never when I feel like it, and for as long as they bloody well please. They are selfish and self-obsessed, like my ex—' I chuckled, then sighed, like a deflating balloon.

'Tell me what was happening in your life a few weeks ago around the time that you stopped crying.'

'I er, well, I had sex with a hot Frenchman—that was nice. I went skiing, also nice. I took two flights in a 36-hour period, although I don't think that affects tear ducts. Oh, and my ex called me, in the middle of the night, to tell me his new girlfriend was pregnant. As I said, I was a bit of a crier before that week. I cry at most episodes of *Buffy the Vampire Slayer* and even some of the more emotive mobile phone adverts used to set me off.'

'*Buffy the Vampire Slayer* is an emotional and dramatic children's television drama series,' she said defensively. She took a sip of water. 'So how do you feel now?'

'Today? Today I don't really feel anything, just numb. Not unhappy, not sad, just nothing. Not hopeless, not hopeful, maybe more hopeless than hopeful. And numb. I feel numb. And I don't think that's entirely normal. I am grey. Grey to black.'

'It's more normal than you realise. The way modern society is structured is not complementary to how we are structured emotionally. For the larger part of our existence on earth we have been in communities with extended families close at hand, three generations living together, purposeful roles, hunting, growing, procreating, nurturing. In the last few centuries the modern world has brought greater incidences of alienation; people living alone, far from family, far from friends, maybe in different countries, alienated, transient, disconnected. Feelings get stuck inside us. They don't find full expression. They are not heard. Eventually they grow tired of waiting, and we become numb.'

'Is it reversible?'

'Of course it is. But we can't change the structure of society so it's important we find other means of expressing ourselves and letting our emotions out. An obvious one is through diaries or even writing letters to oneself. Writing allows people to connect with how they are feeling and make sense of what they are experiencing, which explains the explosion of blogging and tweeting; social media is a way of connecting, reaching out where an extended family and local community would have been years ago. Although I believe it is counterproductive, sitting alone writing, so I recommend more colourful fun things, things you don't even realise are helping you feel better. A passive road to happiness.'

'Well, I am only here for a few days so I won't be able to join a programme or a class but is there something I could try—a small thing, that might take away the grey?'

'Of course, that's very easy, Kate. The next time you have a flicker of desire, take notice of it. Start to really listen to what your body and emotions are telling you. If you want something, go get it. You might be walking past a deli and see the most delicious-looking chocolate cake, or see an item of clothing that makes your pulse race. Or maybe you have an urge to do something slightly reckless, like kiss a stranger in an elevator. Whatever it is, rather than dismiss it and carry on with your day—which is what most of us do most of the time—get in the habit of listening to it. Stop. Take notice of that feeling. And *go with it*. Buy that choco- late cake, or that handbag, or that pair of shoes. Kiss that stranger. Connect with your spontaneous impulsive and truthful feelings. That will begin the process of you feeling more connected to yourself and feeling positive emotions, and it should start to make your life feel more colourful.'

'That's it. You're telling me to shop freely, eat badly, kiss randomly and feel good about it.'

'No, that is excess. That is consumerism. That is promiscuity. I am asking you to pay attention to *how you feel*. When you have a little twinkle inside, a tingle, a flutter, notice it, and go with it. Here,' she said, handing me a small crystal butterfly and hugging me for a really long time before opening the door for me to leave. 'It's not about big gestures, grand plans or group therapy programmes—just listen to yourself a little more. One of the simplest ways to start is by buying yourself flowers; treat yourself, and take note of how that feels. Good luck, Kate.'

I walked back down the corridor, past all the butterflies, the stuffed birds, the dried flowers stuck to wallpaper, and took a taxi back to the hotel. I took myself and my crystal butterfly straight to the hotel bar. It was getting late and New York wasn't quite as much fun on my own as I thought it would be. Maybe the bar, or the contents of the bar, would give me the flutter of my butterfly that I had lost in the cocoon of my caterpillar. Or maybe I should just have a tequila that has a worm in its bottle which is a bit like a pre-butterfly worm. Tequila didn't make me flutter, but it made me tingle, which Madame Butterfly said was a good thing, so I ordered another and another and another.

my hotel room | waldorf-astoria

I woke up the next day with no idea where I was, crystal butterfly in hand. When I realised I ordered room service, it arrived, I ate, I threw up, three times, ordered more room service, it arrived, I ate, it stayed down. I kept my mobile switched off all day and watched reruns of *American Idol*. As night fell I felt as if I were finding my cocoon.

Just before 10 p.m. there was a knock at the door. I hadn't ordered room service. I opened the door wearing a food-stained bathrobe with last night's make-up on my face. He stood there immaculate, fresh faced, highly pressed. He smelt clean. I know this because I smelt stale, as did my room; it gave me away like a weak-willed hostage.

'You look terrible, Kate,' said a stern-faced Peter Parker before marching into my room. Once he was in there I could see he wished he hadn't. He looked around at the chaos; the half-eaten plates of food on every surface, the darkness broken only by the flashing of a TV, my clothes everywhere, underwear everywhere, the mess of me. The corners of his mouth were turned down, as if the entire scene left a bad taste in his mouth; smell in his nose; twitch on his face.

'Kate, you have two options. You can get in the shower, get dressed and meet me down in the hotel bar in 30 minutes or we can meet tomorrow for a 10km run around Central Park.'

'I'll see you in the bar.'

'I thought so.' He marched out.

sir harry's bar | waldorf-astoria

Peter Parker picked the quietest table in the bar, in the furthest corner, by a window, and a very very large potted plant. There were two seats, both very low to the ground, and a low-standing checkerboard table with two glasses of water on it. Peter looked gigantic on the small chair, incongruous and expensive in comparison to me, who had an air of *'all inclusive holiday excess'* about me, fitting in perfectly with the cocktail-swigging crowd. The bar staff eyeballed me suspiciously as I walked in.

'I didn't recognise you with normal skin tone,' I said, sitting myself down only to be engulfed by the overhanging leaves of the large potted plant. 'These days you always tend to have a moody red face. It suited you.' I said this through the shrubbery that was draped all around me. 'And prolific sweating on a regular basis is a great way to expel toxins. It's the basic premise behind saunas.' I was snappish, blunt and defensive, like a hammerhead shark. I was annoyed that he was here. Why bother flying all the way across the Atlantic to judge me in a hung-over state? He could do that every Saturday in London. It was as if my mother had hired him to act as my critical parent in her constant absence. Peter pushed a glass of water towards me and pulled some of the branches from my hair. One immediately swung back and whipped me across the cheek. So Peter pulled me, on my chair, closer to him.

'So...' he began as if reading from a meeting agenda '...first of all I would like to apologise to you.' He sat forward in his chair. He was tracing his fingers along the edge of the table, trying to formulate the best sentence. 'I have not been myself with you for some time. I have on occasion been somewhat rude.' Giant understatement. 'I know that and awareness is step one towards change as written about in... It doesn't matter what book it was in.' He took a breath. 'Kate, there is something about the work you've been doing that's been bothering me. At times I've felt that you've pulled things apart, things that previously made sense to people, rocking the boat, someone else's boat, kissing people all over the place, and I don't think I liked it—' He tapped the table with his finger as if he had finally found his point. 'I don't like it.' Another tap.

'That doesn't sound like a very accurate description of my work. There has been no rocking of boats. There has been the missing of love boats, my own boat, and the re-capturing of love-stolen dreams.' Had he been listening to *anything* I'd been telling him?

'I don't approve of you kissing people,' he blurted out rather loudly. He sat forward resting his index fingers on his lips as if trying to prevent any other noisy words escaping. And I couldn't see the relevance of the kissing. It was the smallest and most insignificant part of what I was trying to do.

'Peter, kissing Mr Patel in Harley Street wasn't exactly a high point for me and to be honest I still get flashbacks as I'm falling asleep at night. But it made Grandma and Beatrice laugh, and Delaware, she used a computer for the first time in her adult life because she wanted to do a *Google Images* search on Mr Patel, which made them laugh even more. Actually it was quite a humiliating afternoon for me at Pepperpots,' I said, remembering the moment they pinned his photo onto the map.

'I've seen the photo, Kate.' Great. 'And, Kate…'

'Yes, Peter.'

'It's Dr Patel. You should really call him Doctor.' Un-believable. 'And you seemed to like kissing Julien…'

'Peter, have you flown here to discuss kissing? Because if you have I've got a few things I'd like to say to you about strawberry-smelling Annabel and the pool party—' Oh, dear God, was I really about to mention this after 25 years? 'It was just after my birthday, Peter. How could you?' Yes, yes, I was. Peter looked confused. 'Annabel... Strawberry *ChapStick*...always carried a *Care Bear* with her...'

'Oh, Annabel! I can't believe you remember Annabel.' I couldn't believe he didn't. 'God, she was lovely. I wonder what she's doing now? Do you know her father won a Nobel Peace Prize in 1987 for his work in particle physics and its specific application to materials that are now used to irrigate land in drought-affected areas of Western Africa?'

'As if I would know that, Peter!' I couldn't believe I'd rekindled an interest in bloody Annabel strawberry lips and her stupid dad. 'Peter, why do you care who I kiss? How did you know Mr Patel is a doctor, and why are you here?' I was snappish. I was tired. I was ill. I was about to become one of those drinkers who needs alcohol to get over the night before.

'I saw your grandma a few days ago,' he said, shuffling closer. 'As always she willingly offered up private pieces of information about other people's lives.' That had *not* been my experience of Grandma recently. She'd been a padlocked vault of secrets concerning Peter Parker. 'She told me about your plans regarding your, er, fertility.' Great. 'She gave me an update on your kissing challenge.' Great. 'And she showed me the map of the world. I'd totally forgotten you had train-track braces.' Great. Great. Great. 'She also said that you'd had a call...from Gabriel.'

Hearing Gabriel's name pop unexpectedly from the mouth of Peter Parker made me wince. We both sat quietly. I mostly looked at my shoes, which were distractingly filthy.

'I wasn't sure how you'd handle the news about the pregnancy. I hoped it wouldn't cause you too much pain, which was completely unrealistic. I just, I don't like the idea that someone has the ability to make you feel sad. And I can't believe there is a man out there who had you in his life and let you go like that, who didn't treat you as you deserve. That made me feel…angry. It still does, which is an unwelcome emotion, and…' He rubbed his eyes as if he was finding the whole conversation challenging. 'Then after last night…' He nodded as if I'd understand. A cold shiver went through my body. Why did he mention last night? What happened last night? Did I see Peter Parker last night?

'Peter, how long have you been in New York?'

'About 90 minutes. I thought I should come, after last night.' There it was again. What happened last night? 'You ask very little of me, Kate, and I haven't been in your life on the many occasions when you might have needed me—' there weren't many occasions, there were maybe two, or twelve, thousand '—and you never call me in the middle of the night asking for help; well, it was the middle of your night, the start of my day, but you are normally very polite and considerate with the timing of telephone calls, although occasionally a little too generous with the making of them. But you never call too late or too early, and certainly never drunk, so that was a first too.'

Vague hazy memories coming back to me: me in my hotel room; curled up by the mini bar; box of tissues, snotty nose, pistachio-nut shells all over the floor, many *many* empty mini bottles of rum and yes, yes, I was on the phone and I was…

'And you have never ever called me before in tears.' And there it was, the door to my memory swung slowly open. I'd been a weeping drunk, a weeping, hysterical, snotty-nosed, drunk lady. 'I'm sorry, Kate, you were right on the phone last night. I have been helping everyone else but pushing you away. You are not the cause of what's going on in my head right now, any confusion I am working through. The past is the past—it doesn't matter any more—what's important is you. You are my oldest friend, Kate, and I'm referring to the passage of time when I say that, not your age, before you have a meltdown about being over thirty.' He reached over and held my hand. 'Kate, I realise that you wanted to have children with Gabriel, that he is the man you wanted to spend the rest of your life with, and I can't imagine what it must feel like to know he's doing that with someone else. So I'm here for you, if you need me. I'm here.'

He continued to hold my hand, watching me with kind eyes, waiting for me to share some piece of my broken, shattered heart. I knew he wouldn't utter another word until I told him how I was feeling, so it was sharing or it was silence, and I think we can all agree that I am not one who enjoys wordless voids…

And just for the record, I totally blame the stupid butterfly lady and her ridiculous *always connect with your desires* nonsense for the resulting tequila incident. Her advice couldn't have been less specific. It left me wide open to misinterpretation, self-sabotage and excess.

'Peter, I just, I feel like every time I start to move on—' I was thinking about the nights spent with Julien '—or I feel a glimmer of happiness, a moment of joy—' same nights '—something always comes up to chop my legs from under me. This time it's a call in the middle of the night to say he's having a baby, next time, what? He gets married? Or has twins? I know what I'm saying is childish and ridiculous. I know it's not nice to want someone else to feel a bit of pain, but as it stands I don't feel like I mattered at all, like I didn't exist. I feel utterly replaceable and insignificant, like, like I am the Insignificant Significant Other—' I stopped myself as Peter flinched at my words, remembering too late that his ex-wife described him the same way. 'I'm sorry, I didn't mean—'

'Don't apologise. This isn't about me, Kate. This is about you and how you are feeling. So, how are you feeling?'

'I feel like, like it doesn't seem fair. None of it seems fair. I was the one who had to leave our home when it ended, move countries, again, with nothing. It was me who had to start all over again. He didn't. He stayed put; same job, same house, same country, family close by, friends around him. He simply found himself another girlfriend who quite literally moved in in my place, and carried on. And I have been trying to learn my lesson. I've taken it all on board. And I am *really* trying to make sure other women don't find themselves in the same position. But what has he lost? Where is his struggle? Where is the great life lesson he's learned? That stupid search for meaning and personal growth that we all strive for after life dumps a pile of shit on our heads? Why is it that I have felt all this excruciating pain and continue to do so and him feel nothing of the sort? It doesn't seem…fair…' I trailed off, into more of a mutter, and a few tears escaped from my right eye; it's traditionally the weakest and always gives out before the left one. But the left one followed suit shortly after, tears streaming silently from my eyes (not that there is normally a musical accompaniment). I realised it was the first time I'd cried (sober) since I found out about Gabriel's baby. Peter took a tissue out of his inner pocket and dabbed my cheeks dry, allowing me to continue.

'What did he lose, Peter?' I mumbled, looking up at him, hoping somehow he knew all the answers. He took both of my hands and held them between his own. His hands were warm, palms dry, skin soft. 'Tell me, what did he lose?'

'He lost *you*, Kate. That's what Gabriel lost. He lost you.' Tears rolled out of both corners of my eyes like an overly squeezed Tiny Tears doll. 'Kate, by the sound of it Gabriel got into another relationship to distract himself, perhaps to fill a gap, the space you left, and now she is pregnant, which I doubt was planned. That is not an enviable situation to be in. It's probably quite scary. It's not something I would wish for myself, or for you or for them. And the situation probably makes him miss you even more, having a poor substitute, a poor man's Kate. I would choose to miss you every day and be alone than try to find a substitute and be stuck with that substitute for the rest of my life. I'd choose heartbreak and healing over that any day.'

We both sat silently for a few moments, holding hands, which was a bit odd.

'Kate, my ex-wife moved on very quickly after we broke up. She met someone, someone very different from me, and never looked back. And while I never doubt that ending our relationship was the right thing, her meeting someone so fast and finding happiness almost immediately, it was a bitter pill. It made me question how important I could have been to her. And I think it actually distracted me from moving on with my life, because I kept focusing on what she was doing, focusing on how she was moving on, focusing on how happy she must be, wondering what that said about me as a man and a husband if I was so replaceable. But this is the ego at work. These are the bits of our brain that we need to shut down, switch off, take control of. You need to tune that noise out. And that is what I did. And that's what you have to do. Given the choice to be with her again, I wouldn't want to. That is not the life I want for myself. And that is the only thing I need to know. And I think given the choice to be with Gabriel again you'd probably say *no* too. Do you want that kind of relationship again?' He twitched, by mere millimetres, while waiting for my response. Just a few extra blinks, a jaw clench, as if he was trying to look casual, just to reassure me how casual the question was, which made me anxious, twitchy and blinky, as if I were on a lie detector and his hand were taking my pulse. Had Grandma asked him to come here to ask that question and assess my response? Was he testing me to see if I was lying? To see if I might snap at any moment and jump on the first flight back to France to beg Gabriel to impregnate me and get married? Was he…? Hang on a minute… Was this post-alcohol paranoia? Bloody Alcohol! It is not the light-hearted social lubricant everyone thinks—damn you, Tequila!

'Kate? Given the choice, would you want to be with Gabriel again?' More facial twitching.

'No,' I said before twitching, blinking, squinting. 'No.' I was about to go for a third *no* but realised I sounded as if I was trying to convince myself. Had I convinced Peter Parker?

'Great, so just keep telling yourself that. Focus on you. Focus on what is good for you and not what someone else is doing. And if you do that you'll start to feel really good about yourself. That's exactly what I did. And I feel great.'

'Peter, how long were those demons in your head making you think you were replaceable?'

'I think about two, no, no, it was at least three days, and then I took control of the situation, and I moved on.' Ah, the simplicity of the male mind. 'Now, Kate, I think you need to get some sleep, drink lots of fluids and if you are free tomorrow maybe we could go to Beatrice's recital together, and talk more about Gabriel if you need to.' He let go of my hand and stood up from the tiny chair. 'Oh, and before I forget there are a couple of other things I wanted to clear up while I'm here—' The corners of his mouth were twitching, which was a sure sign he considered what he was about to say rather amusing. 'Kate, I'll be honest, I am not sure about being a sperm donor for you.' Oh, good God, no. 'Yes, you did ask me that last night and I am yet to get my head around offering out the fruit of my loins in that context, even to you.'

'Understood.'

'And I've arranged a meeting for you at Westminster with the Education Secretary. It's only a ten-minute chat but that's enough time for you to tell him a bit about your Love-Stolen Dreams drop-in centres. He'll let you know if he can take it any further. There is one tiny condition. They asked, no, they insisted that Jenny Sullivan be there. Don't say anything. You will take up the offer and say thank you.'

'Thank you.'

'And something else that feels fairly important to mention at this juncture—' there was a glint in his eye '—although I am slightly perplexed by the confusion surrounding this, but, I am not, and I never will be, gay.'

'Oh?' The word just popped out. I was confused. How could he *not* be gay? In my mind he was shacked up with a bloody great wrestler called Stu.

'You were terribly sad about it on the phone, although you did say the sperm donation would make up for it.' Drunk bartering, excellent. 'Yes, you were very *very* sad about my homosexuality. If I didn't know any better I'd think you had a little crush on me.' I flushed *luminous* red. 'I'm kidding!' he said, gently squeezing my shoulder. 'I'm just kidding—it was a joke. So I'll see you tomorrow?' He gave me a quick kiss on the cheek before turning to leave, walking in what felt like slow motion from the room, walking as if there were a spotlight on him, a 1950s movie star. And there was definitely a spotlight on me too, a spotlight of judgement from the staring bar staff and a maître d', who shook his head every time he looked in my direction. This must have been where I'd been drinking the night before. Wonderful…

I took myself back upstairs to my room, processing the evening's events. Peter Parker wasn't gay. How odd. How unexpected. How confusing. Once again I could feel my universe shift slightly on its axis.

That night I went to bed feeling different, feeling a kind of sepia colour, which is not yellow per se, and it's not white, but it's definitely not black and it certainly isn't grey.

an interval

Dear True Love,

Hi, it's Annie-pants. I wanted to let you know that I went on the basic clothes design course and it was brilliant. I admit the first few weeks I was nervous. I kept getting a last-minute urge to cancel, finding excuses to work late, or go to the gym, or do my laundry—anything to avoid going, which was odd, but I stuck with it and I love it. And I have also been attending a few lectures at London College of Fashion. In fact lots of the universities have free or really cheap one-off workshops that I can just drop in to. Last Sunday I went to a lecture about the history of hat making, which as I write it seems a bit dull but I can assure you it was very interesting.

My boyfriend (the one who hasn't proposed) started to feel like a bit of a lame duck sitting at home by himself on Thursday nights so he finally agreed to join his office football team. At first he was pooh-poohing it, saying,

'It's only bloody five-a-side. I don't know why they all care so much. They go on about it all the time at work. I hate

it. I can't even get up to make a cup of coffee without some-one wanting to talk to me about tackles and whether or not I think the goalkeeper Glen should be dropped, which, by the way, I do. It's like the man has actually oiled his hands.'

But then in the next match, he scored the winning goal. Now he can't stop talking about office five-a-side football and came home with a Man of the Match trophy last week.

The best bit is that the football has got rid of his love handles (an actual miracle). Plus he has so much more en-ergy than before and he's so much more up for...sex! Who'd have thought him running around with a bunch of middle-aged men once a week would have such an impact on our sex life? Actually, I don't want to overthink that...

And, Federico, just so you know, my boyfriend, the one who hasn't proposed, he started taking much more notice of me. Initially he was grumpy that I was so interested in something other than him. Then he went a bit quiet. Next thing I know he asked me to keep a weekend free and took me to Paris for Fashion Week. On the last night he pro-posed! This whole experience has been amazing for both of us. Such a small change has made such a big difference.

Thanks, True Love!

Annie Pants x

central park | new york

'Give me my Romeo, and, when he shall die,
Take him and cut him out in little stars,
And he will make the face of heaven so fine
That all the world will be in love with night,
And pay no worship to the garish sun'
(William Shakespeare, *Romeo and Juliet*)

'But, soft! what light through yonder window breaks? It is the east, and Juliet is the sun.'

Peter had taken me to watch *Romeo and Juliet* at an out-door theatre in Central Park. Hundreds of people were sitting on picnic blankets under the stars, drinking wine and watching the story of the famous star-crossed lovers.

'That's how I always thought love was supposed to be,' I said as the final scene began to play out, an ill-timed awakening followed by an ill-timed death.

'You thought love was supposed to be suicidal? You're very dramatic, Kitkat.'

'No, I thought it was supposed to be two people, drawn

together, in spite of their differences, in spite of life's obstacles, stronger together than the sum of their single parts.'

'Love like that is dangerous, Kate. *Romeo and Juliet* is about two people not wanting to live in the absence of the other. It's weak.'

'You're oversimplifying, Peter.'

'Am I? So what do you think love is now? You said you used to think it was like that.'

'Now I don't think I think about it. Or if I do it's more in the context of Samson and Delilah, love leading to the loss of power, strength and the essence of oneself.'

'That sounds more realistic.'

'It sounds pessimistic. I think I wanted love to be more extraordinary than that, or at least I hoped it would be.'

We were sitting on a blanket and Peter had brought red wine and popcorn. People were dotted all about the dark park doing the same thing, the theatre taking place in the middle.

'So what about you, Peter? What do you think about love?'

'How serious were you about the egg freezing?' he said, trying to catch popcorn in his mouth. His subject changing was getting tedious.

'Well, I would like to give myself the option of having children later on. But there is a certain amount of genetic testing involved, to see if I am carrying any hereditary diseases or abnormalities. I'm not sure how I feel about that.' On the stage Juliet was waking, about to find Romeo dead by her side. 'Did you ever have any tests done to make sure you don't have the same heart condition as your mum? Sorry,

I don't actually know her exact cause of death. Grandma just said she had a weak heart.'

Peter didn't answer and carried on throwing popcorn in his mouth.

'Peter, why did you never get in touch with me after you left England? You wrote to Grandma. And I get it, she's important to you, and she's always seen herself as a sort of surrogate mother to you. I just don't see how hard it would have been to have dropped me a line, or passed a message on through her.'

'O happy dagger! This is thy sheath...' Juliet was taking her own life on the stage, death preferable to a lifetime without her love. *'There rust, and let me die.'*

'I do want to explain certain things about my past, Kate,' he said, sounding very much as if he didn't. 'I just don't really know where to start, or where to end, and to be honest I'd rather just forget it ever happened and start afresh from today.'

'So does that mean you're going to tell me or you're not? We could go back to speaking about my fertility if you like?' Men hate talking about ovaries and menstrual cycles.

'OK, then.' He nodded, shifting in the darkness to face me. 'My mum didn't die of a weak heart. She found out my father was having an affair and she killed herself.'

The stage went dark and the audience started applauding.

This went on for several painful minutes.

'Peter, that doesn't make any sense. Your mum always seemed so happy.'

'She was happy,' he said, flicking pieces of popcorn off the blanket, 'when she was with my dad. Her universe orbed around him. He was her Sun.' He poured us both more wine, then lay back on the blanket, pulling me with him. I turned my head to watch him as he spoke. 'Kate, do you remember when I came to stay with you and Grandma for about three weeks? We were about six. You were still wetting the bed quite a lot.' He always manages to mention at least one humiliating childhood fact when I see him. 'Well, I was only supposed to stay for the weekend. My father had been called to an urgent business meeting in Rome and he had to leave straight away. Mum was supposed to pack his things and have everything shipped over. But last minute she decided she wanted to surprise him, so she booked a flight and took everything herself.'

'I wasn't wetting the bed *all* the time.'

'Kate, your bed was like a water park,' he said, patting my hand, 'and please don't make this about you.'

'Sorry.'

'When Mum arrived in Rome she found my dad with another woman.' He turned on his side, resting his head on his hand. 'Apparently the affair had been going on for a while. It was a serious *relationship*—' he struggled over the word '—and my father had already planned to leave my mum. Well, there's no universe without its Sun and the depression engulfed her. She didn't want to fight it. She didn't try to. My mum didn't want a life without my father so that is exactly what she chose.'

He lay back down on the blanket, staring up at the stars. I reached over and held his hand.

'They say she didn't suffer, which I suppose is a good thing. It would have been just like falling asleep. Of course,

I didn't know any of this. Dad told me she suffered a weak heart and that it had finally given out on her, which in a way is true. It was only when we were selling the house years later that I found some letters from Mum to Dad, some paperwork regarding the divorce proceedings, and some letters sent to my dad from the other woman.' He took his hand away from mine.

'And this happened when?'

'I found this out just before your 15th birthday.'

'Why didn't you tell me?'

'I didn't want to talk about it, Kate. I didn't want to feel the things I was feeling. I didn't want to explain them to you. I planned to run away. But your grandma found me packing—'

'How does she do that? Always turning up at the right moment?'

'Or the wrong moment. Anyway, she knew I wouldn't change my mind about leaving and your grandma is not one to waste her breath, but she wanted me to finish my education, to give myself the best chance to create a good life for myself. She didn't want me to be beholden to anyone ever again. **"Freedom is choice,"** she said to me that day, and I wanted both. So I agreed to let her help me if she promised not to tell anyone where I was going. She knew if she broke her promise I would have just run away. It was a horrible position for me to put her in, I know that, but I was only thinking about myself. Within 24 hours I was in a new school in Switzerland.' He sat up and took a sip of his wine. I was still struggling to put together the pieces of his puzzle. 'I did want to see you, Kate. I did miss you. But you are so connected to my past. I wouldn't have been able to see you without thinking about ***her***.' For the first time since he'd started speaking I felt an actual emotion expressed from Peter Parker, and it was anger. 'Why would anyone give up everything they had because of love?' he said, turning to face me. 'How could anyone be so weak? Punch my dad, yes. Divorce him for everything he's got, maybe. But lie down and choose to die? Because of love? Who does that? Seriously, Kate, what kind of person does that?' He shuddered as the temperature in the park started dropping.

'I'm *so* sorry about your mum, Peter.'

'So am I, Kate, but it was her choice, not mine, and I really *really* want to leave it in the past. It's exhausting carrying this around with me all the time. It's exhausting lying to you—lying on any level is an emotional drain.'

'I can't imagine living like that, Peter,' I said, rubbing my arms to keep warm.

'So Kate Winters has never lied to someone close to her?' he said, taking his jacket off and wrapping me up in it.

'No, Peter, I haven't. In fact the only time I haven't been totally forthcoming with the truth was when things were falling apart with Gabriel, and then I think I didn't tell anyone because I wanted to protect *them*, not because I was protecting myself.'

'I just want things to go back to how they were when we were kids, Kate. Do you think that's even possible? Our lives were so simple then.' I looked into his blue eyes. How could we ever be again who we were when we were children?

'So that's it, Peter? No more secrets?'

'I promise you, Kate,' he said, taking my hand, 'I'm only

ever interested in your well-being.' He leant over and kissed me gently on the cheek. For some strange reason I suddenly felt the urge to kiss him back so, remembering the words of Madame Butterfly, I quickly pecked his cheek, like a little bird looking for worms. Then I felt *really* silly.

'Kate, I'm sorry but do you mind if I gave the recital a miss? I have a splitting headache and I think I need to rest. I'll get the car to take you but I'm afraid I need to leave.' He kissed me on the cheek, this time closer to the edge of my mouth. 'I'm sorry,' he said as he got up, slowly wandering off into the darkness of Central Park.

the juilliard school

The auditorium at the Juilliard School was as impressive as any West End theatre. There were plush red seats sprawling up through the stalls to a dress circle. There was an elaborately decorated gold domed ceiling and the stage was enormous, framed by a thick red velvet curtain. The recital was a mixture of music and song and Beatrice was the third artist to play. Huck gave an introduction and spoke as if he were doing vocal scales, going all the way up and then coming all the way back down. It was slightly hypnotic and sleep-inducing.

'Our aspirations sometimes give way to our obligations,' Huck began. 'What we want to do gives way to what we feel we *should* do. Our expectations for life start out sky high but a rejection, a missed opportunity, a lack of encouragement all have the same effect—we make our dreams a little smaller. Most of us sitting in this room have already begun this process. Someone who came here wanting to be the lead composer for Disney now thinks they'd happily accept a part-time role with Paramount. A violinist aiming for the New York symphony thinks that Boston would do just as good. We are all chipping away at our dreams. And tonight we have a guest who knows this firsthand. She gained a place at Juilliard before the Second World War. But obligation stepped in, a duty to marry, to do the right thing in the eyes of her family and society. Then doubt crept in because what are the chances of her being good enough to be a concert pianist? And just like that she let go of her dream and the ceiling of her ambition was lowered. But she did not give up altogether. Tonight she is going to grab hold of that dream to play here, just as she wanted to over 50 years ago, and for that we are thankful. So the theme of tonight is simply this: to take a break from giving up on our hopes for the future. We must occasionally allow ourselves the opportunity to dream. So without further ado may I introduce you all to Beatrice Van de Broeck, the dreamer who got away. Beatrice Van de Broeck!'

Huck walked off to the wing. To rapturous applause he led a slow-moving Beatrice onto the stage and towards a grand piano at the centre of it. She sat down and the auditorium fell silent. There was a long uncomfortable wait for her to begin. She placed her hands on the keys. I held my breath. She played a chord. It sounded flat. She stopped and withdrew her hands as if the keys had stung her. I was sitting up in the dress circle but I could see her hands shaking. No one knew what to do. I heard people shuffling in the stalls. Beatrice looked out into the audience and squinted against the bright lights. It was horrific. A ninety-year-old lady sitting alone on a stage, too scared to play a note. I wanted to run down there and sweep her off the stage. I was about to do just that when Huck marched on stage clapping loudly and nodding to the audience to do the same. Everyone joined in, clapping furiously. Then he sat himself down next to Beatrice. He put his arm around her and made her look out to the applauding audience. She shyly turned, blinking furiously, as if the audience were a sun. He squeezed her tightly, whispered something in her ear then played a very loud E sharp. She did the same. He played a chord. She did the same. Before I could say Beethoven they were performing the most amazing duet. At the end of it the audience burst into ear-splitting applause. He made Beatrice take three bows and then she played a solo piece. She might have been 90 but that lady's got rhythm. At the end of the evening she was asked to 'jam' with some of the percussion players and they had the whole audience up and dancing for 15 minutes. She was positively radiating by the end.

a fact – the most beautiful colour in the world is the flush of pink on Beatrice Van de Broeck's cheeks the night she performed at the Juilliard School.

After the recital Beatrice and I waited for the hall to empty then sat together on the beautiful stage taking in the space, the room, the smell, giving Beatrice's senses a moment to absorb everything she didn't get to digest all those years ago. We sat silently looking out onto the low-lit auditorium, hundreds of empty seats staring back at us. It was a comfortable silence, where no one is compelled to speak, except me, after a few short minutes...

'Beatrice, how do you think your life would have been different if you had attended Juilliard?'

She took a moment. Took a deep breath. Mulled it over.

'That is impossible to imagine, Kate. And I am starting to suspect it was not my destiny.'

'What do you mean? You were amazing tonight.'

'Had it been my destiny to be a performer, surely my life would still have contained music, even after I chose not to come here? Or at least it should have had more of a musical emphasis. But it didn't. I gave up almost immediately; as soon as the decision was made I turned my back on music. I am sure I could have found some way to study to the same level in England. But I didn't. And the choice to go without was very much mine. I was self-saboteur, active in the end of my music. It's funny but in over 60 years I have never once looked at it like that. But now I see clearly. The kids are here because they wanted it more than me. They are braver than me. What a silly woman I am to have spent my whole life thinking I was something I'm not.' Her voice started to break. 'What a silly silly woman I am.' She took a small embroidered hanky from her handbag and dabbed her eyes. We sat there, without words, without music. 'But I played here in the end though, didn't I?'

'Yes, you did, Beatrice. And you played magnificently.'

'It's time to go home, I think, Kate,' she said, tapping me affectionately on the knee before standing up and slowly walking off.

I couldn't bring myself to say much to Beatrice on the flight home, which was convenient, as she slept the whole way. So I watched her sleep, for hours, in a way that definitely resembled a stalker. What had I just done to this poor old lady? And could Beatrice's revelation of self-saboteur be applied to us all? Even when we found ourselves in circumstances we hated, had we on some level had a choice, either to accept these circumstances or a choice *not* to bring about change? Were we frightened of being more powerful? Frightened of the control we had over our own lives? Frightened of taking more responsibility? Or is it that, if we took responsibility, we would only have ourselves to blame if things went wrong?

As soon as we landed I did something I had never done before and I put in a call to Chad. I wasn't sure how to write up Beatrice's visit to New York because what if *self-sabotage* was the real cause of all this loss?

'We speak about this now, we speak about this for 30 seconds, then we never twatting speak about this again, understood?' I could imagine him pacing up and down as he spoke. 'If I am sleeping with someone I already know it's not going anywhere, right? But I don't actually want to be the one who ends the relationship. I want them to do it. Responsibility Avoidance, get it?'

'No.'

'Look, if someone dumps me then I can be the Passive Recipient, which is a great place to be. I can be like, "What could I do? They ended it. It was their choice." But if I dump them and then I realise I've made a mistake, I'd be like, "Fuck, Chad, you can't trust your own judgement, you fucked up." I'd start to doubt myself. I don't want to doubt myself, Kate. It makes my life more twatting complicated. I'd need a shrink. So, I avoid certain types of responsibility.'

'What if you end up with someone who doesn't take responsibility either? What if they never end the relationship?' I was thinking specifically about Federico and his ability to hang on like a barnacle. 'Do you end up staying together forever?'

'Eventually they all walk away, Kate. It's a constant of life. No one will *ever* stay forever.' He cleared his throat. 'So let's get back to this old piano lady.'

'Beatrice.'

'Whatever. What if Beatrice didn't get married but then didn't make it as a pianist either? What if she married him and carried on piano in some form or other and realised after a couple of years she really wasn't that good anyway? She'd have misjudged herself, her talent, she'd have to admit that she was fooling herself about being a concert pianist. And as a result her life might start to feel a bit twatting meaningless. She'd be all like, "Who the fuck am I? Why the fuck am I here? I'm not good at anything. What does it all fucking mean?" You see? We all need to look for meaning, Kate. We all need to define ourselves by something else. Just like you currently define yourself by being all heartbroken and Love-Stolen Dreams. That is your choice. So if you don't take responsibility in a way you are taking responsibility by pretending not to have much control. Get it?'

I wasn't sure.

'No one wants to take responsibility, Kate. We do, up to

a point, up to deciding what job to have, who to shag, how much debt to put on our credit cards, visiting your nan once a year to make sure she keeps you on her will. But anything outside that, no thanks, missus. Only the Martin Luther Kings of this world want to test themselves and the might of their own power. No one else would want to come up with a revolutionary idea, promise change, promise a better something for fear of not delivering, for fear of it not turning out OK. Millions follow Gandhi, right? No one wants to actually be twatting Gandhi. D'ya get me?'

'Er…'

'Kate, Beatrice isn't the only one. You are also in control of all the shit that is currently out of control in your life, including the fact that I have a certain amount of control over your career development, speaking of which, I expect the copy for this article on my desk by noon tomorrow, and by *my desk* I mean *inbox* and *copy* I mean *digital format*.' He hung up.

Was Chad right? Was Beatrice really responsible for her own undoing? If so, then love hadn't taken anything from her at all. There were no missed boats or love-stolen dreams. There was just a lack of determination or perhaps a lack of genuine and enduring interest.

I once read a book called *The Artist's Way*. It was a 12-week recovery programme for writers who were struggling to create. In fact the book was designed for anyone whose life suddenly felt a little less shiny. It had lots of simple and quick exercises for people to do to help them feel better. My personal favourite was always the *Morning Pages*. The

Morning Pages are three pages of writing that people do as soon as they wake up in the morning; three pages of longhand, stream-of-consciousness writing. There is no wrong way of doing the *Morning Pages*. You wake up, you grab a pencil, you write three pages. That's it. You write about anything and everything. They rarely make sense. They are not supposed to be reread. More often than not they are negative, fragmented and repetitive: worries about your job; the way your boyfriend talked over you the night before at dinner; longings; anxieties. Sometimes I have written *'what am I going to write'* for an entire sheet of A4 before the rest comes out. And it always does. The little bits and pieces that run around your head unmonitored. Writing *Morning Pages* is like taking a morning shower for your brain, leaving it clean, fresh and ready for the day; a little lighter, brighter and open to all that the universe has to offer.

The front section of *The Artist's Way* deals with how people can self-sabotage. How they can block themselves and prevent themselves from doing the things they love. Apparently one of the main blocks is,

'If I really was a **[insert]** I would have **[insert]**.'

So for me we could say,

'If I really was supposed to ***teach people to ski*** I would have pursued a career in ***skiing*** from an early age. I have not done that. Therefore it can't be my thing. I should give up.'

And I've blocked myself before I've even begun, before I've even tried. The book helps you recognise this incorrect and self-sabotaging way of thinking so that you don't become a slave to it, so you don't give up on your dreams. Had love and its absence become my block? Was I incorrectly telling people that love had stopped them doing things too? Was I liberating women or disempowering them? I was starting to become confused…

Regardless of Chad's theory and my own inner turmoil I did not want Beatrice to spend a single second thinking she was not a musician. *'If I was a musician I would have gone to the school or chosen to carry on studying in the UK.'* That's what she'd implied, just as *The Artist's Way* had described. She'd blamed herself, devalued herself, devalued her talent. She had given herself a hard time unnecessarily, incorrectly. So, with a spin in my head and confusion in my heart, I ordered Beatrice Van de Broeck a copy of *The Artist's Way*. Maybe if she read it she'd be able to see that her choice not to study piano was simply a block. She could see how perfectly normal it was. Perhaps it could even show her how to remove the block altogether?

the calm before the storm

fortnum & mason tea shop

'Please don't feel obliged to wait,' I said to Jenny Sullivan, wishing to God she'd just bloody well leave. 'I have to wait because I promised my grandma and my best friend I'd meet them for coffee, so I can just see you back at the office, later on...'

She huffed moodily and continued to stare out of the window. And just for the record she had totally invited herself along. I'd told her I had to meet friends and she'd just silently glared at me until the words 'Would you like to join us?' popped out. Then she'd grumpily agreed to come as if I had just insisted she join us, opposed to her forcing me to invite her through the power of silence, the mentalist.

We were together because we'd just presented the idea for LSD Drop-In Centres to Downing Street (although the first thing they told us was to change the name). Jenny had been smug as the kitty cat in *Alice in Wonderland* (the one with the big gob) as soon as she found out that I needed her.

'You are both twatting going,' was Chad's response to my protests. '*True Love* at Westminster,' he'd cooed. '*True Love* hobnobbing, no, *advising* the men who run this country.' He started to well up. 'My mum would 'ave been so twatting proud.' He pronounced the word *proud* with an A, *praade*, as if being all East End and earthy would distract us from the fact his eyes were weeping like a Virgin Mary figurine from Lourdes.

'Don't fuck it up,' were his parting words as we left the office.

Peter had spent weeks emailing me notes for my presentation. We had created a 50-page proposal outlining the reasons why a nationwide initiative to help young women reach their potential would become the foundations upon which the success of the UK would be built (Peter's words). But when I'd given it to Jenny she'd flicked through it like a cartoon flipbook, preferring to use it as a makeshift fan on the overheated London Underground. And that was probably the most use it saw all day. Because when we arrived at Downing Street the man we were supposed to be seeing, Michael Bates, the *actual* Education Secretary, had been called into an emergency meeting on the salt content in primary school lunches. So Jenny and I met with a different man called Richard Ballentyne, who was *The Shadow* of the Shadow who shadowed the Shadow Education Secretary— which made me think we were in a Batman film. And this Richard Ballentyne didn't give a crap about my presentation. He spoke only to Jenny Sullivan, which was convenient, because when I tried to stand up and start talking she snatched the proposal from my hand and presented it herself—the thunder-stealing idea-sabotaging cowbag that she is. *Even worse* she presented it verbatim. Yes, that's right. She had memorised the whole bloody thing—every single word of it—which meant I had to add *photographic memory* to the never-ending list of her gifts and qualities. And Richard Ballentyne spent the entire presentation staring at Jenny's legs. He used the Q&A to ask her about her contract with L'Oreal, then quizzed her on her recent photo shoot for M&S underwear.

'But what are your thoughts on my idea?' I'd asked the Jenny-obsessed politician.

'It's *cute*, Katherine,' he'd said. 'Cute and rather utopian, because if everyone is constantly checking in with themselves at these centres who, my dear girl, is going to be doing all the work?' Then he'd laughed before shoving a Hobnob in his gob and trying to touch Jenny's left hand.

'Surely,' I'd argued, 'if the government helped people understand the things in life that made them happy and ensured they did these things either outside work or for their work there would be a reduction in stress-related illnesses; in the depression brought about by feeling alienated and unfulfilled; a reduction in the sense of hopelessness so many people feel. Which I thought would be a good thing for the country, economically, and certainly for NHS resources.' Which Federico was *still* concerned about after I accidentally reignited his obsession with MRSA the day I discovered Jenny's husband was a big fat whore. 'Plus if kids actually understood the kind of work they wanted to do, and got into that field, there would be fewer people leaving jobs, a reduction in Jobseeker's Allowance, in recruitment costs, in the cost of temps needed to cover absences from work, a reduction in the amount of sick pay given to people signed off through stress. Economically it makes perfect sense, doesn't it, Mr Ballentyne?' He was staring at Jenny's breasts. 'But it's not a six-foot blonde who models underwear for M&S,' I said, lobbing a Hobnob at his head. 'So how f*****g interesting could it be?'

That's when I was asked to leave…

fortnum & mason tea shop

'Oh, so you *are* going to wait with me,' I said as Jenny continued to sit at my table. 'Well, that's nice…' I nodded as she tapped away on her mobile phone in silence. I racked my brains for things to say. 'Thank you for presenting the idea, Jenny. I didn't think you'd even read the proposal, if I'm honest. But you seemed to be able to recall *every single word* of it…'

'It was a good idea, Kate,' she said, putting the phone down and stirring a complicated coffee concoction. 'Although I think the media has more influence on public opinion than government. You probably should have pitched your idea to the private sector.' Helpful.

She continued to stare out of the window.

I compulsively checked my watch.

Then suddenly, out of the blue…

'Nathanial and I separated.' It had been quiet for so long her words startled me.

'Nathanial?'

'Nathanial…my husband…'

'Oh!' I blushed redder than a burning sun as the image of him snogging in *Liberty*'s burst into my brain.

'It's OK, Kate, everyone knew about the affairs. Everyone but me, although I think even I knew on some level.' She took a small pot of cream out of her expensive handbag and started moisturising her perfect hands. 'Kate, you won't know this about life yet, but sometimes it's hard to accept the things that one doesn't understand. I've spent a long time stuck on the "How could he?"s and the "Why would he?"s and as long as I've stayed stuck I've avoided dealing with the truth. Cowardly I know. Anyway it's hard to ignore things that are *literally* under your nose—' Her voice started to wobble. She took a deep breath and another sip of coffee. 'I am still struggling with the *"How could he?"'s* but I'm not in denial any more.'

She went back to staring out of the window.

I went back to staring at my watch.

I still wasn't sure why she'd come with me or why she suddenly felt the need to start sharing. But if she was in the mood for sharing I wouldn't have minded a bit of the breakfast fruit salad she'd ordered herself without asking first if I might like something. And was it me or was *Avoidance* becoming a common theme in Love-Stolen Dreams?

I'd met women who were avoiding ending a relationship *(We are fine as we are / nothing's perfect)*; avoiding getting into a new one *(I won't meet someone I like / I don't think relationships are for me)*; avoiding intimacy *(things are simpler on my own / my time has passed)*; avoiding truth *(Jenny)*. We seemed so much more in control of our lives than we realised. Which meant Chad's theory of

Responsibility Avoidance was potentially spot on, because even when we knew bad news was approaching, like Jenny, we seemed to have the ability to *choose* to ignore it until we felt ready. How was that possible? How was it possible that I had chosen to ignore Gabriel's behaviour, hurting myself until the very last moment when I could take no more? Why did Jenny *choose* to avoid dealing with her husband's adulterous ways? Avoidance and Choice—they were an odd combination but they seemed to go hand in hand. It was as if they were dating, or at least going steady, and I wondered how many other women were avoiding things at this very minute.

'Jenny, may I ask what will you do now? Is there anything you didn't do because…?' My voice petered out. I wasn't brave enough.

'Is there anything I didn't do because I fell in love?' She raised her scarily perfect right eyebrow. 'Yes. I didn't get to *not* be in love, Kate. There has always been a husband, a boyfriend, another person. What I didn't have because of all of them is not having them. I have done a lot of travelling. I like my work. I'm sure now I'm single I could have sex with different men in different ways and all those other "things" that people say they've missed out on. But most of all I'd really like to be alone, Kate. That I suppose is what love stole from me. Plus my agent thinks the public are very responsive to women striving to put their lives back on track in the wake of a failed marriage. Apparently having a troubled love life makes you more relatable.' She took a small spoonful of fruit salad, then pushed the bowl away as if she was full. It just sat there taunting me with its fruity beauty. 'But my agent said one must rise from the ashes like a phoenix, otherwise one looks like a whiny broken-hearted wimp.'

'You mean like me?'

'Kate, it's important to actually get back up after you've been *sucker-punched* to the floor.'

'I can get back up. I'm up. I'm onto the next round.'

'Really, Kate? Have you? Because you very much seem to be lying on your back on the floor.' I was sitting on a chair opposite her.

She turned back to the window, staring out of it in silence, which was fine. I was bored with boxing metaphors and am actually very comfortable with long, protracted voids of words.

Leah and Grandma *finally* turned up 45 minutes late and walked over to join us at our table. Then they just stared at Jenny, open-mouthed, wide-eyed, also bloody silent. It was as if I were on a silent retreat. Grandma finally stepped forward and shook Jenny's hand enthusiastically.

'It really is a pleasure to meet you, Jenny Sullivan,' she said, pink cheeked. 'I absolutely love your work. You are an inspiration to a great number of women out there.'

'Me too…' gushed Leah. 'Me too, I just love your work. You are so talented. Really really talented.'

Bastards.

'You know, Jenny, and I hope you don't mind me asking you this,' Grandma said, sitting herself down, 'but I have always wondered, what would your advice have been for my beautiful granddaughter? What would you have done if you were Kate?'

'My advice for Kate has been and always will be the same. Not that she has ever asked my opinion.'

'Goodness, Kate, you have this wonderful oracle of women's liberation by your side every working day and you don't indulge in her wisdom and vision?' Was Grandma being ironic? Did ironic mean to Grandma what it meant to Peter Parker, in that I totally didn't get it? 'So what would you do, if you were Kate?'

I actually winced in preparation for her acerbic words.

'If I was Kate I'd go back to France. I'd go back and I'd see this ridiculous Gabriel.'

'What?' Me.

'What?' Leah.

'Inspired!' Grandma said. 'That's *exactly* what you must do. Go back and work out why you abandoned yourself in that relationship. Now that would be progress, wouldn't it?' she said, patting me on the knee. 'It's a wonderful idea, Jenny. A true challenge. And a challenge is just what you need, dear Kate. We have been dancing around this from the very beginning. Time to set yourself free, I think. Jenny, we are very lucky that you joined us today. Very lucky indeed,' and now she was patting Jenny on the knee.

'Yes, we are really very lucky,' muttered Leah, gently stroking Jenny's knee. 'You really are very very beautiful.'

Total complete bastards.

quest | travel back to france to see gabriel

dance studio | covent garden

Jane had asked me to go and see her before her final rehearsal for the Pro-Am dance competition. We were supposed to be talking through an action plan for my imminent and already booked return to France but when I arrived at the studio she was pacing up and down, alone, and she was not in the least bit chatty, or at least she wasn't in the mood to chat about me...

'Where is he? Where the hell is he? We literally have two hours today to practise and that's it. No more time. So where the hell is Julio?' I really didn't know but my phone had just beeped with a message from Leah.

6 p.m.—Karmic Awareness Course—Kings Cross. Don't be late. Lx

'Jane, does Leah ever make you go on these strange courses, and to these strange lectures, and on these weekends spent in remote villages with nudist Buddhists?' Jane stifled a giggle.

'No, she only asks *you* to do those things,' she said, smiling at me. 'Kate, if you just agree to do this past life regression she'll stop. Until you do I suspect all your weekends will be spent in poorly lit rooms with lots of middle-aged women touching themselves trying to find the source of their internal karmic chakra power nonsense. You're doing hard time until you do your past life time.'

'But that's not fair. Past life regression is bloody scary and weird and…scary.'

'I'll tell you what's scary, Kate: scary is the fact that Julio is still bloody missing!' Jane restarted her hypnotic pacing up and down, which is when I became mesmerised by her arse. Because very much in spite of the multicoloured leotard she was wearing that had tiny birds printed all over it, her bum looked magnificent. She caught me looking at it and smiled.

'It's pretty good, isn't it?' She rubbed her bottom with her hands.

'Can I touch it?'

'Sure, go ahead. It's practically solid. My whole body is—have a touch. I've never had a figure like this before and it's just down to dancing. I haven't changed a thing. In fact I have to eat loads more than I used to, and I drink protein shakes.'

'I want to drink protein shakes and have a rock-solid arse!' *Nothing* in this world was fair any more. 'It's amazing,' I said on my knees, squeezing a bottom cheek in each hand.

'Have we progressed from kissing everyone to actually fornicating?' I turned to see Peter Parker sauntering towards us, shower fresh from the gym, his hair still slightly wet. He was wearing amazing jeans and a fitted T-shirt that made his muscular arms look as if they were bursting out of it like a Banana Split. He leant down and kissed me on both cheeks. For a moment I thought I might leap up and bite his sweet-smelling neck. I made myself blush bright red with the thought of it, which confused everyone else in the room, including me.

'So are you all set for France?' he asked innocently. 'Still sure this is the right thing to do? Because you don't have to go. You could do something else. *We* could do something else.'

'Oh, my God?' Jane looked from Peter to me then back to Peter. 'Peter, I've seen a photo of you in Kate's flat,' she said, beaming at him.

'Have you?' Peter said, looking from her to me.

'No, you haven't.' Damn her.

'Yes, I have. It's been there for years. I mean you're a teenage boy in the photo, but I've just realised it's you. You did say his name was Peter but I just assumed it was a picture of a godson called Peter, or a nephew, or—'

'Kate doesn't have any brothers or sisters,' said fact-focused Peter Parker.

'No, she doesn't,' Jane said with a smile that she literally couldn't seem to reduce. 'So you are Peter. You are *all* the Peters. Just you. Where to put this strange piece of information I have just gleaned?'

'I don't think it needs to be put anywhere, Jane—' I chuckled '—except perhaps through an industrial-sized

shredder, or perhaps made into a papier-mâché hat. I don't
know why I think you've put it on metaphorical paper...'

'So, Peter.' Jane beamed. 'The 15-year-old boy from the
photo who is also a bloody great handsome adult male—
what can we do for you today?'

He reached into his pocket and took out two shiny pieces
of paper.

'I have two tickets to a *Take That* concert this weekend,
with back-stage passes to hang out with the band. I just
wondered if Kate wanted to stay in London this weekend
and we could go? You could go to France another time,
later in the year—the weather would probably be better
then. And I could go with you, later in the year, if you
wanted.'

Jane clapped her hands together and laughed at a joke I
didn't get.

'I didn't realise you were a fan of *Take That*, Peter?' I
said, looking at the shiny tickets up close.

'That concert has been sold out for months,' Jane said,
taking the tickets from my hand.

'It is sold out, and I've liked *Take That* for a long time,'
he said, nodding his head. 'Since I was young, younger,
I've been a fan.'

'What's your favourite song, Peter?' Jane asked, barely
suppressing a wave of strange laughter.

'There was a song that came out a few years ago that
I really liked. I don't recall its name. I don't have a good
memory for trivia, Jane,' he said, studying the ceiling of
the dance studio.

'Oh, I think I liked that song too.' Jane beamed.

'Peter, I'm going to France this weekend. Grandma has booked everything and Chad wants me to write an article about it. The working title is "How love can totally fuck you over and make you look like a giant twat". Well I assume we'll change the title before it goes to print.'

'Well, that's great news, Kate. Great, I'm sure it will be great.' Peter looked around the dance studio, hands on hips. 'Well, I have to go now, so have a good one and I'll see you soon.' He strode off towards the double doors.

'Peter, your tickets,' Jane said, holding them in the air.

'Keep them, Jane,' he said, bursting through the doors of the studio, marching past Julio, who took one look at Peter and jumped back against the wall as if in a G-force simulator. He slid along the wall like a mime artist before scurrying past Peter Parker and into the studio.

'OMG!' he mouthed as he reached Jane. 'OMG he's so hot!!!!' He was all swinging hips and blushes.

'Don't *OMG he's so hot* me—where the bloody hell have you been?' screamed Jane.

'I've just been to an audition,' said a beaming Julio. 'And I got it! The first one I have been to in nearly 18 months!'

'Was Edmundo there?'

'Yes, Jane, he was there. We were competing for the same part and I got it.' He sort of collapsed in on himself with giggles.

'Was he horrible to you?'

'Actually after I beat him and was awarded THE LEAD ROLE he came straight up to me and asked me on a date!' Jane and Federico started jumping up and down on the spot, squealing and clapping. So I did the same. But they both stopped and just stared at me.

I will never be accepted into the world of dance.

the blind side

I have a friend who'd been dating his new girlfriend for about six months. When I asked him how it was all going he said,

'Well, I finally met my girlfriend for the first time last week, as opposed to the version of herself she's been choosing to show to me for the last six months, and the real version is a little bit messy, if I'm honest, and a little bit of a self-obsessed bitch. And I'm not entirely sure she was impressed with the neurotic narcissist she woke up with on Sunday morning. It's going as well as can be expected under the circumstances of us finally being truthful.'

At the beginning of a new relationship we are always blindsided. Everything is so heady and golden that there are things you just don't notice; things you just don't see, or if you do you are so vision-impaired you let them slide. But these are the warning signs, showing you the beginning of what will be the end. And the following is the truth about what happened to me.

The first few years with Gabriel were like living in a

dream. The night we met, in a bar on the mountain, we seemed to radiate towards each other like magnets. I was aware of only him. We talked and we drank and we danced but mostly we just stared at each other, all night, just staring, taking in every tiny detail of each other's faces. And I remember his mum calling him that night. He was sitting opposite me when he answered the phone and he looked at me and he said to her, 'Maman, I have found her. I have found the woman I am going to marry. She is here.' And that was the start of our life together; we never left each other's side. We lived high up in the mountains in his chalet. Every night we would fight sleep to keep staring at each other. The mornings were like a reunion. Our world was just about each other: skiing together, being together, cooking for each other, reading to each other. And it remained that way for an incredibly long time.

A few years into the relationship he started hanging around with a different group of friends. They loved to party, they openly took drugs all the time and very occasionally Gabriel would too. But the recreational became frequent, as did the drinking. At the beginning of our relationship any drinking we did seemed to be in the spirit of new relationship; going out for dinner all the time, having champagne, having mulled wine before lunch on the ski slopes. But these were my warning signs, and I'd missed them. His pre-lunch drinking became a daily occurrence, as did smoking weed, which he did every day at work in between ski lessons. Suddenly I found myself with a man whose entire existence seemed to be under the influence of something. But he was fit and he was healthy. He held down a good job. I was still in love with him and confused by the incongruous juxtaposition of health, vitality and great sporting ability with the clandestine drug and alcohol consumption that had somehow become a part of our lives.

I tried to explain my concerns. I found studies and books on the effects of marijuana, on alcohol dependency, even on depression and its expression through drink and drugs. But his personality had already started to shift. If I tried to talk about it, it made him worse. He started staying out all night. He wouldn't come home at all if he thought he'd be coming home to a disappointed and angry girlfriend. Unless I could promise to laugh about the fact that he'd been so drunk he'd fallen asleep on the floor of the ski school; or laugh as he dented his car on a post; or laugh because he was too drunk some mornings to go to work. I was *'not nice'*; because his friends all laughed; they laughed with him; but me, I was spoiling everyone's fun, a concept of fun that I totally didn't understand.

For about twelve months I lived in a constant state of confusion with two completely different men: a charming, doting boyfriend who I wanted to start a family with, and a lairy, abusive drunk. If we fought he could rarely remember it the next day. He'd wake up confused by my anger. He'd blindly apologise for mistakes he didn't remember making. He never once questioned his behaviour or thought for a minute that he should stop drinking or taking drugs. That was never once considered. His friends had normalised it. I had become the abnormal one.

It's all *very* cliché. I know that. And I still feel a great deal of shame that I ended up in that kind of relationship, because doesn't it normally happen to someone else? But I really didn't see it coming. I was blindsided. Perhaps it was my human need for a relationship that overruled my rational mind? Or my attachment to the cherished dreams I had for my future with him? Or maybe he had filled my void? Whatever it was, this bad relationship had crept up on me like a cancer. It made me doubt my judgement, doubt myself, which paralysed me further, preventing me from walking away. I kept asking myself:

'How is it possible I've ended up in this position? I must be doing something wrong. Maybe I'm not seeing things clearly. This wasn't how my life with him was supposed to turn out.'

It was a mathematical equation I couldn't make sense of. So I kept rechecking the calculations, in the same way Jenny Sullivan had. I just kept looking at Gabriel, the man I'd fallen in love with, and thinking how he still looked the same; he still sounded the same; he still smelt the same. But he wasn't the same.

Eventually, I did leave. And I left with nothing, arriving in London with no money, no home, no job and zero self-confidence, and I think I blamed myself. You should always be able to save the person you love most in the world. Isn't that what they teach us in the movies? But this new version of Gabriel, *Gabriel 2.0*, didn't want saving and *Gabriel 1.0* had got totally lost; the love of my life had totally disappeared.

To this day I still can't make sense of any of it. I still can't do the maths. I left him. I've never been back and most of the time it just feels like a really *really* bad dream, like maybe it didn't happen at all, like maybe he is still out there somewhere, my Gabriel, as he was. And if he is still out there, as he was, then he is still the man I want to be with. And that is what I can't let go of, that hope, that possibility. That is what I need to go back and see. I need to know which one of them survived. And I need to let go of the guilt, the guilt that I didn't protect him, that I didn't save him, that I didn't stand by and help the man I loved. I just left. And I still wake from nightmares about him being trapped somewhere in pain, or him crashing his car when he's too drunk, or him hurting himself when he is unable to keep himself safe.

So until I admit that all these things did happen to me and that it wasn't OK, it was scary and heart-breaking; until I forgive myself because it wasn't my fault and it wasn't my job to fix him; until I trust myself enough to know that I will never let it happen again; until I go and see which Gabriel is left, then I'm not sure I will ever be able to move on. Because right now Gabriel still defines me by the very fact that everything I do, every day, is about getting over him, piecing myself back together again and trying to save everyone else along the way. So Jenny is right. Now is the time to end this chapter of my life. It is time to move on. I need to go backwards in order to move forwards. I can see no other way of truly getting over him.

going backwards to go forwards

french alps

Arriving in the mountains was like being dropped into a movie set of my own life. The flight back to France was the same. The drive up the mountain was the same. Our chalet looked the same from the outside; the shops, the buildings, the mountains and streams, all as they were. Even the air smelt the same: fresh, clear, unpolluted, a hint of wood-burning fires and pine. Everything exactly as I had left it.

It was late by the time I arrived. I stayed the night in a local hotel. In the morning I walked through the village to my favourite coffee shop. The mountains surrounding the village were white with snow but the sky was blue, the sun out, warm enough to tan, warm enough to wander through the village without a coat. It was my favourite time of year; white snow, yellow sun. As I wandered back through the storybook of my previous life, like a giant picture book,

I was searching for one thing and I knew exactly where I would find him.

Gabriel and I both love the morning. The best part of the day occurs before 8 a.m. when no one else is awake and the mountain feels like your own. Just as I had expected I found him reading a newspaper at a table outside our favourite coffee shop. As I approached, with a normality that bewildered me, he smiled, closed his newspaper and got up to greet me. He gently held my shoulders as he leant down and kissed me on each cheek, each kiss lingering dangerously close to the edge of my lips. We looked into each other's eyes and I struggled against a volcano of emotions that seemed to have erupted in my chest. All I kept thinking as I looked at his face was, *'He's alive. He's still here. He's real.'*

'I knew you would come here, Kate,' he said in a soft French voice. He looked tanned, relaxed and healthy. His thick dark hair ruffed, fresh from waking up. He was wearing a top I'd bought him. He wore the same aftershave. 'It's been a long time, *non*? You want a coffee? I think you want a coffee. Sit, sit.' He darted off to get me a drink. I sat down at the table. The situation felt totally…normal. He came back with an espresso for me and sat down next to me, shifting his chair close to mine.

'Look at you,' he said, smiling, taking me in, taking a deep breath as he studied my face, shaking his head. 'You look just the same, Kate, just the same.' He took my hands up in his, squeezing them gently between the palms of his warm hands, kissing them, holding them to his lips and kissing them again. 'And your skin smells the same. You feel the same. It's so good to see you, Kate. I've missed you.'

He kept hold of my hands in his lap, gently squeezing them, and looked up at me, the same big brown eyes, the same face, the same everything. He was in touching distance but at the same time he felt totally untouchable. For a moment I tried to breathe him all in, my brain scrabbling to store up the image of him, his voice, his smell, his touch.

'I think I know why you are here, Kate. I called you the other night and I'm sorry for that. It wasn't fair of me.' He took a gentle sip from his coffee, then his hands went back to hold mine. 'She come home and tells me she's pregnant. I didn't expect it. It was a shock.' I assumed the *she* was the new girlfriend. 'You know I chose to be with her because I wanted something a bit more simple, you know, nothing complicated, after you and me, and she chased me, you know. She was so nice to me all the time, and, I was so sad about you, oh, my God, you can't imagine how I was sad about you. So it was easy, you know? But now she is pregnant, so it's not so easy.'

He was talking in such an oddly detached way, like describing a preferred bus route. *'I stopped taking the number 47 because the traffic problems, the number 6 suits me better because it goes across town.'* I felt totally disempowered by his ability not only to reference our relationship in such simplistic emotionless terms, the most significant relationship of my adult life, but also to have thrown his new relationship immediately into the conversation. How could he be sure I wouldn't just burst into public tears at the mention of his new girlfriend? Any other guy would have danced around the subject like Michael Flatley before leaving at the crucial moment, high-kicking his way out of the room just as you finally got up the courage to ask if he's seeing someone then braced yourself for the agonising pain. But he was vomiting it all up like scripted reality TV. And he didn't seem the least bit distressed by my leaving or by me turning back up. It was as if I had just popped out to the utility room mid-conversation, popped back in, and we carried on where we left off.

'I know you, Kate. You are thinking about something. What is it?' He pulled me by my hands closer to him and gently stroked the side of my face. He was a breath away from me, my face, my lips. 'Hey, Kate, don't look so serious, eh.' He kissed me on the cheek. 'I'm here, it's OK, you can tell me anything, anything.' He put my hand on his chest and held it there. I could feel his heart beating. 'You know me, Kate, you *know* me. Speak to me.'

'I just—' My voice immediately broke. I tried to swallow back the tears and focus on what it was I wanted to ask. I hadn't prepared myself for Gabriel 1.0. I had prepared myself for Gabriel 2.0, and an argument. 'Why didn't you ask me to stay?'

I felt pathetic as soon as I'd said it. He gently wiped away the tears from my face and kissed my cheek, staying there, cheek to cheek, breathing me in. 'You didn't try and fix things, Gabriel,' I whispered. 'You didn't try and fight for me to stay.'

'Kate,' he said, staring into my eyes, cupping my face in

his hands, hands that I had held, hands that I had kissed, hands that used to hold me as I fell asleep every single night. 'Kate, you were *so* angry with me, all the time.' He shook his head. 'Really, you were so unhappy with me.'

'Because I didn't understand what you were doing. I didn't understand any of the choices you were making.' I could barely speak through the tears.

'Kate, my Kate.' He kissed my cheek again and again and again, his hands in my hair, pulling me close to him, gently rocking me back and forth. 'Shh, my Kate, shh, it's OK, it's OK, I am here, I am with you. I am here.' I pulled away and wiped away the last of my tears with the back of my hand.

'But you are not here, Gabriel. You are not with me. You let me go. Now you are with someone else.' I took a deep breath, grounded myself and, for once, I didn't fill the silence.

He sat back in his chair, letting go of me for the first time since I'd arrived, and just stared at me. We just stared at each other. This was the fork in our road.

'I didn't want to be by myself after you left, OK. I don't want to be alone. It's not funny to be in this tiny village alone without you.' He signalled for the waiter to bring him another drink and started fidgeting in his seat. 'You know, Kate, there was a lot of pressure for me when you were here. I mean, you moved country to be with me, you know?'

'Gabriel, you asked me to move to France to be with you.'

'I know, because I love you. And I want to be with you. I still love you, Kate, but it was too much for me, all your friends and family in England. And what am I, eh? Some

stupid ski instructor? Not exactly what your grandma want
for you, I don't think. I think she wants you to be with a
nice English boy who wears suits and plays chess. I don't
want to feel like that, Kate, like I am a disappointment to
your family. I don't want that on my shoulders.' He was
upgrading to 2.0. 'It's too much pressure, Kate. I don't
want that pressure. I don't want to be responsible for someone like that. Can you imagine the pressure?' He whistled
loudly for the waiter. 'Hey!' he said, yelling towards the bar.
'Do I need to come and make my own drink? Seriously?
I don't care if I do, just tell me, OK? Then I don't sit here
waiting like an idiot.' He turned back to me. 'I am simple
man, Kate, you know that. I am a simple man. And I want
to do what I want to do. And my new girlfriend, she lets
me do what I want.' The waiter arrived with a large glass
of wine and Gabriel threw some money at him. Gabriel 2.0
was fully installed. He caught me staring at the wine. 'Eh,
don't pull that face at me, Kate. I am always in the wrong
with you. You see. You see! We are together five minutes
and you are already annoyed with me. I want to be free,
Kate, you know, like a bird. I want to be free like the animals in the forest. I want to go out all night if I want. Be
with my friends if I want. Not come home if I want. You
always want me to come home or call you to tell you where
I am. It's too much.' Gabriel 2.0 was revealing himself
like a Venus flytrap, only this time I didn't have my head
halfway inside the toothy flower. 'The animals are free to
do what they want, Kate. No one asks the animals in the
forest where they are going. I don't think anyone calls a

bird and says, "Hey, bird, where are you? Why have you not come home for two nights?" I don't think so, Kate. I don't think so.'

I didn't think so either. I've never once seen a bird with any kind of mobile communication device, except its beak. And I had no idea why he was so obsessed with forest animals. Gabriel 2.0 was officially nonsensical.

'So, Kate, what do you want from me? What are you doing here? I tell you now my girlfriend would not be very happy to know that I am talking with you. And I don't want to piss her off. She lets me do what I want. I am free with her, Kate. I like to be free.'

He necked half the glass of wine, lit a cigarette and nodded to the waiter to bring him another drink. It was 9 a.m. Gabriel didn't seem in the least bit free.

'You are very complicated, Kate. I don't think you know how complicated you are.' He pulled heavily on his cigarette and looked out across the mountains, acting as if I were no longer sitting next to him.

I looked at his face for a final time. There was no avoidance. There was no denial. The truth was staring me in the face, or at least it was sitting next to me staring in the opposite direction. Leaving had been the best thing I could ever possibly have done for myself. I could trust myself. I had saved myself. The only thing now confusing me was the parallels, because for Gabriel 2.0 love was as simple as finding someone to fit around who he already was and wanted to be. But wasn't Love-Stolen Dreams telling women to connect with themselves and never let that go, for anyone?

Did that mean that Gabriel 2.0 was already being what we were all trying to become?

'Seriously, Kate, what are you doing here? Are you here to make trouble? I think so. I told you, the phone call the other night, it meant nothing. I was drunk. It was a shock about the baby, that's all. What? Don't look at me like that, Kate, with your moody eyes judging me. It's just a bloody baby. Everyone has them. My God, you are so dramatic. You are just like the others, you know, always talking, always judging what everyone else does. Talking, talking, talking, like a silly village person. You are just like the stupid village people here. I thought you were better than that but I misjudged you completely.' And now he was muttering away to himself. 'It's just a baby, my God, so what if there is another person living in my chalet? It makes no difference to my day. She can have three babies if she want, I don't care, makes no difference to me.' He knocked back yet another glass of wine. 'Seriously, Kate—' he was getting a bit shouty '—what are you doing here, eh? *What* are you doing here?'

'I think I came to say goodbye, Gabriel, that's what I'm doing here. I came here to say goodbye.' Then I got up from the table and walked away.

I will never understand why Gabriel 1.0 chose to upgrade himself to Gabriel 2.0 but let's just put it out there: I made mistakes. I made him the centre of my world. I gave up everything to be with him. He never asked me to do that. I put that pressure on him, the pressure to be my sun. I was no different from the girlfriends who'd driven their unhappy boyfriends to ask *True Love* for help. Was that the reason Gabriel changed? Did that pressure drive him to drink and drugs? Possibly, who knows? Personally I don't think that's my cross to bear. But taking responsibility for myself and for what I did to our relationship—that was something I was ready to do. And I was ready to make sure it never happened to me again.

So I think this is my moment to offer my Love-Stolen Dreams advice, although I'm not sure it's worth a dime, or a penny or the medical diploma of a celebrity doctor.

number one

be yourself from the very beginning of your relationship and encourage your partner to do the same. That way neither of you will wake up with a total stranger in two years' time with a joint mortgage, joint bank account and joint little else.

number two

ask yourself the Love-Stolen Dreams question religiously. *'If there was no one true love, no happy ever after, no kids, what would and will make you feel happy and joyful on a daily basis?'*

number three

make the most important relationship you have in life the one you have with yourself

you are absolutely your only constant

To: kate@true-love.com
From: Jane Brockley (Formerly Robinson)
Subject: What the F did you do to my husband?????????

Kate Winters....
What did you do to my husband?

I ask because last weekend was our 7th wedding an-
niversary and I came home to find that James wouldn't
say a bloody word to me. He just handed me a bag and
told me to get in the car. Then he drove us to Heathrow,
where I discovered we were flying to Moscow of all places.
He didn't speak to me for the entire flight, pretending to
sleep, and on landing we got a taxi straight to a hotel. Our
bags were sent up to our room, the Honeymoon Suite, and
James rather sternly said that we should probably get a
stiff drink and have a chat. So we went to the hotel bar
where James told me that YOU had taken him to secret
dance classes. (Well, aren't you the secret squirrel these
days, Kate Winters!!!) But that wasn't the worst of it. He
told me that waiting in our hotel suite was a very special
someone from our past who YOU had told him I still think
about! He told me to wait in the bar for 15 minutes then
come up. He said this was all very difficult for him but that
he loved me very much and wanted me to have everything
I'd ever dreamed of. Then he left me in the bar for what
felt like the longest 15 minutes of my entire life.

Eventually one of the hotel staff came over and said,
*'Are you Miss Jane Brockley-formerly-Robinson? The Hon-
eymoon Suite is ready for you now. Gregoire Pechenikov is
waiting for you there.'* Yes, Kate, you heard me correctly,

the hotel staff told me that Gregoire bloody Pechenikov was waiting for me in my hotel suite. If at this point I had been carrying my own passport, instead of James, who insists on carrying all travel documentation and paraphernalia, I'd have made a dash for the border, or the airport, or the nearest port. As it was I had £3.52 in my purse and a Boots Advantage card and I couldn't in the time available work out the logistics of a Russian escape!

Kate, I do not want to get into the ethics of you telling my husband a secret I had entrusted you with. But I will get into it, in detail, at a later stage, and probably more than once.

When I arrived at the suite the door was ajar. I stepped inside what was a huge and very *very* low-lit room and I could just about make out a huge double bed in the far corner. Next to it I could see the outline of Gregoire Pechenikov in the same bloody outfit he used to wear at university. In a very quiet and very thick Russian accent, he said,

'I've never been able to stop thinking about you, Jane. I have always wanted you.'

Then he started slowly walking across the room towards me. Kate, I am easily excited by an accent at the best of times but a Russian accent, in a darkened room, with my adolescent crush Gregoire Pechenikov... It was never going to end well!

Well, Gregoire clapped his hands and music started playing and I was so busy trying to work out where James was in the darkened room that before I knew it Gregoire had reached me and swept me up in his arms. He spun me expertly in circles to the music, pressed against my body, breathing heavily in my ear. And the dancing was wonderful, sensual, just like I remembered it. But all I could do was keep looking over his shoulder because where the bloody hell was my husband and what on earth was everyone expecting from me in this bizarre threesome situation that *you,* Kate, were wholly responsible for? I still hadn't located James when Gregoire whispered something in my ear, something far racier than I would normally share with you but it seems relevant to the story. He said,

'Jane Robinson, get on your knees and show me if you are the kind of woman I think you are.'

Well, things had gone quite far enough. I gave that thuggish Gregoire the hardest slap I could muster. But the resultant *'Ouch'* was high-pitched, hurt and very *very* English. Well, I marched over to the light switch and turned up the lights to find James, my James, dressed up like bloody Gregoire doing some kind of Russian role play, inspired by you, no less, with a bright red imprint of my hand across his face. Kate, he looked like he was going to cry. So I went back over to the light, put the dimmer down to low, restarted the music and let James finish what he had started. And yes, before you or more likely Federico ask, I did get on my knees and show him the kind of woman that you know me to be. James stayed in character for the rest of the night and we did the most erotic tango of my entire life. I have goose bumps just thinking about it. At one point he instructed me to take all my clothes off and pleasure him (he actually used the F-word) before throwing me onto a huge fur-covered bed. I have never given so many blow jobs in my entire life, and, yes, that includes college.

I say again, I don't want to get into the ethics of you telling my husband one of my secrets. You got it right, this time, but probably best you don't make a habit of it. And let's hope for your sake that I don't bump into Peter again any time soon, now that I realise that boy in the picture is in fact the adult Peter in your current life, and the very same Peter I think you were referring to recently when you drunkenly revealed a strange sexual fantasy of yours. Remember, Kate, as you are always saying to us, with great power does come great responsibility...

You are a very *very* bad friend.

Jane x

that's another fine mess you got me in

goldman apartments

I went straight to Peter Parker's apartment on arriving back in London; past the stone-faced concierge, who raised a judgemental eye at the sight of me, up the lift, down the corridor, to once again face the impenetrable front door of apartment 41. I had actually forgotten about the difficulties in crossing the threshold and the secret he kept hidden inside, the one that made him discombobulated and colourful of cheek, and as is the norm he answered the door pink-faced, sweating and out of breath.

'I'm back!' I announced loudly and proudly from the hallway. 'And I'm having a bit of a rethink about my life. I'm thinking of quitting *True Love*.' Bombshell dropped, I just stood there waiting for the Q&A.

'What do you mean you're thinking of quitting?' Peter stepped into the hallway and, as is routine, pulled the door closed behind him. 'You've just started writing your first features. Your reputation is developing. You have your own

column on the *True Love* website. People are really starting
to know who you are and what you're capable of. You've
even got Jenny Sullivan on board! You are not quitting.'

'She's not really on board, Peter. She's just more tolerant
now that it complements her own goal of celebrity divorcee.'

'So what are you going to do instead?'

'I have no idea. That's my point. I found out and recap-
tured Love-Stolen Dreams for so many other people but
I've never really spent any time working on my own. I don't
think I planned further than getting over Gabriel.'

'How was he?' Peter crossed his arms and stepped slightly
closer. 'Does he love you? Do you love him? Are you moving back there?' He put his clenched fists in his pockets and
leant against the wall.

'Gabriel was just the same, in that he was odd and rambling and broken. There is no love and there will be no
moving.'

Peter looked as if he wanted to talk things through but
kept glancing back at his front door.

'Kate, I want to see you and I want to invite you in but—'

'It's OK, Peter,' I said, turning to leave. 'I can meet her,
him, whomever another time, when you're ready. I just
wanted to let you know I was back.' I moped off towards
the lift.

'It's really not what you think,' he said, grabbing my hand
and pulling me back up the hallway. 'I just don't know how
much we'd end up talking about you if we go inside. We'll
end up talking about me and my problem...'

'What problem?'

'OK, so you mustn't freak out, Kate—' he put his hand

on the door handle '—or laugh at me, or appear shocked...'
He pushed the handle down and let the front door swing
wide open. Inside the immaculate penthouse apartment was
in tatters.

'Oh, my God, Peter. Have you been burgled? Why didn't
you tell anyone?'

'I'm exhausted, Kate,' he said, slowly sitting himself
down on the floor in the hallway, resting his head in his
hands. 'I had no idea it was possible to feel this knackered
and this totally out of control.'

I heard scratching, a squeak, then two black and white
puppies came careering into the lounge, skidding as they
cornered at high speed. They both made little yapping
noises before tearing past the seated Peter Parker and bolt-
ing straight down the hallway towards the lift. A rather
desperate Peter Parker scrabbled after them. A few minutes later he strode past me with a snuffling, tail-wagging
puppy under each arm.

'It's like this every single day,' he said, marching into his
apartment. 'Cup of tea, Kate?'

There was nowhere to sit down in Peter's flat so I perched
on the edge of the coffee table in the lounge. He started
clearing a space on the sofa, picking off chewed-up teddies,
dog biscuits, shredded pieces of paper.

'I haven't told anyone about them because I still don't
know if I can keep them. I mean, look at them!' It was
Orwell's *Animal Farm* and the humans had well and truly
lost the war. One of the puppies was peeing in the middle
of the room and I swear to God he was smiling as he did it.
'I've wanted to tell you, I have, but I'd set myself this goal

of somehow having them slightly house-trained before introducing them to you, or at least tidying up a bit before inviting you in. But I just, I can't seem to control them, or teach them to listen to me, or get them to pee in the right bloody place. They just do what they want, all the time, day and night. I have no idea, at all, what do with them.' He attempted to sit down on the edge of the sofa while he continued to remove rubbish off it. 'I don't know how to live like this, Kate. I really don't. I *can't* live like this. Which means giving them up, which is, well, you don't walk away from commitments like that, Kate. You just don't.'

'So having dogs is your Love-Stolen Dream?'

'My ex hated dogs. It was never an option for us to have one but I always assumed after Jake that I would. Your idea inspired me to just go for it.' There was a crash as puppy number one pulled a newspaper off the coffee table, taking three mugs with it and an iPhone.

'Everything is insured,' he muttered to himself like a mantra. 'Everything is 100% insured.' He looked like he was about to cry. 'I only went to the dog breeder for some advice. I can't do anything without ridiculous amounts of research and pre-planning and—'

'Over-planning.'

'There is no such thing as over-planning, Kate. So I went to her to ask some questions about care, routine, exercise, appropriate breed type, insurance policies, jabs and—'

'I get it, Peter.'

'But there was a litter of puppies there. So I started playing with them while the breeder talked to me. And there was this tiny little puppy, all black, with a white diamond on his chest and one white paw. And he had these little dog freckles on his pink nose, a bit like you. Not that you have a pink nose, although it does tend to go very red in the cold, and when you have too much caffeine, or alcohol—' I waved him on. 'And then when I went to leave, I didn't want to. So I sat there for another couple of hours, watching this puppy play with its brothers and sisters. And there was this other puppy he played with more than the others, a little girl puppy—they were a bit like you and me actually. He was the smarter of the two, obviously, and she was always watching him and copying him and chasing after him, trying to get his attention and—'

'Peter, seriously, just tell the story.'

'Well, I thought how sad it would be when it came to separate them. Then the breeder explained that sometimes it's easier to take two puppies rather than one because they keep each other company—'

'And she makes more money if she sells two.'

'Don't be cynical, Kitkat. Although you're right, because the next thing I know I'm back in my apartment in the centre of London with not one but *two* puppies and, well, I haven't had a night's sleep since. In hindsight it was a rash decision involving no pre-planning, preparation or research, which, if I may say so, proves without doubt why all of those things are actually incredibly important.' He attempted to lie down and stretch out on his large leather sofa. 'So you see, Kate, as I have mentioned to you on numerous occasions, your Love-Stolen Dreams idea can actually cause totally bloody chaos in other people's otherwise ordered and functional lives.' He pulled a chewed-up remote control from under his back. 'I just didn't realise how hard this would be. I didn't realise how totally *uncontrollable* they would be. I think I just need to get some sleep. Then I can come up with some kind of puppy-training schedule.' The puppies jumped up on the sofa, landing on Peter's groin. He doubled up in pain and fell off the side of the sofa.

'I'll go and make us some tea,' I said, leaving him lying on the floor, the puppies jumping on his head.

'Don't judge me on my cleanliness, Kate!' he cried out as I walked into his kitchen, which was an absolute shit pit.

The black marble work surface was covered with dirty utensils. Every fork, knife, spoon, and plate, mug, glass and bowl had been used and not washed up. On the island in the middle of the kitchen were empty food cartons, biscuit cartons, milk cartons mixed up with old takeaway containers. At various intervals I could see open books on dog training. I spotted a self-help book called *'Crisis Management: How to function with no sleep'* and there was a spotlessly clean litter tray by the door to the roof terrace. There were a million different things on the black stone floor, from chewed boxes and tissues, to what looked like important letters and post, to shoes and sports equipment. Everything had been chewed up, peed on, ripped up.

'I would get a cleaner,' he said from behind me, resting his hands on my shoulders, 'but I'd need to clean up before the cleaner came round and I just don't have time!' He was squeezing my shoulders quite hard. 'So this is how I live now. I live like this, like a, like a, I don't even know what the word is for someone who lives like this! I think this was a mistake. It was. I can't do this by myself. I'm obviously limited and faulty and unable. My ex was right—I should just stick to living by myself.'

'Why do you have to do this all by yourself?'

'Because that's what I do. I am self-sufficient. I'm capable. I'm—'

'Standing in dog poo.' He looked down at his foot. 'Peter, you are definitely standing in a dog poo.' He looked as if he was about to cry, again. 'Peter, no one else does this all by themselves. No one. They have dog walkers, and vets, and puppy trainers and cleaners. Or at least everyone with full-time jobs in London seems to. You don't have to do everything by yourself all the time.'

'I just. Well. I always have.'

'Peter, I have an appointment I have to go to now but, after, why don't we take the puppies to my house for the night? There is nothing of value there for them to destroy, at all, and you can get some sleep while I look after them. I love dogs. I loved Jake.' One of the pups was on my foot, chewing it. 'And I know this great non-judgemental industrial cleaning company. I can arrange for them to come in and sort this place out while you stay with me. Don't worry—their tagline is, "We won't judge you, you dirty little fucker".' I snorted with laughter at my own joke. 'Then tomorrow we can come up with a long-term action-plan. I think Grandma knows some dog trainers and dog walkers. And she can definitely organise for regular cleaners. She can organise stuff. Stuff and staff. That's what she does. She manages.'

'Thank you,' he said, leaning down and engulfing me in an enormous hug. 'Thank you, thank you, thank you, thank you, thank you, thank you, thank you.'

man becomes what he thinks about

'Kate,' Bob began, stirring sugar into his fresh mint tea, 'the boundaries and limits in our lives are always self-imposed. You can only live the life you can imagine. Sugar?'

'No, thank you,' I said, looking at my watch. I wanted to be back with Peter within the hour.

'You are sweet enough, I'm sure.' Bob beamed before adding another three spoons of sugar to his own tea.

I'd made an appointment with Bob (the life coach from *Fat Camp*) to discuss making a change. I told him I was ready for something new but needed help. So we met in his office in Chelsea, an airy studio space with a large glass atrium, and he'd invited me to sit on a brown leather sofa then poured me the aforementioned mint tea. We drank from tall glasses with metal handles and it reminded me of being in Morocco before all the bombings and discontent.

'You say that you want your life to go in a different direction but you don't quite know what that will be,' he said, wiggling in his seat like a maths professor about to solve complicated algebra. 'Kate, when you currently think about your future life, can I assume you are imagining the life you have now but a slightly blacker or slightly rosier version of it?'

'I think so, yes. Certainly I can't imagine how anything will ever be *dramatically* different. I hope that things will improve but I can't really see it, if you know what I mean?'

'For me,' he said, touching his chest, 'I think people focus too much on what they *haven't got*, or what they *don't want*. They obsess over these things; about a lack of abundance; about feeling sad; or being rejected; or maybe freaking out because they don't know *how* to achieve change.' I nodded along. 'And that actually keeps them stuck where they are. All their thoughts are on the negatives so life has no opportunity to manifest change. Your life is limited to the life you can imagine. If you imagine badly that's what you'll get. I want to tell you something, Kate. I want to tell you about a friend of mine. He said to me, he said, "Bob, whatever you think you can do, begin it; action has magic, grace and power in it."'

I didn't want to tell Bob that his friend was quoting Goethe.

'The important thing here is to imagine without limits, so I want us to do a little exercise. It's one of my favourites. Will you indulge me? Great. I want you to daydream your dream life, a day in the life of your dream life, and every time you find yourself dismissing something, and saying to yourself, "Well, that's ridiculous, Kate," or, "That's not possible, Kate, you could never do that," then consciously remove that block and let yourself keep imagining, just for a second, that it is possible and what it would feel like.'

'I think I did something similar with my cleaner, Mary. She wanted to be a mechanic.'

'Well, that's great news, Kate. So let's do it for you this time. Get comfortable in your seat.' He started wiggling again as if he were getting comfortable on my behalf. 'Close your eyes, relax, take a deep breath and let yourself day-dream your perfect existence, your perfect day. Where does it start? Where do you wake up? What is the bed like? What colour are the sheets? When you get dressed what clothes do you put on? What would you love to wear if you could wear anything? When you leave the house turn around— what kind of house is it? What kind of house would make your heart soar? Do you get in a car? What kind of car is it? Where are you driving to? What do you drive past? What is the weather like in your perfect day? Where do you eat lunch? Who do you eat with? Does someone call you? You are really happy to hear from them. What do you talk about? What do you do in the afternoon? What are your plans for the weekend? You can go anywhere, so where are you going? If all things were possible, Kate, if you were allowed anything, if you could have anything, if you could achieve anything, who would you be, Kate? Who would you be? Who would you be? Who would you be?' Images were flick-ing through my head, objects, people, places, sports, foods, colours, cities, experiences. 'Remember, Kate. You…Have… The…Power.' He said this last bit in a deep breathy voice, as if he were blowing the magic power my way. I hoped that he was, that clever son of a gun. I kept my eyes closed and with the magic dust all around me I let my imagination go wild: a life without boundaries, without constraints, without lim-its. What would I do? I happily melted away into a world of

golden happiness. After about 10 minutes I could hear Bob
shift in his seat. I was pretty sure he was wiggling again.

'And come back to reality, Kate,' he said very quietly. I
opened my eyes. 'Welcome back, Kate,' he cooed as if he
knew where I'd been, as if he'd been there too, watching,
like a Willy Wonka of dream states. 'That exercise should
start to give you a sense of the things you are drawn to?'
Every Californian sentence ended with what seemed like a
question. 'The images are all important and we will make a
list of those images in just a moment. But we will also make
a second list. Because the exercise should also make you
aware of the *feelings* you are seeking, and by that I mean
the feelings that you are wanting to experience in this life,
be it feelings of happiness, feelings of strength, feelings of
fitness, heaven knows, perhaps you want to feel more sexy!'
He slapped his thighs in excitement. 'These are your cues,
Kate; they are your markers. They are important. Because
these feelings can be attained in a variety of different ways.'
He paused and just as I was about to ask he said, 'Let me
give you an example. An alcoholic may find an escape in
his drinking. Being drunk may offer him the opportunity
to run away from his problems; he feels free of life's constraints; he feels liberated. It's a false sense of freedom but
for the alcoholic it's the only activity that makes him feel
free. A soldier in the army may crave the exact same feeling of freedom, but he gets it by throwing himself out of a
plane and skydiving. A mother of three might get that same
sense of freedom when she salsa dances. I might get it when
I run along a beach. We are all seeking the same feeling and
we have each discovered a different method for feeling it.
Do you understand what I mean?'

I did, and I didn't.

'So what I want to do is make a list of the physical aspirations that you have identified in your daydream. You might have been riding through your dream on a Vespa; you might have been sprinting at high speed, physically really strong and fit; perhaps you were receiving an Oscar! After that we are going to make a list of the emotional aspirations, all the feelings you had in your perfect day. Then we can sit back and take a look at your picture. What your dream life looks and feels like. Then we start putting together small steps to work towards realising your dream life. And it's the smallest steps in life that can bring about the biggest and most powerful changes. Once we have fully identified who you were in your dream life, I want you to spend five minutes every day closing your eyes and being that person, and feeling what it feels like to be that version of yourself. You could do it while sat on the train, while in the shower, just as you wake up. The key here is to feel how you would *feel* if you were that person. If you find it tough the first few times try this. When you are in the shower each morning close your eyes and imagine how you would feel if you had 50 million pounds in the bank. When you close your eyes imagine you can see your bank statement and see your name at the top, your address, and the balance at the bottom says 50 million pounds. Know that it's yours. What would that feel like?'

I started beaming. I felt elated, excited, naughty even, as if for the first time in my whole life I knew I would be OK. 50 million quid!

'I think you get the idea, Kate. It's that emotion, that wonderful feeling that I want you to home in on. I want your body to get used to feeling like you have 50 million pounds in the bank. I want your body to get used to feeling like you did in your perfect day. I want the universe to feel you feeling like that. And the universe will respond to you. Remember, as clichéd as it sounds, you get back what you put in. It's not rocket science. Let these positive feelings of your perfect life out into the world every single day.'

'If it's that easy, Bob, then why aren't we all doing it? Why don't we all have everything we want?'

'That's a great question, Kate. There are two main stumbling blocks. One is that people focus on the things they don't want, the other is that they go to all the bother of thinking positively, then let the negative voice of doubt creep in, and most of the time it's noisier than the positive voice. I have a great example of both.' He was off again. I decided to rename him ChatterBob. 'I have a wonderful Italian friend from Rome. For as long as I have known her she has always said to me, "I will never date an Italian man, especially a man from Naples. Men from Naples are horrible. They are uncouth, they are philistines." And what happened? She met and fell in love with a man from Naples. Why? Because she focused all her energy on what she didn't want. So the universe kept hearing over and over again, "date an Italian man" or "boyfriend from Naples". And that is eventually what she got. The other people get the first bit right, they focus on what they want, imagine it for a moment, and then they dismiss it. They think to themselves, "Well, that would be lovely but that's not really going to happen," or, "What are the chances? I'm not that lucky," and that is what the universe hears. It hears you saying, "I will always be poor. I will always rent horrible flats; my job will always be rubbish. I won't be able to make that change." And they immediately undo all of their hard work.'

'ChatterBob,' I said to ChatterBob, forgetting he wasn't aware of his new nickname, 'I have done *both* of those things.'

'If you are ever in doubt,' said ChatterBob, 'take a moment and think about the following. If you decide to drive from New York to San Francisco you can't see the whole road ahead of you. It's over 2,900 miles. In fact you can't see more than about 200 metres ahead of you. But I bet you never doubt that you'll get there. You never think, "I can't see the whole entire road ahead of me. How do I know I will make it? I can't imagine a road 2,900 miles long. If I can't see it I can't travel on it." No, you decide you'll drive from New York to San Fran and you just *know* you will get there. You focus on the destination, not the road ahead. That is what I need you to do with your dreams. Forget the road, just focus on the destination. The universe will do the rest.'

I didn't fully understand the physics of ChatterBob's idea, and I didn't fully understand ChatterBob, but I was happy to give it a go. He got out a pen and paper and we started to make a list; of the things that had happened in my perfect day and a list of the feelings I'd felt. When we were finished I had a much clearer idea of what I needed to do for my very own Love-Stolen Dream.

I admit I could see a few immediate problems emerging, and they all fell under the heading of *money*. Because most of the things I wanted to do were far too expensive. The main one, the one that really would make me happy for years to come, would be qualifying as a ski and snowboarding instructor. After Gabriel and Julien, this was something I was certain of. To spend five months of every year teaching people on the mountain; being outside doing physical activity all day, going back to my chalet at the end of the day, eating cheese and speaking French—just the thought of it makes me feel lighter than air. But the training courses for qualification are expensive, tens of thousands of pounds, in fact, and tens of thousands of pounds isn't hiding behind the excuse of money, it's trembling in the shadow of the mountain of money I didn't have. And that was before the intensive French immersion language course I wanted to do, and the chalet I'd need to buy to live in and, if we are making a list, and apparently we are, a round-the-world ticket, and a car. I could also do with some new ski equipment, and no girl says no to a makeover, and a wardrobe-replacing shopping spree. Bob was chipper, but he wasn't bloody Jack in the Beanstalk. So what I needed was another way. And I didn't have a clue what that other way would be. So with not a bean in my pocket or a Jack to my name I did what ChatterBob told me and set my positive intention to the universe; feeling how I would feel on the ski instructor training courses; feeling how I would feel when I passed the courses; feeling how I would feel when teaching people to ski, and speaking fluent French, and wandering around my chalet, and wearing wonderful clothes and driving a big black Range Rover with a pet dog called Spot who was ironically named because he's totally black. At least that's my sense of irony.

Bob's version of the universe felt very much like QVC but I liked it, and I was more than happy to give it a try.

my apartment | east london

I found a dog walker. I booked industrial cleaners. I found a puppy day school, dog kennels, a vet, a behavioural specialist for the boy puppy (who I think likes to defecate on expensive pieces of furniture) and I bulk ordered dog food and biscuits. For once I was a chip off the old block that is Grandma. I even spent as long as was physically possible in the local park in the hope I could tire out the relentless puppies. When I finally got back to my apartment I found Peter exactly where I'd left him, completely fast asleep on my bed. The puppies immediately jumped on him and started licking his face.

'I'd prefer it if a beautiful woman woke me up like this, not an unruly pair of dogs,' he said as one of the puppies started chasing his hand before getting distracted by its own tail, chasing that, then falling off the bed. 'I can't normally sleep at other people's houses,' he said drowsily, propping himself up with some pillows. He patted the bed for me to lie next to him. 'Kate, do you remember when we were little and we used to have sleepovers at your house?'

'Are we talking pre-teen sleepovers,' I said, lying down, 'or adolescent ones when I was lucky to get through the night without you pouncing on me?'

'Pre-teen Kitkat. Your grandma would always tell us off for talking too much. What on earth did we have to say to each other until four o'clock in the morning?'

'You were probably giving me a lecture on the pros and cons of animated facial expressions with a focus on smiling and its wrinkle-producing effects. Or the Industrial Revolution.'

'But we did used to be such an industrious country, Kitkat,' he said, turning on his side to face me. 'So, tell me what you plan to do if you quit your job,' he said sleepily, his eyes once again fighting sleep.

'Well, I think I have some ideas, or the beginnings of ideas. I have idea embryos.'

'Do you want me to fertilize them for you, Kate? Honestly, you are always asking me to contribute my bodily fluids to make things for you. It's disconcerting.'

'Seriously, Peter, I've been so focused on fixing everyone else I didn't formulate a proper plan for myself. But now I think I know—as I said, I have idea embryos. I am on the road, even though I can't see the road, there are no street lamps, but apparently that's OK.'

'Very cryptic, Kitkat.' One of the puppies climbed onto my stomach and fell asleep. 'Ah, look at that,' Peter said, having noticed the puppy. 'Well, I'm afraid now you can't move,' he said, gently stroking the dog's head. 'They rarely if ever sleep so if it's sleeping on you then you are staying exactly where you are. I'm afraid you're going to have to sleep next to me.' He stopped stroking the dog and laid his arm across me, pulling me close against him. 'Talk to me while I fall asleep, Kitkat. Your voice always had a sedating effect on me.' He chuckled to himself before kissing my hand and squeezing it tightly. 'Stay here with me,' he said quietly.

I watched his face for a few minutes, the perfect complexion, lack of frown lines, even skin tone. The genetic lottery wasn't the least bit fair.

'Kate, I know you are watching me,' he said, his lips twitching. 'And it's really, *really* disconcerting. And something I thought you'd grown out of. You used to do the same thing when we were kids.'

'It's not the same at all. Your mum had just died and you used to cry in your sleep. It was legitimate staring.'

'So what kind of staring is this?' He had his eyes closed but I could tell he was waiting for my response.

'I don't know what kind this is.'

We both fell silent.

'It's disconcerting, Kate,' he said, stifling laughter. 'That's what kind of staring it is. Dis-con-certing. I think we should nickname you Stare Bear.'

'Peter, I think that almost counts as smiling. I think I just saw you smile.'

'Never. No smiles. It's not my thing.' He kissed my hand and pulled me even closer to him. We both went very quiet. I thought he'd fallen asleep but he reached up and gently stroked the side of my face, his finger tracing lines along my cheek, my nose, my lips. My face moving mere millimetres, responding to his touch like a petal starved of sunlight. He ran his finger gently along my lips. I found myself holding my breath, watching his beautiful face. I was waiting, wanting…

'I don't know how to do this,' he whispered.

'What did you say?'

'I don't know how to have you in my life in the way that I want.' He still had his eyes closed, but he was frowning.

'What do you mean? I'm here. Peter. I'm here.'

I waited for him to utter another sentence but a few seconds later he fell fast asleep.

family times are happy times

As my parents don't celebrate Christmas, or any kind of religious festival, and I don't like to celebrate my birthday, Grandma Josephine's birthday is one of the few occasions when we attempt to be in the same country as each other and sit down for a delightful family meal. My parents had flown in 10 days earlier, a brief visit before an 18-month stay in Kazakhstan, and I'd managed to avoid seeing them until this evening. I was hoping Peter's attendance would provide a buffer between me and their intrusive questioning and undisguised disappointment.

the floating restaurant | pepperpots

I arrived in the floating restaurant to find Peter sitting in silence at the table. He scowled at me as I walked in, pulling me into a whisper as soon as my bum touched my seat.

'You didn't tell me your parents were going to be here!' he shout-whispered.

'I didn't?' I said innocently, knowing full well that *no one* agrees to come to dinner if they think my mum's in town. 'Sorry, I must have forgot…' I said, trailing off because Peter looked explosively angry yet at the same time slightly tearful. For a split second he resembled his 9-years-old self.

My dad noisily cleared his throat.

'Sorry,' I said, turning to them. 'Hi, Dad. Hi, Mum,' I said in a teenage mid-tone. My mother glared at me. 'Sorry. Hi, Richard. Hi, Regina.'

'You're not allowed to call your parents Mum and Dad?' Peter whispered.

'I'm an individual, Peter, not a vessel for the creation of future generations,' shrieked my octave-crushing mother, elbow-deep in a bowl of peanuts. 'I am a person with a name, not a job description. You wouldn't call Kate "Writer", would you?'

'It's not everyone calling you "Mum", Mum,' I whinnied. 'It's just me, your actual daughter, who wants to call you Mum, and they'd call me Feature Writer actually.' I couldn't help myself. My mum rolled her eyes and clicked her fingers for the waiter to come over. Grandma kissed me on the forehead before taking her seat at the head of the table. The Vietnamese pool boy snuck in and pulled up a chair next to Grandma, gently placing a hand on her knee. It was a classic Winters family dinner, with my parents who didn't raise me, Peter who raised himself, Grandma my primary care giver, and the pool boy whose role was somewhat undefined.

'Darling, tell your mother what you have been doing at work,' Grandma said, serving the pool boy with some wine. 'Kate has been brilliant at *True Love*. She's doing some ground-breaking work.'

'I've been following her writing,' my mum snapped, peanut crumbs on her face.

'Have you, Mum, I mean, Regina?'

'Yes. I was surprised you hadn't called me to ask what I gave up for love.'

Peter knocked over his glass of wine.

'Well, I was saving that for tonight,' I lied, passing Peter a napkin. Not at any point since I first conceived of the idea had I ever, ever thought about asking my Regina. 'So, Regina, what would you have done at my age if you didn't think you would fall in love, have kids and settle down? What did love steal?' I beamed at her in an idiotic way.

'Well, I'd done *all* those things by the time I was your age. All of them.' She shoved an olive in her mouth and some oil dribbled down her chin. I noticed Peter holding his fork so tight it looked as if he was going to stab someone. 'But I suppose if I were to be alone forever I would have liked to be a camel racer.' Bloody typical. I am sure she does this for attention. 'They have a very intense race programme, more races per season than Formula 1. The prize money is substantial. The best racers are celebrated as heroes, well, in the Arab states. And I was very talented. My first boy-friend, Abdal Malik, was keen for me to race his family's herd.' She shoved an asparagus tip in her mouth and it dribbled butter on her chin. By this point there were so many different food groups on my mother's face I was surprised Gillian, that aggressive nutritionist from the TV, didn't pop up and start laboratory tests on my mother's skin.

'So, Peter,' my dad mumbled, a way of speaking he has learnt from years of being spoken over by my shrieking mother, 'how is your father?'

And now my mum had knocked over a glass of wine.

'Actually I don't know,' Peter Parker replied, loudly. 'My father and I don't speak.' His jaw was clenched.

'Since when?' I said, turning to Peter.

'Since I was 15.'

'Oh, Kate, you always buy me my favourite things,' Grandma said, unwrapping her present. 'I feel very spoilt. Thank you.'

'I'm glad you like it,' I said, watching my mum, who seemed to be watching Peter, who seemed to be watching her. She seemed transfixed by him, or more precisely by the fact that he had his arm along the back of my chair, his hand on my shoulder. While it was nice that he felt he wanted to touch me it felt more as if he was clutching my shoulder for stability than offering parentally appropriate mealtime affection. He left his hand there for the entire dinner, my mother staring at it every second minute. By dessert my mother's questioning turned to him.

'So, Peter, you've not said much this evening. How are you? What's new in your life?' She was talking to his hand, not his face. 'Is there anyone special in your world?' My dad shuffled uncomfortably on his chair. The table was oddly silent. I realised I was holding my breath. Peter was staring at my mother with what could only be described as murderous intensity. He took a large gulp of his wine before speaking.

'You always were overly interested in the love affairs of my family, weren't you, Regina?' He spat the word *Regina*. I turned to face him. I felt as if I had just switched tables, dropping into a totally different dynamic, one with undertones, undercurrents and a general lack of understanding on my part. It was like the bloody *Sopranos*. 'Are you checking up on me, Regina? Hoping I have found some semblance of happiness from the ruins of my broken childhood?' Peter took another large swig of wine. My mother had gone quite pale.

'Goodness, that was dramatic, Peter.' I giggled. 'It was like you were reading from a Dickens novel!' I chuckled nervously, looking around the table to find no one else the least bit amused.

'It was an innocent question,' my mum said. 'I ask Kate the same thing all the time.'

'She really does,' I whispered to Peter.

'I think you're more concerned I will tell your daughter about you.'

Peter's words hung in the air like celebratory bunting. My mum, dad and grandma all seemed to be intently studying the contents of their plates.

'Tell me what?'

'Peter, please.' My grandmother's voice was gentle. 'I don't think tonight is the night for this conversation.'

'There is no good night for this conversation!' he barked at Grandma.

'What conversation?' I asked, apparently invisible to the rest of the table.

'Maybe you are worried, Regina,' Peter continued, glaring at her, 'that I am going to implode like my mum, a destructive force of nature, taking your daughter with me. Don't worry, I am pretty sure my emotions were switched off around the age of, oh, I think around the age of seven, if memory serves me.' What the hell was going on? '"Give me the boy until he's seven and I'll show you the man." Isn't that the saying, Regina?' Peter downed the contents of his

wine glass. 'Well, I wasn't a man at seven, Regina, but I
certainly was one by the age of fifteen.' He poured himself yet another glass of wine and pulled me on my chair
closer to him.

'I just wanted to know Peter's relationship status.' She
laughed nervously. 'Isn't that what they call it on Facebook?
I was just being polite. I mean, you could be dating Kate for
all we know. So? Are you? Are you two dating?'

'Why do you care what I do with your daughter?' Peter
said incredulously. 'Are you worried you'll have to see my
dad at the wedding?'

'Wedding! What wedding?' I said in a high-pitched giggle.

'Because I don't think my dad will be getting an invite
to the wedding.'

'There's that word again!' I beamed at the table. 'Wedding!'

'Or are you jealous, Regina? You don't want Kate to have
what you couldn't. Because Dad didn't want you any more
after she died. I know that. I saw the letters. He didn't want
you any more.'

Oh, my God…

I turned to Peter.

'Peter, what's going on?' But he was still looking at my
mum, who was staring at Grandma so fiercely I thought
her eyes were going to shoot across the table like missiles.

'Well? Should Peter and Kate be seeing each other?' my
mum asked Grandma, gesturing towards Peter and me. 'Isn't
anyone else thinking what I'm thinking?' Mum shrieked.

Peter looked from my mum to my grandma. It was as if
he was trying to do the maths but it wasn't adding up. Then
I heard him catch his breath.

'How long were you having an affair with my father?' His words were barely audible.

My mum wouldn't look up from her plate.

'HOW LONG?' he yelled, slamming his hand on the table, sending the plates and glasses flying.

'Well, it wasn't a bloody holiday romance, Peter!' she screamed back at him.

'Before I was born?' he asked her. 'Before *we* were born?' he said, grabbing onto my arm as if I were a prop. By now I felt pretty dizzy and it wasn't on account of the wedding chat.

'Ten years,' my dad said solemnly. 'She was having an affair with your father for ten years.'

'No.' Peter started shaking his head. 'No, no, no.' He was shaking his finger at my mum. 'NO!' he yelled, stumbling backwards, away from the table, clutching his head in his hands. Then he put his hands over his mouth, took a deep breath and turned to face me. I didn't know if he was going to lunge for me or run from me. For a second I thought he was about to break down, there and then, crumble to the floor in tiny pieces, but instead the emotion burst out of him like a bomb. 'NO!'

'Peter, calm down.' Grandma tried to get up but the Vietnamese pool boy kept her back.

'Are you fucking joking me?' Peter yelled at my mother, pacing backwards and forwards, each turn looking back at me. 'ARE YOU FUCKING JOKING?' he yelled at the top of his voice, pointing at me but speaking now to Grandma.

Luckily only a tenth of the other ancient diners in the restaurant had noticed the yelling, shouting, pointing and pacing. Two or three of them had turned to stare. Their

Parkinson-induced hands appearing steady in comparison to the trembling hands of Peter Parker. At that moment I was more fuzzy-headed than any senile dementia sufferer in the room.

'Did you know about this?' He turned on my grandma. 'Did you know?'

'Peter,' my grandmother said very calmly, 'I didn't know the length of their relationship until last week. It was Regina's wonderful birthday gift to me, wasn't it, darling? You gave me your dirty laundry as a present.'

'But is it possible?' he pleaded with her.

'Peter, I just don't feel in my heart that it's the case, OK.' She was very matter of fact, as if she thought he would accept her opinion, sit back down and finish his lemon meringue pie.

'But it's possible?' he asked her again. 'It is possible?' Peter's face was a mixture of pain and disgust. He was falling apart before my very eyes.

'Yes, it's possible!' my mother shrieked. 'I was sleeping with them both when I fell pregnant with Kate. Far better someone bloody well mentions this now before we have a herd of six-fingered children running about with ogle boggle eyes and learning difficulties.'

'Regina, I have never raised my hand to a woman,' my father said, throwing his napkin on the table, 'but I swear to goodness that if you don't shut up I will ruddy well do so tonight.'

By this point Peter was standing, practically catatonic, staring at me, his jaw clenched so tightly I feared it would ping off at the joints and explode out of his head. Slowly he turned to face my mother. In a disgusted whisper he muttered,

'How could you?'

She blinked back emotion before lifting her defiant chin high in the air and saying,

'Because I was in love, Peter. I was totally in love with your father.'

'So was my mother, Regina!' he yelled. 'So was my mum!'

Then Peter Parker did what Peter Parker does best and he left, just as all the staff in the restaurant brought out a birthday cake for Grandma singing 'Happy Birthday'. The strange thing was, we all stayed sitting at the table. Grandma blew out the candles and made a wish. My father refilled all our glasses with wine. We finished eating our desserts. Everyone agreed that the chocolate fondant was a better choice than the cheese and biscuits. I had a quick espresso. Then I put my napkin on the table, got up, pushed my chair neatly under the table and finally put on my coat ready to leave.

'Dad,' I said, walking to his side of the table and crouching down next to him. 'I'm sorry for you, I really am,' I said, kissing him on the cheek.

'You can't help who you fall in love with, Kate,' he said, not looking at me.

'No, Dad, you can't. But you can choose just about everything else.' I stood up and turned to face my mum.

'I don't think we will be seeing each other again, Regina.' It was the first time I had felt more comfortable calling her by her first name. 'So take care of yourself, as I am sure you will, please don't contact me, and definitely *definitely* don't try to contact Peter. Grandma, I will be waiting for you in your villa.'

grandma's villa | pepperpots

It was like the direct-eye-contact 700lb-bomb-detonation scenario all over again. No one could look at each other. And by no one I mean me. My eyes were ogle boggling all over the room trying desperately not to land anywhere near Peter.

'You weren't even sick,' Peter said, pacing up and down the room.

'Excuse me?'

'Sick—you haven't been sick. You threw up at Mary's house when you thought I had a girl in my apartment. You felt sick after finding my letters to your grandma but this, this happens, we find out we might be related and what, not even a bit of nausea?'

'I can't believe that is what you are focusing on,' I said, staring at floor.

'Well, I don't understand it. Why weren't you sick?'

'I don't feel sick, Peter, because I don't think there is a reason to feel sick. I just don't believe we could be…er… siblings.' Had he looked at the difference in our complexions?

'But you can't look at me? If you don't think it's true then why can't you look at me?' He was right. I had been talking to a magazine stand slightly to his right.

'I don't want to look at you until we have this all straightened out. I don't want to have *any* images of you in my head when you could have been my... I just think it's best I keep my eyes on the floor.'

'Oh,' he said, mulling it over. 'Oh!' he said, both of us swinging round to face opposite walls. 'I really wish you'd told me that's what we were doing,' he said as we stood back to back.

'Peter, I can't process any of this, that it was *my* mum who took away your family from you. I just, I don't know what to say—' Peter stayed silent. 'I miss her too, you know, Peter. I miss your mum too. I still remember playing with her, and the picnics when she would cut sandwiches into funny shapes, and hide-and-seek in your garden. I still think about her.' Still nothing from Peter. Just his back against my back, solid, constant. 'You should have told me.'

'Would you have wanted Regina in your life if you'd known?'

'No!'

'Well, I wanted you to have a family. I wanted you to be happy. And from a purely selfish point of view I really didn't want to see the look on your face when I told you. I wouldn't have been able to bear it. So Josephine and I decided it was best if you didn't know. I went away. Problem solved. And I wanted to start over. I'm sorry, Kate, but I did. I needed a fresh start. It was the right thing for me.'

'Was it as bad as you thought, my face tonight when I realised—was it as bad as you'd imagined?'

'Actually it wasn't. You were still giddy from talk about imaginary weddings.'

'There was no giddiness! The restaurant was overly warm. And the giddiness I feel now is mostly nauseous.'

'But you don't feel sick?'

'Peter!'

'Kate, I wanted you to have a relationship with your parents. I wanted you to have a mum. There was no point both of us going without. And you *were* giddy.'

'I don't have a relationship with my parents. I never have. Grandma has always fulfilled that role. And my mum, my Regina, well, she's just so, she's so…horrible.'

'She really is horrible.'

'I don't know how you can look at me without thinking about what she did.'

Peter stayed *very* silent.

'Oh.'

'It gets better, with time. It is better. The more I am with you, the less there seems to be any connection between the two of you, any similarity, except when you were wandering around kissing everyone. That wasn't a happy place for me.'

I rolled my eyes, although no one saw. He always had to bring up the kissing.

'Peter, how did you plan to continue spending time with me without sharing any of this? I specifically asked you in New York if you had any other secrets.'

'And I told you that your well-being was my priority.'

'But you stayed at my house last night!' I squeaked. I wasn't really sure why I needed to bring that up. It's not like we'd had sex. We'd lain platonically next to each other, two puppies between us, me acting like a giant Stare Bear. Oh, God, the nausea was coming back.

'So,' Grandma said, marching into the room carrying two clear plastic bags and an envelope. She did a double take as she saw Peter and me standing back to back, then she handed me one of the bags, which contained what I recognised as my hairbrush.

'I thought I'd lost that, Grandma!'

'You didn't lose it, darling, but you could afford to use it a little more often,' she said, passing the other bag back to Peter.

'You're a tealeaf, Josephine,' he said as he retrieved a hat I recognised as his.

'Well, thank goodness I am. Now I say once again that I just don't in my heart of hearts think this is possible. But when Regina turned up last week and found out you were in contact she decided to share her hideous news with me. So I just wanted to make sure. Now, the results came back today. I haven't opened them because I didn't know whether to tell you first or just find out the result myself.' She held the envelope out towards us. Peter snatched it off her, then perched on the edge of the sofa, staring at the envelope, jaw clenched. Grandma came and held my hand. Then Peter tore open the envelope. I could see his eyes scanning through all the words on the page, desperately seeking the results. He found them. Taking them all in. Processing them. Then he placed the letter on the coffee table in front of him and sat back in the sofa. He put both his hands to his mouth, then slowly looked up to meet my panic-filled eyes.

Peter got his wish that night, about the sickness thing, because I did eventually throw up, and I did it right in front of him. It reminded me of a time when, 17 years of age, I projectile vomited across the lounge of my then boyfriend's parents' house. I'd had way too much cider and, if I'm honest, a little spliff. But this was more controlled vomiting. I managed to do it straight into the bin. But Peter was in the room. He saw it. He heard it. It was a joint experience, excuse the pun. It happened right after he'd read the results of the paternity test. Right after he'd read the letter but before he exhaled heavily and said, *'Thank God.'* The vomit started as he began to exhale, because I thought that was a sign of bad news. He should have just said, *'We're not related!'* straight away. But he paused. He stared. He inhaled. Then he exhaled. By which point I had totally freaked out. I bent down. Threw up. Stood up. Got light-headed. Passed out. It was like a strange dynamic yoga move. I came to to find Peter cradling me in his arms, his hand stroking my face, him all around me, holding me, rocking me. It was like Romeo and Juliet on their deathbed, but with vomit, paternity tests and duplicitous parents.

And he didn't let me go from that moment on. In the taxi I slipped in and out of heavy sleep, exhaustion sweeping over me like a storm cloud, Peter's arms around me at all times, the beat of his steady heart almost hypnotic. He carried me into my apartment and laid me down on my bed, but still he didn't let me go, holding me all night, close to him. He held me so close it was as if he thought I might disappear. But when I woke the next morning he was gone.

big fat presents for big slim fat camp

the boardroom | true love

'Well, it looks like only half of you bothered to turn up today,' was Chad's opener to the last meeting of *Fat Camp*. 'Only half of you…half of you…because you have all lost so much weight… What the twat does a man have to do to get a laugh around here?'

The room was silent. There were furniture-creaking noises and tumbleweed rolled across the heart-shaped table. Federico broke the silence by clapping loudly and nodded for everyone to follow suit.

'Look, girls, I have never had a problem with my weight,' Chad continued. 'I'm not an athlete, or a body builder. I don't even know if I have any distinguishable muscle tone on my body. But the point is, I've never been a fat twat. I have never questioned my desirability. I have never given up on my self. I've never felt desperate or alone or over-looked. I can't imagine feeling like that and if I did I don't think I'd twatting tell anyone. But you lot, you were really

fat, weren't you? Do you remember the first day you all arrived here and we had to take you up in small groups in the
lift? Oh, that tickled me—' He spun one circle in his chair
and slapped his thigh. 'Happy times.' He grabbed a red
apple from a fruit bowl. 'But now—' he looked around the
room at all the women sitting around the table '—now we
get the lift together…' He took a moment to let his words
sink in. Federico started clapping again but the applause petered out pretty quickly. 'Look, you all know that if I keep
speaking I will fuck up. I will say something to make one
of you cry, or offend someone, or hurt someone's feelings. I
am in a fucking tank of oestrogen right now, you included,
Federico, and I am fucking drowning. So let's make this
quick. You all look fucking terrible—' Federico coughed
loudly. 'Sorry. Let me start again. You do look terrible—'
The room groaned. 'But!' He tried to talk over them. 'But
looking great can be expensive. Once you get started it's
easier to maintain but initially, well, I bet none of you have
a single thing in your wardrobe that actually fits you.' I
looked around the room. They did look like the dreary cast
of *Les Misérables*. 'I think you've all been twatting marvellous throughout this whole process. You turn up every day.
You push yourselves. You don't complain. So I wanted to
do something for you. To say thank you.' He rocked back
and forward on his heels, rubbing his hands together, waiting for the right moment. 'I have asked one of my friends
to come in. He's pretty good with fashion and all that twatting jazz. He's been given £5,000 to spend on each of you.
The only condition is that you have to agree to be in his
show, which has a few quite specific conditions of its own,

but I will let him tell you about that…' Everyone looked at each other, confused. '*Fat Camp*, I think you are twatting brilliant. Thank you.'

Chad opened the door of the boardroom and at that exact moment the elevator doors pinged open. Out of them stepped Gok Wan[12] followed by yet another camera crew filming us as we filmed them.

Then Gok Wan yelled from the top of his voice, 'Are we ready to look good naked?' as the *Fat Campers* sprinted across the office to engulf him in a pile-up of oestrogen, happiness and healthy BMIs. Most of the screaming I heard was from the mouth of Federico.

'Winters!' Chad growled as I tried to run after Federico. 'I think you and I need to have a little chat, don't you?' He opened the door to his office where a guilty-looking Bob was sitting waiting for us. 'So Bob tells me that you are thinking of twatting leaving?'

'ChatterBob! I thought your sessions were supposed to be confidential?' I barked at ChatterBob. He beamed at me and shook his head from side to side.

'Apparently,' Chad continued, 'you are thinking of quitting and pissing off around the world, learning the abomination that is the French language and doing some kind of skiing course.' Bob excitedly wiggled in his seat. 'Six months of self-indulgent nonsense is apparently what you're after.'

---

[12]**Gok Wan** – British Fashion Stylist with his own TV show, books and fashion line. Women fell in love with him because he wanted us to fall in love with ourselves. Each episode of his TV show is an emotional roller coaster ending with the happiest of all endings—a podgy woman exposing her totally naked body to millions of viewers.

'Nothing *at all* has been organised. I planted a seed. Or Bob planted a seed. Something was sown.'

'Well, it's just gone into bloody bloom, then, hasn't it, like ivy and now it's all over the front of the twatting house. Kate, you can go on your own LSD, you can fuck off for six months but I don't see any reason why you can't continue to investigate Love-Stolen Dreams while you're away. It could add a different angle. We could break into the North American market,' he said, looking off into the middle distance, 'and Canadians are very responsive to print advertising. This could totally twatting work. At least that way I can justify spending thousands of pounds of *True Love*'s money sending you to a bloody ski school.' ChatterBob was excitedly patting Chad's back. 'Bob, I keep telling you. I am not a twatting people person. Stop with the touching. So, Kate, I still expect an article a week on our LSD website. I want a feature each month for our print edition and I want you to thank me personally in everything you write from this moment onwards, something along the lines of, "Thanks to Chad, the owner of *True Love*" or, "My mentor, Chad" or even, "Relationship expert Chad". You get the twatting idea. No, don't, no, don't come over here, I don't want a hug, I don't, oh, for twat's sake.' I gave Chad the biggest, hardest bear hug I could manage. ChatterBob had a go too. 'Oh, and I forgot to mention, you leave next week. You start at the Canadian ski school, then to a French language school, and while you are based on continental Europe you will go wherever the twat else I ask you for any LSD features we are writing. And I expect a two-year commitment to the London office afterwards. Well? What the twat are you waiting for? Pack up your stuff, get yourself organised and get Loosie to book you a flight out of Heathrow. Go!' he yelled, before shoving me out of his office.

I turned, beaming from ear to ear, to find Peter Parker standing outside Chad's office. He was carrying a huge bunch of flowers and had two puppies sitting obediently at his feet.

'I thought you might want to have lunch with us,' he said quietly. 'But I can see you are very busy with your work, as you should be.' He looked at the floor. 'So six months of travelling?' he said, nodding his head. 'That's, well, that's really…well done, Kate. It's a great achievement.' He carried on looking at his feet. 'Well, I should—' He gestured towards the exit. 'We need to—' He pointed to the puppies. 'Well done.' He turned and walked off. The puppies kept turning back to look at me as he led them towards the door. He chucked the flowers in the bin as he left Reception.

the last supper

'Well, Len keeps coming to my mechanics classes with me,' Mary said, passing me a Strawberry Cream from a Tupperware container filled with arse-enlarging Quality Street. We were sitting having tea on the decked terrace of the floating restaurant, waiting for Grandma to allow us inside for my hastily arranged leaving party. 'At first Len said it was because he wanted to make sure I wasn't being ripped off, but now he's enrolled himself as a student and he's there three times a week.'

'How does he get on with Jefferson?'

'Well, it was like peacocks at dawn! All chests out, spanners in hand, who knows the most about spark plugs and chassis. Then Jefferson asked Len if he wanted to go and look at the Formula 2 cars he works on. He runs the pit lane on race days. Well, my Len nearly collapsed with excitement. Now they are best friends. Len is going to spend the day in the pits with Jefferson this Sunday making tea for the engineers and watching how everything works. And when he talks about Jefferson he gets a little flushed in the face. I have no idea why he's blushing—it's quite ridiculous.'

I smiled to myself. Mary's face was practically volcanic the first few lessons we had with Jefferson.

'Don't you want to go with them, Mary, to this pits lane thing?'

'All that noise, and chaos, and those skinny girls wandering around with petroleum company logos on their boobs. No, thank you. I am quite happy with my regular car mechanics, thank you very much. I've actually got quite a bit of work here at Pepperpots,' she said, waving to some of the elderly residents on the shore of the lake. Personally I've never been terribly comfortable with the unsteady, and occasionally unsober, Pepperpots residents whizzing about the private roads in their expensive and generally over-sized cars. It's like bumper cars when you get a few of them driving at the same time. Once Mr Bordel drove head first into the lake after mistakenly putting his automatic in reverse. The lake is only two-foot deep but I read somewhere that it's possible to drown in less than three millimetres of water— that's the liquid equivalent of a spill of tea. I admit I don't fully understand the physics of that but let it be a warning to us all. The dangers of caffeine are far-reaching and absurd.

'Actually Len and I have been looking to rent a garage, you know the ones, under the arches?'

'I remember them, Mary, from our *Power Mary* chat.'

'Well, one came up for rent—what are the chances? There's not been one of them on the market for at least 10 years, but I passed a man in the shop and I overheard him saying he wanted to get rid of his, so we are probably going to take on the lease.' She was struggling to suppress a smile. I watched her pick up her cup of tea, take a sip, then place it back on the table. Mary was warming her own breastbone these days. 'Well, you must come straight round to see me as soon as you get back from your travels, little Kate. We'll all miss you, especially poor Peter Parker. He always has a twinkle in his eye when he talks about you.'

'He doesn't twinkle, Mary. He squints and frowns, mostly in confusion at the nonsense I tell him.'

'Well, he'll be quite lost without you. I don't like my Len going away for one weekend, let alone six months of travels.'

'Peter's not exactly my old Len!' I guffawed, shoving another Strawberry Cream in my mouth. 'He's just a friend, Mary. But if I didn't know any better I'd think you were meddling, and we both know meddling never ends well.' I wanted to think of an example when meddling didn't end well, but couldn't, so hoped the silence would do the talking.

'Enough said,' she said, pulling me in for a big cuddle, planting a kiss firmly on my cheek. 'Well, good luck on your travels. We are all very proud of you. And remember, come straight round to see me when you get back. I am sure we will have so much to tell each other!' She patted me on the knee and got up to get another cup of non-breastbone-warming tea. I watched her walk off, one half of a pair, Len the other piece of her puzzle. Would I feel like a complete puzzle after six months devoted to the pursuit of my own happiness, or would a piece of my puzzle still be missing? And why did that piece feel more and more as if it belonged to Peter Parker?

Since that day in my office and the revelation of my impromptu plan to disappear for six months Peter had made himself incredibly busy, with puppy day care, reinstating his penthouse to pristine condition, building a new water conservation plant in West Africa, which seemed plain old selfish seeing as I was going away for six months. And his preoccupation with his own life left me to deal with my own, which consisted of overwhelming anxieties about not seeing him. Did I like Peter too much to go away even though we weren't a couple? Should I tell him? Should I seek out the advice of my friends and run the risk of them publicly shaming me like a fraudulent expense-claiming politician? I could already see Chad's gleeful face. *'Fall of the already fallen angel,'* he'd yell. *'How to make the same twatting mistake time and time again to the financial gain of your magnificent twatting boss.'*

Personal choice, honouring one's own dreams and ambitions, choosing to do things that bring you joy in the absence of everything else; true, sustainable, healthy, freestanding happiness. I wanted to feel the contentment of reaching my true potential. These were some of the most basic lessons I'd learnt on my Love-Stolen Dreams journey yet they were proving to be the hardest to apply. I was choosing to take myself far away in order to fulfil personal ambitions. It should be easy. I knew it made sense. The maths added up. But the voice in my head kept saying over and over and over again, 'If you go away Peter Parker will meet someone else.' And by this point I didn't want Peter Parker to meet anyone at all. I wanted him to be a piece in my puzzle.

'What on earth are you doing out here?' Grandma demanded, having burst out of the double doors of the floating restaurant. 'Absolutely everyone is waiting for you inside!'

She tutted, then stomped off. I had no idea how *everyone* had managed to get inside without me noticing *any* of them walk past, or how my grandma could be annoyed at me for following her instructions to the letter and waiting exactly where I'd been told, which made it official. I was unable to interpret people or situations. When Peter Parker turned up I would definitely *not* tell him about my all-consuming thoughts about him, or about my inability to stop eating Quality Street Strawberry Creams, because it was very possible I had misinterpreted and misunderstood both.

inside the floating restaurant

'*Is* there a second bridge?' I asked Federico after walking into the floating restaurant to find over 200 people waiting inside; 200 people who had miraculously managed to walk past me without me noticing a single one. How deep in thought had I been on the terrace? Had I gone into a Peter-Parker-induced thought coma? Federico looked confused.

'Federico,' I whispered again. 'Is there another bridge, here? Is there another way?'

'Is this a test?' he whispered excitedly. 'Is there another bridge?' He opened his eyes so wide I thought they might pop out.

'What?' I said.

'What?' he said back. 'You know, Kat-kins, I've always thought there were lots of *ways* and lots of *bridges*,' he said, frantically nodding his head. 'You are like a poet, Kat-kins,' he said, kissing me on the cheek then wandering off, muttering to himself, 'There is *always* another bridge, Federico Cagassi, you just remember that.'

'We're going global, darling,' Grandma said, marching past me and locking the restaurant door so no one else could get in, or out. I didn't know if Peter had arrived or if the Tupperware container of Strawberry Creams had safely found their way to the buffet table…

Grandma pressed a button on a remote control and I turned to see all the electric shutters on the windows close. It left us in total darkness. Bright lights suddenly burst on and my grandma seemed to be wearing a headset and carrying a small clicker. She pressed it and an enormous map of the world (once again with a headshot of me in the middle, early 1990s, after a disastrous perm) moved slowly through the air until it was behind her with spotlights on it. It was the first time I had ever looked at the ceiling of the floating restaurant. It had more cables, wires and lighting installations than the O2 arena. What on earth did they use this place for when they weren't eating here?

'Everybody, may I have your attention?' All the lights went down, except a spotlight on Grandma. Dramatic music started playing. Who was coordinating all of this? 'Can everyone please take a seat?' Everyone did. All the hundreds of people who utilised an entirely different means of entry to me sat on seats, at my strange leaving party. I could see *Fat Campers* mixed up with pensioners, Julio and Edmundo and the LSD Dance Crew, Beatrice talking to Jane and James. Mary was hovering near a plate of sausage rolls. Leah had a sleeping Henry in her arms. Chad was standing close to Delaware, staring at her; Loosie was furiously scribbling notes. Even Jenny Sullivan was there with her very own camera crew filming goodness knows what. I could see the faces of friends, family, colleagues, women whose lives had hopefully changed for the better. The only face I couldn't see was Peter's.

'We have all watched and participated in this thing called Love-Stolen Dreams,' Grandma began. 'Looking closely at ourselves and our lives; reassessing our choices; taking back things we may have lost when we fell in love. Some of us have been changed by it,' she said, looking to Mary. 'Some of us have helped others,' she said, looking to Federico. 'All of us have been moved or affected by it in some way. Whether that be by the realisation that there was a part of ourselves we'd forgotten about, or the acknowledgement that love had not always brought us joy, or by having to stand up and say that we did the best we could do, under the circumstances, with the knowledge and experience we had at the time. I personally feel privileged to have met the women I have met.' She looked around the room. 'To have watched the experiences they have had.' Everyone was nodding along, including the pensioners, and not in a sleep-fighting kind of way. 'To have seen the challenges they faced and the obstacles they had to overcome. And I have faced my own challenges. Reassessing my own ideas about what love is, how powerful it can be, how negative and, conversely, how wonderfully positive it can be.' Different faces across the room kept looking over to me and smiling. What would they think if they knew the real me, the founder of Love-Stolen Dreams, had learnt nothing at all and was desperate for her childhood friend, a man she wasn't even romantically involved with, to burst in the room and ask her to stick around so they could continue to hang out, maybe from time to time lie platonically next to each other in her bed, eventually, one would hope, rip each other's clothes off and turn each other's faces bright pink through non-conventional aerobic exercise. I was like Judas at the Last Supper, sipping from the Cup of Life when secretly I'd already had a Big Mac and Diet Coke with King Herod at the local drive-through. 'So today marks the end of an era,' Grandma continued. 'The end of the first chapter.' Chad was nodding along as she spoke. 'We are beginning to make an impact in the UK, so now we are going global!' Everyone started cheering. The pensioners were loudest of all. 'And we are starting by sending Kate to Canada.' Yet more whooping. I was starting to feel nauseous. 'Kate, here is your phone, laptop and GPS so we can locate you *at all times*. Our job is to find women all across the globe, women who have lost themselves, whether in love, out of love or while they are waiting for love to arrive. With Chad's help and the dedicated team of scouts here, we will locate and make contact with these women. The writers at *True Love* will capture the stories. We are going to make change through action. If every woman we help goes on to help another woman, the domino effect could be far-reaching. This is a movement. Welcome to Love-Stolen Dreams *Goes Global.*'

Everyone started cheering. I looked at the madness all around me. It was bigger than anything I could ever have imagined and somehow I no longer felt a part of it. All I could think about was Peter. Why wasn't this quest, this thing I fought so hard to start, to maintain, to grow, why wasn't it enough for me any more? Was I a giant void of a person, a black hole, continually sucking things into my endless bottomless abyss? Is that why I couldn't stop eating Quality Street? Because of the black hole in my soul that now wanted Peter Parker as well as everyone's love-stolen dreams. Did I have an emotional, actual and metaphorical universe-devouring eating disorder?

I slipped away from the madness, out of the nearest door, back onto the decked terrace and the cool night air. Chad followed me a few moments later, lit a cigarette and hovered by my side, both of us staring out at the dark and peaceful lake.

'First the pendulum swings one way. Then it swings back the other way. Eventually, you hope it stops somewhere in the middle.' He rolled back and forwards on his heels and took a big drag on his cigarette. I had no idea what he was talking about.

'Chad, is this about the second secret bridge and all the other access routes? Because I think Federico misunderstood me.' Actually I didn't think it, I knew it. He totally misunderstood me, as per normal.

'There is always another side to a story. There is always the other side of the coin. Everyone goes to the dark side before going to the light.' Oh, God, this was awkward. He was talking total and utter rubbish. 'Nothing in life is without confusion and struggle. No man is an, oh, for twat's sake, Kate—' He flicked his half-finished cigarette in the lake and immediately lit another one, then he sighed heavily and turned to face me. 'Did you really think this was going to be enough for you forever?' He nodded to the door to the floating restaurant where the sounds of laughter and animated conversation were seeping out like beams of light around a door frame.

'Chad, I have no idea what you are talking about.'

'You're not a fraud if you are worried about leaving this Peter Parker. I assume he is the cause of your sullen-looking face tonight? Personally I expected you to be high-fiving everyone and chest-bumping your grandma but he's not here, and your face is like that.' He waved his hand in front of my face.

'My face isn't sullen. It's a look of concentration. It's a… It's… I don't know what it is.'

'Kate, there are very few certainties in life, and most of them you learn as a child. Sporting ability, good looks and even being very funny can get you some kudos but they are all to a degree God-given, dished out at birth, rarely to the most deserving. And if you don't have those things when you are a young boy—and you are a young boy who already knows he's gay—there is only one thing that helps you fit in, and that's money. Money can buy you acceptance, respect, adoration. Money can protect you in all kinds of ways. And *True Love* has given me money, status, power. And that has always felt like it was enough for me. Until I started watching you do the exact same thing.'

'I am the least money-orientated person I know.'

'I'm not saying you are chasing money. But working as you do, taking back things that other people lost, you are controlling the controllables. And it's been the best thing that's ever happened to my magazine, and it might just be the best thing that's ever happened to me, to watch people being brave and pushing themselves out of their comfort zone, everyone accepting each other even if those people have none of the twatting qualities I grew up believing were important. Well, let's just say it's been more fulfilling than when our main feature was the percale content of bed sheets in honeymoon suites. Just don't wait too long, Kate, to let the uncontrollables back into your life again. Don't switch off your feelings and your emotions for too long, don't try and control them, because, I promise you, it's not like riding a bike. It gets harder and harder to open yourself back up to someone, to allow yourself to feel. And for some people, eventually, it becomes impossible.' He took a heavy drag on his cigarette. 'Everyone is scared of having feelings, Kate. Everyone is scared of being hurt, abandoned, *rejected*, but people need people. You must have seen that, throughout this whole journey, that one absolute constant. People need people. The pendulum swings one way. Then it swings back the other way. But eventually we hope it stops somewhere close to the centre.' He flicked his cigarette in the lake and wandered back to the party.

I stood on the terrace for several minutes, breathing in the cold night air, listening to the laughter and joy coming from inside the floating restaurant. It was a million miles from the cold night in France when I had packed my bags and left Gabriel, a million miles and a million stories. Was I finally ready to start my own? And was it going to be the story I had imagined?

**'never apologise for showing feelings
for when you do so you apologise for the truth'
(benjamin disraeli)**

Two-fold plans. I'd learnt all about them watching *The A-Team*. Fold one normally requires many complicated things to happen, at exactly the right moment, against all odds, and those things then allow fold two to take place, which involves an explosion and driving through some kind of barrier. And then, when all the folds have been folded, the leader of the A-Team, who was called Hannibal long before that cannibal Hannibal was named as such, he says, *'I love it when a plan comes together,'* and what he meant by that was, *'Thank goodness my two-fold plan worked.'*

So I had come up with a two-fold plan, all of the folds involving Peter Parker although my goal was less distinct than the A-Team's, which normally involved blowing something up, escaping from something or making impressive pieces of machinery from small cardboard boxes. There may be a moment when I yell, *'I ain't gettin' on no plane, you fool!'* but that was very Mr TBC.

So Fold One was that I had decided to tell Peter Parker that on occasion, or in fact most of the time, I thought of him in ways that weren't *100%* platonic. In fact they were the exact opposite of platonic. If platonic had a nemesis it lived in my head in the part of my brain where thoughts about Peter lived. So I was going to get it out there, be brave, be vulnerable, hope that the pendulum stopped somewhere in the middle. Fold Two was the kiss that I hoped Peter might offer me after I told him I thought he was special and handsome. That was my brilliant two-fold plan. After which I was going to fly to Canada to train as a ski instructor. Or I was going to stay in Peter's apartment kissing him until my lips were chapped and I'd run out of saliva. Either way fold one of the two-fold plan was about to happen. Kate Winters was stepping up to the plate of love, or honesty, or kissing. I was stepping up to the plate of something. And all of the above seemed like a really clever idea until Peter Parker had actually answered his front door, a cool ice-pop fridge magnet in a super-fitted T-shirt and no such enthusiasm for two-folds or new plans.

'Aren't you supposed to be at your leaving party?' was his initial flat-toned, smile-free comment when he saw me standing, once again, in the hallway of his apartment block. He looked beautiful, and fresh, his top skimming over what I already knew to be an exquisite torso.

'Aren't *you* supposed to be at my leaving party?' I chuckled nervously as I followed him into the immaculately clean apartment. We walked into the lounge and he stood cross-armed next to one gigantic sofa. I stood next to the other one. He didn't invite me to sit down, so we just stood there.

I looked about the place, as one does when things are a bit awkward and tense.

'Sorry, I was going to come to Pepperpots but I was having trouble with the dogs so…'

We both looked at the dog basket where the puppies slept as if they'd been sedated. 'Well, they were disruptive earlier,' he said, rubbing his hand through his hair and frowning. 'They were more energetic pre-10 p.m.'

'Peter, I leave in two days and I haven't seen you, at all.'

'Well, it's a really busy time of year for me,' he said, gesturing towards his laptop, which was switched off on the coffee table. He registered its dark screen, then looked at the floor and sighed heavily. 'I was thinking things through before starting work,' he muttered. The apartment was eerily quiet. I could hear the London traffic on the streets outside.

'So how are you?' I said, trying to sound super casual, my vocal cords sounding as if someone were pinching them together.

'I'm good, Kate, same as always.'

'That's great news. Good stuff. Well, I just wondered if, I thought maybe you would, perhaps we could spend some time together before I go away? Maybe do something together?'

The last thing I'd done with Peter was fall asleep with him wrapped all around me. It was pretty much all I'd been thinking about ever since.

Peter stared at me from the other side of the room. I found myself nervously fiddling with the hem of my dress. He watched my hands.

'You're going away for a long time, Kate. Don't you think

it's a bit stupid to spend every day together if we're not going to see each other for six months? There's not a lot of consistency there. And it's been proven that both humans and animals benefit from consist—'

'I don't care what's been proven, Peter. I just want to know if you want to see me before I leave, get a coffee. We could talk about *stuff*.' I shrugged, as if *stuff* were mere bric-a-brac as opposed to crossing the cavernous divide from friendship to people who kiss and sniff each other's necks.

'Well, let's have a coffee now and talk about this *stuff*—' bric-a-brac '—then it's done and you can get back to preparing for your trip.' He strode off towards the kitchen. The noise woke the puppies, who immediately tore after him before noticing me and tearing back the other way. They came to a skidding halt at my feet, then started running after each other. I watched the girl puppy chase the boy puppy with unabating enthusiasm; she just chased and chased and chased, her quest for his attention relentless. I sat down on one of the sofas. Through the huge windows the lights of the London skyline twinkled in at me; the financial distract; the dome of St Paul's nestled among the skyscrapers; the old with the new; visual reminders of different eras. Was I about to enter a new era? Was I trying to cling to Peter as a safety net? Was that why I felt as if I wanted to kiss him until I ran out of breath?

'Here you go,' he said when he finally wandered back into the lounge, handing me a hot mug of coffee. 'To your new life,' he said, clinking my mug, then sitting himself on the sofa opposite. He picked the further possible point away from me. The puppies ran over to him, jumping up onto the expensive sofa.

'They are as well trained as ever,' he mused, stroking them. 'They definitely know I'm the boss,' he said as the boy pup jumped up and tried to bite his nose. The girl pup was desperately trying to climb up Peter's chest and lick his neck. I watched him take a sip of his coffee. He watched me. I wanted to start on fold one.

'I will miss you, Peter,' I said quite forcefully. I had officially turned into the girl puppy.

'I think when you get to Canada you'll find you miss very little about your life here.' He took a sip from his coffee and looked out of the window. 'But it's nice of you to say something. Very sweet,' he said, still looking out of the window.

'I just thought that, well, things have been pretty intense, what with the whole "Are we related?" drama, and now I am going away for six months it doesn't really give us a chance to get things back on track, back to normal, so I thought that if you wanted me to delay my, I mean, if you prefer me being around, more than me not being around to work through what has happened or not happened, or because of certain feelings that one or both of us may or may not have…'

'Sentences are hard to understand when they contain double negatives, Kate.'

'What I mean to say is that you are important to me and I would reconsider what I'm doing if it was the best thing to do for…us…for you and me, you know, if you prefer that I am around so we could do things together.' Like kissing. 'For example, you could tell me your thoughts and feelings and then I could tell you my thoughts and feelings and then we could, adjust things, things aren't set in stone, if you know what I mean.' I didn't, and it was my speech. I'd do better to get down on all fours and start yapping.

'Kate, I'm not entirely sure what you're saying,' he said, putting the puppies on the floor, 'but my interpretation of it sounds like you're saying I could have an influence over your travel plans,' he said, frowning. 'Is that what you're saying? You'll delay your trip or?'

'Cancel it…?' Was he asking me a question or asking me to finish his sentence?

'Or cancel your trip for me?'

'Peter, I haven't actually thought everything through. I just wanted you to know that you are important to me. I like you in my life…' yap…yap…yap '…I would prioritise your well-being when considering my plans, and, I would like more of you in my life. I need you, how you are, your perspective on life, I like it all, all of it, all of you, you are…nice.'

Well, what an impressive wordsmith I was. Of course Chad would hire me to rewrite the words of other humans. I had absolutely none of my own; I was word poor; I was living below the word poverty line. But at least I'd said it, sort of. I had taken the higher ground. I'd been brave, stepped up to the plate, put myself and my feelings out there, in a confusing, vague and self-protecting way.

'Are you saying you'd stay for me, Kate?' he said, glaring at me. Then he shook his head, rubbing his eyes and his forehead. He suddenly looked very tired. 'And what do you mean you *need* me? You don't *need* me, Kate. And I'm

really sorry to say this but I definitely don't *need* you.' He
sat back in his seat and crossed his arms. 'I don't need anyone, Kate. And neither should you. You really should know
better than that.'

'Don't give me that speech, Peter, about not needing anyone. It's bullshit. I think you like having me in your life.
What I want to know is if you have feelings for me, other
than friendship.' He shuffled uncomfortably in his seat. 'Do
you? Do you feel *anything* at all about me? When you stayed
at my house? When we spend time together? Anything?'

'It's been nice getting to know you a bit, after all this
time.'

'That's it? That's all you want to share? It's been nice
getting to know me *a bit*?'

'Well, what do you want?' he said, getting to his feet. 'Do
you want me to tell you to stay? So we can have some kind
of emotionally painful goodbye when you eventually decide to leave? Or maybe,' he said, grabbing the coffee cups
off the table, 'maybe you could stay and then blame me for
it afterwards.' He marched off towards the kitchen before
turning on his heel and marching back. 'I have a much better idea. Let me become the source of all your happiness
and joy. Let's do that. Then you can fall apart all over again
when you realise I do not have the ability to make you feel
complete. Seriously, Kate, you come here basically telling
me that you would change all your brilliant and exciting
plans, plans that are important to you, for me. And you expect me to be excited at the prospect of that? What kind of
man do you think I am?' I thought he was a really handsome
and nice man, obviously, and I hadn't committed to a plan

change. I'd only committed as far as the speech, and the kissing. I was a short-termist; that's how I got into credit-card debt at university.

'Kate, it's late and I'm really tired so if you don't mind I'd prefer if you left.'

'Peter, we haven't finished talking about this.'

'We have and I want you to go.'

'There is nothing brave about denying your feelings, Peter! There is nothing brave about how you're being. It's OK to want someone else to be around, Peter. People need people.' I couldn't believe I was quoting Chad.

'You can show yourself out,' he said, marching off into the kitchen and not coming back out. The puppies sat on the floor in the space between us; neither one knew which way to go.

The pendulum swings one way, then it swings another, and you hope that eventually it lands somewhere in the middle. But it doesn't always. Sometimes it just keeps moving.

a short interval

theresa—62 years old—second time's a charm

Dear True Love,

When I first read about Love-Stolen Dreams it didn't connect, at all. Before I got married I did all the things I wanted to. The late 1950s were not a period in history when all young women went off on their own to live abroad but my parents actively encouraged it. My European travels are still some of my fondest pre-love memories and when I met the man I eventually married I never once thought I was disengaging from myself in any way. But the fact is, 10 years into my marriage I was utterly miserable and I didn't recognise myself any more. I was no longer financially in-dependent. I had no career. Theresa had left the building. So in truth, love showed up and, yes, the balance started to shift, slowly, in barely tangible ways, and ultimately that was very detrimental to me, and to my marriage.

Do women actively give up their dreams when they fall in love? I think the dreams become more and more dream-

like until you almost forget you had them. Do women waste time before they fall in love? I don't know. I didn't.

My advice for women is quite boring and quite practical. But I tell you with all honesty and all sincerity that being financially independent has been the single most significant factor in the reclamation of my own happiness. I am answerable to no one. I am financially free of any other person. It's taken me until after my 60th birthday to achieve it, but that independence is the cornerstone of my personal happiness. It also contributes to the success of my current relationship.

I spend lots of time with my wonderful boyfriend. At the weekends we travel together, we have fun, we kiss, we have great sex, we relax, eat great food, see friends, play sport, all the best parts of being in a relationship. After the weekend we both go back to our work and back to our separate homes. And we have never ever been so happy. Oh, I should probably mention at this point that the new man in my life is my ex-husband. Twenty years later, two marriages and seven step-kids between us, we are back together, for all the right reasons.

Life really can get in the way of love. Not feeling good about yourself really does get in the way of love. My lack of self-worth during the relationship; my lack of 'having my own shit going on' as our youngest son would put it, played a massive hand in the failure of my marriage. But my boyfriend/husband/ex-husband/father of my children, whatever you want to call him, really was the love of my life. We were meant to be together. Two marriages and forty years later I am so happy that I can finally have the relationship of my dreams with the man of my dreams. But being with someone doesn't have to mean being together all the time. A committed monogamous relationship doesn't have to mean living in each other's pockets, or living together at all. We know we are going to be together for the rest of our lives but living apart means we get to have the homes we want and the lifestyles we want. We never speak about laundry; what food is in the fridge; whose turn it is to take out the trash or clean up the bathroom. When we were married we even used to fight about whose turn it was to pick up the dog shit in the garden! I'd feel hard done by because I did all the housework so the least he could do was clear up the garden. He'd feel hard done by because he was working all the time to financially support the family. He felt a burden. I felt a burden. No one felt happy. Now our time together is precious; it's just about enjoying each other's personalities, conversation, bodies. It's the ultimate relationship because it is actually about the relationship and not about all the shit that sometimes comes with being in a relationship. We are in a privileged position. I know that. Our kids are grown up so we are free to live any way we please, but my advice for Love-Stolen Dreams would still be the same. Work for your financial and emotional independence. Get your financial and emotional independence. Keep your financial and emotional independence. It saved me and gave birth to the most wonderful relationship of my life. I also highly recommend living apart.

karma

the basic theory that the universe runs according to certain laws of cause and effect; your actions create your Karma; whatever you do comes back to you; what goes around comes around...and there is no earthly way of changing this.

heathrow terminal five

It had arrived. The day I finally returned to Heathrow Terminal Five, hopefully with less luggage (metaphorical and literal) and a lot less tears. As I crept across Departures like a cartoon mouse trying to avoid a cartoon cat I was certain every security guard in the building was watching me, which made the familiar face of the check-in girl even more disconcerting.

Tabitha Jones had been at playschool with me and Peter Parker. She had one green eye and one brown eye, which was, let's be honest, going to single her out for mild teasing and alienation at preschool. She'd fallen in love with

Peter when she was 4 years old and hated me from age 4¼. That was around the time I'd discovered a drawing she'd made of her and Peter kissing under a rainbow. She called it *'Peter & Me forever'*. She'd even made a feature of her odd-coloured eyes. I'd never thought to make Peter a picture and was jealous of her original creative thought. So I decided to stick the picture high up on the blackboard for everyone to see, just out of Tabitha Jones' reach. She cried and she wailed as she jumped up and down trying to grab it before Peter Parker caught a glimpse. The other children laughed. She lashed out at me with a green crayon and threw her Mr Men lunchbox at my head. Eventually Peter did see the drawing and, the good-natured boy that he was, took the drawing down and gave it back to her. He then gave her a big hug and told her it was a beautiful picture, which riled me even further. And I'm sure everyone else moved on after the hug, emotionally speaking, but I never did. To this day I still feel ashamed and it's the only time I have ever done anything that could be considered bullying. The memory of it is stuck on my heart like crude oil on a small seabird. But I thought feeling bad about something *forever* would be enough of a punishment. I mean, what were the chances that the woman who was quite literally checking me in for the next stage of my life would be Tabitha Jones? It was karma, proving to me that it existed, waiting for this poignant moment, then sucker-punching me in the face. Not that I'd ever doubted the power of karma, just that I'd been more interested in what it might do to Gabriel.

'You are *so* familiar to me,' she said as I passed her my ticket and passport. She smiled genuinely as she picked up my documents and typed my details into her computer. 'Do you fly with us regularly?' She stopped typing to look at me, open-faced, interested. I shook my head.

'No, I don't normally fly to Canada.'

'Oh, my God! It's you! It's you!' she said, pointing at me then ducking down under the desk. She came back up with a copy of *True Love* in her hand. 'You're her! You're the girl, the LSD girl!' The airport police glanced over. 'Oh, I *love* you! I've been following you in the magazine and I love the *Fat Camp* video diaries on the website. They even have uploads on *YouTube* now! You are doing such a great thing,' she said, handing back my passport. But just before she'd finally released it from her green-crayon-yielding fingers I felt a pair of heavy male hands on my shoulders. The hands squeezed my shoulders gently before the arms slid around my waist and I could feel the warm breath of Peter Parker on my neck as he whispered quietly in my ear.

'I'm so sorry, Kate.' He wrapped his arms all around me. 'I'm so *so* sorry.' I extracted myself from his embrace and turned to face him. He took my hand and pulled me closer to him. I stared at him. He stared at me. 'It doesn't feel nice when people leave, Kate.'

'I know that, Peter. It doesn't feel nice when friends lie about things that happened to them and ask you to leave their apartments.'

'I'm sorry. But I didn't want you to go away without saying goodbye.' He gently kissed me on the cheek, leaving his face against mine, then he scooped me up in his arms, holding me so tightly I could feel his heart beating in his chest. I hoped he couldn't feel the speed of mine. My bodily functions were always giving me away.

'What I want to say,' he said, releasing me only slightly,

'is that it doesn't feel nice when *you* leave. Kate, the night I stayed in your apartment, I told you that I didn't know how to be with you, and, well, I don't. I don't think I am naturally very good at being with another person. I didn't do well when I was married, but, what I'd like to do, what I really want to try is, oh, my God, Tabitha? Tabitha Jones?' Oh, no. 'Tabitha Jones, is that really you?' Karma. 'I'd know your eyes anywhere in the world, Tabitha Jones. It's me,' he said, touching his chest. 'It's me, Peter Parker.'

She looked at Peter as if she were going to combust with longing.

'I know who you are, Peter Parker,' she said with a twinkle in her eye and the beginnings of a smile. Then her eyes flashed to me. 'You!' she said, pointing a scary crayon-yielding finger in my face, snatching back my passport to look inside. 'You are Pirate Kate? You! The child torturer! The school bully! The picture stealer!' It seemed as if she had a fairly good idea who I was. 'What are you doing here? Why are you going to Canada?'

'Kate is going for work, which I am very supportive of, which is something else I wanted to talk to you about,' he said, turning to me, 'because—'

'They are sending you to Canada?' she screeched. 'For work! Is there no God? Is there no karma?' I wanted to tell her that there absolutely definitely was. 'Just typical of British society that bullies are rewarded with good jobs and free holidays. They said as much in the *Daily Mail*. And Peter Parker as your boyfriend! Is there no bloody justice?'

'Oh, Kate isn't my girlfriend. She's my…' He stopped and looked at me.

'She's your what?' Tabitha demanded.

'I'm your what?'

'Your wife! I knew it! I knew you two would get married!'

'We're not married!' we said in unison.

'Oh,' Tabitha said quietly, looking between the two of us, her odd-coloured eyes trying to work out the dynamic, something I'd given up trying to do.

'Karma,' I muttered under my breath, wishing she had never drawn that stupid picture.

'Karma,' Tabitha said as she stared at me, her spiteful eyes plotting, hatching a plan. Whatever it was I was doomed. Tabitha now had the power over my future life because I had messed with her past.

'Tabitha, I was just wondering,' I asked as casually as I could manage, 'am I properly checked in because I don't think you gave me a boarding pass and you, er, you still have my passport.' She looked down at her hand; her knuckles had turned white where she was clenching the passport so hard. I knew I wasn't going anywhere. Chad was going to go ballistic when he found out I'd missed my flight on account of some primary-school indiscretion. Tabitha composed herself and looked up.

'Peter, are you going to Canada to work?'

'No,' he said, tucking some of my hair behind my ear. 'I am not going to Canada to work.'

'How long are you going for?' she barked at me. 'How long, Kate?' Her supervisor looked alarmed and smiled reassuringly at the long queue of passengers behind us.

'I'll be gone for about six months.'

'She will *definitely* be gone for six months,' Peter said proudly, squeezing my shoulders, completely misjudging the tone of the situation. 'She has lots of important work to do. She's on her own Love-Stolen Dreams mission and—'

'Canada is horrible, Peter. You'd do well to stay in London. I live in London. Perhaps I could take you out?' She gave me back my passport and signalled for me to step away from the check-in desk with dismissive hand-flicking gestures reminiscent of my duplicitous mother. 'You are checked in, Kate,' she said menacingly. 'You are very very checked in. Make your way to the plane.'

As we walked away from the desk she yelled out, 'Message me on Facebook, Peter!' but he didn't seem to notice as he had slung his arm over my shoulder and was once again doing something that could be called 'affectionate' with my hair.

'Do you have time for coffee before you fly?' he whispered quietly in my ear. His warm breath on my neck made my whole body tingle. I didn't know if I had time or not. I wasn't aware of anything other than Peter and his strong arm pulling me close against him as we walked. 'And not a coffee like the other day, a proper coffee. We really need to talk.'

He walked me all the way to the departure gates still with an arm around me, but I wasn't sure how we were going to have this mythical coffee as all the cafés were now a long way behind us. The only thing that constituted a refreshment stand was the tray of bottles that had been forcefully removed from poorly prepared infrequent-flyers; the ones that apparently had the ability to make a bomb from 101ml of Fanta and a tub of Boots Anti-ageing face cream. Perhaps Peter had brought a flask and we were going to picnic by the gates? Or perhaps there would be no coffee, just a hug and a back pat before he shoved me through the gate yelling, *'See you some time next year, Kate,'* then messaging Tabitha bloody Jones. But Peter Parker kept walking, all the way up to Passport Control, reaching into his pocket, taking out a passport, then walking straight through to the gate. Frozen to the spot, I watched him as he finally turned and reached out a hand for me to follow him.

'Are you coming with me or not?' he said, walking off towards the mini shopping mall that was Departures Heathrow Terminal Five.

gate 11

We had been sitting next to each other for what felt like a decade, on a row of plastic seats, in a deserted area close to the gate. My flight had started slowly boarding. Peter had bought me a coffee but still hadn't said anything. Neither had I. As the last remaining passengers got up to board he finally turned to face me.

'Kate, I don't have an abundance of role models in my life showing me how to be in a relationship. In fact I don't have any. I had my mum, and your mum, and you, at least you before me, you with Gabriel. And none of it seems all that positive. So when you tell me you need me, well, it makes me want to run away, and I'm sorry, but I really *don't* need you. I will never need anyone.'

I couldn't believe Peter Parker had come all the way to Heathrow Airport to reiterate that one point. It was the one point I had zero chance of ever forgetting.

'I get it, Peter. I got it that day. You really didn't need to come down here to say it all over again.'

'Kate, I keep telling you that I don't know how to do this and yet you keep getting annoyed when I say the wrong thing!' He cleared his throat and started again. 'Kate, I don't need you.'

'Peter, you are like a broken record! They were thinking of you when they invented it!'

'*But* given the choice, I'd *choose* to spend my time with you. I'd choose you. I choose you.' He took my hands and squeezed them gently, shuffling in his seat. 'What I am *trying* to say is that I am happy with you. I am happier with you than without. It feels normal and it feels right and it feels complete. And what I realised is, that's different from need, it's choice, it's personal preference. So I came here today to give you a choice. I am giving you the choice, to…' The words seemed to get stuck in his throat.

'To what?'

'To do all this with me.' He edged closer to me. 'Kate, I have arranged everything. And I mean *everything*. Everything is taken care of. It's totally possible. So I am free for you, if you want me to be. It's your choice. The question is, do you want me to come with you? Do you want me to come to Canada with you?'

He looked me deep in the eyes and time stood still.

I am not sure how long we stared at each other. I didn't want to break his gaze. And when I spoke the sound of my voice surprised me, as if I had been in my own head for a very *very* long time. But what surprised me even more was my answer. It was clear. Short. Without explanation.

'No.' I took a sharp intake of breath after I said it. Peter stared at me, impossible to read.

'No, I don't want you to come with me.' I said it again, more to confirm it to myself than to him. Why couldn't I just say *yes* like any normal girl? Why was I so complicated and inconsistent? I realised my hands were shaking from the adrenaline and hid them in my pockets. Peter still didn't speak. His blue eyes just gazing at me.

'Last call for Flight 7098 to Calgary, Canada.' I recognised Tabitha's voice on the loud intrusive tannoy. 'That's last call for any remaining passengers for Calgary, Canada.'

'Peter, I need to feel *The Thing*, that Mary's felt, and Leah and Annie. Because otherwise I think you will become *my thing*, like you said in your apartment, you were right, and while I really like the sound of that, I can't. I can't do that knowing all I know, having learnt all the things that women have bothered to share with me. So I need, no, I *want* to do this next stage alone. I'm sorry.'

'This is the last and very final call for any remaining passengers travelling to Calgary, Canada.' Tabitha's voice was as strained as my own. I could see her in my peripheral vision, pacing up and down at the gate, eager to get me on the plane and away from Peter Parker, whose use of words now rivalled his use of smiles.

'Peter, please say something.'

He didn't. He just stared. I felt very aware of my constricted throat and tear ducts that were on red alert.

'Peter, six months doesn't seem like a long time to be apart in the grand scheme of things. Surely we could have other shared experiences in the future? And if your interest in me is so fragile that a six-month work project could ruin it then it probably wasn't an enduring interest anyway. This isn't a test. I promise you. It's just…six months; six months doesn't seem that long.'

Peter still didn't speak, and there wasn't really anything else I could say. Of course I could ramble on and on for ten to fifteen minutes, share all kinds of peculiar things, but I didn't feel I had any more to comment on the current subject. I would have to walk away, and live with the consequences of my decision, a decision made from somewhere so deep inside me that it was stronger, more powerful, had more clarity than the woman I knew myself to be. I stood up and picked up my hand luggage but he stopped me, taking the bag and putting it back down on the floor.

'Six months isn't a long time,' he said taking my hands.

'It's not!' I squeaked. 'It's not a long time, Peter! There are series of *X Factor* that run for longer than six months, and that's an annual returning TV show!' He was frowning slightly so I was fairly sure he didn't know what the *X Factor* was. 'I'm sorry, Peter. It was an amazing gesture, although quite *out there*, quite extreme—you haven't quite got the hang of the pendulum concept.'

'Kate, I *keep* telling you that I don't know what I'm doing. And please don't say sorry—you don't need to be sorry. It was win-win for me. If you said yes then I could spend six months with you on a mountain and if you decided to go alone then I would be, *I am*, incredibly proud of you. Although the *no* part was slightly more painful than I'd expected but that's a feeling which is a good thing in itself,' he said gently squeezing my hands. 'Kate, for as long as you know me you will never *ever* have to compromise any part of any dream for me. I promise you that. And I promise to always be argumentative if you try.'

'Wonderful. The promise of an argumentative Peter.'

'And I think it's reassuring to know that we're not like our parents.'

'You mean it's nice to know I'm not exactly like your mum, or my Regina.'

'That's mostly what I mean,' he said as he pulled me by my hand closer to him. I caught my breath as our bodies touched, Peter gently tucking some of my hair behind my ear. He had a look of concentration as he studied my face, gently running his thumb along my cheek bone, down my neck. As he tilted his head ever so slightly I found myself mirroring him, breathing at the same rhythm, at the same rate. He was a breath away from me, from my lips, from kissing me; a millimetre away from crossing the line, a heartbeat, then finally, after 29 years of knowing each other, Peter finally took the last step, moved the last millimetre and bridged the final gap, and he leant down and he kissed me, Peter Parker kissed me, in the most perfect, gentle, dizzying way.

'This is absolutely the last and final last call for passenger Kate Winters flying to Calgary!' a hysterical Tabitha Jones squealed into the tannoy. 'If passenger Kate Winters is listening she should know that it's very selfish to keep everyone else on the plane waiting. Just because she writes for a magazine does not give her the right to treat other people like crap. Not now, not ever!'

'I know you want to say it, Kate,' Peter whispered, pulling away from me slightly, 'and it's OK.'

'I don't know what you are talking about, Peter.'

'You want to say it, just once, I know you. We're at the

airport. You're going away for a long time. You want to say it. You need to say it.'

Peter was right. I did need to say it. And Madame Butterfly told me to always connect with my desires. So I took a deep breath and prepared myself. I closed my eyes and as authentically as I could I said,

'I ain't getting on no plane, you fool.'

'My God, it's like you are actually channelling Mr T,' Peter said, mesmerised. 'It's like I am in an episode of *The A-Team.*'

'I know. It's a gift.'

'I mean you sound *exactly* like him. And you are a small white female. Do it again.'

'You ain't getting on no plane, you fool,' I said, grinning.

'Astonishing. Does he actually live in you?'

'You ain't getting on no plane, you fool.'

'OK, that's probably enough, Kate,' he said, cupping my face in his hands and kissing every inch of it before pulling me into a hug.

'It's never too late to be who you were supposed to be, Kate Winters,' he whispered in my ear. 'I am so *so* proud of you.'

As he leant down to kiss me again, and I prepared to tumble into a world of Peter-Parker-filled kisses, one karmic-filled Tabitha Jones marched up behind me and pulled me, by my arm, through the departure gate to the plane.

'I'll come and visit you, Mr T,' Peter yelled just as the doors of the gate were locked behind me. And I wasn't positive but for a second I thought I saw him smile as he waved goodbye.

flight 7098 to calgary, canada

As I sat on the plane in the smallest and most uncomfortable seat Tabitha Jones could find, the one that won't recline even though the passenger in front can, I took the brochure for my new ski school out of my bag. This ski school was my choice. My decision. My reason to say *no* to Peter Parker. It was the hundredth time I had looked at it. And every time I felt *The Thing*. I hugged the brochure to my chest and closed my eyes. I was about to realise a long-cherished dream. Finally this was my moment. Then I noticed something glistening in the bottom of my bag, something unfamiliar, something I definitely hadn't packed. I pulled out all my clothes, my magazines, my books and toiletries, trying to get to this mysterious addition, a present wrapped in gold paper. I unwrapped it like a child, and found a family-size pack of *KitKat*s and a small white envelope. I opened the envelope. Inside there was a Polaroid photo and a small card. On the card were written the words:

'It's never too late to be who you were supposed to be.'

And when I looked at the photo it was of the one thing I had waited most of my life to see again. It was a photo of a smiling, no, a positively beaming Peter Parker.

epilogue

chad decided to take a back seat at *True Love* and concentrate on his new career as a relationship expert—he has his own show on a central London talk radio station. After the success of *Fat Camp* he set up *Fit Camp*, *Date Camp*, *Dress Camp* and *Camp Camp*. He also funded the opening of the first LSD Drop-in Centre. Its alumni already include several famous singers, an Olympic athlete and numerous female mechanics.

federico finally ended his relationship with Chad after a dramatic and very public argument in the *True Love* office. He started dating an air steward called Brian. Chad had what could only be described as a full-blown emotional breakdown, gave Federico the Editor job at *True Love* and asked Federico if he wanted to *get the twat engaged*. Their civil ceremony is next month. Federico is now running the 5th session of *Fat Camp* and they have a series on Channel 7.

One of the previous *Fat Campers* is now an inspirational speaker having lost 8½ stone on the programme.

mary & len got the lease on the arches and have a second garage up at Pepperpots. Both have given up their day jobs to concentrate solely on their mechanical careers. Both are still under the mentorship of *Mechanics R U*. Mary also set up and still runs basic mechanics courses at the LSD Drop-in Centre.

jenny wrote a book called *'Go on admit it, you married an idiot'* and is currently touring America publicising it. HBO are thinking of making it into a film for TV. She was recently nominated for the *Woman of the Year* award and is a regular on *Oprah*.

jane & james bought a second home in Moscow and are currently on a two-week holiday discovering the former communist state. Jane won the Pro-Am dance competition with Julio and they have been asked to perform at the Royal Albert Hall. James continues to dance with Mustafa at a specialist dance academy (I was refused admission). Both have lost an incredible amount of weight.

delaware decided that if you can't act, teach, and if you can't have children, mentor some. The childless Hollywood actress now teaches acting classes at the LSD Drop-in Centre. Her lessons are fully subscribed for the next 24 months.

beatrice started to play piano recitals at Pepperpots and Delaware sometimes duets with her. A *YouTube* video of them went viral and Simon Cowell has asked them to perform at Elton John's next charity event. Beatrice recently had her application accepted to study piano at the Juilliard School of Music and she starts there in a few weeks.

leah set up her alternative therapies practice and is well on her way to becoming a doctor (in the non-traditional sense). I have finally agreed to have past life regression and we are due to travel to Sicily next year. Apparently we are going in search of evidence of our former selves. But that's an entirely different story for an entirely different book.

peter parker still has two dogs, and a stray cat called Cat. He swapped his penthouse apartment for a house with a garden and swapped his high-powered job for a freelance consultancy role. He works between London and a chalet in the mountains. He's unlikely to win any Biggest Smiler awards but they are definitely getting more frequent, especially when he runs with his dogs.

and me, well, I completed the skiing and snowboarding instructor course in Canada. I was bottom of my class, in everything, and 12 years older than almost every other student, *but* I passed all my exams and it was the best experience of my *entire life*—I start a 5-month teaching placement in Switzerland next winter. I still write for *True Love* as a freelancer and I'm allowed to print articles under my own name.

In fact next week I am being sent to China with a love-lost reader who wants to run along the Great Wall. Peter Parker knows an awful lot about running, and about China, where he was instrumental in the success of a recent proposal to develop solar energy along its northernmost border, so he is going to come with me. And then we will probably go home, together, and share a *KitKat* and a lovely cup of tea.

the relationship that broke me, didn't
the love of my life, wasn't
my life now, wonderful.

love is a thief
for before love
for during love
for after love

this is the end
and this is your beginning

it's never too late to become
who you were supposed to be

* * * * *

ACKNOWLEDGEMENTS

Every good story begins with a broken heart and ends with a group of wonderful friends and family, inspirational women and men, who share their own experiences and their own pain, who offer a shoulder and who lead by example and show you the way to put yourself back together again. I was Humpty Dumpty and you were the king's men. I love you all.

Thank you to Aikten Alexander and in particular my agent Charlotte Robertson, who took a chance on me and my embryonic manuscript and who has the uncanny ability to make perfect creative sense to my muddled creative brain, and to my publisher, Harlequin MIRA—you are both the key to a giant impenetrable door I have spent many, many years trying to open. Thank you. You made all my dreams come true.

AUTHOR Q&A

Who are your three favourite characters in the book? Why? What inspired you to write them?

Federico, Kate and Peter Parker. Federico because I think he is a manifestation of the internal monologue in my own head. There's no filter to the things he says, it's like he's constantly playing a strange word association and I love that. I love the realness and rawness of Kate's feelings. What's not to love about someone who feels with that level of depth and who, out of her own sadness, seeks only to help others? And Peter Parker because I know him to be ridiculously handsome, and tall, and fantastic smelling; and because once upon a time I fell in love with a boy who never smiled (although he was slightly shorter).

Do you think Love is a Thief?

I love love. I'm a love lover. But I do think love's arrival can create a shift in the balance of a person's life, mine included, and sometimes that shift can lead to a loss of certain things or a disconnection from one's sense of self. Or maybe it's simply a time management issue? If we choose to spend several hours a day snogging the face off someone handsome, we probably can't fit in our Tuesday-night yoga class.

If there's one thing you'd like readers to take away from *Love is a Thief*, what is it?

I think my overriding obsession is with people reaching their full potential. People so often write things off, or decide to just make do, and life doesn't have to be like that. It's not about shooting for the stars or doing something ground-breaking. It's just about people taking time to think about the simple things in life that make them happy, in the absence of love, and making a little time for those things. I'd also like to make people laugh a little bit.

Where do you find your inspiration?

As a general rule, through spirit-crushing heartbreak. Every book I've written started with me weeping about some guy. The questions I ask in this book are the questions I asked my broken self aged thirty; questions about love, about kissing, about the calorie content of Quality Street Strawberry Creams and about why handsome men can be so goddamn distracting.

What do you love most about being a writer?

Sitting and writing is the only time I feel a hundred per cent like myself, like the person I was born to be. I don't feel like my brain was wired to do anything else. My mum always said *there is nothing better than being the person who loves what they do* and I have spent the last ten years slowly working towards that goal and I hope I am starting to make steps towards that. I also like the fact that as a writer I can legitimately work anywhere in the world, including on a sun lounger by a pool; that it's 'important' for me to spend hours and hours lying around daydreaming; and I like that I have a whole other bunch of other friends and handsome men living in my head.

Where do you write? Are you a paper/pen girl or a laptop in a coffee shop?

I don't like white paper at all, so I always write on yellow. Paper is for planning and brainstorming. The rest of the work is done on laptop. I write anywhere and have always had a full-time job while writing, so I work on train journeys, in coffee shops before work, in the tiny spare room at my dad's house at weekends. In fact my parents held an intervention because they didn't think it was normal the amount of time I spent by myself typing. They didn't know about all my imaginary friends and boyfriends in my head.

How often do you write?

After my first novel was rejected I didn't write much at all for nearly two years. But slowly I started again. I used to spend my annual leave sitting on mountains developing different ideas, but was never totally convinced any of the stories were quite right. *Love is a Thief* gave me a better work ethic, because I felt like the universe had dropped something in my lap. I felt passionate about it in a way I never had before. I wouldn't have been able to live with myself if I didn't write it. So I reorganised my life to make it happen and lived for two years on blind (borderline crazy) faith that if I sacrificed to make it happen everything would work out OK.

One piece of advice to aspiring writers…

I don't in any way feel like I've got it sussed, so I'm reticent to advise anyone. I can tell you that, for me, the moment I took myself more seriously and said 'I am' rather than 'I will be' things started to change. Also I had, and have, a very clear vision about what I want to achieve. I have always wanted to be commercially successful. I have never wanted writing to be a hobby. I asked my agent early on, 'Can you sell this?' and she said, very, *very* nervously, 'I think so', so I said 'Cool, I'll send you the book when it's done' and did so about eighteen months later. If she'd said it wasn't commercially viable, I probably wouldn't have written it.

Do you believe in love at first sight?

I want to believe in love at first sight. My natural predisposition is towards the idea of one great love, one that transcends universal time, space, geographical boundaries and fluctuating weight issues. But the older I get, the louder the niggling voice of doubt becomes as I hear more and more people speak of love and relationships in a way that sounds very much 'settling'. I want The Thunderbolt, but I'm starting to feel like a little girl at Christmas who is about to find out Santa doesn't exist. I want to keep leaving out mince pies.

Do you believe in happy-ever-after?

I watched a TED talk recently about happiness. In it the speaker said that even when humans end up with their second choice they grow to love and prefer it. They did an assortment of different tests, including tests on amnesiacs who kept forgetting what their preference was, and in every scenario people came to prefer, love and then be grateful for the things they ended up with. So on that basis yes, the science says we will all inevitably end up *happy ever after*. Which is pretty cool. It certainly takes the pressure off my next boyfriend.

What was the first book you loved?

Roald Dahl's *Revolting Rhymes*. Does that count? My mum used to read it to my brother and me before bed. We'd all end up weeping with laughter. That and *The Enormous Crocodile*. It's Roald Dahl all the way for me.

Champagne or a cup of tea?

Champagne.

Winter or summer?

At a push winter, but not a British winter. I'm thinking snowy mountaintop in Canada or France.

Topshop or Gucci?

Topshop.

Do you have a guilty pleasure?

My guilty pleasure is that I have so many guilty pleasures. I'd wrestle a man to the ground for an After Eight or Ferrero Rocher. The soundtrack to my early twenties was Phil Collins. I feel a lot of guilt about that. Teen Fiction. How am I expected to get through a copy of *Lolita* when I could get in bed and read the *Twilight* series?

Tell us a bit about your next book...

At the moment I am quite preoccupied with the idea of having it all and what that means for women. My ovaries are also quite preoccupied by that. So the next book is looking at that theme.

PLAYLIST TO *LOVE IS A THIEF*

These are the songs that either I was listening to on repeat when writing and editing the book, or that contain lyrics that I felt resonated with the story or scene I was writing. I'm not exactly at the cutting edge of the music scene, but they are for me irrevocably attached to the book. There are actually more than the ones listed below, but I'll be honest—they are all quite slow and depressing… The two in bold are the songs that for me sit at the beginning and end of the book.

I'm Not Calling You a Liar
– Florence & The Machine

High Love – James Vincent McMorrow

This is What Makes Us Girls – Lana Del Rey

Clocks – Coldplay

Babushka – Kate Bush

Keep Your Head Up – Ben Howard

Never Tear Us Apart – INXS

***Every Teardrop is a Waterfall* – Coldplay**

The depressing extras…

Turning Page – Sleep at Last

Have Yourself a Merry Little Christmas – Coldplay

Colourblind – Counting Crows

Old Joy – Noah and the Whale

What has love stolen from you?

By now, you're probably asking yourself
'What has love stolen from me?'

Join our community to **share your own
'stolen dream' story**, and read about what
other people have given up in the
name of love.

Facebook.com/loveisathief

@ClaireGarber #Loveisathief

Three superstars. Three secrets.
Who will fall first?

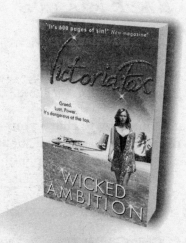

Some will do anything for fame.
Others will do anything to bring
the famous down.

For Robin, Turquoise and Kristin, the spotlight
shines brightly. They've reached the glittering
heights of stardom, but in the shadows lies the
truth... An exposé could be their end.

'It's 600 pages of sin'
Now magazine

M335/WA2

Welcome to Paradise.

*Only the rich are invited…only
the strongest survive.*

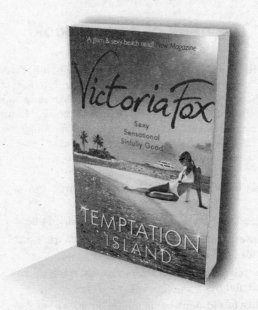

Three women drawn unwittingly to the shores
of Temptation Island, all looking for their own
truth, discover a secret so shocking there's no
turning back. It's wicked, it's sensational.
Are you ready to be told?

M261_TI